I DON'T DATE HOCKEY PLAYERS

BY

LOLU SINCLAIR

ISBN: 978-1-965155-09-7 (TPB)
ISBN: 978-1-965155-08-0 (KIN)

lostlust.com

Music Playlist

We made an awesome playlist to accompany our story!
We know you will love it.

Scan the QR code to listen for free.

SKATEFUL SHREDDERS
— vs. —
THE FREEZERS

Contents

1. Do We Have a Shot This Year? 1
2. Everybody Decent? 13
3. He's A Firecracker, Isn't He? 24
4. What Is That? Soccer? 34
5. All of This Is Off the Record 42
6. Does That Say . . . Mealworms? 50
7. He Loves My Biscuits 58
8. Chaos Drill 68
9. Release The Kraken 77
10. Sorry, Did You Want This? 85
11. This Thing Is Dumb 94
12. The Juice Is Loose 102
13. He's Up to No Good, I'm Telling You 109
14. Ready For Some Healthful Exercise? 115
15. I Was Told You Would Be Wearing a Lot Less Clothing 123
16. Are You Gonna Bid on Me? 132
17. We Need an Orchestra 140
18. You Mean Like Spy a Little Bit? 146
19. Actually, Make It a Large 154
20. Why Doesn't She Water Her Plants? 162
21. Notorious Batman Villain Poison Ivy 171
22. Seven Minutes in Heaven 184
23. Goal 193
24. It Was Strictly a Standard Level of Jolly 207
25. Call Me When You Start Acting Like a Freezer Again 215
26. We Need Our Evil Queen 224
27. Sink or Swim 229

28. Compensating for Something   234

29. Not Even Vancouver is Safe   244

30. Another One Bites the Dust   252

31. Never Bargain with a Horse   261

32. A Voyeuristic Raccoon?   267

33. Why Is Your Dad Sending You Links to
Cheese Graters?   280

34. Why Are You Being So Normal?   290

35. The Cat Who Ate the Canary   299

36. Actually, Where Is Belize?   307

37. I'm Afraid That's All We Have Time For   316

38. I Am Not a Duck   323

39. Get Over Here and Let Me Punch You   333

40. Are You . . . Paying Attention to the Game?   340

41. Give It Your Best Shot, Stick Head   345

42. Can We Do This in the Back?   349

43. I'd Rather Talk About Hockey   360

Six Months Later   373

Also by Lolu Sinclair   381

Chapter 1

Do We Have a Shot This Year?

ANNA

My secret is that I never watch the first puck drop of the season. I lean back against the plastic curve of my chair, the scent of the ice in my nose and the chill on my cheeks. From the Coliseum's vast windows, a fiery Portland sunset drapes across the ice. I like to sit dead center—high enough to melt in with the fans, low enough to see the players' furrowed faces.

I close my eyes, drawing out the moment. One last heartbeat where anything could happen. Suddenly, the little disc hits the ice and the stillness explodes into a tornado of scraping sticks. The crowd roars, I open my eyes.

The hockey season has begun.

The once-tranquil ice swirls with activity as the red and navy players of my team, the Portland Freezers, clash against the orange and teal of last year's PCHL champions, the Skateful Shredders, battling over the barely visible puck. Then a forward on the Shredders nabs it and sends it sailing across the rink.

I sigh, that buoyant feeling I had moments before already miles away. The Freezers were not off to a good start. But I hadn't yet asked the expert.

I lean forward in my chair and tap the shoulder of the wiry man in front of me, his gray hair almost entirely concealed underneath a red and navy beanie: Eddie Mullins, the Freezer's oldest fan. He claims he'd been coming to games at the Veterans Memorial Coliseum since it was built, although I was skeptical.

"Well, Eddie, what do you say? Do we have a shot this year?" I ask. I met Eddie during a publicity event I had coordinated several years ago for season ticket holders. Even at eighty, his slap shot is as lethal as his opinions.

Eddie squinted at the ice through his coke-bottle glasses. Then he turns to me, shaking his head. "Sorry, hun. I'd say we've got about as good a chance as an ice rink in hell."

The white-haired woman seated next to him in a hand-knit red and navy scarf whacks him on the shoulder. I can't help but grin. Ramona Mullins is their second oldest fan.

"Don't you say that. The Carolina Hurricanes didn't have much of a shot either and look where they ended up."

Eddie shakes his head vehemently. "You need an Eric Staal for that. Do you see Eric Staal out there?"

"See? You can't see anything anymore," Ramona huffs and turns to me. "You just tell them to play their best, dear. We'll be here."

Eddie scoffs and gestures toward the Coliseum with its many empty blue and red seats. "We will, but will anybody else?"

The seats are filled with mostly fans sporting the opposing team's colors. A pit forms in my stomach. I was pretty sure Eddie was right. The Freezers' ticket sales are down for the third year in a row, and it shows. Too many of our die-hard fans have not forgiven them for last year. And, after the phone call I got first thing this morning . . .

"You know what they say," Eddie continues. "Oregon has two hockey teams. One good one—" He pointed over to the Shredders.

"And the other one," I finish for him. This is the first game of the season, and I've already heard it three times. It takes all of my publicist training to plaster a polite smile on my face. The Shredders—based in Beaverton—are just a quick fifteen-minute drive away. And since we are neighbors with the best team in our league, we can count on more Shredders fans than Freezers ones.

Ramona whacks Eddie again. "Don't rub it in her face. It's not her fault."

I glance down at my dad, knowing exactly whose fault Eddie and Ramona think it is that the Freezers are at the bottom the Pacific Coast Hockey League's Mountain Division, making them the laughingstock of the minors. Coach Peter is in his usual position, behind the Freezers bench with his arms folded, standing completely still. Only his eyes move, bouncing like tiny pucks.

He's been the Freezers' head coach for as long as I could remember, and even when they lose, he always pours his heart and soul into the team. *This year even more so than usual.* I notice the heavy bags under his eyes and remember the sleepless nights he'd spent at the office, determined not to repeat last year's mistakes. This morning, before I'd had a chance to tell him about my phone call, he pulled me aside and told me he was sure this year would be "the one."

I knew exactly why he thought this year would be different, although I wasn't sure I agreed. My gaze traced one particular red-and-navy blur across the ice.

I lean back toward Eddie and Ramona to point it out as it barrels down the rink, blowing past the Shredders' defenders. "Don't count us out just yet. We've got a bit of a secret weapon this year."

As they all watch, veteran announcer—Ike the Mic—squeaks excitedly from up in his booth. "Oh, would you look at that? An early shot by Freezers' new first-line center, Blake Tyler, and it's blocked by the Shredders goalie—but wait—he gets it on the rebound! What a play!"

The crowd cheers. I grin. Maybe my dad was right after all. New to the team this year, Blake Tyler dominates in practice, though this was the first time I saw him in competition. I had to admit he did not disappoint.

The team whoops in shocked celebration and "We Will Rock You" pours from the speakers. The Queen song is in honor of our mascot Freddy, a googly-eyed, mustachioed

Refrigerator-Freezer combo that we'd been stuck with since we had the unfortunate idea to let fans vote for their mascot. I have to admit, Freddy doesn't seem as silly when he is rocking out to the first point of the season.

Not bothering to celebrate, Blake whips past his cheering teammates and skates back to the center line. He is a beast for sure, but as I watch him flying solo across the ice, I wonder if we could keep this beast contained. I have dealt with a lot of hockey players over my many years with the team, but none quite like Blake.

He is ruthless on the ice, committing with a laser focus that gives me chills. Most of the players talk big, but off the ice they are just goofy kids, excited they get paid to whack into people. For the few months I've known him, I have never seen Blake turn off. He is unpredictable since he is as tightly wound off the rink as on. My dad wanted a wild-card, and he got one.

Pulling myself out of my thoughts, I lean down and grab my SLR camera. Doubts aside, it is time to do my job and grab some publicity stills for our social feed.

I zoom in, capturing the intense look in Blake's dark brown eyes as he waits for the puck to drop. I feel a little thrill studying those eyes, but quickly chalk it up to excitement about the game. Anything else is firmly off-limits. I need to stay professional. I constantly interact with the players, setting up press conferences and coaching them on how to handle prying questions. Image isn't everything, but bad press can kill a team almost as quickly as a bad season. It is my job to keep everyone's feet out of their mouths.

Which is exactly why I tried to set up media training sessions with Blake multiple times. Blake does not hold back on the ice, and, from his clips online, he doesn't hold back with reporters either. The Freezers are clinging onto their spot in the PCHL by a thread, and the only viral videos we can afford are players doing TikTok dances. But try as I might to meet with Blake, my dad keeps pulling him back to the ice to run drill after drill. I want the team to win just as badly as Coach Peter does, but sometimes I wish my dad would take my job more seriously. At least he agreed to keep Blake out of the post-game press conferences until I can work with him.

I line up the perfect shot of Blake's chiseled brow. I don't know what to make of him, but he can't look bad in a photo if he tried. A human whirlwind thuds into the empty seat beside me, throwing off my aim.

"Sorry I'm late! Did I miss the coin toss?"

I roll my eyes at my best friend Alison. "It's called a face-off."

Alison waves a dismissive hand as she digs through her New Seasons tote bag. I love my friend to death, but a hockey expert, Alison is not. Still, I admire her adventurous sense of fashion—her cool pompadour pixie, cropped black vest, wide-legged pants, and the icy-silver eyeliner that perfectly complements her skin tone.

I tug at my wavy chestnut-brown hair, which refuses to be styled, and glance down at the "uniform" I wear throughout hockey season: a poly-blend blouse in signature Freezer red and dark jeans. Compared to Alison, I feel like the opposite of cool.

I sigh.

"What was that for? Are we losing already? Here, these should cheer you up."

Alison extracts the tin of cookies from her tote and drops them in my lap.

I stare down at the delicate lacy waffle-like cookies tinged a mossy green. "For your information, we're actually up by one. What are these?" I pop one into my mouth and close my eyes as the mixture of bitter and sweet flood my taste buds.

"Matcha pizelles. Italian-Japanese, just like me!" Alison declares, grabbing one herself.

"Ooo, they are delicious, and they are now my dinner." I clutch the tin possessively, watching my friend light up at the compliment. "Are you going to have them at Munch?" Munch was *the* up-and-coming eatery in Portland, and thanks to its impressively styled Instagram account, it is getting lots of attention from both locals and celebrities. Thanks to Alison's funky creations.

Alison nods. "Figured it was time to shake things up again. If Sal will let me, that is."

"Please. Sal's never turned down your ideas once."

"That's because he knows what's good for him." Alison winks. "So, what's this about you guys not losing for once?"

I point back to the ice. Blake has the puck once again, and he is pushing it through the neutral zone, ignoring his two wingers, even though Chad on the left is wide open.

"Hot dog, look at that speed, folks!" Ike calls out.

"Well, hello. Who is that?" Alison asks, leaning in as Blake races up the ice. "And more importantly, is he cute?"

"Alison! That is beside the point," I insist, my voice pitching up an octave.

Alison simply raises an eyebrow at me.

I refuse to meet Alison's eyes. Sure, Blake has dark-brown hair and piercing eyes that accentuated his sharp, sculpted features. And his constant scowl gives him sexy, bad boy vibes. When Coach Peter asked me to give the new player a tour at the start of the pre-season, Blake gave me a stare so intense it made me shiver. He is a little bit dangerous.

I'm not sure that is a good thing.

The whistle blows, drawing our attention back to the ice, as the referee calls a penalty on Blake for slashing at the Skateful Shredders' center. As if to prove his point, Blake is screaming in the ref's face. Henri, their longtime French-Canadian referee, is screaming right back in very fast-paced French.

Ike chimes in with his opinion. "It looks Blake disagrees with the ref's call, but I tell ya, folks, that seemed like a pretty clear penalty to me. Boy, oh boy, this man does not want to hit the penalty box. That reminds me of the time when . . ."

I cringe, glancing at my dad, who is doing nothing. Coach Peter believes a little rowdiness is what the people pay for, but Blake isn't going to make my job easy.

Eddie leans back, waving for my attention. "Looks like you got your Eric Staal."

Ramona shakes a finger at him. "That's no Staal. That's a Tiger Williams. Get your head on right."

The couple descends into yet another argument, and I

send a prayer to the hockey gods that Blake is not about to break Tiger Williams' penalty minute record. Meanwhile, the Shredder's center skates behind Henri, waving mockingly at Blake, who looks about ready to murder both of them.

I clock the number on the Shredder's jersey and groan. Charlie "Chuck" Haskell. The next few minutes of this game won't be fun.

"Blake might be cute," I sigh, "but he's handed the Shredders a power play."

"I don't have any clue what that means, but you *do* think he's cute!" Alison trills.

I ignore the second half of Alison's comment. As Blake fumes his way to the penalty box, I point out the army of Shredders—led by Charlie—whipping the puck back and forth across the blue line toward the Freezers defensive zone. The red and navy defenders can barely keep up. "They've got five players, and now we've only got four. Their offensive line won them the championship last year. I guarantee you their center's going to chuck it."

"He's going to what now?" Alison asks.

"Just watch," I tell her. "Trust me."

Sure enough, Charlie executes some artful dangling, faking, and twisting through the Freezers' defense, passing the puck with his wingers as he speeds toward the goal. Shredders fans in the crowd chant, "Chuck, Chuck, Chuck!" Sure enough, he transfers his right-handed hockey stick into his left hand and chucks the puck toward the net at top speed. Charlie's signature move is highly difficult, and he executes it with swashbuckling flair. The

9

puck sails through the air and straight into the net. The goalie didn't stand a chance. Charlie is swarmed by Shredders as the crowd erupts. The Grateful Dead's *Truckin'* blares in celebration as the Shredders fans sing along, shouting "Chuckin'" instead. Their mascot—Ted the Shredder with his tie-dye shirt and guitar—high-fives two shirtless fans with teal and orange torsos.

Charlie skates in a wide circle, blowing kisses to the crowd. His sandy hair sticks out from beneath his helmet, and he has the most contagious grin.

Alison giggles. "Ooo, he's fun. Is he cute?"

"Please don't root for the enemy," I say. I remember the only time I had ever talked to Charlie, and how badly it had gone. "Charlie is nothing but a showboat, biding his time before the NHL picks him up. Our players have heart."

"You are most certainly right," Alison says, watching Blake burst out of the penalty box and back onto the ice. "And very nice faces to go along with their hearts."

I shake my head. "You know, if you ever actually watched a game, you would learn there is more to it than the players' jawlines."

Alison rolls her eyes. "I will admit there's more to hockey than hotties if you admit there's more to life than the Freezers," she counters. "Every season, you disappear into this game and the same old publicity routine your dad always demands."

"It is my job," I argue, even though I know Alison is right that I forfeit my social life to hockey every October through April. If it weren't for those pizzelles, my dinner plan would be the cardboard meal waiting in my tiny, over-full freezer. That is if I didn't settle for a bag of microwave popcorn.

"Then tell me," Alison says, fixing me with *The Look* she always gives me before speaking hard truths, "have you talked to Coach Peter about your ideas yet?"

I look away. Despite our bleak ticket sales and the very troubling phone call this morning, I have not gotten up the nerve to talk to my father.

Alison relents, knowing how hard this was for me, and squeezes my shoulder. Then she frowns down at her phone.

"I gotta go. Sal just texted me 'bread emergency,' and I'm afraid to know what that means. Is it halftime soon? I'll stay if I can see the zambini."

I roll my eyes. "There is no halftime, and there is no zambini. It's a Zamboni, and you already missed the first one."

"Zamboni? Ooo, that sounds like an Italian sandwich. A little prosciutto? A little mortadella? Maybe sneak in a little wasabi aioli? I think we've figured out tomorrow's lunch special at Munch." Alison grabs her tote and climbs out of the seat. "Love you! Be back later for Stinker!"

"We'll be here!"

Babysitting Alison's ridiculously cute dog gets me through the long days. I wave as my friend scurries away, trying to shove aside the thoughts Alison had evoked. Hockey is my life. I grew up around the ice. It kept me and my dad going after mom had passed away, and I wouldn't trade it for the world. Of course, if we don't deal with the news from this morning, there will be a lot less hockey in our future.

I return my attention to the ice. Blake is at the boards, battling with Charlie for control of the puck and shoves into him hard. I bite my lip. He is toying with another penalty.

I wonder where Blake's anger comes from. Some of it probably has to do with Charlie. I mean, even I wouldn't mind wiping the grins off the Skateful Shredders' faces every once in a while, but the Portland Freezers don't have much of a chance from the bottom of the league.

Blake gets the puck away from Charlie and slices it into the net. Another goal! The crowd erupts. I smile to see Eddie heave himself to his feet with Ramona's help.

"Well, I'll be jitterbugged. What a game this is turning out to be!" Ike calls out to the energized audience.

Watching Blake, I smile and get caught up in the excitement for a moment. Maybe this season will be different.

Chapter 2

Everybody Decent?

ANNA

I take a big breath and brace myself as I open the doors to the Portland Freezers' locker room. "Everybody decent?"

As expected, the question is met with a deafening round of hooting and hollering. I duck my head and push my way inside. The locker room is in full-on party mode. Twenty very sweaty men with an average height of six foot one are leaping up and down on benches and belting the team's unofficial fight song, Queen's "Don't Stop Me Now," at the top of their lungs. Even Gordie, the tall twenty-something inside the Freddy the Freezer mascot costume, is wailing on an imaginary guitar. I catch embarrassing glimpses of my dad in the center of it all, conducting like the whole thing is a very off-key orchestra.

I have come on business, but am pulled into the maelstrom. Wingers Chad and Vlad, who look nothing alike and are not related, grab my hands and get down on their knees to serenade me.

I try to extract my hands from their grasp. "Great game, guys! The Freezers are back! Just don't forget, you also have a press conference in twenty minutes!"

"Bring it on," Vlad cries. "We are the champions tonight!"

They all cheer, and the group descends into a new round of Queen.

I stare up at Leo, always shocked by how tall the goalie is up close. "Your team's off to a good start, captain." I say, and mean it.

Leo smiles, but he is a bit less enthusiastic than the rest of the rabid crew. "Everybody played well . . . when they had a chance to." His eyes slide to the corner of the room, and I turn.

There is Blake, toweling off his bare torso as he watches the melee. He holds himself apart from the group, even though the celebration is very much because of him. I wonder again what is going on in his head.

I nod at Leo and make my way through the sea of players, trying not to count the abs rippling up Blake's bare abdomen. There are just so many. His eyes never leave my face. In fact, I always feel like he looks at me with the same intensity as he does the puck.

"Blake, congrats on the win. You guys really crushed it out there."

Blake shrugs. When I get closer, he looks away. "The

team could use some speed drills, but they've got me now. If those reporters don't think I'm gonna get us to the championship, they've got another thing coming."

I bite my bottom lip. Humility is one of the issues we were going to have to work on. Blake might have skill, but the Freezers need more than skill to get through this season. Coach Peter must have forgotten to tell Blake that he won't join any press conferences until he has more media training. Now I have to tell him. *Just great.*

Blake stands up, stepping very close to me, and my breath catches as I am treated to a front-row view of his abs. Then he pivots around me to reach his locker, and I force myself to focus.

"Blake, listen, Coach and I think you should sit out the press conference tonight—"

Blake frowns. "Why?"

I hesitate, trying to think of how to answer diplomatically. His intensity and confidence are very alluring. It just isn't that press-friendly.

Thankfully, Coach Peter has finally noticed I am in the locker room and bounds over.

"What'd I tell you, Anna? What a game!" he whoops, ruffling my hair in a mortifyingly dad way. Still, I am happy to see him so jubilant after last season. I remember with a twinge that I still have to break bad news to him tonight. But first things first, the press conference.

"Congrats, Coach," I said. "I was just telling Blake why we thought it would be good to save him for a later press conference."

Coach Peter does not pick up on my hint. "Oh, yeah,

we did say that, didn't we? But that was before we won. Did you see him out there? He's a natural. We gotta give the people what they want, right?"

My dad claps Blake on the back, and the two of them look at me expectantly. Coach Peter trusts me to work publicity miracles, but even I am skeptical I can get Blake reporter-ready in the next eighteen minutes. I try one more time.

"He was great, but we already made the arrangements—"

"Oh, he can have my spot. I hate these things."

Before I can marshal up another argument, Assistant Coach Sylvia makes her entrance, and the whole room devolves into hooting and cheering again. I wince, wondering how quickly a person could go deaf.

Coach Peter takes off, leaving me with Blake, who gives me the full blast of his dark stare. Seventeen minutes to go.

"Glad that's settled," I say breathlessly. "Maybe we can run through some practice questions?"

Blake nods. "Sure. I just gotta hit the showers. Then I'm all yours."

Fifteen minutes—and as many crises—later, I still haven't talked to Blake. It isn't for lack of trying. But then the AV system has issues, an intern has laid out the chairs wrong, and every time I check, Blake is still in the shower. I am ready to fight anybody who says women are the ones who take a long time to get ready.

Hopefully, these last two minutes will be enough.

I have just finished reconfiguring the folding chairs in the press room when an older woman with wireframe glasses and a stunning spiral of gray hair atop her head peers inside. I leap forward, ushering her to a seat in the front row.

"Quite a game, don't you think, Ms. Cornwallis? The Freezers comeback would make for a great human-interest story, wouldn't it?" I gush. If Tricia Cornwallis covers you for *The Oregonian*, people pay attention. The woman is a legend. I still don't know how she broke the Hockey Canada scandal, one of hockey's biggest Me Too moments. Without her and her fellow journalists, the organization might still have a slush fund using membership fees to pay for sexual assault claims.

Tricia gives me a once over and sniffs. "We'll see. We will be speaking to the new center, yes? Mr. Tyler?"

I nod hesitantly. "Of course. You're gonna love him," I promise, hoping that is true. I try to back away, aiming for the door, but Tricia holds up a finger.

"I would like to speak with you as well, at the next junket. The challenges facing women in sports and such. My assistant will schedule."

I nod, not trusting myself to speak. My own interview with Tricia Cornwallis! I have done interviews before, but prefer to stay out of the spotlight. Still, when Tricia Cornwallis asks, you don't say no. I don't know if I am more excited or nervous.

I make another beeline for the door, but it is too late. The players are already filing in with a proud Coach Peter herding them along. I hurry over. Chad and Vlad cheerfully salute as they pass me.

Leo leans close. "I tried to go over some basics with him."

I squeeze his arm gratefully. "How'd it go?"

Leo only clears his throat and moves past me.

I glance over at the Shredders players coming in and purse my lips at seeing Charlie. Of course he would be here, but I am not looking forward to his bragging. If he acts like the last time I met him, we are in for it.

I catch Blake's eye at the doorway and make a last-ditch effort to prep him. "Just don't forget to smile and keep your responses positive. This is a team victory."

Blake pauses and gives me a small smile, as if testing it out. In the few months he'd been with the team, I haven't seen him smile very much. It warms up his whole face.

"Just like that," I tell him, smiling back.

Blake opens his mouth to say something, but Coach Peter has caught up. "Come on, let's get cooking!"

With that, Blake breaks away and heads for the stage. I watch him with bated breath. This multipurpose room with its stained wall-to-wall carpeting and its buzzing track lighting is *my* arena, and press conferences can make or break the season almost as much as the games.

Coach Peter throws his arm around me and pulls me close. "It'll be great," he tells me. "You worry too much." I hope he is right as I step forward to open the conference for questions, but Blake is way ahead of me. He scowls out into the crowd, eyes dark and brow furrowed, looking like he's never smiled in his life. He clears his throat and glares at the reporters.

"Who wants to start?"

So much for those thirty seconds of media training. The room fills with a cacophony of voices, all hurling questions at once. Blake, unphased, points directly at Tricia.

"Tricia Cornwallis, *The Oregonian*. Mr. Tyler, to be frank, no one expected the Portland Freezers to win tonight. Can you speculate on what led to this surprising victory?"

I cross my fingers. At least this is an easy one. All Blake has to do is say some nice things about the Freezers.

Blake leans into his mic. "To be honest, I didn't see much skill out on the ice from the Shredders tonight."

I wince.

"You do realize the Skateful Shredders won the league championship three years running," Tricia states, eyebrows raised.

Blake shrugs. "Yeah, well, that's cuz the Freezers didn't have me last year. If the Shredders wanna win again this year, they're gonna have to take on a real challenger. I'm getting pucks deep. I'm getting them in the net. So far, the Shredders don't seem to be doing the same."

From my spot by the door, I watch fingers flying on phones all around the room with rising dread. The Shredders on stage don't look thrilled, and neither do Blake's own teammates. Within one minute, he insulted them all. At least Coach Peter seems to be enjoying himself.

Blake's hot temper is entertaining during the game, but

this is exactly why it won't fly off the ice. The last thing I need is for the Freezers to be branded as the villains of the league this season. I try to catch his eye.

Hands shoot up all over the room. Reporters jockey for the next question, including two burly dudes practically climbing over their chairs in the back. I stare, trying to place them. They look familiar, but I thought I had every reporter in the circuit down cold. I look closer and see flecks of orange and teal paint clinging to their shirts.

Then I realize they had been in the stands near their mascot, hollering like hyenas. They aren't reporters. They are Shred Heads. Wondering if this is going to be a problem, I skim the room for the stadium's sorry excuse for a security guard, but he is nowhere to be found. Of course.

Oblivious, Blake points at the next reporter, as Charlie spots the enthusiastic bros.

"Nick and Nate? You're not press. Who the hell let you maniacs in here?"

One of them waves his press pass defiantly. "We started a podcast so we could ask you why you sucked so much tonight."

"Yeah, tell us," says the other one.

"Ladies and gentlemen, my two biggest fans," Charlie announces drolly. "Please, dear god, does anybody else have a question?"

The room echoes with laughter, and even I bite back a grin. I shouldn't be surprised Charlie is a clown off the rink too. At least he is drawing attention away from Blake's last answer. My grin fades as the next reporter stands up.

Kyle Brodie's long gray beard makes him look like a lovable Oregon mountain man, but that stops at his eyes, which are as dead as a shark's. He is just as predatory, selling hot takes to anyone with enough money.

"Same question. Why did you suck tonight?"

I tense, feeling bad for Charlie. I don't like him, but I like Kyle even less. Leave it to Kyle to turn a joke into a gotcha question.

"Well," Charlie replies, keeping his face neutral, "All I can say is my team played their hardest. We had four lines going hard all night, and we've got good depth on the team, but we didn't stick to our systems. The Freezers put up a really great game and took some great shots. We're excited about our reception here tonight and look forward to playing at the Coliseum again soon." He leans close to the mic, locking eyes with Blake. "And, of course, we look forward to our colleagues here on the Freezers teaching us how to skate."

The reporters laugh again, and I sigh. That was, unfortunately, a perfect answer. The story tomorrow isn't going to be the Freezers win, so much as Charlie's charm. *Drat.* We really need the extra boost.

I look at Blake and see thunder brewing behind his eyes. He clearly does not like getting one-upped by Charlie. I grit my teeth, cursing again that my dad never takes the need for media training seriously.

I study the two men side by side. They couldn't be more different. Blake has thick, dark hair and dark eyes to match. His face is all sharp angles, as though it had been carved from granite. He moves across the ice like he has been destined for it. Meanwhile, Charlie has sandy blond hair that never stays in one place, sparkling blue eyes, a broad face with a strong chin, and a healthy natural tan. He is more like an easygoing lumberjack who wandered out of the woods and onto the rink, then happens to be great at hockey. I am sure his wide grin has melted many hearts, although it doesn't seem to have that effect on Blake.

I can tell whatever Blake wants to say now is going to cause a big storm, so I leap to my feet. "I'm afraid that's all the time we have for today, folks. Thank you so much for coming by, and we look forward to seeing you at the next game."

By the time I make it back to the locker room, the mood has turned gleeful again. I seek out Blake, hoping for a quick moment to debrief.

"Hey, Anna." Chad waves at me from one of the benches. "You're gonna drop your rule about not dating hockey players, right? Now that we're winners? Because a queen like you deserves a king like me." He strikes a pose, one leg up on the bench and his hands on his hips like some kind of Halloween pirate.

I laugh. "Sorry, boys, but comments like that are exactly why I have my rule in the first place." I know Chad is joking, but that rule saves me from a lot of awkward encounters. Not only does the league frown on manager-player relationships, so does my dad. Besides, my ogling of Blake's abs aside, I have yet to meet a hockey player evolved enough to tempt me into compromising my own professional ambitions, and if I ever do, it definitely won't be Chad.

Chapter 3

He's A Firecracker, Isn't He?

ANNA

After the players finally filter out of the locker room, Dad settles behind his mess of a desk and pours himself a finger of the "good scotch" he saves for when the Freezers win a game. To be honest, it's the same scotch he drinks when we lose, but tonight, it goes down smoother. He says he feels in his bones we have a chance to go all the way this season. Of course, he's had that feeling before. The start of every season comes with a bit of amnesia about the previous one, if we're being honest. Last season is not one he wants to remember.

I knock softly and lean against the doorway. He still always seems surprised I'm a poised and fully grown adult now. Gone are the days of the five-year-old with blue raspberry popsicle lips, loudly declaring to my grandparents that I am going to play for the Vancouver Canucks right out of college. That was the last time Granny ever brought up figure skating.

This was also the moment dad knew I was going to be a fighter. He realized the two of us were going to be okay after Mom died from a stroke.

I give him a similarly defiant look now, minus the blue popsicle juice lips. He follows my gaze to the telltale bright pink box peeking out from below a pile of papers on his desk. He nudges the paper stack to cover the box completely, I just shake my head.

"More Voodoo Donuts, Coach? Really? Didn't you promise Dr. Phillips you'd start watching your sugar?"

"Those are from this morning," he swears, even though Zamboni Zane snuck them in right before the game. "Besides, hockey is a burning thing, and I need my fiery ring," he sings poorly, adapting the lyrics to his favorite Johnny Cash song to go with his favorite "Ring of Fire" donut. I cover my ears as I sink down into the chair in front of his desk.

"Please don't bring Johnny Cash into this. His donuts have nothing to do with your win tonight as much as you wish they did."

"*Our* win tonight. The guys played a great game, didn't they? Did you see our shooting percentage? Off the charts. I'm telling you, Anna, this is gonna be a good season. I mean, you saw the press conference. Weren't they eating us up?"

I consider how to answer this. Apparently me and my

dad had not seen the same press conference. "Blake certainly makes an impression." I finally say.

Coach Peter grins, settling back in his chair, earning a squeak from the long-suffering springs. "He's a firecracker, isn't he?"

He scouted Blake from the Czech Extraliga, a high-level European minor league circuit, and the kid had been happy to head back to United States soil. Not that anyone would ever describe Blake as happy, exactly. Dad loves his team like they are my twenty rowdy brothers, but sometimes the boys need a kick in the pants, and Blake was exactly that.

"Sure," I respond, "but I'm worried he's a bit too fiery off the ice. Those kinds of antics can backfire with the press."

Coach Peter shrugs. "The press love the drama just as much as the fans do. You worry too much, Anna Banana."

I wrinkle my nose at the nickname. "It's my job to worry, remember?"

I watch my dad in his classic 'coach pose,' kicked back in his chair with a wry grin and a determined look in his eye. I always envied his cool confidence. Despite his easy demeanor now, it had been my dad's job to worry during my childhood, raising me as a single parent with a grueling hockey schedule. My grandparents helped, but he had been the one who was there, day in and day out, for every school recital, every sports game, and every childhood tragedy or triumph. We might have our differences, but we are a team of two.

My dating rule is "no hockey players," but the truth is I

haven't been on a date with anyone in quite a while. Me and my dad never talk about it, but I know the standards he sets for anyone who might want to date his "Anna Banana" are way too high. Like Alison had said, running the Freezers with my dad is my life, and I'm not ready to risk it.

Coach Peter waves me off, oblivious to my line of thought. "Trust me, Blake is just what the Freezers ordered. I promise I'll clear some time for you to do your press training with him, but I'm sure you'll see. Remember, 'confrontation simply means meeting truth head-on.'"

I laugh. "Don't you quote Coach K at me. You know he was not talking about penalty box minutes." Trying not to show my concern, I took a deep breath. "Listen, Dad, I got a call this morning from Plaid Pantry. They're pulling out. They said they love us, but they can get more bang for their buck with teams like the Shredders."

I study my dad's face, but he keeps his feelings masked as he takes another sip of his post-game scotch. Plaid Pantry was our biggest and only major sponsor left after Salem Lumber and PNW Realty dropped out last year.

Dad puts on a smile. "Come on, we'll be okay. We've got ticket sales, and we can put out some new Freddy merch. People love that stuff."

"Sure okay, but listen, I've been running the numbers. With the overhead for salaries, rink, and equipment, plus the travel schedule this year, our current ticket sales aren't going to cut it. We might not make enough to get to next season."

There. I had said it. The elephant in the room had

finally been acknowledged. Unfortunately, the trickiest part is what I have to say next.

"Now, I know you don't love doing anything that's too non-traditional when it comes to our outreach," I continue, trying to push past his skeptical expression, "but this is Portland—"

"Exactly. This is Portland." Coach says, drawing out the name. "The last time we tried something new, we got a refrigerator-freezer combo for a mascot."

I knew he was going to say that. Having a dancing gray box with a mustache at all our games has been great for merch sales, but the *New York Times* picked up the story, and he still has not recovered from the deluge of national mockery. I try again.

"I know, but I have some ideas this time that I really think could work."

"Anna," Coach Peter stops me gently. "You know I love the enthusiasm, but I think you're worrying too much again. We've been in tight spots before. Hell, what's a minor league team without money troubles? This year is different. We've got Blake. We just got the first win of the season, against the Shredders of all teams. Our ticket sales will pick up. We'll be fine."

I fake a smile. He is hesitant to try new ideas, so I figured the conversation might go this way, but I had to try. My dad is right that we had been in tight spots before, but this year I am really worried. My dad lifts his glass toward me.

"Cheer up hon. It's all just another chapter for the memoir: *Cold as Ice: The Coach Peter Story.*"

I groan. "Okay, Boomer."

"Excuse me! I'm Gen X, missy, and you know it."

"Sure, Coach." I stand, stretching out my back. My work night is far from over.

"Hey, Anna Banana? Has anyone ever told you . . ." He trails off.

"Told me what?"

"You're as cold as ice—!" he sings off-key.

I bolt for the door before he can finish the verse. Safe in the hallway, I head for my cramped office, passing Zamboni Zane on his way to Coach Peter's office. The sixty-five-year-old Portland native is an institution on the rink, and my dad's best friend.

"How's the ice, Zane?" I ask.

Zane kisses his calloused brown fingers and crinkles his eyes. He has the most expressive crow's feet of anyone I've ever met. "Like silk, my friend. I got a real clean sheet for you this time."

"You always do. And how are the stocks?"

Zane grins at my knowledge of his other passion. "The Dow is down, but my spirits are up."

He waves as he disappears into my dad's office, and I slide into my own office with a sigh of relief. The space is postage-stamp tiny, and I have inherited my dad's penchant for mess, but during hockey season, it is home.

My sigh was greeted by a loud thumping.

"Stinker!" I cry, scurrying around my desk.

Stinker's tail thumps harder. The medium-sized super mutt with scruffy salt and pepper fur gazes lovingly up at me. His sleepy, soulful eyes peer out from under bushy eyebrows matching an equally bushy dog mustache and tufted ears. He would be quite the distinguished gentleman if it weren't for the giant tongue lolling out of his mouth as he panted.

"Hi, buddy," I coo, scratching Stinker on his favorite spot behind his ear. His eyes flutter in appreciation. Since Munch's kitchen isn't exactly dog-friendly, I happily volunteer to dog sit whenever I can. Our pre-game walks help me de-stress, and I am jealous of his ability to nap the entire length of a game.

Freddy the Freezer may have won the internet poll, but Stinker is the real Freezers mascot. Whenever I feel intimidated by the massive hockey players I have to boss around, I remember how high-pitched their voices get while talking to the dog.

I give Stinker a last scratch and drag myself over to my desk chair to update the team socials with footage from the post-game interviews. I open my laptop, its screen as messy as my desk, and pull up the file.

There is Blake, his strong jaw clenched and his eyes brooding. I scroll through his interview, debating what clip to pull, but he comes across as so unsportsmanlike the entire time. I haven't been able to get to him in the locker room after the conference before being pulled away for yet another crisis. I wish my dad would take my concerns more seriously, but I'll just have to figure it out, like always.

I fast-forward past Blake's answers and into Charlie's. I let the clip play, watching Charlie joke with his rogue fans. As much as I don't want to admit it, he has the exact warmth and professionalism I need from Blake. Although

I really doubt "be more like the Shredders" is a piece of advice Blake will listen to, or one I could bear to give. After all, Charlie is all showboat and no substance. I'll have to find another way to bring out the charming side of Blake. I know it's in there. Hopefully, we won't be going up against the Shredders again anytime soon.

Stinker's tail thumps again, even harder this time, and I look up.

Alison is in the doorway, holding boxes of food. "Hi, Stinker. Hi, my stinky baby," she coos.

Alison plunks the takeout box next to my laptop and bends down to give Stinker a thorough belly rub. He wriggles around in glee, his tongue flopping.

I open the takeout box, mouth drooling at the fluffy focaccia inside, which contains a rainbow of deli meat and shards of pepperoncini. "What's this slice of magic?"

"That, my friend, is the Zambini. Tomorrow's lunch special. I figured you got first dibs for helping inspire it."

"Zamboni."

"Zamboni? No, you said Zambini."

I sigh. "Just make sure Sal does the specials board, okay?" I take a bite. "Oh, this is heaven."

Alison grins. "If I don't feed you, no one will."

I make a face and set the sandwich back down, accidentally hitting a key on my laptop. Charlie's interview begins to play again.

Alison perks up. "What are you watching?"

"Nothing." I quickly stop the video. "Just work."

"Oh, really? You don't sound like that when it's just work. Let me see."

Alison stands up from the tangle of Stinker's paws, but I snap the laptop shut, keeping my hand over it protectively.

"It was that cute hockey player, wasn't it? Blake? He's got a good voice."

"For your information, no, that was not Blake."

"A different cute hockey player?" Alison tries to read my expression and remember the other hockey players. "Was it . . . the goalie? He's a snack."

"Yup, the goalie. Leo's a good guy. You should meet him sometime."

I hate to lie to my friend, but I want to end this conversation. I wasn't sure why I didn't want Alison to see Charlie. It was my job to review press conference footage. But somehow, I feel guilty for watching him. Charlie was the enemy. "Why don't you come by practice, and I'll introduce you?"

"Right, hockey practice. Of course." At that suggestion, Alison quickly retreats to Stinker, pulling his leash out of her pocket.

I blow out a breath. If there is one thing that is her friend's kryptonite, it is the thought of paying attention to hockey.

"You know, if you ever actually did come to a practice, you might realize hockey is a lot of fun to watch. A huge percentage of hockey fans are women."

"And I love that for them," says Alison, tugging on Stinker's leash to get him to stand. He rolls over instead. "Are you taking him tomorrow?"

"Assuming I can ever get out of here."

Alison gives me a look. "At least eat the sandwich. If I can't get you to live your life, the least I can do is keep you alive."

"I swear on Stinker's silly face that I will," I say, then take another massive bite. Alison blows me a kiss and trots off with Stinker, his nails clicking as they head down the hall.

I open the laptop back up. The video refreshes, bringing me back to Blake. He leans down to the mic, his brown hair falling onto his forehead. I feel an urge to push the strands away from his furrowed brow. My dad's words ring in my mind, telling me not to worry so much and that Blake and the team have this. I hope he is right, but I also know how much can happen during a hockey season. I'll stop worrying after the championship in April and not a second earlier.

Chapter 4

What Is That? Soccer?

BLAKE

As I shoulder my way through the doors of Ground Kontrol, the damp chill of Portland in October is replaced by a blast of hot air and a cacophony of dings, whistles, and chimes buzzing nonstop from the barcade's rows of vintage games. My eyes adjust to the dim blue light as I hunt for the rest of the team.

I had heard them shouting about coming here as they were packing up. They had been around the corner, not realizing I was in earshot. I don't usually go with them to their incessant after-practice outings, but when I looked down at my duffel in the quiet locker room, I didn't feel like going home. So, I figured I'd surprise the gang with an appearance from their star player.

I press through the crowd, heading for the bar, which is

bathed in an orange glow. The Friday night crowd is rowdy, but being six-foot-two and mostly muscle has its advantages. I easily lock eyes with the bartender, a guy with a nose ring and tattoo down his arm of the Pac-Man characters chasing each other.

The bartender clocks my Rangers jersey and nods. "What is that? Soccer?"

I lean in, ignoring the question. "Gimme a Rainier."

The bartender shrugs and goes to grab the beer. I've been in Portland for a few months now, but I still don't really "get" the city. I bounced around a lot as a kid, my parents' divorce and subsequent moves sending me to three schools in four years before I finally ended up with my grandparents. But none of the cities I've lived in have ever been as unabashedly "weird" as Portland. Someone needs to sit me down and explain what is so charming about this place because I find it annoying.

I grab the beer and look around again, hoping to spot a flash of chestnut brown hair above a red silk blouse, unwilling to admit how significant a role that played in my decision to come here. From what I hear, Anna sometimes joins the team after the games.

I am still kicking myself about our conversation—or lack of conversation—from earlier. Getting nervous around a woman is new for me. I planned on impressing her during our post-game media training, but I'd been so determined to look good that I took way too long in the shower and missed my chance.

Instead of seeing Anna's brown hair anywhere, I see a flash of pink hair above an artfully ripped black T-shirt. I turn the other way so quickly that I almost spill my beer. I should have known Mabeline would be here tonight.

Praying she hasn't seen me, I head toward the herd of bulky silhouettes bent over a pinball machine. I once again elbow my way through the crowd, grinning in anticipation. My team is going to be psyched.

They are huddled around a game called Medieval Madness, cheering on Chad or Vlad. I can't tell which one from the back. Everyone is screaming about trolls. I wonder if Portland has any normal bars.

I lean forward, tapping Vlad—I'm pretty sure it is Vlad—on the shoulder. Vlad jumps and mistimes hitting his paddle. The ball sails down the drain. A chorus of groans ricochets around the machine.

"Hey. Thought I'd join you." I step forward, revealing myself to the team and waiting for their reactions.

The rowdy group goes quiet at the sight of me. Chad and Vlad exchange looks that I can only assume are of awe.

Leo clears his throat and steps forward to clap me on the back. "Good to see you, man."

I nod. I knew they'd be psyched. "I thought we could grab a table. Figured we should go back over the game. I think defense was pretty slow tonight. I've got some pointers."

"Sure, we can talk pointers. I think we need to work on our passing game," Leo says.

I nod emphatically. "Totally agree, man. We need to work on creating more opportunities for your guys to get the puck to me. Second period was a mess."

Leo plasters on a polite smile.

"You know what? Let's save it for practice. I think the guys are pretty focused on pinball tonight."

"Sure, I can do pinball," I say, cutting in front of Chad and grabbing the Medieval Madness levers. "Let's go."

I pull the plunger, sending the pinball zinging through the machine. It hits the castle and zooms back toward the bottom. I immediately button-mash the flippers, but the ball slides straight through them and down the drain. I curse and dig in my pocket for coins.

Chad leans forward, offering a baggie of quarters.

"You know, it's actually better if you only hit one at a time—"

"I got it," I snap, grabbing the quarters and shoving some into the machine. I yank the plunger. The ball shoots out again. This time, I hit it back up a few times before it rolls onto the castle's drawbridge and then down the drain.

I swear and grab for more quarters. Stupid pinball. Stupid city. Maybe it is a good thing that Anna isn't here until I figure this out.

It takes me three more games to get a decent score. But when I turn around to high-five Chad, there is only a very scared busboy grabbing my empty beer. I shrug it off. The team knows not to bug me when I am in the zone. I'll grab another beer, then see if someone wants to go head-to-head.

I prepare to wade back through the crowded room to get another drink, and turn back to grab my quarters first. In front of the game, where I swear nobody was standing a second ago, is Mabeline.

She is easily a foot-and-a-half shorter than me, but that is the only thing about her that is small. Her wild hot-pink hair frame a fierce face: smoky eyes lined heavily in black, nose piercing, and blood-red lipstick. She has on a vintage Black Sabbath T-shirt, tiny shorts, and fishnets. She is the Freezer's biggest fan, and she terrifies me.

Mabeline smiles widely. "Blake, is that you? I didn't know you were here." She punches me on the shoulder in a friendly gesture that is way too hard. Leo told me that Mabeline plays for the Rose City Rebels in Portland's roller derby league. He said her derby name is "Mabel the Destroyer." I believe it.

I grunt in response and try to go around her.

Mabeline quickly steps into my path. "Great game tonight. Really great. You played amazing. That last shot in third period was really *wow*." Now she is petting my arm like it is a small animal. Her long acrylic nails are painted as red as her lipstick, and they gleam dangerously in the low-blue light.

It isn't that she is wrong. I appreciate she can recognize talent. I just wish she was a little less . . . Portland. I look around, trying to find the guys, but they all have disappeared.

"What are you drinking? Can I buy you a drink? They have a great drink here called the Levitating Woman." She winks. "And then maybe we can talk about the game. Or I can play you in pinball? Or what if we just get out of here? It's so loud." She leans close to make her point.

I make one more desperate scan of the bar, but some-how, a bunch of massive hockey players have vanished into the crowd. I put my hands on tiny Mabeline's shoulders and carefully create distance between us.

"Wish I could, but I can't. Gotta get home to the lady."

Mabeline's hopeful face plummets. "Oh. Gotta get home . . . to the lady?"

"Yeah. She hates it when I'm out too late." I can picture the glare Iris is going to give me when I get back.

"Well," Mabeline sniffs, "she sounds really possessive. I don't have a boyfriend right now. Just so you know."

I know. I nod like this is new information and, not knowing what else to do, give her an awkward pat on the head. She smiles at me in a way that would be quite cute if Mabeline wasn't so damn menacing. It is very different from the warm smile Anna had given me earlier in the locker room.

Mabeline opens her mouth to say something else, but I turn and almost run out of the bar.

I drop my keys on the table and flick the lights on in my small apartment. The walls are white, but the predominant color in the space is green. Plants sit on every surface they can. Tall fiddle leaf figs grow in large pots in the corners. English Ivy spills from the sides of my TV. A peace lily reigns on the coffee table. I've moved around a lot, and it's been hard to make cheap apartments feel like home. I learned I could always add plants. It makes even the ugliest apartment feel like an oasis.

I grab a mister and spray. My oldest fiddle leaf is shedding leaves like crazy, but I think I finally got it back on track. I check its soil gently. There is a faint jingling behind me, and I turn to find Iris watching me. Glaring, as predicted.

"Hi, pretty baby. I know. I'm so sorry."

Iris ignores the apology, turning and strutting away from me. Her voluminous tail flicks as she walks, and I wonder if I'll find any poop in my shoes. Iris, the stunning white and brown Persian cat I rescued from a vacating neighbor several years ago, does not appreciate my long hours and always makes it known.

I set down the mister and head for the kitchen, knowing the surest way to win my cat over. The cans of sardines sit in a neat stack next to my windowsill herb garden. Everything in my apartment is neat, though aside from the plants, it is mostly undecorated. I bought some frames for my hockey pictures, but I left the stock photo of a waterfall in one of them. I think it makes me look adventurous.

Iris leaps onto the counter the second I crack the sardine top and looks at me with her big, blue eyes. I stroke her cloud-soft fur.

"Guess who won the game tonight, my fuzzy princess? I had better stats than Gretzky. And then we all went out for beers," I coo at her as she inhales the sardines. I don't mention the team hadn't actually invited me or spent much time with me. I know they are intimidated by me, but I hope to find more friends on the Freezers than my old team, or back on my college team, for that matter.

I set those thoughts aside, and my mind drifts back to

Anna. She is so beautiful with her long, wavy hair and her big hazel eyes. I can tell she is intrigued by me.

"Anna's going to love you," I tell Iris, who purrs. "Next time, I'm definitely going to ask her out." I don't know why I get so tongue-tied around Anna. I am usually great with girls. Then again, she is a lot smarter than the women I usually go for. And there is that pesky little rule about her not dating hockey players.

I scoop up Iris and carry her over to the couch, where she sprawls in my lap. I grab my phone and hunt for game highlights. The first thing I see is a clip Anna posted of my post-game interview. A thrill goes through me that she's been thinking of me tonight, too. She said something about being more positive with the reporters next time, but I disagree. I showed everyone I am a man to be reckoned with.

I resolve that the next time I have a chance, I will sweep Anna off her feet and make her rule a thing of the past. It is game on.

Chapter 5

All of This Is Off the Record

CHARLIE

I'm running late as I slip through the entrance to the Veteran's Memorial Coliseum, slowing down as the rink comes into view. I admire the glow from the wraparound windows and the way it makes the ice glisten. Ever since I was a kid, I've been coming here to catch games. I know most minor league players dream of the big time, but playing here for the first time with the Shredders felt like making it.

Zamboni Zane is out on the ice, and I give a little wave. Zane sends a salute back. I won the pre-game lottery to ride on the Zamboni with Zane back when I was about twelve. I felt like the king of the world.

I shake off the memories and head into the labyrinth of hallways behind the rink, trying to remember everything

Coach Ryan wants me to say in this season-opener interview. My coach did not appreciate my improvisation the night of the Freezers game. He felt it distracted from others taking the team seriously. I often wish the coach would lighten up. I feel hockey is at its best when everyone is having fun. However, goofing around is not in Coach Ryan's vocabulary.

I poke through the hallways until I nearly run into a frazzled assistant whose eyes narrow into slits when she sees me.

"You're late."

"I know. I'm sorry, I got—"

The assistant isn't listening. She grabs my arm and practically hurls me into the same room I'd done the last press conference in. This time, *The Oregonian* and a few smaller outlets are interviewing players one by one. Tricia Cornwallis had asked for me specifically.

I tumble into the room to find Tricia waiting, hair coiled tight and back ramrod straight.

She gives me a once-over. "You're late."

I nod. "I know." I settle into the chair and smile a sheepish grin. Tricia does not smile back, but she doesn't push the issue. I suppose she feels I wasted enough time already. I try to remember Coach Ryan's talking points, knowing it isn't good for the championship team to lose its very first match to an underdog like the Portland Freezers.

The losing didn't bother me, although I wouldn't have minded getting one over on the Freezers new center. I can't remember his name, but that guy was begging for a fight.

"Now, Mr. Haskell, the Shredders won last year's PCHL

championship by four goals," Tricia states, looking down at her notes.

I nod, pulling my mind back to the interview and knowing exactly what was coming next. But before Tricia could ask the rest of her question, the door opens. I look up.

Standing there, looking confused, is a woman in a red silk shirt. She has chestnut hair that spills past her shoulders in glossy waves, large brown eyes framed by an explosion of lashes, and high cheekbones dusted pink. I swallow. She is quite beautiful. A puzzled line appears at the center of her forehead as she looks at me. I recognize her from the press conference at the Freezers game, but I have a nagging feeling we have met before.

The assistant bursts in after her, looking at Tricia apologetically.

"I'm so sorry. This is Anna Green, the publicist from the Portland Freezers. You were supposed to be done with *him* by now." The assistant glares. I offer another sheepish grin.

"Should I come back another time?" Anna asks, taking a step back.

Tricia Cornwallis glances between Anna and me with a gaze that would be more at home on a lioness assessing its prey. She points at Anna with a long, graceful finger.

"You," she says, freezing Anna in her tracks. "Join us."

"What?" both Anna and I ask in unison.

"I would like to know how a team with a track record like the Freezers managed to beat the reigning champions in the first game. Perhaps having a representative of the

Freezers will keep you from filling this interview with drivel about soft ice and player injuries, Mr. Haskell."

I frown. Those were exactly the reasons Coach Ryan had prepped me to give. The assistant drags over a second folding chair with an unpleasant screech.

Anna sits tentatively.

I watch Anna's hair bounce as she sits, taking in the graceful line of her face, and the single beauty mark on her cheek. She must see me as the enemy, though I'd like to win her over. I have no bone to pick with the Freezers publicist, and I am pretty good with women. Suddenly, the images flood back to me. I snap my fingers.

"I know where I know you from. We met at last year's All-Stars game."

I remember it perfectly now and smile at the memory. She had been coordinating team photos before the match over in Rapid City. She'd been going by Annie then. While I waited my turn for photos, I played a game of pickup soccer in the hallway with a few of the Peach State Puckers and Bangor Blizzards I'd gotten to know playing college hockey. Anna and I had literally bumped into each other while I was diving for the ball, and I had challenged her to join the game, figuring it would do her good to blow off steam. She might be a publicist, but she sure as hell held her own with a soccer ball. I was impressed.

Anna clears her throat. "Did we? I don't recall."

My heart sank. Maybe that moment hadn't made an impression on her. I try again. "You know, before the game? The All-Stars? In the hallway? With the soccer ball?" I stop, realizing how much I sound like I am playing Clue. Anna just shrugs. So much for winning her over.

Tricia watches us with something akin to amusement on her face. She points her slim finger at Anna again.

"Since Mr. Haskell seems inclined to stall, Ms. Green, would you care to offer an explanation as to the Shredders' underperformance?"

Anna clears her throat before answering.

"Well, the Shredders are an excellent team," she starts, ignoring my megawatt smile at the compliment. "But the Freezers have really been putting in the work this year. I think it's possible for a team that's been at the top for so long to underestimate their competition."

"Mr. Haskell, do you feel that this is the case?" Tricia asks, swiveling her gaze to me.

"I, well, I think we take every game very seriously," I respond, not thrilled at how Anna's eyebrows go up when I say the word 'seriously.' "The Freezers played well for a first game—"

"For a first game? So, you're saying you don't think we could beat you again?" Anna asks.

"I, uh, that's not what I—" I stammer.

"Because, if I remember correctly, our goals per game and our save percentages are actually better this season than the Shredders' percentages from this time last year," Anna says sweetly, batting her eyelashes at me. "Or, is that not right?"

"Well," I say, trying hard to hold on to the numbers in my head instead of getting lost in those eyelashes.

"I believe that is correct," Tricia volunteers. "Mr.

Haskell, are you concerned you might be at risk of losing the championship this year?"

"To the *Freezers*?" The words were out of my mouth before I could stop myself.

Anna pivots in her chair to face me fully. "Yes, that's right. To the Freezers," she says. "I know most people look at the Portland Freezers, and all they see is that we have a refrigerator for a mascot. But our team has heart, and we've been working our butts off. We've been drilling our forecheck systems, our power play systems, our edgework. While other teams might be content to rest on their laurels, we plan on going all the way this season."

I admire Anna's passion while kicking myself for getting talked into a corner. But I wasn't about to let Anna have all the fun. "Heart is one word to describe your players," I say. "Lots and lots of heart. Speaking of statistics, can you remind me of your PIM per game? I just have this memory of some of the guys having a little trouble staying out of the box." I turn to Tricia. "Or, is that not right?"

Anna glowers.

Tricia, meanwhile, is taking copious notes that I very much wished I could read. "Would you say you have a strong team this year, Mr. Haskell?"

"Oh absolutely," I respond, trying to get the interview back on track. "Gilly Patterson's one of the best power forwards outside of the NHL, and you haven't lived until you've seen our goalie Tony do one of his split saves." I catch Anna's raised eyebrows. "What? He's very bendy."

"Uh-huh. I'm just surprised you didn't list yourself."

"Yeah? You think I'm that good?" I ask, hoping the pink

on her cheeks is a blush. But she surprises me by taking the question seriously.

"I can't deny that you're good," she acknowledges. "But I think you could be better."

"Really? I'm all ears," I say, intrigued.

"I think you play well. Your speed's good, your puck control is sharp, and you have great instincts." Now Anna is definitely blushing. "But you play to play. You don't play to win."

I sit back in my chair, stunned momentarily silent by hearing Coach Ryan's words coming out of Anna's much prettier mouth. So, I like to have fun on the ice. It isn't a bad thing not to treat every game like life or death, like certain Freezers' players do. At least, I didn't think so until now.

"It's not every day you get advice from your rivals." I say, trying to smile gallantly, not wanting it to look like she had gotten to me. "I just might have to take it."

"By all means." She smiles back at me. Despite her surprisingly impactful words, seeing that smile makes me look forward to finding an excuse for a rematch with this fascinating woman.

Anna holds her hand out for a handshake, and my large hand closes over hers. We remain like that for a second, looking into each other's eyes, the interview forgotten.

Then Tricia claps her hands, and we both jump. Her eyes are glittering. "I am looking forward to this season," she says. "Wouldn't you agree, Coach Ryan?"

My stomach drops. Coach Ryan is standing behind

Tricia, along with Coach Peter. I have no idea how long they'd been watching the interview, but Coach Ryan's glare could slice my skates in half. A few other journalists had apparently snuck in and hovered in the corner, looking back and forth between the Coaches.

Giving me a look that said: 'I'll deal with you later.' Coach Ryan grunts and says to Tricia bluntly, "All of this is off the record."

He then turns to Coach Peter. "Keep your people away from my players," Coach Ryan growls.

"What's wrong?" Coach Peter asks. "Are you afraid of us, Ryan?"

Coach Ryan's nostrils flare. "No. I just don't want any undue interference," he says, sneering at Anna.

Coach Peter steps up, going toe-to-toe with Coach Ryan. "Believe me, my people don't want anything to do with your players."

There is a tense beat as the two coaches glare at each other.

"You know what?" Anna says quickly, coming to her father's side and tugging firmly on his elbow. "I think the best place to settle this is on the ice."

"I couldn't agree more," I chime in, pivoting my coach toward Tricia's chair to remind him they have a renowned journalist listening to every word. "The Shredders are looking forward to our next game with the Freezers. We definitely won't underestimate them this time."

Chapter 6

Does That Say . . . Mealworms?

ANNA

I stand outside in the blustery October weather and try to keep my thoughts under control. It isn't easy. Ever since a press contact told me that journalist Kyle Brodie leaked Tricia's silly little interview with Charlie, press requests have been flooding in.

Are the coaches *really* bitter enemies? Do the Freezers *really* think they can beat the very team that dominated them last season? How do I feel about Charlie Haskell's responses? This growing rivalry between the Freezers and the Shredders is good for the team, but I wasn't used to being part of the story. And I don't know how to answer all these questions about Charlie, the man I am determined to dislike. *Mostly*.

With difficulty, I force my thoughts back to my current

task. I skim the gray streets of the Alberta Arts District for any heads that stand out above the rest. And there he is, dark hair towering above the Saturday shoppers.

I have learned that not all hockey players move gracefully when off the ice, especially when using only their feet against the hard ground. But Blake moves with a liquid efficiency that almost has me checking for skates. His long gray overcoat flaps open to reveal the hockey jersey underneath. I notice he lives in hockey jerseys, like he never wants to get off the ice. My mind flashes to the muscles I know lay hidden beneath the polyester. I wonder how he'd look in a tight T-shirt and leather jacket. For press purposes, of course.

My cheeks heat as Blake stops in front of me, his dark eyes gazing down into mine. Then he looks up dubiously at the building behind me.

"Ice cream?" he asks. "In October?"

"It's Salt & Straw," I say, by way of explanation. "Trust me. You'll love it."

I turn and tug open the glass doors, ushering Blake into the warm wood and brick tones of the ice cream parlor. I breathe deep, letting the waffle-cone-scented air fill my lungs. Of all the Salt & Straw locations across Portland, the OG is my favorite. Alison's eatery, Munch, is definitely my happy place, but this is a contender. I hope the sweet smells and the promise of sugar will soften the conversation I need to have with Blake about his media training. Besides, this isn't just your average ice cream.

Blake studies the chalkboard menu with a frown.

"Are there any non-fat flavors?" he asks, lowering his

voice to a growl and trying to make the question sound manly.

I lean in close and give him a devilish grin. "They have dairy-free, but trust me, the full-fat experience is worth it."

Blake nods, dragging his gaze back to the board where there are Halloween-inspired flavors for October. One is called Creepy Crawly Critters. He squints at the ingredients.

"Does that say . . . *mealworms*?"

I grin. "It's better than it sounds, I promise."

As I step forward to order, Blake pivots away from the bug-filled ice cream specials, skimming the classic flavors which include Strawberry Honey Balsamic with Black Pepper and Pear with Blue Cheese.

Blake sighs. "Do they have vanilla?"

Ice creams in hand, we settle at a rickety table inside the shop. I gleefully dig into my Candycopia, and Blake inspects his Salted, Malted, Chocolate Chip Cookie Dough for rogue bugs.

I look over and clock his barely-picked-at ice cream. "You don't like it?"

"No. No. It's really . . . good," Blake says and shoves a large spoonful in his mouth. He drops his spoon and grabs his head as if he got brain freeze.

I nod, studying him with pursed lips. "Listen, Blake. I really appreciate you meeting me here on your day off. It's just so hard to get a moment to really talk at the Coliseum, what with everything Coach Peter is putting you guys through."

Blake grunts in agreement, rubbing his temples.

"Practice has been good too," he manages. "We need it."

I watch him. "Yeah? You think so?"

"I mean, I'm good," Blake says. "But the team's gotta work on speed and holding onto the puck. I can't score if we keep getting stuck playing defense. I told Chad and Vlad if they wanna stay on the first line with me, they've gotta stop getting caught on the boards."

"You did?" I ask. "How'd that go over with them?"

"Uh, I think they got the message," he says and gives me his signature grin. His dimples are on full display, and I smile back.

I really do like seeing Blake smile. It softens his sharp face, and I am a sucker for dimples. Maybe I can convince him to smile more for the press. Since I don't want him to get defensive, I choose my words carefully. "Blake, I think your attitude has been really good for the team," I start, and am immediately rewarded with another dimpled grin. "Everybody's really thrilled about our victory against the Shredders. But—"

"I saw the interview you did with that Charlie guy and the coach. They're gonna pay. Nobody looks down at the Freezers." Blake's face darkens again.

I nod, wishing once again no one had seen that interview. I got caught up in the moment of ribbing Charlie, and I am still dealing with the fallout.

Blake reaches out and puts his hand on my arm. "I mean it. He doesn't get to talk like that to you."

I am a little flattered. I definitely do not need Blake

fighting this battle for me, but there is something sexy about knowing that angry scowl was all for me.

"Don't worry about Charlie. I'll handle that. I am glad you brought up the press conferences, though."

"You want me to do more of them?" Blake asks.

"I do, but before we set that up, I think we should talk about how the press perceives you," I say. Judging from Blake's blank stare, he didn't know what I was getting at. "With your intense practice schedule, we still haven't gotten a chance to do any real media training, and I worry the reporters aren't seeing the best version of you."

"They see me winning games, don't they?" Blake asks.

"Sure, but that's not all they see," I try to explain. "They also see it when you fight with the ref or with the other team."

Blake shrugs. "So?"

"So, they don't always like that. They don't respond well to players who fight too much or brag too much about their wins. They like players who are humble and share credit for their victories. Like—" I stop myself. I was about to say, like Charlie but I don't think that will go over well. "Like Leo. He's really good with the press."

"Leo's fine, but he needs to work on stopping rebound shots."

"Okay, sure. But that's not the point."

"Why not? I'm the one who won the game. They don't want to talk about that?"

"It's just that you didn't win the whole game, right? The team did. It's more sportsmanlike to give everybody credit.

If you hog credit and trash-talk the other team too much, you come across as arrogant."

"You think I'm arrogant?" Blake asks, rearing back.

I am losing him. "No, of course not," I assure him hastily. This is not going the way I had intended. Blake has barely touched his ice cream, which has turned into cookie-dough-studded soup. I feel bad. He is arrogant, but I am convinced there is a lot more under the surface that just needs to come out. I need to try something else. "Why did you get into hockey in the first place?"

Blake shrugs. "I dunno. It was something to do."

Blake's walls are up, but there has to be more to his fierce love of the game than that. I try again. "Did your parents take you to hockey games when you were a kid?"

Blake looks away. "My grandparents. My grandad loved hockey. He was a Rangers guy. Took me to my first game, Rangers against the Flyers. We won."

I nod, watching another small smile warm Blake's face. I took a second look at his jersey. Rangers number eleven, the iconic center Mark Messier.

Blake continues, my wide eyes encouraging him to keep going. "I moved around a lot when I was a kid, after my parents got divorced. I guess hockey was one thing I could do everywhere. When I moved in with my grandparents, my grandad came to every game."

I swallow a sudden lump in my throat. I know what it is like to have your childhood disrupted and be raised by a different group of people. I love my dad and my grandparents, but it is hard to fill the hole left by my mom. Like Blake, I had sought solace in hockey from the second I could strap on skates. Out there on the ice, you can forget everything else. It is your own private world. Working for the team, I still feel that way."

It is my turn to reach over and put my hand on Blake's arm. "I'm glad you told me. That's the side of you I really want the press to see. I think they'd love to know things like that. I know I do."

Blake shrugs, staring down at my hand resting on his sleeve. Maybe we were finally connecting.

He reaches into his pocket and pulls out a crumpled paper bag. He hesitates for almost a full minute before sliding it over. "Here."

He watches me unfold the bag with apprehension. I reach inside and pull out a small flat square of worn wood.

"It's a hockey puck," he blurts, unable to wait, "from the 1870s. My grandma found it at an antique shop when I was living with them. Crazy, right? They're really rare."

I make to give it back to him, and Blake holds up his hand. "I want you to have it," he says grandly.

"Wow. Thank you," I say, not entirely sure what else to add. I always enjoy learning little tidbits about hockey history, and figure that Blake wants me to show off the puck to his fans. In fact, it could be a sweet way to humanize him. I gently place the puck in my bag and say, "This is really very cool, Blake. We should display it at the Coliseum, or maybe we can do a feature on it for our social. What do you think?"

"Sure, if you want," Blake says, watching as the puck vanishes into the depths of my purse.

Blake stands abruptly, and I struggle to get to my feet.

This meeting has gone awry, although I can't quite put my finger on what happened. The puck really is a unique piece of history, although he didn't need to give it to me. I hope it is a sign that he is coming around to media training.

He fixes me with his intense eyes. "Thank you for the ice cream."

He quickly gathers our trash and sweeps out of the store before I can respond. I watch him go, intrigued despite myself. The mystery of Blake Tyler will have to be solved another day.

Chapter 7

He Loves My Biscuits

ANNA

"That's really a hockey puck?" Alison asks, staring down at the worn wooden block on my desk. "It's square."

"That's how they used to make them," I explain, messing with my iPhone portrait settings as I line up a shot. "Before this, they were using balls, but those tended to bounce out of the rink and whack people in the face, so they switched to these in the late 1800s. Cool, right?"

Alison shrugs, still eyeing the puck. I reach over and make an adjustment to my desk lamp, causing the puck to cast a long shadow across the vintage hockey photographs I have underneath it. The puck is a fascinating piece of hockey memorabilia, but it isn't easy to make a wooden square look interesting in a photo. I didn't know if the post for our feed would get much engagement, but I had promised Blake. I'd hate to disappoint him.

"Actually, some of the earliest hockey pucks were frozen cow dung, so this was an improvement."

Alison wrinkles her nose. "I'm really glad he didn't give you one of those."

"They didn't tend to last long." I laugh. I sit back and flick through my shots. They are all almost identical images of a piece of wood resting on old photographs. I tried, but the most interesting ones feature the photographs instead of the puck. I sigh.

Alison leans over and picks up the puck, taking a closer look. She holds it down for Stinker, who lifts his bushy face off his bed to give it a polite sniff. Deeming it not to be food, he settles back down. "So, Blake Tyler gave this to you? To keep?"

"It's a unique part of hockey history. He said his grandmother found it in an antique shop." I glance up and catch Alison staring at me.

"And you're sure the only reason he gave it to you was for you to post it on Instagram?" Alison asks.

I blush and look away. "Of course. It's all part of my job."

That is the reason, isn't it? It was a very sweet gesture, given how much he cares about the puck. I start to wonder if the brooding Blake wants more from our relationship, he is always so quiet around me.

"Besides, he knows my rule. They all do."

Ignoring Alison's eye-roll, I lean over and stick my fork into my friend's latest creation, a jiggly tiramisu-inspired Japanese cheesecake, which feels like eating a coffee-dusted cloud. The airy sweetness melts in my mouth. Then I grab the photos I took at the Freezers-Shredders game to find a few of Blake to post with the puck.

Alison snatches the portfolio away. "This is him, right?" She thumbs through the photos of Blake, his nearly black eyes glaring out at the ice from under his heavy brow and his cheekbones sharp enough to cut glass. She lets out a wolf whistle. "Remind me why you have this no-dating-hockey-players rule again?"

"First of all, because the league frowns upon members of management dating players, and rightly so. It risks preferential treatment," I remind her, trying to snatch the pictures back. Alison holds them just out of reach. "Besides, workplace romances are never a good idea. Remember Amy and T.J.?" Amy had been the team's doctor several years back, and T.J. was Peter's assistant coach before Sylvia. Their relationship had not ended well.

"That was five years ago! And based on what you told me, T.J. deserved to have his car keyed. If the only real issue is that the league 'frowns upon' manager-player relationships, then I don't see the problem. If I didn't date anyone that people frowned upon, I would still be a virgin." She winks.

"Yeah, well, even if the league's stance wasn't a legitimate concern—which it is—there's also the fact that my dad coaches my prospective hockey dating pool. It's kind of a buzzkill."

"I'll give you that," Alison allows, "but what about someone like this guy? He's not on your dad's team. Problem solved." She holds up a photo of Charlie Haskell that I had forgotten was in there. I didn't plan to take any photos of the Shredders, but Charlie had been goofing off with some young fans, and I grabbed my camera on instinct. It is another example of him not taking the game seriously, but his exuberance is palpable.

"Problem very much not solved," I reply. "My dad made the Shredders our unofficial rivals for the season. If I dated someone like Charlie, I think his head would explode right off his shoulders."

Alison laughs. "Point taken. I guess you'll just have to date Blake then." She holds up another photo of Blake, a black and white shot of him racing across the ice, with his jaw clenched as he chased the puck.

I cannot deny that Blake is an incredibly handsome player. He is filled with a focus and determination I find impressive. He lives and breathes hockey. I think back to what he said about his past and how hockey was the one constant in his childhood. I felt another pang of empathy. His arrogance is clearly grounded in something deeper. Maybe . . .

I shake my head, clearing my thoughts. Dating Blake or Charlie or any player is out of the question. I take a long sip from the iced coffee Alison brought for me, along with the cheesecake.

"Nice try, but it's not going to happen. Why do you want me to date a hockey player, anyway? You hate hockey. If I date a hockey player, it just means more hockey in your life too. Wouldn't you rather I date a chef or something?" I ask.

I try to date, but mostly in the off-season when I have actual time to spare, and my dad isn't breathing over my shoulder. I would honestly love to date a chef, but meeting anyone these days is so hard. Two years ago, I ran into a Freezers fan at an NHL game, and we really hit it off. Until I realized he was dating me to get to the players. After that, I got a lot less enthusiastic about looking for relationships.

"Well, if I had a choice, I'd really rather you date a celebrity who's looking to invest in a new line of bake shops." Alison says grinning.

"I'll try," I promise. "Remember when Ryan Reynolds came into Munch that one time?"

"He said he loved my biscuits!" Alison sighs. "If he wasn't married, I would have proposed on the spot. I almost did anyway." She leans down and gives Stinker a few scratches behind the ears. He thumps his tail. "Look, I don't really care if you date a hockey player or a famous person or anyone at all. I just want you to be happy. Are you happy?"

I poke at the cheesecake, contemplating the question. No one is happy all the time, are they? I love my job, but it also drives me crazy worrying about my dad or how the team is doing or whether our ticket sales are enough. There is more I can do for the Freezers if he lets me, but it is easier to stay in my lane. Nothing wrong with playing it safe, right?

"Of course I'm happy."

"And you're sure that this absolute smoke show could not increase your happiness?" Alison asks, making Blake's picture dance. "Remember what our good friend Ellie says, 'You should do one thing every day that scares you.'"

I make a face at Alison. "You're not allowed to use Eleanor Roosevelt to try to get me to date Blake."

"Why not?" Alison asks. "I bet she would have grabbed him in a heartbeat. Saucy minx."

I laugh. My friend is not wrong, not about the feisty former first lady we love, nor that Blake scares me. I found a good rhythm in my life. Is it worth breaking my rules for someone like Blake, even if his intense gaze makes my heart flutter? Still, what if it all goes wrong? He is far from a safe bet for so many reasons. I am afraid to risk it.

Seeing the argument is going nowhere, Alison hands back my photos. "These are really good, you know."

"Maybe for an amateur. We have a pro who takes the real photographs." I remind her.

"These *are* real photographs," Alison insists. "They almost make me care about hockey. You're really good at your job, babe."

"Tell that to my dad, who is not interested in using any of my ideas."

"Still?"

I shake my head. "I kinda get it. They're risky, and he doesn't want any distractions while we're still in the running. Which would be fine if our ticket sales pick up, and they're starting to. But if we don't hit our targets, I'm not sure what we're going to do."

"You know what our good friend Ellie would say to that?"

"More stuff about doing things that scare us?"

"A woman is like a tea bag," Alison quotes. "You can't tell how strong she is until you put her in hot water." She lifts up her chai latte.

"I'll cheers to that." I grab my iced coffee, and we clink our takeout cups.

"Oh, Anna, is that an iced coffee I see?" comes a disappointed voice from the hall. Zamboni Zane leans on the doorframe, watching us. I quickly drop my arm, hiding my cup behind the desk.

"No?" I lie.

"It's forty degrees outside." It is Zane's long-standing belief that my addiction to iced coffee is terribly misguided. I have seen him drink coffee so hot the Freezers players couldn't even hold a mug of it. A byproduct of a life on the ice.

I bat my eyes at Zane. "Iced coffee just tastes better."

"Did you at least make it at home? I sent you all those links about those cold-brew pitchers you can keep in your fridge." It is also Zane's long-standing belief that I spend way too much money on my addiction. If I am going to drink blasphemously, I should at least do it for less.

"Yes?" I lie again.

Zane shakes his head. "Don't make me break out my graphs again," he threatens, referring to the very impressive chart he made of my coffee habit last season. It didn't change my mind, but I framed it and hung it up in my condo. "Anyway, I heard there was cake."

Alison holds out the half-eaten tiramisu cheesecake and a fork. "We come in peace."

Zane ambles over and takes a bite. "She," he says, jabbing his finger at Alison, "can drink whatever she likes."

I pretend to pout, but I have to laugh. Zane bends down to pay his respects to Stinker, who drools in happiness.

"What's new, girls? What's the gossip these days?" Zane asks.

"The lack of gossip is that Anna refuses to date any hockey players for me," Alison laments.

"Because it's a bad idea, Zane. You tell her." I insist.

Zane regards us both, scratching his chin. "I think you should do it," he declares. "You're too young to be so serious. You need to go have some fun. Just pick a hot coffee drinker."

My jaw drops. Alison cheers. Stinker, unsure what the excitement is for, thwaps his tail.

"Don't worry, Zane, I know just the guy," Alison promises. She picks up Blake's hockey puck and tosses it over to me with an exaggerated wink.

The temperature has dropped by the time I finally make it home for the night. I hurry to the door, digging for my keys that must have sunk to the bottom of my purse. I cast a quick, apologetic glance at the mostly dead plants sitting on the low half-wall surrounding my condo's terrace. They are my attempt at creating a peaceful green space at home, like the self-help books recommend. But I have once again forgotten to water them. No plants of mine ever survive hockey season. I keep trying, though.

Keys located, I push inside and breathe a sigh of relief as my condo's heat warms me. It is only October, and already time to break out the heavy coat. I forget how quickly the weather turns in Portland since I spend winter holed up in the Coliseum, buried in my job.

I dump my stuff on the oversized chair of my cozy—but mismatched—living room set and make a beeline for my small kitchen. Since I'm not much of a cook, its size doesn't bother me. I yank open the freezer and debate if I want to crack open yet another frozen meal or douse a leftover baked potato in cheese. The only frozen meals I have are healthy, so baked potato it is.

Alison's question pops back into my head. Was I happy? If I wasn't, it was from being overworked, not from being single. Besides, the thought of adding another big, sweaty man into my life right now is way too complicated. I have enough on my plate.

I stuff my dinner in the microwave and return to my bag. I have a few fundraising appeals to finish before I can call it a night. Digging around, I fish out Blake's hockey puck. I had shoved it in my bag, hoping to snap a better IG pic later. I pluck it out and hold it in my palm. After everything Alison had insinuated, I felt a little guilty for taking the puck that meant so much to him, even if he had insisted. Did he want something more from me? Do I want something more from him? He can be gruff and arrogant, but he clearly has a sensitive side. I like the idea that I could be the one to bring that out in him.

I tug open the drawer of my vintage side table and toss the hockey puck inside. I'll find a way to give it back to Blake as soon as I can figure out how to do so without it being awkward.

Chapter 8

Chaos Drill

CHARLIE

I fly across the ice, welcoming the cold air as it whips through my hair and stings my cheeks. No matter how many times I strap on my skates and lumber onto the rink, this sensation always makes me feel like a kid again. I flip around so I am skating backward, bending low and willing my stiff quad muscles to limber up for the grueling practice ahead.

Coach Ryan watches from the sidelines as his players zigzag across the ice. He stands ramrod straight, arms folded, with a permanent frown etched across his jaw. Behind his back, I joke that Coach has resting-drill-sergeant face. None of the players remember ever seeing him smile. Today, I know, would be no exception. Despite winning our last two games, Coach Ryan has not gotten over the loss to the Freezers.

Coach nods curtly, and his assistant coach, Jared, blows two sharp notes on his whistle. I like Jared even less than Coach Ryan. Our coach is harsh, but good at his job. Jared is harsh because he wants Coach Ryan to like him.

The players stop, turning toward the whistle to find out what torture awaits.

"Chaos drill," Jared announces, a nasty gleam in his eye.

Everyone stifles a groan and splits into two groups, heading for opposite sides of the ice. I grab a puck and skate randomly, waiting for the whistle to send us all sailing across the ice at top speed. Chaos drills are the worst.

My teammate Quentin skates by. "Hey, Charlie! So what are you going to underestimate today?" he laughs. "Probably your body's pH balance," he calls, waggling his dreadlocks as he skates. Last season, Quentin had gone all in on exploring his Vietnamese culture and made the most incredible bánh mì for the team. This season, he's fallen down a macrobiotic rabbit hole. His organic brown rice gruel is a lot less tasty.

I hold up my glove to give him an awkward middle finger. Quentin laughs and skates away. The team has not let me live down that clip of my interview with Anna.

Jared blows the whistle, and I turn my attention to the goal across the rink. Ten players barrel in my direction.

"Show me those dekes," Coach Ryan calls out. "And keep your heads up."

I feint and dodge, moving my puck across the ice. I nearly slam into Alex, our youngest player, who is too focused on his stick handling.

"Head up, Alex!" Coach Ryan shouts. "It's not rocket science."

"Sorry, Charlie!" Alex calls, drawing out the 'o' with his Canadian accent, as he jerks his head back up.

"No problem, Alex!" I holler back, pivoting fast as Gilly sails toward me. My friend is easily the tallest man on the team. He wastes no time in hip-checking me and trying to steal the puck. Gilly is great off the ice, but on the ice, he is the Shredders scariest enforcer, and he makes no exceptions for me.

"You're playing a little off today, Chuck. Ya' sure there hasn't been any undue influence on you?" Gilly teases with a grin, showing off the dentures he has earned from years of getting his teeth knocked out on the ice.

I ignore him, too focused on executing my signature move. I switch my right-handed stick to my left hand and chuck. The puck sails toward the net as intended, but Tony —the goalie—easily slaps it aside.

"Getting sloppy, Charlie!" Coach Ryan shouts.

I mentally kick myself as I swing around and skate the other way. In truth, I can't get that interview out of my head either. Actually, I can't get *Anna* out of my head. Those wide eyes with long lashes twinkle at me from my dreams. I feel her hand—soft and warm—in mine. But what sticks the most is her telling me I need to step up my game.

"Alex! Keep your head up, or I will come out there and

do it for you!" Coach Ryan roars, interrupting my thoughts. I glance at Alex, who collides with Quentin, once again too focused on his stick. Poor kid. He is fresh out of college and still talks to his parents on WhatsApp every day. His desperation to prove himself and get a spot on the lineup often ends in sabotaging himself. He has yet to score a goal in any of our scrimmages. I'm not sure if Coach Ryan will ever let him off the reserve list.

Assistant Coach Jared blows the whistle, and the frantic energy on the ice stills suddenly. Coach Ryan surveys us with a clear look of disappointment.

"Stations," he announces, summing up his disdain for us in a single word.

The team splits up once again. Gilly, Alex, and I veer back toward Tony for shooting practice, while everyone else heads to their various agility, defense, and edgework stations.

Gilly eyes me as we skate. "*Has* there been any undue influence on you, brother?" he asks. I try to ignore him, but at six-foot-six, several inches taller than NHL giants Anders Lee, Juraj Slafkovsky, and Alex Ovechkin, Gillis Patterson is very hard to ignore.

"No undue influence whatsoever. That girl didn't even remember me," I swore, still surprised that Anna had forgotten our meet cute from the year before. Was I really so forgettable? I aim for the net and chuck the puck. Tony doesn't even have to move to swat it away.

"Yeesh," Gilly remarks. "My sister plays better than you."

"Your sister plays better than all of us," I retort. Gilly's sister Hollis is a rising star in the Professional Women's Hockey League. She can skate circles around me.

"True." Gilly grins. "But you are off today. You wanna talk about it?"

I shake my head, focusing on my footwork. It is too hard to explain. It isn't just that Anna is gorgeous and knows her stuff when it comes to hockey. She has also called me out on things I can barely even admit to myself. I have always been naturally good at hockey, and I love the rush of sailing across the ice with four other players who have your back just like you have theirs. The world narrows down to my teammates and my breath as we battle it out over a three-inch black circle.

I have friends who have made it all the way to the NHL, living and breathing the ice to the brink of exhaustion. I know if I push myself that hard, I can be good enough too. But something holds me back.

"Alex!" Coach Ryan snaps. "Hit the net next time!"

"Sorry, Coach," Alex calls, his face turning pink. His puck flies wide, shooting across the ice into the back corner. He tries again, and this time his puck goes straight into Tony's stomach.

"Sorry doesn't cut it, Alex," Coach Ryan booms, loud enough for the whole rink to hear. "Get it in the net or go home."

"Yes, Coach," Alex says meekly. Gilly claps him on the back in sympathy. I wonder, not for the first time, if my own hesitation comes from wanting to stay out of Coach Ryan's way. So long as I keep my head down and play a good enough game, I avoid the wrath. Unfortunately, Alex isn't so lucky.

The whistle blows again, and we head back to the neutral zone. I skate up beside Alex. "Ignore him," I say. "If he doesn't meet his yelling quota for the day, he dies."

Alex smiles. Usually, I would leave it at that, but Anna's challenge that I don't play to win rings inside my head. There is more I can give to my team.

"Listen, you're a good player," I say. "You're just in your head. Don't think about shooting to score. Think about shooting to miss Tony. And you're small, you can use that. Get in low and go for it. Trust me, it'll work." I smile encouragingly.

Alex nods. "Try to miss Tony?"

"Try to miss Tony. Don't even think about scoring."

The whistle blows again. It's scrimmage time. I put myself on Alex's team, although it means facing off against Gilly, which is never a good idea.

Myself, Alex, and Quentin barrel down the ice, passing the puck backwards between us as we try to clear the neutral zone. Quentin slices it over to me, and I dance it over the blue line into their offensive zone.

Gilly comes straight for me, slamming me into the boards. I know exactly where I'll have bruises tomorrow. I will my screaming muscles to behave as I work to create space, keeping myself between Gilly and the puck. I fake to the left and then look right, searching for openings. Alex is closest to the goal. I take the chance and send the puck flying toward him.

Alex catches the puck and goes straight for the net,

ducking low like I said and throwing off the defender coming up to check him. Alex lines up his shot and slaps the puck, sending it soaring straight past Tony's outstretched arm and into the net. Goal!

I cheer, impending bruises forgotten. Me and the other players swarm Alex, and hoist him into the air. We spin him around, whooping in glee. His first goal! I catch a glimpse of Coach Ryan and Jared. Jared is sulking, like always, but there might have been a ghost of a smile on Coach Ryan's face.

The party continues in the locker room after practice. We are as rowdy as if we had won a real game. Quentin runs around handing out macrobiotic treats that no one wants, and Tony throws them into Quentin's discarded helmet whenever he isn't looking. Alex is up on Gilly's shoulders, which means they have to hunch to keep Alex's head from going straight through the ceiling. He is on top of the world as he cheers, "I missed Tony! I missed Tony!"

I am proud my advice helped make that happen. I knew Alex could do it if Coach Ryan got out of the kid's way. Coach Ryan built the team from scratch seven years ago after the previous Shredders coach, William Farmer, had presided over two losing seasons in a row. Coach Ryan put us back on top, but he'd done it by screaming at us until we bent to his will. The constant verbal abuse works, but I hate it. I know other coaches in the PCHL, like the

Freezers Coach Peter, are beloved even when their teams lose. Surely, there has to be a happy medium. I feel a glimmer of what that is. Maybe the mysterious Anna Green really is right. I should try more often. Nothing feels better than helping my teammates.

I clear my throat, banging on the locker room floor with my hockey stick. The team quiets down, and Gilly turns so that he and Alex face me. Coach Ryan hates sticking around the locker room when we are goofing off, so he gave me his announcement to deliver. I plan on doing it in the way Coach Ryan will hate the most.

"Hear ye, hear ye," I cry, attempting a terrible British accent. "The Knights of the Locker Room have spoken. We hereby declare that today shall henceforth be known as Alex Gonzalez Day."

The players hoot and stamp their feet in response. Gilly spins Alex around in a circle.

"And furthermore," I shout, banging on my hockey stick, "King Ryan has issued an official edict. Alex, you are a Skateful Shredders reserve player no more." I pull the official game team jersey from behind my back. "Welcome to the roster, kid! You're on the lineup!"

The noise in the locker room is deafening. The whole team has been rooting for Alex, and they are over the moon. I reach up with my stick and tap Alex on each shoulder and then toss him the jersey. Alex wastes no time yanking it on, glowing with pride.

I step back, enjoying the utter chaos of my teammates. Like she has done about four million times over the past few weeks, Anna pops back into my mind. She might not think much of me, but I wish she could see my team now. The real Shredders . . . and the real me.

Chapter 9

Release The Kraken

BLAKE

I stare at the oversized diaper in horror. Surely there must be some mistake. I hold the plastic-draped clothes hanger in my hand and look around for somebody—anybody—who can fix this.

Anna speeds out of the multipurpose room, looking frazzled. She sees me standing and gives me a harried smile.

"Blake, hi, I'm so sorry we're running late. We had another, um, accident," she says. Her eyes fall to the hanger. "Oh, good, you found your outfit. Get changed and we should be good to go in five."

She hurries away before I can say a word. Specifically, the words "there's no way in hell I'm wearing this." Now I am alone with the diaper again. I stare at it, reminding myself this will get me a full hour with Anna.

It has been an entire month since our date at Salt & Straw, and our relationship is moving like expired molasses. I expected her to set up a time for us to post the hockey puck to the team socials, but then I saw she'd already done it. The puck looked incredible, of course, but I thought she'd suggested it as a ruse to spend more time with me.

I blame Coach Peter. The season has picked up, practice has beyond intensified, and I get the sense Coach told her no more media training was required. Which makes sense, since I always crush it with reporters, but still. The hockey puck should have worked by now, and the only reason it hasn't is because I can never get time with her.

So, when this opportunity came up, I signed on right away. I take a deep breath and tug off my shirt. The things I do for love.

I frown as I stand there naked except for a bulky white diaper pinned with a heart, massive pink glitter wings strapped to my back, a gold glitter halo headband, and Nike sneakers.

"Is something funny?" I ask her.

"I'm so sorry, Blake," Anna forces out between giggles. "This is incredibly unprofessional of me."

I'm not used to women looking at me and bursting into laughter. Especially when I am wearing this little clothing.

If a man was laughing at me like this, I would punch him in the face. But it is Anna, and I get a little giddy seeing her laugh so hard because of me. My face cracks into a small smile.

"Cupid is a god," I tell her. "That's no laughing matter."

She laughs even harder, and I feel invincible. I strut over to the photo backdrop of fluffy clouds and glitter hearts and strike the manliest pose I can in a diaper.

"I can see why you picked me for February." I was flattered when I found out I was getting the Valentine's month in the calendar. It confirmed everything I've been hoping.

"Oh, I know, I'm so sorry," Anna says, trying hard to catch her breath. "After Chad and Vlad got in a fight over who got to be a pilgrim last year, we had to make it a random drawing system."

My smile falls. She didn't choose me for February? Surely, this isn't a coincidence. Maybe she's just pretending the drawing is random to keep things professional. I won't let that ruin this moment for us.

"It's a good month for me anyway," I tell her. "I'm a very romantic guy."

Anna wipes her eyes on her sleeve.

"Sorry?" she asks.

"I can show you how romantic I am."

"Oh, yes, you're right, we should get started," Anna says, glancing at the time. She picks up her camera and knocks on the side door. "We just need your accessory."

I wonder what on earth we could possibly add to this abjectly awful outfit. A bow and arrow? That would be good, actually. I can shoot anyone who walks in and sees me.

But instead, an older woman in a shirt that says Oregon Dog Rescue comes in holding a very squirmy white and brown puppy. I take an involuntary step backward.

"Ooo, that's the cutest one!" Anna squeals.

I feel a surge of pride.

"You say that about all of them." The rescue coordinator laughs.

I deflate.

The woman holds the wriggling ball of fur out to me. "We're calling this one Kraken after the Seattle Kraken," she says. "We're so thrilled you guys partnered with us for your calendar this year, so all of these puppies are getting NHL names."

I take Kraken carefully, holding him underneath the dog's bony elbows. The puppy stares at me with huge mismatched blue and brown eyes and massive ears unfurling on either side of his head, like Baby Yoda. Then, true to his name, he tries to eat my hand.

"Looks like you two are getting along great," the coordinator says. "Call me if you need me." Then she disappears back into the side room amidst a cacophony of barks.

Once we were alone again, Anna grins at me. Even with the massive diaper, I am an incredibly handsome, shirtless man holding an utterly adorable puppy. But I hold Kraken as far away from my body as possible, like the puppy might explode at any second.

"You can hold him a little closer," Anna suggests.

I reel in my elbows, bringing the puppy about a foot closer to my body. Kraken shifts from trying to eat my hand to trying to eat his own ear. They are big enough that I think he might actually do it.

"Um, is that comfortable?" she asks me. "You can relax a bit."

"I'm more of a cat person," I grumble.

Anna grins. She sets down the camera and hops on the set before lifting the puppy away from me. Kraken gives her his biggest happy puppy smile.

"Maybe hold him like this." She demonstrates, cradling the puppy like a baby. He lay there like a fuzzy angel.

I step forward to take the puppy, and Anna is once again right up against my bare chest within kissing distance. Unfortunately, the second I take Kraken back, the puppy wriggles like he'd swallowed an Energizer Bunny, and Anna takes a giant step back.

"So, you're a cat person? Do you have any cats?"

"I do," I say, holding my face away from Kraken's tongue. The puppy seems extremely desperate to lick my mouth.

"Aww," Anna coos. "What's your cat's name?"

"Iris," I answer. "She's a full-bred Persian."

"I bet she's gorgeous," Anna says, snapping pictures.

"She is. I groom her myself. She loves it. You should hear her purr." I'm as proud of my cat as I am after scoring the winning goal in a game. "Do you like cats?" I ask.

"Oh, I do, but I'm actually allergic," Anna explains.

"I didn't know that. I'm sorry," I say, my daydreams of

Anna putting bows in Iris's fur shattering to pieces. I'll just have to buy a lifetime's supply of Benadryl.

Anna waves off my apology. "What else do you like?" she asks.

I shrug. Kraken sneezes on my shoulder.

"Come on," Anna prods. "I know there's more to you than cats and hockey."

I am pleased Anna is so interested in me. Almost pleased enough to overcome the horror of puppy snot. "Plants," I say.

"Plants?"

"I like plants. I have a lot of them."

"That's cool," Anna says. "What kind of plants?"

"Oh, all kinds," I reply. "I'm expanding my tabletop herb garden right now. I haven't bought herbs from the grocery store in years. It's been a bit touch-and-go with the parsley since I moved here, but I think I've got it under control now."

Anna keeps taking pictures as I talk. This shoot is turning out great. The puppy stares up at me like he is in sheer awe of me. If she keeps the diaper out of frame, it could even be a cover shot.

"Actually, Anna," I say as she clicks away. "I've noticed you don't have any plants in your office. Do you want me to get you one?"

"Oh, you don't have to do that," Anna says.

"No, I'd like to," I say firmly. "I'll bring you something good."

"I like getting to know you better, Blake," she says.

I smile.

She snaps another picture, then says, "I'd love to see you open up more at the press conferences too, you know? I think you could really get the reporters to fall in love with you."

I beam. This is exactly what I'd been hoping for. A signal from Anna that she is interested. The press conferences are one of the few places we get to spend time together. And reporters falling in love with me? Clearly, that means her. I know she'll drop her no-hockey-player rule eventually. For me.

I clear my throat and look directly into her hazel eyes. "Anna, listen, I've been meaning to ask you—"

Sensing an opening, the puppy lunges for my mouth, landing a full doggy French kiss.

Horrified, I let go of the puppy, who thankfully falls onto his floppy feet, then meanders over to my ankle, lifts up his leg—

And pees.

Anna laughs so hard she can barely breathe now. I don't know whether to melt down more about the puppy saliva in my mouth or the puppy pee on my leg. I settle for hopping one-legged around the set, wiping my tongue on my arm. Kraken bounces after me, happily leaping after my diaper and fluttering glitter wings.

The rescue coordinator must have heard the commotion because she comes rushing in to scoop up the gleeful Kraken, while Anna watches, completely helpless with laughter.

"Don't—worry—Blake," she wheezes. "These—are—the—best—pictures—ever."

But I'm not laughing. Yet another moment with Anna completely ruined. And the puppy peed on my favorite Nikes. This is the kind of mesh you can't put in the washing machine. I need to get out of here before things get any worse, so I can figure out a new plan of attack.

I muster up any remaining dignity I have. "Thank you, Anna. We good? I just remembered I have this thing to get to."

Not waiting for an answer, I turn and stride out, head held high.

Chapter 10

Sorry, Did You Want This?

ANNA

I can never go into Munch and only buy one thing. The eclectic eatery—home to Alison's edible creations—is too enticing. I love the funky industrial space, with its turquoise concrete walls covered with art from local Portland artists. The only exception is the wall in the second-floor area, which is a massive chalkboard for café patrons to add their own.

I beeline for the pastry display case and its rows of colorful confections, where classic eclairs jockey for space next to marionberry mochi donuts. Baskets of fresh breads sit above the glass, their just-baked aromas wafting enticingly. I have my eye on the huge sundried tomato focaccia for my lunch. I barely finished the dog rescue calendar on time and have two more massive charity projects fast approaching. Today is definitely a focaccia day.

Sal is helping a customer, but he gives me a friendly wave and leans over his shoulder to shout, "Hey, Alison, your better half is here!"

I grin. Sal is a massive hockey fan and has loved me from the second I scored him Freezers season tickets. Alison emerges from the back, her thrift-store pinstripe vest and denim apron dusted in flour. I know Alison is in charge of Munch's soundtrack today, because Chappell Roan pours from the speakers, crooning, "Good Luck, Babe!"

"Gluten Morgan," Alison trills at me. It is her favorite shop greeting. As adventurous as Alison is with flavors, gluten-free is not in her vocabulary. "What do you want today? I just made some cannoli tayaki, and they are delicious, if I do say so myself."

Alison points to several rows of tayaki—fish-shaped pastries brimming with sweet ricotta and covered in chocolate—in the case.

My mouth waters. "Um, yes, please. One of those and then maybe just an assortment? There's a staff meeting today. Just make sure there's at least one donut for Coach Peter."

Alison salutes and goes to get a pastry box.

"Oh!" I say, "And one of the focaccias."

I reach for the last of the pillowy breads, but instead of feeling focaccia, my hand brushes against someone's hand. I jerk back. "Oh, I'm so sorry—"

I turn and stare right into Charlie's bright-blue eyes.

"It's you," Charlie says, and I swear his eyes light up. Is he excited to see me after everything that happened at the interview? I don't know how I feel about seeing him, but my heart is beating a little faster. I wish my hair was better behaved today. I didn't sleep well, and look like a total mess.

"It's me," I reply. "Sorry, did you want this?" I gesture to the focaccia, trying not to look at it longingly and failing.

Charlie laughs. "You know what? I meant to grab a baguette. My mistake. Please, take it." He reaches the opposite direction toward the bouquet of baguettes at the other end of the counter. I know that could not have been what Charlie was reaching for, but I appreciate the gesture. And I want the focaccia.

"Thank you," I say, snagging my favorite bread. "It's just, I love focaccia. It's kind of like a very fluffy pizza." Then I blush. Charlie doesn't need to know my silly opinions on bread from when I was seven.

"Oh, I make an excellent pizza," Charlie responds, then winces. "Not that you care about that of course." It seems I'm not the only one blurting things out today. "But you're right. Very fluffy pizza."

We grin dopily at each other.

"So—" he said.

Someone shouts from farther down the line, "Hey, look, it's Chuck!"

"Charlie! Hey, Charlie!"

Charlie turns to Nick and Nate, the rowdy couple who crashed our last press conference.

"Hey, Charlie, when are you going to come on our podcast?" Nate shouts.

"Name the date, fellas," Charlie calls.

"Yeah?" Nick asks, delighted. "How about now? Nate, start a voice memo."

As the two men surge forward, fumbling with their phones and apologizing to the other people in line, Charlie shoots an exasperated look at me, and I try to mask a grin.

"You have interesting friends," I comment.

"'Friends' is a very strong word," Charlie replies. He turns to Nick and Nate, who had made their way up to the top of the line and are now eagerly standing in front of him, holding their phones up to his face. "Don't you want to do this in a recording studio or someplace more controlled?"

They look at each other. "Nah. This is more authentic." Then Nate notices me and his eyes go wide. He elbows Nick.

"Hey, it's that girl from the video. The Freezers girl. *The enemy.*"

Nick's eyes narrow as he swings his phone over to me. "What are you doing here? Are you trying to exert more undue influence on Charlie?"

I hold up my hands in surrender, amused as I say, "No, I swear. Just trying to buy bread."

Nick and Nate study me. They aren't buying it.

Charlie groans.

"Not just any bread. She's buying focaccia," Charlie says, desperate to turn the conversation around. "That's the G.O.A.T. of breads, in my opinion. What do you guys think?" Nick and Nate slowly turns back toward him. Charlie keeps going. "I'd say it's a pretty good contender for my desert island box."

Nate frowns. "Desert island box?"

"You know," Charlie explains. "The stuff you'd take with you if you were marooned on a desert island. You only get one food. Mine's focaccia. Or maybe pizza," he amends. "What's yours?"

"Oranges, obviously," Nick states. "For the scurvy."

His husband shakes his head. "Dude, what about Thai food? You could give up tom yum soup?"

Nick's brow furrows. "But what about scurvy?"

Charlie turns to me before they go further down this Vitamin C rabbit hole. "What about you? What's your desert island food?"

"Well, focaccia's up there," I say.

Nate shakes his head. "Charlie's already doing focaccia. You should pick something else. Spread out your resources."

"Got it." I grin, playing along. "Well, in that case, I'd probably have to say ramen. I'd hate to give up ramen."

"Excellent choice," Charlie says. Nick and Nate nod at my selection. I could tell they were forgetting their crusade against me and keep going.

Charlie turns to the very tall, very blond man standing in line behind them, who just finished ordering. "Excuse me, sir, if you don't mind me asking, if you brought a single food with you to a desert island, what would it be?"

"Ah," says the man with absolutely no hesitation and a thick Northern European accent. "Rijsttafel, of course."

"Of course," says Charlie, shrugging as if he has no idea what that is. He glances at me, and I shake my head, equally clueless. "Ridge . . . staple. What is that, exactly?"

"It is Indonesian food we make in the Netherlands, very tasty. A series of small plates with rice. Do you have Indonesian food here in Portland? I have already tried the Voodoo Donuts," the tourist says. "I am Jan," he adds, holding out his hand.

"Dude, yeah, this place called Wajan on Burnside," Nick answers, shaking Jan's hand with enthusiasm. "It's sick."

Charlie's eyebrows spike. He didn't realize Nick and Nate were such foodies.

Jan nods, then points at Nick and Nate's phones. "You are recording a podcast? It is about food?" he asks.

"Kind of," Charlie says quickly, before Nick and Nate can remember their original purpose. "Food and ice hockey."

"Ah," Jan says, nonplussed. "Ice hockey I do not care for, but field hockey, yes, that is very big in the Netherlands. On my team, I am—how do you say—an attacker."

"Ooo, dude, you should come on our podcast," Nick says excitedly.

As Nick and Nate swarm Jan with their phones, Charlie and I back toward the register, where Sal has been patiently waiting.

"For the record," Sal says to Charlie, "I'm a Freezers

fan. But the Shredders aren't half bad. That's seventeen fifty for the baguette and the sandwich."

"We do okay," Charlie says, handing over his credit card. "I'll get her food as well."

"Oh, you don't have to," I say, my face split between pleasantly surprised and guilty. "I ordered kind of a lot. It's staff meeting day."

"Please, it's the least I can do for subjecting you to that," Charlie says, jerking his head toward Nick and Nate. "And for everything else."

"If the man wants to pay, let the man pay," Sal interjects.

I smile. "Fine. Thank you very much."

Charlie grabs his sandwich and shoves his baguette under his arm. "Will I be seeing you at the Peewee Players Day next week?"

I nod. "We're hosting it this year so the Freezers will definitely be there."

"Then I'm looking forward to it. We Shredders could use some good competition." Charlie gives me a grin, then turns reluctantly to go. He pauses by Nick, Nate, and Jan, who are still talking animatedly as they wait for their orders. "Jan, nice to meet you. Guys, another time on that podcast?"

"Sure, sure," says Nate, shooing him away.

I watch as Charlie is waved off by his fans and heads for the exit. He turns for a quick glance back as he reaches the door, and he winks at me. I feel a little flutter in my stomach. He really can be charming.

Alison materializes out of nowhere with my box of

sweets. I suspect she has been lurking nearby and eaves-dropping.

"What was that thing he just asked you about? Are you going on a date?" Alison asks eagerly.

"Nooo, it's part of this year's PCHL league-wide Charity on Ice. All the teams come together to coach kids' hockey for a day. It's also why we're holding that benefit I was telling you to come to, remember? The fancy dinner with the auction? It's the same week."

"So, that's kind of a date?" Alison asks, and I roll my eyes. "Oh, come on, are you saying you wouldn't date that absolute tree trunk of a man?"

I laugh. Charlie is very tall and broad shouldered, and he does have the air of the woodsman about him. His tousled hair and massive grin get underneath my defenses. I am impressed by how he handled that situation, distracting his fans with foodie talk. He could easily have let me squirm like I had made him with Tricia Cornwallis, but he didn't.

"I guess he's kind of cute," I admit, and Alison squeals. "But he is the absolute last hockey player I should ever date," I remind my friend. "Coach Peter is on a mission to defeat the Shredders this season, come hell or high water." Plus, I remind myself, I still don't want to date a hockey player. Especially not a showboat like Charlie, who doesn't take anything seriously. If it makes sense to date anyone, surely it should be Blake, shouldn't it?

I notice Alison watching me. My friend can probably tell my thoughts are more conflicted than my words. I grab the pastry box from Alison, dropping my focaccia and tayaki on top.

"Anyway, I've got to go. Staff meeting, then I've got a ton of stuff to do for these charity events. Youth hockey's even crazier than the minor league, if you can imagine."

Alison nods. "Sure. You wouldn't be throwing yourself into work to avoid thinking about one or two big, beefy hockey players, would you?"

I shove the tayaki in my mouth to avoid answering, biting down on the creamy ricotta filing and backing away. "Okay, bye!"

Chapter 11

This Thing Is Dumb

ANNA

I've never heard the Veterans Memorial Coliseum quite so loud. There are over a hundred eleven and twelve-year-olds sprinting through the rows of seats, shrieking and shouting while they wait for the Peewee Players event to begin. I leap back as a gaggle of them race past me and wish I'd brought a bullhorn. I love kids, but putting this many hyped-up little hockey players in one place feels like a disaster waiting to happen.

I glance over at Blake, who is watching the kids run with his brow furrowed.

His gaze locks on me. "Are you sure this is worth our time?" he grumbles. "We're losing a day of practice."

I nudge him lightly. "Charity is always worth our time. It'll be fun, I promise." At least I hope it will. Blake doesn't strike me as someone who has a lot of experience with kids, but he seems a little less freaked than with the puppy. Maybe he is finally coming out of his aggressive shell. This will be good for him.

Blake goes back to scowling.

Michael, the beleaguered gray-haired PCHL official, and my co-coordinator, steps up to the ice and waves the other adults over. I scan the group, which includes players and management from across the league's mountain division. I see a burly Salt Lake Cave Bears goalie, a Nevada Dragons coach, and the massive Oklahoma Oil Rigs enforcer who Blake got into a fight with in the last game. I keep searching, trying not to admit that there is one face I am hoping to see. The Oil Rigs enforcer steps forward, and suddenly there is Charlie, standing next to Coach Ryan and looking straight at me.

I immediately snap my attention back to Michael, who is desperately trying to get the kids to quiet down. "Excuse me. Excuse me!"

Charlie puts his fingers to his lips and lets out a loud wolf whistle. The hoard of children immediately stops, and silence reigns.

Michael smiles gratefully. "Welcome to the fourth annual Peewee Players Tournament, where the stars of today come together to shine a light on the stars of tomorrow," he shouts in a reedy voice. "If you kids can please get into your assigned teams, we'll get started."

The shrieking resumes as the kids elbow each other, diving and weaving through the chairs until they form into eight groups of varying colors, like a rowdy rainbow.

Michael looks back down at his paperwork. "Now," he announces, with a glance toward me. "We're going to do things a little differently this year."

I frown. What is he talking about?

"In the spirit of sportsmanship and inter-team cama-raderie, I'm mixing up our coaching pairs. That way, each group gets the wisdom of not one but two different teams. Isn't that fun?" Michael looks around for an enthusiastic response.

The kids look unimpressed. The adults look less than thrilled. Next to me, I feel Blake tense.

Michael returns to his notes. "Let's start with the home teams, shall we? Blake Tyler, you're with Shredders Coach Ryan Roberts for the red team. Charlie Haskell, you're with Freezers publicist Anna Green for the green team." Michael chuckles at his little color joke.

I turn to Blake as Michael continues through the coaching pairs. "I'm sorry. He did *not* tell me he was going to do that."

Blake shrugs it off, trying to mask his disappointment. "I'll manage. I'm just sorry you're stuck with *him*," he growls, glaring past me. He steps in close and puts his hand on my shoulder. "If he bothers you, you let me know."

I nod, looking up into the dark wells of Blake's eyes. It is sweet that he is concerned. I didn't dare tell him about the flurry of complicated emotions that bubbled up inside me when Michael announced my name with Charlie's.

Shortly, Charlie approaches me and Blake and forces a smile. He holds out his hand to Blake. "Good to be back on the ice with you, Blake. Not exactly the rematch we expected, is it?" he says cheerfully.

Blake simply grunts and shoves past him, ignoring his hand. Charlie pivots, directing his hand toward me, his grin turning sincere. My hair is pulled back in a ponytail, and I am wearing an oversized Freezers jersey. It is probably the first time he's seen me in anything but my business attire. My chest tightens as I take his hand.

"Fancy meeting you here." He winks. "What do you say we go inspire some stars of tomorrow?"

I laugh. "We can try. So long as we get through this in one piece, I'm happy."

"Come on, isn't your dad the Freezers coach? I'm sure you're a natural," Charlie assures me as we make our way over to the green team, which is a blur of kids tugging on skates, gloves, and helmets.

I wrinkle my nose. "I'm not so sure it's genetic. What about you? Have you done a lot of coaching?"

"Not really," Charlie admits, "but my sister's sixteen so I know my way around these little monsters." He beams with pride when I look impressed.

"I didn't know you had a younger sister," I say.

"Oh yeah. She's much smarter than me already. It's terrible," he jokes.

We reach the kids, and Charlie clears his throat. "Alright, listen up you Mean Green Hockey Machines," he hollers, earning some giggles. "We're here today for two reasons. We're gonna play some hockey, and we're gonna have some fun. If anybody doesn't like fun, please tell me immediately, and I'll get you assigned to a different team asap. Is that clear?" The giggles increase. The kids are into it.

He turns to me. "Ms. Green, I was thinking maybe it would be the most fun if we had the kids take off all their hockey gear and run a bunch of laps up and down the stadium for, I dunno, about an hour? Two hours? How does that sound?"

I pretend to think about it as a chorus of nos come from the kids. "I don't know, Mr. Haskell. They already have their skates on. Maybe we should let them get on the ice?"

Charlie scratches his head, mocking confusion. "Really? That's more fun than running laps? Kids, are you sure?" He frowns as they all agree. "Fine, fine, get out there. Show me what you got."

The kids cheer and pour past Charlie and me, spilling onto the ice. I watch as Charlie organizes them into a passing drill that involves shouting their names so everyone can learn them. He is really in his element with the kids, and some of my hesitation melts away. I have always dismissed him as a ham—all swagger and no substance— but there is a lot of heart in his happy-go-lucky antics.

I glance over at Blake and Coach Ryan across the ice. Their team is running speed drills, racing around their section of the rink in silent concentration, while the two men yell out corrections—using their numbers—to the players.

I glance back at the chaos of the green team, where the passing drill has devolved into a game of tag. Blake and

Coach Ryan certainly have a better command of their team. I've never seen a group of kids so focused on a task. Blake also looks like he is in his element, whipping around the ice, dark eyes flashing as he and Coach Ryan call out orders. I admire his drive and his passion, but it doesn't look like the kids are having fun.

Charlie skates over to me. "Blake and Coach Ryan certainly seem to be vibing."

"That they are." I laugh.

"He's a good player. A little intense."

"Yeah. But he's a nice guy when you get to know him," I say.

"So are you and he—"

My eyes widen. "Me and Blake? Oh, no." Charlie looks more than a little relieved, and I am flattered. "Actually, I have this rule. I, uh, I don't date hockey players," I explain, then immediately wish I hadn't told him that. It's important for him to know, isn't it? There are so many reasons he shouldn't ask me out, not that he was going to. He is just being friendly.

"Right," Charlie says, his face carefully neutral. "That's a good rule. We're a bad bunch. Sweaty. Loud." He swivels back toward the kids and notices one of the boys drifting along the edges, not participating.

"Hey!" He waves the kid over. "It's Devin, right? I know you. You're Coach Ryan's son, aren't you?"

Devin nods. Coach Ryan enrolled his curly-haired son in the demanding L'Etoile French immersion school, planning on shipping him off to Canada the first chance he gets

—to season Devin and make sure he goes pro. Coach Ryan never does anything by half.

"So, what's the deal?" Charlie asks. "Why don't you get out there? Show the other kids what you're made of?"

"Whatever." Devin shrugs, scuffing his skates on the ice. "This thing is dumb."

"Devin, do you not like hockey?" I ask.

He shrugs. "I'm not good enough."

Charlie and I exchange looks. It must be hard to be the son of a taskmaster like Coach Ryan. If he is hard on the team, he must be even harder on his only son. No wonder the kid isn't enjoying himself.

"Okay, here's the thing," Charlie says, crouching to Devin's level. "There are only two rules today, and the one rule I absolutely cannot bend is the having fun rule. So, we have to figure this out together." He glances at me, wheels turning. "I bet you're plenty good at hockey, but if that's no fun for you, then I have an idea. Why don't we make you Ms. Green's assistant? You can be the Green Team's publicist. You don't have to play if you don't want."

Devin looks up, skeptical but intrigued. "What would I have to do?"

"It's not easy," I say. "Publicity is all about storytelling. We've got to make the Green Team sound better than any other team here. So, you've got to get to know the players really well, find out their strengths, and see what kind of story you want to tell about the team. Are we the underdogs? Are we the class clowns? I think it'll be easier if you stay on the ice."

Devin nods slowly. "Okay, I'll do it." He skates back

toward the group and falls into conversation with several players, already looking more animated.

I smile at Charlie.

He pulls away and heads back toward the kids. "Okay, let's see your footwork! Who here knows how to dance?"

I watch him go, touched by how he handled the situation with Devin. The more time I spend with him, the more I realize he is not the person I thought. There is no way I can date a hockey player, especially one who plays for my rival. But for the first time in my life, I can't quite remember why.

Chapter 12

The Juice Is Loose

ANNA

Twelve pairs of eyes stare up at Charlie, waiting for him to say something inspirational. He glances over at the scoreboard, stalling. We are going into the last period of the last game, and the green team has tied the game against Blake's red team.

Charlie bends low, and the kids huddle closer. He studies them, face grave. "Alright, it's the last period, and time's running out. It's now or never, kids. What's it gonna be?" He turns to Devin. "Have you all decided on a team name?"

Devin nods, equally serious. "We are . . . the Green Juices!"

Charlie's eyebrows went up. He glances at me, struggling to keep a straight face. "The Green Juices? That's what you want?"

The whole team nods. "No one wants to drink us, but we're the best. And our mascot can jump out of the Freezer mascot's refrigerator costume."

"Wow," Charlie says. "That's actually awesome. I mean, of course it's awesome, Green Juices. I would expect nothing less. Anna, is it senior publicist approved?"

I smile. "It's perfect. I can already see the sponsorships. Great job, Devin."

Devin beams. It is incredible how much he's come out of his shell. He even seemed to have fun playing hockey and supplied the assist to score their tying goal last period.

Across the ice, Coach Ryan bangs a hockey stick, glaring. "Let's go, Green Team, stop wasting time!"

"That's Green Juices to you!" Charlie hollers back, ignoring Coach Ryan's incredulous look. He turns back to the kids. "Go on and play your celery hearts out, Juices!"

The kids cheer and swarm the ice. Charlie turns to me. "Celery hearts. Get it? Celery? Hearts? Because they're the Juices."

I roll my eyes. "That is awful."

"No, *peas* don't say that." Charlie puts his hand to his heart. "You're *kale*-ing me."

I laugh. After spending the day with Charlie, all my assumptions about him have gone flying out the window. Sure, he is a goofball who doesn't take this game too seriously, but the Green Team is having the time of their lives. He's gotten improvements out of every single player, without them even realizing he was coaching them. It inspired my work with Devin, and honestly, I was quite wowed by the kid. I promised to let him do a takeover of the Freezers's social media feed to post content about the Peewee event, and I can't wait to see what he does.

Ted the Shredder, the giant felt rock-n-roller with a tie-dye shirt and an electric guitar, skates over to me and Charlie and pops his head off, revealing a woman in her late fifties with a shock of curly red hair.

"Hey, Carla, what's shaking?" Charlie calls. "Have you met Anna? Anna Green, meet Carla Manfredi, our goalie's mom and the scariest member of the Shredders team."

Carla ignores Charlie and holds out a felt hand for me to shake. "I had to meet the lady who's keeping Charlie on his toes."

"I don't know about that, but it's great to meet you," I say, shaking the oversized fake hand. "I'm always happy to see more women out on the ice."

"Oh, yeah. I love to pop off my head and freak out the big burly man-fans. They really can't wrap their heads around the fact that a grandma can skate circles around them." Carla winks. "My son says I'm crazy for doing this. I'm an ER nurse by day so I have a high tolerance for crazy. Besides, us ladies have to show 'em how it's done, don't we?"

I grin. Carla is my kind of gal.

Out on the ice, one of the Green Juices is battling it out on the boards against not one but two on the red team. Charlie leans all the way over the half wall of our bench, practically out on the ice, hollering encouragement.

Carla nudges me. "He's a keeper, that one."

"Oh, we're not together," I say, embarrassed. What had Carla read in my gaze?

Whatever it is, Carla isn't buying my denial, and she simply shrugs. "Too bad. You'd make beautiful babies."

Beet red, I turn back to the game. The red team has stolen the puck and is racing down the ice toward the green team's goal. Charlie is now shouting encouragement at our defense, but the red players are relentless. It is some of the best skating I've seen all day. Even so, Coach Ryan and Blake are screaming for the kids to skate faster with spit flying.

I wince. Blake's coaching style gets results, but he takes things too seriously, even when it comes at the expense of his team. Being paired with Coach Ryan didn't help, but I hoped today was a chance for Blake to have fun and work on his softer side. I know he has it in him, but Blake doesn't let his softer side show, even for the kids. I sigh. It is disappointing.

Devin makes a valiant effort to check the red team, but they dodge him and take a shot at the goal. The green team's goalie completely misjudges the angle and tries to butterfly, getting on his knees to block the puck, but it sails straight past him and into the net. Cheers go up around the crowd. The red team has won.

I move over to Charlie, who is applauding. I hope he isn't taking it too hard, but when he turns to me, he is grinning from ear to ear.

"Did you see how our kids did out there? What a game!" he whoops. I smile. His enthusiasm is infectious, and I feel a flutter in my stomach at the phrase "our kids," remembering what Carla had just said about babies.

The Green Juices skate back over to the bench, and I am relieved that they too are grinning from ear to ear.

Charlie bows low. "Juices, you crushed it," he declares. "We may not have made it to the top shelf, but you played your berry best. I knew I could be-leaf in you." The kids groan, but I can tell they love it. Charlie gets serious for a second. "No, really. You should be proud of yourselves. Today wasn't about winning some game. It was about playing good hockey. And what I saw out there was great hockey. Don't ever forget that."

The kids glow at the compliments.

I step forward. "He's right. You guys are a true team. You helped each other, you made each other better, and you came up with the best team name of the day. Any of you ever want Freezers tickets, come see me and they're on the house!"

The kids cheer. Devin turns to his teammates. "Green Juices, blend!"

The kids all put their hands in the center and then skate around in a circle, chanting, "The Juice is loose! The Juice is loose!"

They finish their cheer and swarm me and Charlie for hugs.

Across the ice, I see Blake looking for his players to congratulate them. But his team is no longer on the ice. They had all abandoned the rink for their family members in the stands, and were yanking off their skates and shoving their trophies into duffel bags and backpacks.

The PA system squeals and Michael's reedy voice blares out of the speakers. He found the A/V booth. Everyone covers their ears.

"Congratulations, Peewee Players. You're all winners today!" Blake rolls his eyes. The announcement continues. "Before you leave, stop by the tables out front where your coaches will be signing jerseys for you. And parents, don't forget to buy your tickets to this weekend's gala and auction! All proceeds go right back to youth league equipment and scholarships."

Blake beelines for the Coliseum's atrium, and reaches for an empty chair behind a table filled with a rowdy line of kids waiting for autographs.

"Oh, Blake," I say. I clear my throat as I point. "Your table's actually over there. We've got your jerseys all laid out for you to sign."

Blake glances at a table a few spots over that only has a few people waiting.

Blake turns back to me. "Come help me sign?"

"Oh, um," I say, looking at Charlie's table. I should go with Blake. He is a Freezer after all, and he looks like he really wants my help. As sweet as that is, I can't shake the image of him and Coach Ryan berating a team of 11-year-olds. "I'll just be a minute. Some of the Green Juices want me to sign their jerseys, too."

I pull away, sliding into the empty seat at Charlie's table. The flow of kids is endless. It is heartwarming but frustrating. The second there is a gap, Charlie pivots his chair to face me, evidently not sure what he wants to say. I look back at him with a hopeful expression on my face.

A throat clears in front of us, and Charlie reluctantly turns back to look. Coach Ryan is standing in front of our table, his hand on Devin's shoulder. Devin's face sports the closed-off surly look he wore at the start of the day. My heart sinks.

"Charlie, a word about how little you had my son skating today—"

"Coach Ryan," I jump in, surprising Charlie. "Can I just say that your son is a natural leader? He rallied the entire team, and I don't think they would have played half as well without him." I leave out Devin's duties as assistant publicist, assuming his dad won't see it as positive. Even so, Devin brightens up at my words.

"I completely agree," Charlie adds. "Any failings on that rink were mine. Devin's our MVP as far as I'm concerned." Charlie holds out his hand to Coach Ryan. Coach Ryan hesitates, but closes his mouth and takes Charlie's hand. Devin beams.

Charlie turns back to me. "Listen, Anna, today was really special. It's gotten me thinking."

"Yes?" I reply, my mouth suddenly dry.

"I don't see why we should stop at just one youth event each season. There's only so much we can do in a day, but if it was a year-round charity, I think we could really make a difference with these kids. What do you say? Maybe we can meet up and figure out how to keep the Green Juices alive?"

"I think that's a great idea," I say. "Let's set it up." Charlie gives me another grin, and we turn back to the kids in line, leaving me to wonder why I feel disappointed.

Chapter 13

He's Up to No Good, I'm Telling You

BLAKE

The Freezers have taken over one of the long picnic tables inside Wayfinder Beer, which is lucky because the massive brick brewery is now packed with Portlandians drinking West Coast IPAs and sours. I sit hunched at the end of our table, staring into my drink like I am the only one in the world, let alone in the bar.

"Hey, B-man!" Chad calls over. I look up. "You wanna join us? We can talk about the game. You can give me some pointers on my edgework."

Vlad glares at Chad, but I just shake my head and go back to staring at my glass.

"See?" I overhear Chad say. "That man is sadder than a mosquito in a mannequin factory."

"I wouldn't wanna talk about the game either," Vlad points out. "Not if I spent half of it in the sin bin."

It is true. I am no stranger to the penalty box, but I was in rare form against the Boise Brawlers. On every other play I was boarding players, charging them, and instigating fights. The crowd loved it, but we were constantly short-handed against the Brawlers. We might've lost the game if it wasn't for Leo saving so many goals. We barely scraped by with a win, and the only thing I have to show for it is a black eye.

Leo sighs and drags himself over to my spot at the end of the table. "You okay, man? You look a little down."

"Yeah, I'm great. Really great," I say. "It's just this bar is lame, you know? I don't know why we come here."

Leo grits his teeth before answering. "Well, it's pretty close to the Coliseum, and everybody else likes it. But we were thinking of heading west and hitting up Ground Kontrol. Playing some pinball. You wanna come? We can have a Medieval Madness rematch." The last time I went to the barcade with the team, I insisted on playing everybody at the one pinball machine I thought I had mastered. The team seemed to enjoy watching me lose until I stormed out because the game was malfunctioning.

I shake my head. "Those pinball machines are messed up. I'll just hang here."

Leo claps me on the shoulder and stands. He rejoins Chad and Vlad at the other end of the table. "I tried," I hear him say. "Let's bounce. Bride of Pinbot waits for no man."

Chad downs his beer and hops up on the bench,

summoning the attention of the team with a wave of his empty glass. "Pinheads! We ride!"

The team cheers and streams toward the exit. With one more glance at me, Leo follows.

I barely even notice they leave. I stare deep into my third drink. Wayfinder is a brewery, but I opted for one of their scotch cocktails and have been drowning myself in it.

My Peewee team won and the Freezers won, but I can't shake the feeling I am losing. Images of Anna and Charlie laughing on the ice and gazing into each other's eyes at the merchandise signing table, keep popping into my head without warning.

Everybody on the Freezers team knows Anna doesn't date hockey players, but Charlie hasn't gotten the message. I wonder if Anna just means that she won't date me. It is almost unthinkable. What does Charlie have that I don't? Wouldn't Anna rather be with a winner? I think she knows how I feel about her by giving her my hockey puck, but since then, our interactions have been strictly professional. It doesn't make any sense. Any other woman would be falling all over me. Just look at Mabeline.

Shuddering at the thought of Mabeline, I push off the bench and wobble unsteadily toward the bar. The only thing that makes sense right now is getting another drink.

"Blake Tyler, right? You played a hell of a game tonight. Can you believe that ref? Such bad calls. You think they should fire him?" a bearded guy asks, sliding into the spot next to me and leaning on the bar.

I turn, trying to focus my bleary eyes. "I know you. You're that reporter guy."

Bearded guy keeps a smile plastered on his face and holds out his hand. "Kyle Brodie. I'm a big fan."

"Did Anna send you?" I ask, perking up. After all my penalties, Anna banned me from the post-game press debrief, sending Leo and another player. She must have sent this Kyle guy for a more intimate one-on-one. Maybe she is still thinking about me after all.

"Sure, Anna Green. Great gal," Kyle replies.

"She is great, isn't she?" I slur, my eyes going glassy as I stare at the wall.

"Great is the word," Kyle agrees. "So, listen, what do you think of your team this season? Do you think they're pulling their weight? Because from where I'm sitting, you're the one getting the most shots into the net. You didn't hear this from me, but people aren't happy with your team captain. What do you say to that?"

"Leo?" I ask, trying to focus. "He plays a lot of pinball."

"Instead of hockey?"

"He's not as good as me, though."

"At hockey?"

"At pinball. And hockey." I down my drink and try to flag down the bartender again.

Kyle tries again. "How about that Coach Peter? After the Freezers' failures last season, people are saying he's lost his touch. Would you agree with that?"

"Coach Peter is Anna's father. She's great, isn't she?"

"Yup. Great gal," Kyle repeats.

"Great, great, great," I agree. "She's smart, and talented, and she likes ice cream, and her hair is really soft."

Kyle's eyebrows rise. "So, you two are together, huh? How long has that been going on?" he asks.

"Me 'n Anna? Hah. She doesn't date hockey players."

"Really? That's a shame. I bet you two would be fire together. The star Freezers player and the team's publicist. That's a power couple right there."

I nod, forlorn. "I know. I even gave her my hockey puck. That's supposed to mean something, you know? But she's been ignoring me ever since. Even at the Peewee game. She was supposed to come to my table. It's that guy. He's messing with her head."

"What guy?" Kyle fidgets with his beard.

"That guy. That . . . that guy," I say. My head feels fuzzy, and the name of the man stealing Anna away from me hovers just out of reach. Chester? Kevin? I give up. "He's up to no good, I'm telling you."

I stand, swaying. My eye hurts, the world is spinning, and I am pretty sure I have another game tomorrow. I need to get home.

Kyle stands with me, grabbing my arm. "Listen, I've been looking for a story to do. Just a fluff piece about the people behind the players, you know what I mean? Anna sounds like the perfect candidate."

I nod emphatically. "Anna's amazing. She's the people behind the players, for sure."

"Of course," Kyle continues, "I'd need to do a lot of research on her, for background. Follow her around a bit, see what she's up to. See if she's spending her time with any guys."

My attention snaps to Kyle. All my brain cells go back to firing. "You'd be able to find that out?"

Kyle shrugs. "It depends. No guarantees, of course, but I find out a lot of stuff when I'm doing research. I could find some things out that might be helpful to you."

"Like where she put my hockey puck?" I ask.

"Exactly. Stuff like that. I'd be happy to pass any info along, especially if you're involved in the story. If I can tell my boss you're one of my sources for the season, he'll have no problem with me sharing anything useful I learn."

My eyebrows furrow, and I give the much shorter Kyle the full force of my signature glare. "This is just for a fluff piece, right? You're not doing anything sketchy?"

"Blake, I'm a professional. Of course, this is all above board." Kyle puts his hand on his heart, pretending to look wounded.

"Good. Then you've got a deal." I reach out and put my hand on Kyle's shoulder, leaning on him a little too hard. The world is spinning again. "I just need to–"

I turn and bolt for the men's room with my hand clamped over my mouth.

Chapter 14

Ready For Some Healthful Exercise?

ANNA

The empty roller coaster looms over the skyline like a sleeping metal beast, biding its time until spring. Closed for the winter, Oaks Amusement Park takes on an eerie air, as though the silent rides are under a spell that can only be awakened with a kiss.

I shiver in the chilly December air, peering into the forlorn park and wondering why I am thinking about kisses. Charlie asked me to meet him here to brainstorm expanding the PCHL's work with underprivileged kids, and this is going to be a purely professional discussion. Okay, maybe a few days ago I thought about a relationship with Charlie, but I think I'm right to have my No-Dating-Hockey-Players rule.

It would be absolutely crazy to date Charlie. He'll be

out of state half the time for away games, crammed on an overnight bus, or in a tiny hotel room with three other players. Even when he is home, he'll be at hockey practice or playing. Not that I have time anyway since my days are filled with publicity work for the Freezers. I barely have time for this meeting, given that the Charity on Ice Gala is only three days away. I still need to secure more silent auction items before the programs go to print, and this morning, the DJ dropped out.

My life is crazy enough without embarking on some wild hockey romance. I don't want to think what will happen if my dad ever finds out about my interest in Charlie. I doubt he could handle me dating a Freezer, and as Coach, he'd go through the roof if he knew I was even considering dating a Shredder. The season is stressful enough, and I have no desire to poke that bear or encounter the wrath of Charlie's Coach. Coach Ryan probably hasn't forgiven me for my interview with Charlie. He stared daggers at me at the Peewee Players tournament. Yep, there is no way I can date Charlie, and that is that.

I don't even know if he is interested. For all I know, he has a serious girlfriend. I may have gone on his social media for research purposes and not seen any evidence of a girlfriend, but that doesn't mean one doesn't exist.

I wonder why Charlie wants to meet here if we are just planning to talk about youth sports logistics. The hand-carved carousel and the Cosmic Crash bumper cars bring back fond memories from my childhood, but it doesn't seem like a business-oriented meeting spot. Also, it is closed for the season. Maybe he is thinking of bringing the kids here?

I hear footsteps and turn. Charlie is jogging up the path in a light windbreaker and worn jeans. It is a casual look, but he wears it well. His eyes light up as he grins and waves.

I hold up my hand in greeting, but when he approaches, he pulls me into a bear hug, enveloping me with his strong arms and pulling me to his firm chest. I smell aftershave and soap before he breaks the hug and steps back. It was a quick hug, but I didn't want to let go.

"Hey, sorry. I hope I didn't keep you waiting," Charlie says.

"Don't worry, I haven't been waiting long. But I hate to tell you that the park is closed."

Charlie laughs. "I know. I kind of love seeing it like this, though. I bring my sister here every summer, but in the winter, when it's quiet, it looks like this giant sleeping animal." My eyes lock on him. "Sorry, I know that sounds crazy."

"No," I say. "I actually was just thinking the same thing."

Charlie holds out his hand. "Well, shall we?"

My brow furrows. "Shall we what? Are we breaking into Oaks Park?"

He laughs. "Nope. We're going skating."

"Skating?" I ask. "You dragged me all the way out here just so we could go back to the Coliseum?"

"Not *that* kind of skating," he says with a wink. Then he grabs my hand and tugs me around the corner.

Just behind the candy-colored Tree Top Drop that once made me lose the funnel cake I had just begged my dad to buy me, looms a large white building with green trim. In big block letters, it says: *Oaks Rink Roller Skating. Healthful Exercise. Delightful Pleasure.*

"Ready for some healthful exercise?" Charlie asks.

I laugh. Then I give him a questioning look. "This isn't a date, right? We're just talking about expanding the kids' program? Because I told you, I don't date hockey players."

"Of course," Charlie swears, giving me an innocent look. "I just thought what better place to talk about kids skating than where we started skating as kids?"

I am skeptical of his explanation, but I turn my attention back to the building. "Maybe you came here as a kid. My dad had me on the ice by the time I was three."

"I'm going to need those pictures," Charlie says, and he pulls me inside.

Our coats off and our roller skates on, Charlie takes my hands in his and guides me out onto the polished wooden rink. I can skate backwards down the ice with my eyes closed, but it has been decades since I roller-skated, and my balance is way off. I cling to Charlie and wobble as a bunch of seven-year-olds fly by, shrieking.

"Showoffs," Charlie tells me. "Just keep your eyes on me, and you'll be a pro in no time."

I nod, but looking into his piercing blue eyes makes me

wobbly for an entirely different reason. I take a few tentative glides, slowly finding my rhythm.

Charlie guides me carefully down the rink, enjoying the feeling of his hands clenching mine. I am already getting the hang of it, but I need to get out of my head. "So," he says to distract me, "should we talk about the kids?"

"Right, the kids," I say, reminding myself that this isn't a date. "What did you have in mind?"

"Well, I think the division-wide event is great, and you did an amazing job organizing it, but it's only once a year and it's not always in Oregon. We've got two professional minor league teams who play right here in Portland."

"Portland does have the Winterhawks youth league," I remind him. I am more confident on the skates now that the conversation is keeping my nerves at bay.

Sensing that, Charlie lets one of my hands go, so we can skate side by side. "I know, and those kids are incredible," he says, "but not everyone can afford that. I've been asking around, and there are at least a few Shredders players who'd be up for donating time to teach kids who might not otherwise get to play."

My heart swells as he talks about helping kids with such passion. Despite my hesitation, he is a genuinely good guy.

"It was pretty incredible what you did with the Peewee kids in just one day," I tell him. "You're a natural as a coach. You really hadn't done it before?"

"Beginner's luck," Charlie jokes, deflecting.

I turn to look at him, my face serious. "I don't think so.

I've watched my dad coach my whole life, and it's not easy to break down hockey for adults, let alone for kids. You found a way to speak their language. You're really talented."

He clears his throat, no longer paying attention to his surroundings. I glance forward, realizing we are heading into the wall. Trying to pivot, I over-correct and trip over my skates. I tumble to the floor, pulling Charlie with me.

Charlie falls on top of me, doing his best to brace his weight.

"Oh my god," I howl with laughter, tears in my eyes. "Do NOT tell my father! I'll be so fired!"

Charlie laughs, too. "Freezers publicist falls on skates! Scandal of the century."

I giggle, trying desperately to catch my breath. Then Charlie pushes himself onto his feet and helps me back up.

"For the record," he says, "your dad would never fire you. You're way too good of a publicist."

I purse my lips and skate ahead. Having gotten a fall out of my system, I am much more comfortable on my skates.

"Maybe," I say, "but he's not always a fan of my ideas."

"Really?" Charlie asks. "How is that possible?"

"They're risky," I admit. "I think if we want to reinvigorate our ticket sales, we've got to think outside the box. Recruit new populations to get interested in the Freezers. Women are one of the fastest growing groups of hockey fans, and we barely target them."

"That's a really good point," Charlie says. "I don't think the Shredders cater much to our female fans, either."

"Plus, Portland's a unique place. We've got a refrigerator for a mascot. Why not be the team that keeps Portland weird? Get some unconventional sponsors. Do some funky fan events. Get people to dress as their favorite Voodoo Donuts. Have the fans try to score using fruit for a puck. Do a TikTok dance night. Try to break a Guinness World Record. It's silly," I say.

"That's not silly. Those ideas are awesome. I wish we did more stuff like that. I'm sorry Coach Peter's not interested, but you shouldn't give up. In fact, if we're going to get this kids' charity off the ground, we'll need your brilliant publicity mind to promote it. Get the word out about the Green Juices."

I turn back to smile at Charlie, buoyed by his confidence in me. "I'll see what I can do. We should keep talking about this." I have to get back to the Coliseum soon, and the time I spent with Charlie has flown by.

Charlie holds out his hand, but before I can take it—

"Look out!" A group of women in purple kneepads burst through the gap between us, skating so fast they are almost a blur. I jump back, nearly losing my balance.

The woman at the back of the pack with fire-engine-red hair slows to steady me. "You okay?" she asks, blinking.

I do a double take. "Mabeline? It's me, Anna Green. The Freezers's publicist."

"Oh! Hi!" Mabeline pulls me in for a hug. "This is my roller derby team. The Rose City Rebels." She points to one of the many tattoos on her arm: a rose with a knife stabbed through it, dripping blood.

Knowing what I do about the Freezers biggest fan, this makes a lot of sense. "That's awesome. I'd love to see you guys play sometime."

"Absolutely. Hey, maybe you can bring Blake. I'll set some tickets aside under Blake. Can you tell Blake I said hi?"

"Yes, of course," I say, not sure whether Blake would be thrilled to hear it. I have seen him hide from Mabeline before. Seeing Mabeline on her skates, I think she and Blake have a very similar energy. "I have to head back to the office now, anyway."

I glance at Charlie as I say that, and Mabeline follows my gaze. Mabeline's eyes narrow the second she recognizes Charlie. She isn't the Freezers number one fan for nothing.

"You—"

"We were just discussing some hockey charity work," I say quickly, kicking myself for getting caught having fun with a Shredder. What was I thinking? What if my dad finds out? Charity work is one thing, but flirting on roller skates is another thing entirely.

"Anyway, great to see you, Mabeline!" I skate toward the exit as fast as I can, and Charlie struggles to catch up. "I gotta go," I shout back to him.

"Oh, okay," Charlie says, sounding disappointed. "I'll see you at the gala?"

"You bet!" I call back, resolving not to spend time with him at the gala. It is entirely too easy to get swept up into Charlie. I can't let my guard down again.

Chapter 15

I Was Told You Would Be Wearing a Lot Less Clothing

ANNA

"Remind me never to help you again," Alison grunts, as she bends her knees and prepares to pull once more. I take the same stance on the other side.

"Three, two, one, go!" I pant, choosing not to respond. We both yank upward with all of our might. The heavy machine teeters and finally lurches high enough for us to slide it into the van. We collapse into the van along with it. My gaze drifts to the funky pink cartoon mural covering the back entrance to Music Millennium, the oldest record store in the Pacific Northwest.

I reached out to the owners a few weeks back about donating to the Charity on Ice benefit dinner and silent auction, hoping for a signed Soundgarden poster or maybe a few Frank Zappa records. Instead, they surprised me by offering a vintage jukebox that someone had gifted the store. My MINI Cooper is no match for it, but fortunately Munch is the proud owner of a delivery van, and Alison has the keys.

Bernie, the record store clerk, was planning on helping us, but Millenium has an in-store show to prep for tonight. It is a band out of Austin named Fried Polyester that plays something Bernie calls "cowpunk." I didn't realize jukeboxes were so heavy. It is like a boxy metal hippo.

Alison rolls onto her side so that she is facing me. "I think I'm dead. Did we die? I can't believe I died doing something hockey-related."

"The noblest sacrifice of all. Come on. Let's get this back to the venue, and I'll make some of the Freezers come help us unload it. Shirtless."

Alison perks up, then turns back to Music Millennium longingly. "Is there time to shop first?"

"Wait, do you even own a record player?" I ask.

"No, but I like the album covers. That one with the baby?"

"Nirvana?"

"Oh, that's Nirvana? Never mind."

I smile. "Good one."

"Good one, what?" Alison asks.

I press my lips together to keep from laughing. I heft myself up. "Moving on. We can shop later."

Alison sighs and drags herself to her feet.

"It's all for a good cause," I remind her.

"More hockey is not a good cause."

Together, we slam the van doors shut and head for the front cab. I calculate how many errands I have run in the last 36 hours. Between finding a new DJ, having to change the catering menu last minute, running into issues with the venue's insurance, and finding a typo in the signage, I am exhausted and I am still a few auction items short. To make matters worse, I've been wildly distracted ever since my not-a-date with Charlie at the roller rink. I'd be about to do something and then slip back to thoughts of him. I'd completely forget what I was doing.

Like right now. Alison is sitting in the driver's seat and staring at me, and it is clear she just asked me a question.

"Sorry, what?"

"The keys? You still have them."

"Oh, right." I dig into my pocket and hand them over, embarrassed. I'm not a schoolgirl with a crush. I am a grown woman with a full life, and a very long list of really good reasons why me and Charlie should not be together. So why can't I stop picturing him on top of me at the roller rink, propped up on his hands, gazing down at me with those mischievous blue eyes? Why can't I stop feeling the weight of his body pressed into mine in all the right places?

I come to, and notice Alison is still sitting there, staring at me. My cheeks go pink. What have I missed this time?

"You're thinking about him, aren't you?" Alison asks with a sly grin.

"What? Who?" I am mortified. Was it that obvious? I haven't even told Alison about the not-a-date.

"Blake, obviously," Alison says, starting the van.

"Oh, him." I lean back, both relieved and surprised I haven't been thinking about Blake much at all.

"Yes, him. The devastatingly handsome man who clearly has feelings for you. The one you have about two dozen pictures of in that portfolio there. Who else?"

"No one else. You're right," I say, picking up the portfolio and fidgeting with it. I brought the folder, thinking maybe I'd pick one or two photos of the team to blow up for the gala. Yet another thing to add to my to-do list.

I flip through them, trying to find a good one of the entire team. Blake's eyes blaze up at me from his chiseled, serious face. But it isn't his picture I stop on.

Allison catches a glimpse of the photo in my lap.

"Who's that?" Alison asks, all innocence.

I slam the portfolio shut at the speed of light, looking guilty. "No one."

"Oh, really? It's not that Shredder player you did the kiddie tournament with? What's his name? Charlie something?"

I clear my throat, looking anywhere but at Alison. "Charlie Haskell. And, no, it isn't, because he's a Shredder and that is not going to happen."

Alison sighs. "Babe, why are you torturing yourself? If you like him, you should go for it."

"Yeah? Do you want to be the one to tell my dad? Do you want to be the one to explain to the PCHL why it's not a problem that I'm dating a player?"

"Absolutely. I will just tell them that love conquers all."

I roll my eyes. "Maybe in a rom-com, but this is real life. Besides, when was the last time you followed your own advice?" I'm not the only perennially single one in this car.

Alison tosses her hair. "You know most men cannot handle all this. Not many women can either, unfortunately." Even in the Portland dating scene, people find Alison's high-fashion androgynous vibe, her crazy baker's hours, and her no-bullshit take on life to be incredibly intimidating. That doesn't mean I'll let her off the hook so easily.

"Well, if you think hockey players are so great to date, you'll have your chance when you come with me to the gala. For the live part of the charity auction, we're letting everyone bid on a date with the men."

"Are you serious? Absolutely not," Alison shrieks.

"Really? After everything you've said to me about how fabulous it would be to date a hockey player? You don't want a night out on the town with Chad and Vlad? They're perfect for you. I think one of them can even juggle."

"Not in a million years. I have no interest in dating a guy whose chosen profession is slamming into another guy so that he can chase a tiny ball with a big stick," Alison declares.

"Oh, but it's okay for me?" I retort.

"Yes, well, you like that stuff," Alison grumbles. "I don't even know if I want to go to this stupid thing."

"Please!" I beg. "Didn't you tell me to do one thing every day that scares you? You have to come. I need you there."

"Fine," Alison says with a heavy sigh, pretending that she is making a huge sacrifice. "I'll consider it. I *am* excellent company at parties."

"You absolutely are. And . . ." I say, looking decidedly guilty.

"And what?" Alison asks.

"I might need another favor," I admit, looking sideways at my friend.

"Oh, no you don't!" Alison cries. "The current favor nearly killed me, remember? Just two seconds ago?"

"It's just that we're a few auction items short, and you make such beautiful cakes, and it's an amazing advertising opportunity for Munch, and I love you very much," I say, giving Alison my biggest puppy dog eyes.

Alison turns the corner and our destination, the century-old McMenamins Crystal Ballroom, comes into view. Alison pulls the van into the loading dock and throws it in park so that she can turn and glare at me.

"Has our whole friendship just been an elaborate lie? Are you using me for cake!?" she asks.

"In my defense, you make really good cake," I plead. "I just want the people of the gala to know it too."

Alison sighs. "I bet you want it to be hockey-themed, don't you. Maybe some sugar work for the rink. And I do love decorating with silver." Her gaze falls back upon my portfolio.

"Did I already mention how much I love you?" I ask.

"I will do it on one condition," Alison declares.

"I'm not dating Blake or Charlie to get you to make this cake," I warn.

"No," Alison allows. "But if you want me to do something that scares me, you've got to do something that scares you too. You said you still need a few auction items, right? Put your photos in."

"My photos?" I ask, looking down at the folder. "I can't just toss a manila envelope of snapshots onto the auction table."

"Give them to me. I'll make a book of them," Alison offers. I am still skeptical. "Come on, they're more than just Instagram pics. Let people see them."

"Fine," I agree. It makes me squirm to think people would judge my silly social media photos, but I did really need Alison to make that cake. "But don't put my name on the book, okay? I don't want the humiliation when no one bids on it."

"Trust me, people will bid on it," Alison promises. "Now, let's please get this wretched machine out of Sal's van so that I can go make the world's most gorgeous hockey cake. I don't want you thinking of any more favors you need from me."

I laugh. "Deal." I check my phone. "Some of the guys should be popping out to help take it in for us."

"Shirtless," Alison reminds me. "You promised."

I laugh and dutifully add the request to my text, pretty sure that the men would not think she was serious about half-naked furniture unloading in December. We jump out of the van and circle around to the back. I open the doors and am relieved that the jukebox has made it there in one piece.

"Well, hello, lovely ladies," a voice calls.

We turn to find Chad, Vlad, and Leo making their way to the van, shirts unsurprisingly still on. The trio huddles over Leo's phone as they walk. I wonder what boys look at on phones. Meat recipes?

"Hey, Anna, this place is awesome," Vlad calls as they get closer. "Did you know that Little Richard fired Jimi Hendrix in the Crystal Ballroom?"

"Yeah, that's why I picked it," I reply wryly.

Alison then folds her arms and frowns at the men. "I was told you would be wearing a lot less clothing."

Leo points, recognizing her. "You're Anna's friend who doesn't like hockey."

"What?" Vlad asks, shocked. "Who doesn't like hockey?"

"Normal people of normal intelligence who enjoy cultural activities that don't sanction men beating each other up on ice skates," Alison replies, smiling sweetly.

Leo accepts the challenge. He steps up to Alison and folds his arms in response. "You're right," he says. "There's no skill, dexterity, or strategy involved in hockey at all. It's much more intellectual to view us as mindless meat puppets, only here for your shirtless enjoyment."

Chad pushes past Leo, saunters up to Alison, and whips off his shirt. He strikes a pose, leaning against the delivery van with as many muscles flexed as he can.

"Hi, Anna's very hot friend," he says. "I just want to let you know that I am available for your bidding pleasure at the charity gala. I would be honored to show you that not all hockey players are mindless meat puppets like Leo here."

"Really?" Alison says, acting intrigued. She shoots a

triumphant glance at Leo, then asks, "Tell me this. Can you juggle?"

Chad's grin widens. "Why yes, I can, little lady. I can juggle anything you like."

Leo pulls a confused Chad away as Alison bursts into laughter. He then holds out his phone to me. "You should probably see this."

I take the phone apprehensively, praying it is just a meat recipe. It isn't. It is an article about the Peewee tournament.

Most of the news that came out of the charity event had been sweet, human-interest stories about the kids. But this one has Kyle Brodie's byline, and it reads like a hit piece. My insides twist when I see Blake has provided most of the quotes.

I hand Leo back the phone and cast an apologetic look at Alison. "I should probably go deal with this."

Chapter 16

Are You Gonna Bid on Me?

CHARLIE

Standing at the bar is the absolute last person I want to see tonight. I have been looking for Anna ever since I arrived at the charity gala, but she is nowhere to be found. The gorgeous gold and green ballroom is packed with elegant guests dressed to the nines, laughing and mingling beneath the grand chandeliers. Glowing lights run along the wall trim, illuminating the room's vast arched windows and ornately painted wallscapes. It is a sight to behold, but I don't care. Not until I find Anna.

I catch a flash of chestnut hair by the bar and hurry to catch it. The spring-loaded dance floor makes it feel like I am floating and chasing a dream. The dreamlike feeling intensifies when I pass Freddy the Freezer handing out hors d'oeuvres. But when I make it through the crowd, my heart sinks. No Anna. Just a tall figure with pale skin and dark hair leaning against the bar, cutting a sharp silhouette in his all-black suit. Blake swaps an empty glass of scotch for a full one.

I thought I caught Blake's death stare more than once during the post-Peewee Tournament shirt signing, but dismissed it. Until Kyle Brodie's latest article, that is. I don't totally know why Blake despises me, although I have an inkling. Still, for that chestnut-haired inkling's sake, I play nice.

"Blake, how's it going?" I ask, grabbing a glass of wine and approaching. Blake nods but does not reply.

I try again. "Congrats on the Brawlers game. It sounded close."

Blake shrugs. "I wasn't worried. Their coach is an idiot."

"Yes, well, at least they're not coached by a—how did you phrase it—a slow, second-rate has-been?" I can't stop myself from bringing up the Peewee article. My politeness only stretches so far.

Blake grunts. "I call it like I see it."

"Oh, listen, chirping's part of the game, don't get me wrong," I say, referring to the usually more good-natured, trash-talking players hurl at each other. "But I'm guessing doing it in the press hasn't made you the most popular player? Did Niederman give you that?"

I point to the fading yellow and purple bruise encircling Blake's right eye. I'm not the only player Blake has aired his strong feelings about. Niederman is the Brawler that Blake had called "a bender who belongs in a beer league."

Blake straightens, sets his scotch down, and takes a menacing step toward me. "Why? Do you wanna take a shot?"

"Whoa, hey," I say, holding up my hands. "No offense meant. Just trying to offer some friendly advice. Players don't always love it when you take the trash-talking off the ice. I want to beat you fair and square next match. Not because some Boise player broke your nose."

Blake shrugs and downs his scotch, signaling the bartender for a third. "I don't need your help."

"Actually, it's good advice," comes a melodic voice from behind me.

I turn and nearly stop breathing.

Anna stands behind me in a midnight-blue, floor-length, figure-hugging satin gown with a sweetheart neckline and a high slit that flashes miles of smooth leg when she shifts. Her hair is twisted off her neck into an elegant chignon, and diamonds dangle from her ears. Her creamy skin glows in the light of the chandeliers, and I think she looks like a goddess.

"You look . . ." I start, mouth dry and at a loss for words.

"Beautiful," Blake finishes.

For the first time, I agree with him. Anna gives us a shy smile.

The bartender drops off Blake's latest scotch. He picks it up, and Anna's smile slips.

Blake frowns. "What? First, I can't talk to the press, and

now, I can't have a drink? We're at a party," he says, taking a gulp so large he chokes slightly.

"All Charlie's saying is that you aren't doing yourself any favors by bad-mouthing other teams in the press. And he's right. We don't all have to be enemies off the ice, do we?" Anna says.

I appreciate Anna coming to my defense, but I worry about what her concern for Blake might mean. She said she and Blake weren't together because of her rule against dating hockey players, but that doesn't mean she isn't interested in him.

I yearn to pull her aside to talk to her, but she instead steps toward Blake, gently placing her hand on his elbow. "Anyway, I came here to steal Blake. The live auction's about to begin." Anna casts an apologetic look at me. "I'm sorry, Charlie. I'm guessing you didn't come to bid on any of the players."

"Oh, don't worry about me," I say, trying not to feel so gutted. Watching her walk away arm in arm with a slightly swaying Blake cuts like a knife.

"Are you gonna bid on me?" Blake asks Anna.

"We'll have to see," Anna says, pushing him in the direction of the auction. Every hockey player in the room might be staring daggers at Blake, but the women are staring for very different reasons. Honestly, a few of the men too.

I swallow hard as Blake's arm goes around Anna, and I kick myself for watching them for so long. I force myself to turn around, meandering to the back of the ballroom, where the silent auction items sit on several rows of tables.

I have no intention of buying anything, but perhaps it will keep me distracted through the bidding on Blake. Surely Freezer staff aren't allowed to bid on their own teammates?

Anna has clearly outdone herself with the silent auction, and I am more distracted than I expected to be. There are items and offers from dozens of local businesses on display, including a very cool vintage jukebox that would most certainly not fit in my apartment. I marvel at a gorgeous three-tier cake wrapped in edible silver netting that is evocative of a hockey goal, with shards of blue isomalt glass jutting out of the top. I hesitate over the year's supply of Voodoo Donuts, then notice that Coach Peter has put a bid down and crossed out all the other spaces.

But it is the last item that makes me stop in my tracks: a book of black-and-white hockey photos from the season so far. I flip through it in awe. I'm not one for fine art or bringing hockey home after work, but the energy in the photos is electric. They capture the essence of how I feel on the ice—flying and free.

I glance at the bidding sheet. There are several bids already. I wince at the current price.

"Thinking of putting in a bid?"

I look up. A woman in a sleek black halter jumpsuit with tuxedo accents looks me up and down like she is the proctor of an exam I didn't know I was taking. I think she looks familiar, but I can't place her.

"Sorry," I say gallantly. "Are you trying to win it?"

"Hockey's not really my thing," the woman says with disdain, sipping from her champagne glass.

I laugh. "Then this is a strange place to spend your evening."

She shrugs. "The things we do for love, right?" She gives me a searching look, then seems to come to a decision, and nods. "If you like the book, you should bid on it. It's worth it, I promise."

I didn't know quite what to make of that, but I turn back to the book. Something about it calls to me. On impulse, I scribble down the highest number I can on the sheet, hoping I won't regret it tomorrow.

The woman nods, satisfied. "I'm Alison," she says.

"Charlie."

"I know," she replies with a smile, shaking my hand. Before I can ask how she knows, a rather drunk guest meanders over to us, turning toward Alison. His poorly tied tie and three days of stubble suggest an unattached guy who does not have it together. I guess single dad or recent breakup.

"Hey. I just bid on your cake. I'm gonna win it," he slurs.

"That's your cake?" I ask, impressed. "It's incredible."

Before Alison can respond, the Schlubby Possibly Single Guy cuts back in. "That's what I said. It's really sexy. Hey, you wanna get out of here?" he asks, leaning way too close. Any sympathy I have for him evaporates. He steps forward, but Alison is faster.

"Yes, you do make me want to get out of here. So, bye," Alison says with distaste, downing her drink, then turning and walking in the other direction. She heads back toward the auction, making eye contact with me as she passes me. "Is there anyone good left to date in Portland?"

As I ease away from the schlub, my mind swims right back to thoughts of Anna. I glance toward the auction and tune in just in time to see Freddy the Freezer lead a surly Blake onto the stage. There are a few boos from the players in the crowd. But when auctioneer Zamboni Zane bangs his gavel to begin the bidding, a number of attractive women's hands shoot straight up. I groan, but Blake's expression suddenly looks a little less surly.

I move toward the excitement, scanning the crowd for Anna and praying that she isn't among the women jockeying for a date with Blake. It is too packed for me to be totally sure. At least she isn't the tall blonde up front who seems determined to win Blake as Zane leads the bidding well into the hundreds.

I find Alison again, leaning on a cocktail table and working her way through another glass of champagne. She hiccups.

"Joining the feeding frenzy?" I ask.

"For him? No. From what I've seen tonight, he's not who I wanted him to be," Alison declares. I am dying to know what that means, but I'm too polite to ask. "Are you going to bid on him?" she asks.

"Not sure I can afford him," I say wryly. The bidding spikes to over a thousand. The blonde has her bank account pulled up on her phone and is doing some math on her fingers. I try one more time to see if Anna is in the running.

Zane bangs the gavel. "Sold!"

A woman with fiery red hair and black lipstick shrieks in glee, bouncing up and down in a low-cut red velvet corset gown that shows off her many tattoos. I recognize her as Mabeline, the roller derby maven from Oaks Park. Blake looks horrified.

Freddy the Freezer reappears, dragging a shocked Blake off to make room for the next player: Leo. Freddy prompts Leo to do a few muscular poses for the ladies.

Alison snorts. "See? All you hockey players are such jocks. Very hot but dumb as rocks."

"Hey now," I say, mock offended. "Don't be mean to rocks. Dumb jocks can be fun, you know. You should give Leo a chance. I guarantee he won't try to smash you over cake."

"Oh, for sure," Alison says, raising her hand. "Look at me! I'm bidding on my very own hockey player! I just love talking about sticks and pucks and zambinis all day."

The gavel bangs. "Sold!" Zane points at Alison. She lowers her hand, her mouth falling open. From the stage, Leo smirks, grabs Zane's gavel, and does a quick bit of juggling.

"Did I just buy a hockey player? Did I just buy *that* hockey player?" she whispers. I nod. "Can I give him back?"

"I think he's yours for life," I say with a straight face. "Just don't forget to feed him."

Alison buries her head in her hands. I pat her shoulder consolingly, but my mind is elsewhere. I wonder what would happen if I got up on the auction block. What kind of price would I fetch? And who would bid on me?

Chapter 17

We Need an Orchestra

ANNA

I sink into a seat on the balcony, completely exhausted. I had put out several fires tonight, everything from the caterers nearly serving Alison's auction cake, to the DJ wanting to play "Ice Ice Baby" every other song. Nor had I expected to be Blake's full-time babysitter as well. I let out a long sigh, ready for the night to be over.

Below me, the last of the guests collect the auction items they won as the caterers break down tables and chairs. The night has been a resounding success, with over eighty thousand dollars raised for underprivileged kids to play hockey. A record. But after spending the evening running between gala disasters and Blake disasters, I am done. My back aches, and my feet are screaming.

Usually, the pain and the insanity only serve to invigorate me, just like playing a game of pickup hockey with my dad. Tonight, though, I just feel hollow. I spent the whole night determined not to look for Charlie, but knowing dating him is a bad idea doesn't make things any easier. I remind myself he is a goofball who never seems to take anything seriously and probably isn't even interested anyway. Still, when I saw him by the bar, I wanted to dump Blake-babysitting duty onto Freddy the Freezer and spend the rest of the gala with Charlie. But now the night is over, and I missed my chance. Perhaps it is better that way.

A chair squeaks as someone plunks into a seat several spots down. I look, and my heart leaps. It's Charlie. Devastatingly debonair in a classic tuxedo, he is like a broad-chested James Bond.

"Incredible night," he says. "You should be proud."

"Thanks," I reply, feeling both thrilled and awkward at the compliment.

"Do you do birthday parties?" he asks. I laugh. He always knows how to break the tension.

We lapse into silence, looking at each other.

The way Charlie is looking at me gives me such butterflies. His face is still and serious. His eyes lock onto mine. I don't think I've ever seen him so focused. I have to get out of here before I do something I will regret. Standing abruptly, I grab my heels.

"Well, I should go. Goodnight." I move quickly, determined to stick to my rules. I just need to brush past him and out of the row first.

"Anna, wait, please." He stands, setting down a book he has in his hands.

I glance at it and do a double-take, stopping directly in front of him. He has my photo book. "You bid on that?" I ask, shocked.

"I know," he says. "It's not like I need more hockey stuff, but something about the pictures just spoke to me. They're so vivid, so alive. It made me feel like what we do is art."

I stare at him, emotions swirling through me. This man I have dismissed as a showboat, whom it would be a bad idea to date on every level, has just seen into my soul. My certainty cracks as a tiny voice in my heart asks, "What if the real mistake would be to run away from this?"

Charlie takes a step forward. "Anna, listen, I know what you're probably going to say, but I—"

"No one's ever looked at my photos like that before," I say.

His eyes widen. "These are your photos? I had no idea."

I nod, gazing up into his crystal blue eyes, no longer trying to get past him. I know what will happen if I don't leave right now. Everything will change.

Charlie takes another step forward.

We are now only a heartbeat away from each other, our clothes lightly brushing. I can see every detail of the stubble on his jawline. I can sense it when he swallows. The pull I feel toward this man is almost unbearable.

"Those photos are beautiful," he says thickly. "They are brave, and they are bold, and fearsomely intelligent, and funny. And if you tell me to walk away, I will do it right now. But these past few months, you have lit up my life, Anna Green. I find you utterly enchanting."

My heart feels impossibly big. I've never been called enchanting before. I've never met anyone like Charlie before. I've been so certain sticking to my uncomplicated life is the right thing to do. Every time I am with Charlie, he turns my world upside down.

The scary thing is, I might actually like it.

I can barely move, can barely breathe. I feel like I have floated away from my real life into this magical moment, and I am terrified something will break the spell. I am silent for a long beat, working up the courage to respond.

I whisper, nearly voiceless, "I don't want you to walk away."

That was all Charlie needed to hear. His eyes heat as his gaze drops to my lips. Millimeter by millimeter, he leans toward me. I feel the gentle heat of his breath intertwining with mine, and my heart thunders in my chest. I close my eyes. Our noses touch. A brief dance of skin on skin. Our lips haven't even come together, and this is already the most spectacular first kiss I've ever had, standing here awkwardly in the narrow aisle with my legs digging into the hard balcony seats.

"We need an orchestra," he murmurs.

My eyes open. "What?" I ask.

Charlie lifts his hand, running his fingers down my hair and cupping my cheek. I feel a thrill run through me.

"Imagine there's music," he says, then hums a few bars of the last song—Frank Sinatra's "The Way You Look

Tonight"—that played at the gala. His rough tenor vibrates the air between us, as we sway slightly to the sound. I think Charlie is wrong. No orchestra could compete with this.

He leans forward and presses his lips to mine.

Heat bursts within me as our mouths meet. All my fears, all my thoughts melt away. The kiss is soft at first, tender and sweet, my lips answering. A conversation in touch, low, and slow, and searing.

Fireworks thunder through my body as the dam breaks, months of longing and denial giving way to sensations that swirl hot and tight in my core. A part of me knows once this is over, I will second guess everything about this moment, but my mind is filled with music and real life feels so far away. I never want this to end.

I need more. I press into Charlie, threading my hands through his thick sandy hair, deepening the kiss. He answers my need by wrapping his strong arms around me, one cradling my neck, the other tightening on my waist. I had no idea how much I wanted this. I arch into him. My mouth parts and our tongues meet in an urgent dance.

A soft moan burst from his throat and I gasp into his mouth, thrilled by how much he wants me.

After what feels like a century and an instant, we finally break apart. Even then, our bodies cling to each other, refusing to separate. Charlie leans against me, pressing his forehead to mine. He stares down at me, his pupils dilated, his breath shallow, his muscles taught, and a grin across his face.

I grin back, floating in his arms. I know I have just

taken my neat, ordered little world and shaken it like a snow globe. Tomorrow will bring back all the thoughts and fears I chased away when Charlie's lips hit mine. But right here, in this moment, I feel like I can soar.

Chapter 18

You Mean Like Spy a Little Bit?

KYLE

Anna Green is the most boring person on the planet, hands down. I have been keeping tabs on her for over two weeks, and I have never had a harder time staying focused. She wakes up every morning, buys an iced coffee, takes the MAX to the Coliseum, works until some ungodly hour, then returns home to her cute little condo, and goes to bed. That's it.

On exciting days, she stops by her friend's house in the morning to walk the woman's scraggly mutt of a dog. Even the dog is well-behaved when he walks with Anna. The only time I ever saw it bark was when I got too close the first morning I was tailing them. When Anna wasn't looking, the dog gave me a snarl that said, "Get any closer, and you'll become reporter-a-la-mode." I do not like dogs.

146

Anna doesn't smoke, I barely see her drink, and she even put change in the bucket of a Salvation Army Santa on her way to work. I've chatted up several of her friends, tried to get the dish from old colleagues, and snooped on her social media. By all reports, she is a genuinely nice and hardworking person who cares about friends, family, hockey, and not too much else. No sex, no drugs, no bribery, and no embezzlement. There is nothing I can sink my journalistic teeth into.

Such a disappointment.

My one shining moment was the afternoon that I followed her to Oaks Amusement Park. I was hungover and not in the mood to stand under a tree twenty feet from an amusement park that had been closed for over a month. I stuck it out only because Anna never deviates this much from her routine, and no one can be up to any good at a closed amusement park. I certainly wouldn't be.

My instincts had proven right when Charlie Haskell showed up, all big smiles and puppy dog eyes. This had to be the guy that a drunken Blake had yammered on about; the one that Blake thinks is stealing Anna away from him. The two certainly had a nauseating amount of chemistry as they flirted their way over to the roller rink. I subtly snapped several photos of them holding hands as Charlie helped Anna get her balance, and a money shot of Charlie perched on top of Anna in a very compromising position after they took a tumble.

I was hoping for more. At least a kiss, preferably with tongue. But afterward, when I tracked down the scary woman with the painfully bright red hair who talked to

Anna and Charlie, all she said was that Anna told her they were discussing hockey charity work. Then she and all her roller derby teammates glared at me until I made up some excuse and ran away.

I was disinclined to believe the redhead. No one talks about charity work at a roller rink. An office or a coffee shop maybe, but not on a cutesy little retro roller-skating date. They are way too annoyingly adorable to just be colleagues. There is something going on there.

Unfortunately, when I snuck into the Charity on Ice gala to spy on them, Anna kept her distance from Charlie all night, focused entirely on keeping the event running smoothly. She was depressingly professional once again. In fact, Charlie seemed more interested in hitting on Anna's friend with the dog. I lost track of them toward the end of the night and gave up. The following week just returned to Anna's maddeningly dull work routine.

If Anna and Charlie are actually dating, I'll be all set. Not only did the PCHL hate player-management relationships, but a secret affair unfolding between management and a player on two rival teams? I could turn the entire season on its head. But what I really want, what would make my career, would be a Blake-Charlie-Anna love triangle. It practically makes me salivate to think about it.

I don't have proof anything is actually going on between Anna and Charlie, but I'm not about to let Blake know that.

Adjusting my coat against the cold and staring out at the river, I check my phone for the time. I arranged to meet Blake back at Wayfinder Beer. It has become our usual spot. Blake is a gold mine for snarky quotes and hot takes on his fellow hockey leaguers. Most of the other players have long ago gotten the memo to be vague and diplomatic with reporters. Blake's memo seems to have gone straight into his brain spam. I am determined to keep the kid in my pocket as long as possible.

Of course, I won't mind if Blake shows up on time for once. The hot-tempered player has proven increasingly erratic, and while it is great content for my stories, it is not great for writing them.

Finally, after forty-five minutes of waiting, I spot Blake striding toward me out of the fog. Tall, hunched, and angry, like he always is.

"Hey, buddy—" I start, but Blake brushes right past me, heading for the door.

"I need a drink," is all he says.

I sigh. This should be fun.

I find Blake inside, flagging down the bartender. It is early, so the bar is fairly quiet. Perfect for illicit conversations.

"Hell," Blake growls at the bartender, pointing to one of the appropriately named Wayfinder taps.

"Same," I say quickly, hoping Blake will pick up the tab.

The bartender pours, and Blake takes a long pull of his beer, draining nearly half of it before he wipes his mouth and turns to me.

"I don't have long. What did you want to talk about this

time?" Blake asks. "Today's just a travel day," he continues. "We're heading to Wichita and Tulsa. Should be easy pickings. Those teams have a bunch of dusters."

I want very much to hear more of Blake's thoughts on Wichita and Tulsa, but I force myself to stick to the script. "Oh, I bet you're going to crush them, man. But I brought you here because I've got an update on my Anna article."

I have never seen anyone sit up so fast in my life. Blake's beer would have sloshed all over his jersey if he hadn't drunk so much of it already. Does this kid really not own anything other than hockey jerseys?

I signal the bartender for another, and head for a table by the wall, reeling in my prey. I haven't said much about my research on Anna since I started meeting with Blake, mostly because there was so little to say about the mind-numbingly nice woman, but I know it is all Blake wants to hear. I needed time to come up with a spin to keep my fish on the hook.

Blake slouches across from me, his eyes boring into mine. "What about Anna? How's the article going? Can I read it?"

"Uh, no, the article's still in early stages. But I've spent some time looking into her, and she's an amazing woman. Really fascinating," I lie through my teeth. Blake nods. "The thing is . . . my editor's just not sure there's enough for me to keep going."

Blake looks shocked. "What? Why? What's wrong with her?" He leans forward as if he will pound me into a puddle of reporter goo if I suggest Anna is anything less than perfect.

"Nothing, nothing," I assure him. "It's just that she doesn't have a lot going on in her life that we can cover, outside of her work with the Freezers. Oh, and the time she's been spending with that Charlie guy," I add casually, setting the bait.

This time, Blake does spill his beer. In fact, he nearly chokes. I lean over to pound him on the back and wait.

"Charlie? Charlie from the Shredders?" Blake coughs out.

"Oh, yeah. He is on the Shredders, isn't he?" I say, playing dumb. "They've met up a few times since that Peewee thing. She hasn't mentioned it?"

Blake shakes his head. "What were they doing?" He practically spits out the question.

"Well, I didn't want to invade her privacy by getting too close, but it seemed more personal than professional if you know what I mean."

Blake picks up his coaster and begins systematically shredding it. "Could you get closer?"

"What? You mean like spy a little bit? Take some pictures?" I act completely surprised by the thought.

"Pictures?" asks Blake, intrigued. "You can do that?"

"Oh, sure. I can't print them without permission, but I'll take pictures for research. Of course, it's hard for me to keep going with the article if my editor's not interested. I gotta pay the rent, you know?" My rent is actually quite low because of another set of compromising pictures I have taken, but Blake doesn't need to know that.

Blake sits back on his stool, obviously distracted.

He looks up. "What?"

"I'm just bummed I have to stop looking into this. I know you were interested, but my editor wants me to move onto other stuff. If he's not paying for it, I can't afford to keep going," I explain, staring at Blake.

Blake looks down at his empty glass.

"Kyle, look, I don't trust this Charlie guy. He's bad news, and if he's hanging out with Anna, he's up to something. I bet he's using her to find out about Coach's systems before we play them again," Blake declares, appearing more and more convinced as he says it.

"You think so?" I fake a shocked frown. "That's terrible."

"Yeah. Tell your editor that, and he'll have to let you do the story."

I'm annoyed. Blake isn't getting it. "Actually, he'll probably want proof, which I can't get without spending more time looking into Anna and Charlie. Which I can't do without someone paying me to do it." I hope that hint was obvious enough.

Blake finally gets the hint. "Maybe I could pay you? Just till your editor gets interested again?"

My face splits into a relieved grin. "That's a great idea, Blake. You sure you don't mind?"

Blake holds out his hand for me to shake. "Hey, man, I'm glad I can help you out. Your editor seems like a real dick."

I take his hand. "Yeah, he's the worst," I say. The imaginary editor has come in handy more times than I can count. I check my phone again and stand abruptly, pretending I have just seen something urgent. "Listen, I have to go. I'll text you later to work out this Anna stuff. I think you're doing the right thing. This Charlie sounds like he's no good." I decide to split before he expects me to pick up the tab.

Chapter 19

Actually, Make It a Large

ANNA

I will never, ever tell Alison, but there is one place I go to even more than Munch. I step through the doors and inhale deeply, letting the rich coffee aroma permeate my senses and calm my nerves. The Stumptown on 3rd Street, near my condo, is one of my happy places. This was why, when Charlie asked to meet up, I told him to come here. It also happens to be a place where I rarely see other members of the Freezers, which is another reason Munch is very much not an option.

At least until I figure out what on earth I am doing about Charlie.

Even Alison would have to begrudgingly admit that Stumptown makes the city's best coffee. The shop is pure Portland. Gig posters for musicians, along with funky local art, covered the white-washed brick walls. The bright front windows are decked out for the holidays, featuring snowmen with big mustaches, tattoos on their stick arms, and clinking their espressos.

I do a quick scan of the coffee shop for Charlie but don't see him. I guess that makes sense because I wasn't able to sleep and got here absurdly early. I join the long line to order, getting behind a businessman deep in a phone call about quarterly earnings, a student with massive headphones and an even bigger backpack, a teen with his hair shaved down to a multicolored mohawk, and the resident neighborhood hipster who rides past my condo every morning on an oversized unicycle. Stumptown unites us all.

I want to turn and point that out to Charlie, which sends a flutter of nerves through my system. Our kiss was absolutely magical, a moment suspended in time, like my own private fairytale. I left the Crystal Ballroom floating on air, my tired feet so light I felt like dancing. I fell onto my pillow that night and dreamed of him.

Then, the next day, as my hazy mind had woefully predicted, I woke up in a cold sweat, all my anxieties crashing right back down on me. Had I really kissed Shredders' center, Charlie Haskell right in the middle of the ballroom? Every single member of the hockey community was at that event. What if somebody saw us? The memory of his body pressing into mine, his arms wrapped around me, and his mouth hot and wet against mine pulled at my heart and made me warm and giddy. But it wasn't enough to dispel the fear. Of all the hockey players I shouldn't date, he is numero uno—written in bold, all caps, and underlined—on the list. I half-expect to see a skywriter fly past, painting the words "Don't Date Charlie" above Stumptown.

Not knowing what to do, I threw myself back into work. Usually, I crash after the charity gala, but not this time. I stayed at the office later than Coach Peter. It was so late that Zane actually came back to check on me, with hot coffee in tow. I've been avoiding Alison, who can tell something is up, but fortunately hasn't pried. Actually, I wonder if Alison is avoiding me right back. We have yet to talk about the fact that my hockey-hating best friend had gone and bought herself a date with Leo. I am not about to let that drop for the next century. I am thinking of ordering them His & Hers hockey jerseys.

But first, I need to figure out what to do with my own love life. My heart and my head are pulling me in two very different directions. Then Charlie texts about meeting up to talk.

I looked at the text so many times that day that I nearly ran the battery down on my phone. Half of me wanted to rush out of my office and run straight into his arms, but the other half wanted to sprint in the opposite direction. I am scared by how much I am drawn to him. This man who could turn my neat, well-ordered life into a panic at the disco. This man who kissed me like there was no tomorrow.

Finally, I told him to meet me at Stumptown, conveniently picking the day after the Freezers left for their streak of away games. I initially planned on going but begged off the trip at the last minute. My dad was disappointed—he finds the away trips a great chance to subject me to his music playlists—but he didn't question it.

The door swings open, and I whip my head toward the blast of cold air, pulling my coat tighter around me. It isn't Charlie, instead just some bearded guy with a hat and glasses who walks straight to the band posters. I think he looks vaguely familiar; maybe he was at Music Millenium. I turn back to the barista, who gives me a friendly smile.

Nayeli, with her heavy blue eyeshadow, purple lipstick, and about a dozen face piercings winking in the light, is my favorite Stumptown employee. Today, she is wearing a Keep Portland Weird T-shirt, and a pin scrawled with the words Save the Snails. I am afraid to ask what they need to be saved from.

"The usual?" Nayeli asks.

"Actually, make it a large," I tell her.

Nayeli gives me an appraising look. "Big day, huh?" I flash her a nervous smile. Nayeli input my order and tells me, "I get it. Venus is entering Scorpio. That's always a crazy time. Embrace your relationships and avoid casual flings. Oh, and don't make any big financial decisions."

I nod, not sure how to feel about that impromptu horoscope. My biggest financial decision of the day is probably splurging on the large coffee. Does embracing my relationships mean taking the leap with Charlie? Or throwing myself back into hockey? That Charlie could be some casual fling is exactly what I am afraid of. I don't want to take a risk and have it blow up for nothing.

Thinking about him being more than a casual fling is

also terrifying. Whatever Charlie is, he is way outside my comfort zone.

I pick up my iced coffee, deep in thought.

"Iced coffee in December?" asks a warm, resonant voice that vibrates straight through me.

I look up, and can't help but melt a little at the sight of Charlie's sparkling blue eyes and his easy grin. Despite my reservations, the knot of stress in my chest immediately dissipates.

"Guilty," I say sheepishly, bracing for the forthcoming lecture.

But Charlie simply grins wider. "My kind of gal."

I fall a tiny bit in love with him for that.

Charlie nods toward the crowded shop. "Think you can fight off some of these hipsters for a table? I'll grab a drink."

I grin, pumping my free hand into a fist, then turn toward the tangle of tables and laptop cords. I watch Charlie chat with Nayeli from the table I pounce on after an aspiring writer's computer dies. Even from a distance, I can feel his charm. When he locks eyes with me as he picks up his drink, I feel a jolt so strong it is like the kiss all over again.

He makes his way to me and sits down, clinking his iced drink to mine. "To cold drinks and good company," he says.

"I'll cheers to that." I smile, nervous all over again. I spent enough time around Charlie that our conversations usually flow easily, but this is different. I feel like a middle schooler, afraid to talk to the boy at the homecoming dance.

We sit there for a few seconds, neither sure what to say.

Finally, Charlie speaks. "Anna, listen, I know you have a rule against dating hockey players, and I want to respect that."

"It's not just my rule," I point out. "The PCHL doesn't like it either. I don't want you to get in trouble."

"I don't want you getting in trouble, either. But I like you so much. And I think you like me too. That or you're just a really, really good kisser."

I laugh, my cheeks warming. "I am a pretty good kisser."

"Believe me, I know," Charlie tells me, his own cheeks turning pink. He grew serious, looking at me. "I don't want it to be just that one kiss. I want to be with you. Do you want to be with me?"

I take a deep breath. "I do," I admit. "But it's not that simple. We'd have to keep it quiet from the league, maybe even from our own teams. Can we pull that off? Do we want to? Then there's our schedules, which are both crazy. And, of course, there's my father."

"Give me the phone right now," Charlie says. "I'll happily talk to your father."

I laugh, but this time there isn't much humor in it. "Now you're really underestimating your opponents." All my fears about what my father would say if he ever found out his precious baby girl was dating a rival hockey player clamored in my brain. Murder charges are a distinct possibility. More than anything, I hate the thought that Coach

Peter would be disappointed in me. I am talking myself out of dating Charlie more and more by the second.

Charlie reaches out and takes my hand in his. We sit there a moment, marveling at the way our hands fit together. His, large and calloused. Mine, small and soft. Charlie traces his thumb over my knuckles, sending shivers down my spine. It is amazing how this tiny touch goes straight through me. I waver, deeply torn and not wanting to leave this moment for the realities of the world.

He gently lets go of my hand, and I feel hollow without it.

"Maybe we shouldn't make any decisions right now," he says. "Take some time and think about it."

I nod, glad he found a way out of the conversation. That feeling mixed with disappointment that he didn't jump onto the table and declare he'd fight for me through all obstacles. Despite my attraction to him, unless something changes drastically, this is a relationship that doesn't make sense on paper. Even if both of us feel it, time to think won't change that.

"Charlie, I just don't know," I say, deciding to rip off the Band-Aid. "I mean, we don't know each other that well. I'm not sure it's worth all the trouble just to go on a few dates," I explain, staring into my melting iced coffee and willing myself to believe it.

"Anna," says Charlie in a voice that makes me look up and meet his clear blue gaze. He looks at me like there is nobody else in the crowded, noisy coffee shop. Like there is nobody else in the world. "Trust me. You are worth it. And if I have my way, it will be more than just a few dates."

Those words and that gaze sears straight into me. I feel them in my soul. And I want to believe them so badly. But still, I am afraid of what they mean.

Charlie continues. "If I have to wait until the end of the season to prove that to you, I will. If I have to wait until your father retires, I'll do that too."

"I believe that will be when hell freezes over," I quip.

Charlie grins and shrugs. "That'll be a perfect time to take you skating again."

I smile. I came here convinced there was no way this relationship would work, and I'm still not sure. But I'm not quite ready to kick Charlie out of my life just yet.

Chapter 20

Why Doesn't She Water Her Plants?

BLAKE

"Hey buddy, you gotta play or you gotta move."

I blink up at the server as I rest on the Medieval Madness pinball machine. A gaggle of annoyed geeks stand behind the waiter, like a bunch of kids who have tattled to the teacher. I lurch up, grabbing my mostly empty drink.

"Whatever. Didn't wanna play the stupid game anyway," I mutter.

The night started out okay. Practice was good. The team seems invigorated after the winter holidays. We haven't lost a game yet, and the championship is feeling more attainable by the day. Anna seems in good spirits too, and I convinced myself she was over the temporary insanity of her interest in Charlie Haskell. I started researching office plants to buy her for Valentine's Day. Before the Charlie fiasco threw me off, I was so close to asking her out. A Valentine's gift will be the perfect way back to that conversation. There is no way she can stick to her no-hockey-player rule when I give her vanda orchids.

I tagged along with the team to Wayfinder to unwind. Then stupid Kyle shows up like the overdue Ghost of Christmas Past. He drags me into a dark corner to reveal badly framed photos of Charlie and Anna at a coffee shop, holding hands. The guy is grinning like a cat who brought home a dead canary and wanted praise for it.

Seeing the photo confirmation dumps ice water onto my soul. I harbor these ideas I can win Anna over, but can I really? Whenever I get her attention, she only wants to talk about work. She is always off doing her job. What is that even about? It is probably so she can rush off and spend time with Charlie.

I thought she was different. I was reluctant to give her my hockey puck. It is a piece of my heart. But I had done it anyway, and she treated it with all the care of a pencil. She probably just shoved it in some drawer and forgot about it.

I still remember the day my grandmother presented it to me, carefully wrapped and tied with a bow. She was so proud of her discovery, and how the antique store owner hadn't even thought to haggle. She couldn't even wait for me to open it before blurting out what it was.

Between the divorce and starting new lives with new partners, my parents didn't take much interest in me. To have someone care so much about me that they went out of their way to find and wrap up such a unique gift meant more to me than anything. As I uprooted my life to play hockey, traveling across the country, then across continents, I took the puck with me. It is my good luck charm and makes the loss of my grandparents a little easier to bear. No matter where I am, it is a piece of home.

When I met Anna, I felt like I finally found someone who could understand me. She grew up on hockey and loves it as much as my grandparents. I have never been great with words, so giving her the puck was my way of telling her how I felt. It is a good luck charm for our future together. I assumed she'd see how important it is to me, be touched, and fall into my arms immediately. Instead, she used it to bring good luck for her fling with the Shredder. I hate the idea that Charlie is reaping the benefits.

In fact, I should ask for my puck back. Yeah. The more I drink, the better this idea seems. I should do it soon, before she throws it away. Maybe she already has. If I insist she gives it back, then maybe she'll realize how she's hurt me and run back to me. The idea burrows deep into my brain and sticks there.

By the time the Freezers move over to Ground Kontrol, I am four drinks deep. Leo suggests I slow down and join the team in their pinball tournament. I join but decline to slow down my drinking, which means I don't make it very far in the tournament. Then I blink, and here I am being evicted by a bunch of skinny tattooed toothpicks.

I stand, waiting for the world to stop swaying, then move toward the exit. Vlad drove me, but that ride is long gone. I need to go home. Fishing out my phone to call an Uber, I hesitate, fingers hovering over the screen. Isn't there something else I wanted to do tonight?

I blink again, and there she is in front of me, like a purple-haired vampire in the night.

"Hi, Blake!" chirps Mabeline. "I was wondering where you were. Going somewhere?"

"Yep, gotta go," I say, looking down and refocusing my eyes to find the Uber app.

"Want a ride?" she asks hopefully.

I look back up at her, an idea forming.

Mabeline pulls her Jeep to the corner of a quiet condo complex, her painted red lips pursed in confusion.

"I didn't think you lived in this neighborhood," she says. "Not that I know where you live. Not exactly anyway," she adds quickly.

"I need to get something from here," I explain. "It's important."

"Okaaay," Mabeline says. "Do you want me to wait? I don't mind. I've got nothing else going on tonight. I mean, actually I was supposed to meet some friends for a birthday party. But I don't mind. Or I can wait, and then we can go to the party together? Or not go to the party together? Maybe this can be our date that I bought. Remember how I bought a date with you, and we haven't scheduled it?"

I shake my head. If all goes according to plan, I won't be coming back out for a while.

"This is something I need to do on my own," I tell her.

Mabeline nods gravely, her purple hair shining in the moonlight. "I understand. But if you need me, you can always call me. Or call me to set up our date. Actually, do you have my number?"

I don't answer. I am already out of the car and stumbling my way toward the condo complex. Each unit is separated by cute little low-walled terraces.

"Anna," I mutter to myself, slurring. "You have something important from my grandmother, and I want it back. It's not just a pencil to me."

I stop, feeling like that isn't quite right. "I want my grandmother's charm back before you throw it at Charlie." That sounds better. I probably won't have to finish the speech before she realizes what she's done and throws herself into my arms.

I pull her address from the Freezer holiday card list, and I squint for the right number. This would be easier if they weren't all spinning. I find it, straighten up, and ring the bell.

"Anna, you have my grandmother," I rehearse, waiting for her to come to the door. But nothing happens. I try again, rapping on the wood for good measure. Still nothing. I amble around to the back, thinking maybe the front door is broken.

There is a light on inside, but while most of the units have cars parked behind them, Anna's MINI Cooper is nowhere in sight. I vaguely remember she was still in her office at the Coliseum when everybody else emptied out. Maybe she isn't home yet. A voice in the back of my mind says maybe she isn't here because she is at Charlie's, but that only makes me more determined.

I stand there, swaying and trying to think. Suddenly struck by an overwhelming fear that she is on the brink of throwing my puck away, I need to do something. If I don't get it back this second, it will be on its way to the dump tomorrow morning.

I should at least try to see if she is home. Leaning over the low terrace wall, I try to peer through the sliding glass doors on her patio, but the closed curtains block my view. There is a small gap in the curtains, but I can't get a good angle to see through from this side of the pesky wall. The only thing that makes sense is to climb over the four feet of stucco and get a better view. Of course, even when I am inside the terrace and can peer through the gap in the curtains, I still can't see Anna's entire living space. Well, I can see most of it. Maybe she is inside the closed coat closet, doing some reorganizing. It only makes sense to try to open the door, just to make sure I'm not missing her.

I try the handle, but the door doesn't budge. I apply a tiny bit of my hockey strength, just in case it is a sticky door. Something snaps and cracks, but the door slides free.

I take a quick glance behind me to see if anybody is watching. There might be movement in the shadows across the street, but otherwise, I see no one. What I am doing might look a tad suspicious, but I'm not really breaking and entering. I am dropping in on a friend, and the door was stuck. No surprise there since her lock has somehow gotten broken. She is lucky it is me finding it and not some burglar.

I ease my way into Anna's living room.

"Anna?" I call. There is no answer. She isn't hiding in the closet or in any of the other rooms. I am alone in her apartment.

I look around, curious about the secret hidden world of Anna's home life. I'm not terribly impressed. Her TV is too small, she is messy, and I wonder if she realizes her furniture is mismatched. To my relief, I don't see any evidence of a man spending any time here. There are no men's shoes or jackets floating around, and only one toothbrush in the bathroom. Unfortunately, I don't see any evidence of my hockey puck either.

I was hoping that when I got here, I'd find it displayed somewhere prominent and important as a sign she understands how much it means to me. But the puck is nowhere to be seen. I grow more and more upset. She framed some scribbled graph about iced coffee, but she hasn't appreciated the significance of a rare piece of hockey history? Who does she think she is?

My casual looking around turns more and more frantic. I shove stuff off tables, shake out her blankets, and uproot her couch cushions. I even dig through her trash. As a last resort, I pry open her drawers one by one and dump them out on the floor. I am desperate to find the puck, panicking that she has taken my treasured possession and drove it directly to the garbage dump.

Just as I am about to root through her clothing dresser —which I am curious about for other reasons as well—I notice that her little vintage side table has a tiny drawer I have overlooked. Tugging it open, I sag in relief. There is my puck, safe and sound. I run my fingers over it, then tuck it gently into my front coat pocket, next to my heart.

I look around at the living room, feeling a little guilty. I caused a bit of a mess during my search. It wasn't the most organized place when I walked in, so maybe she won't even notice. Besides, if I try to clean it up, I'll put things back in the wrong places, and I hate when that happens. After I make a half-hearted attempt to shove the cushions back on her couch, I drape the blanket over some of the chaos. There, that is better.

Car headlights flash past the window. I need to get out of here before Anna gets home. I have my puck, but realize I have forgotten my speech. I might lose my moral high ground if she finds me here like this.

I turn and tiptoe out the sliding door and to the low terrace wall. As I heft up my leg, I kick the small row of slowly dying potted plants on the patio wall. One teeters precariously on the edge, and I throw myself back to make the most heroic save of my sports life, catching the pot before it shatters.

I hug the small fern, relieved I have not killed a plant tonight. While giving it a quick examination to make sure I have not broken any leaves, I notice it is under-watered. That will not do at all.

I make my way back into Anna's condo to carefully water it. Looking under her sink, I find an empty spray bottle and fill it with water. I bring the plant back outside and gently set it on her small outdoor table, then mist it and her other plants. When I give Anna my speech about the hockey puck, I'll tack on a section about proper plant care.

Feeling satisfied, I set the spray bottle down by her plants, flop back over the terrace wall like a giant drunken fish, and stumble my way into the night. I am proud the evening is back on track.

Chapter 21

Notorious Batman Villain Poison Ivy

ANNA

My condo must have exploded. This is my first thought when I get home from the late-night post-work drinks Alison had talked me into. I drop my bag and stare at the utter chaos. All my things are on the floor, all my drawers pulled out and emptied, and even my couch looks more like abstract couch art. I try to get my tipsy mind to comprehend it, but the only idea that comes to me is that a gas main beneath my living room must have burst, sending all my belongings flying. No, that is crazy. Clearly, a very tiny tornado must have blown through my condo complex. I didn't even realize we had tornados in Portland.

Then my mind finally rolls around to the most likely explanation that I didn't want to be true. There are no tornados in Portland, and no signs my floor had ruptured in a gas explosion. My condo has been broken into.

My knees go weak, and I try to sink into the nearest chair, but it is covered in the contents of my spice rack. I simply slide to the floor instead. I have always felt so safe in this neighborhood and in Portland in general. Not to mention, I don't own much I would consider very valuable. Has a burglar really broken into my condo? Why?

Not knowing what to do, I dig into my pocket for my phone and hit the first number in my favorites.

The gravelly voice answers on the first ring. "Hey, Anna, I'm just going over some tapes for next week's game. It's late. What's up?"

"Daddy?" I ask, my voice trembling.

"Sweetheart? Are you okay?" my dad asks, concerned.

"I think . . . I think my condo was broken into."

"Oh, Anna Banana," he says. "I'm so sorry. Are you safe? Have you called the police?"

"Uh-huh," I say. "And, nuh-uh."

"Okay," Coach Peter says, taking charge through the phone. "Call 911, tell them what happened, and stay put. Don't touch anything. I'll be right over. It's going to be okay."

"Thanks, Daddy," I say, feeling about five years old again. There is no one I trust more in these situations than my dad.

I call the police to explain what happened, realizing as I talk to the operator that I'm not even sure what actually happened. My front door was locked. How had they gotten in? The voice on the line promises that officers will be over shortly, and I force myself to stand back up so I can figure things out before they get here.

I wade through my living room, trying to avoid the various knickknack landmines and the other debris of my life. Stepping over board games, books, blu-rays, records, exercise equipment, sports memorabilia, and all the random stuff I shoved in drawers and forgotten about over the years. Is that a VIP concert pass from the Jonas Brothers tour? All of it swirls together on the floor like some kind of insane Anna collage. I didn't even realize I own this much stuff until I see it strewn all over my living room.

My phone buzzes, and I glance down, wondering if Alison is checking to make sure I got home okay. It isn't Alison, but Charlie, sending me a silly hockey gif. Between the holidays, work, and my uncertainty, I haven't seen Charlie since our quick coffee at Stumptown. But he texted me a picture of him drinking iced coffee the next day, and naturally I had to send one back. We haven't stopped texting since.

Mostly it is just silly memes, TikTok videos, and hockey gossip. I appreciate that Charlie never pushes the conversation into something more serious because I still don't know about pursuing the relationship. With Freezer ticket sales still sluggish and Blake still glaring at any reporter who even thinks of asking him a question, Charlie's random texts are the highlight of my day. Just seeing his name bubble on my phone screen makes me feel better.

Below the gif, Charlie is typing something else. *In your*

neighborhood, comes the text. I told him where I live when we were arguing about which parts of Portland are the best. Three more dots dance across the screen. Then, after an eternity, the question: *Want to grab a drink?*

My heart skips a beat, but I don't have time to process the question or what it means for us. I text him quickly that I am dealing with a break-in. Even putting it into a text makes it all a little too real, so I hit send before I can think too much about it and shove the phone back into my pocket. There is an answering buzz from Charlie, but I decide to look at it later. Right now, I need to figure out how someone got into my home.

I look at my back door, but it also seems perfectly fine. Then I notice my patio screen door isn't quite closed. Sudden guilt ices over my insides. Had I forgotten to lock the patio door? I hurry over to look and realize the latch is broken. I don't touch it, but I see it is hanging loosely at the wrong angle. There is also a crack in the glass pane next to it. The burglar must have yanked the flimsy door hard enough to break the lock. The guilt eases, but fear takes over. Someone really broke into my condo. Why would anyone want to do that?

There is a knock at my front door, and I let out an involuntary squeak before remembering that burglars don't knock. I hurry to answer, hoping it is my dad and not the detectives. I want to see a friendly face before dealing with the police. But it is neither.

It is Charlie.

I stare at him, surprised and confused, but the emotion I feel strongest is pure relief. I hadn't realized how much his presence comforts me. Seeing his tall, broad frame standing in my doorway and his soft eyes filled with concern, I feel safe again.

"I did say I was in the neighborhood," he explains with a bashful smile. "Is it okay that I'm here?"

"Actually, I'm really glad you are," I say.

Charlie's smile deepens, and I step back to let him in. Instead of going around me, he steps forward and pulls me into a bear hug. I let him hold me, drinking in his warmth and the firmness of his chest underneath his sweater. I need this, and I don't want to let go.

While he holds me, he looks around, taking in the chaos.

"You had a break-in? How can you tell?" he asks. I give a low chuckle. "I mean, I didn't realize you were quite this messy, but I'm not one to judge."

I wrinkle my nose.

"Honestly, this is a really cozy space," he tells me. "I'd love to see it under better circumstances." He blushes, and redirects his gaze to the art on my walls. "Is that ... a graph about iced coffee consumption?"

I finally give a real laugh. "Zamboni Zane made that for me. He doesn't agree with our lifestyle choices."

Charlie's eyebrows shoot up. "Zamboni Zane and I are going to have words." He turns his attention back to the burglary. "Do you know what happened?"

I point toward the patio. "Looks like they forced the door. See? The lock is broken, and the glass is cracked."

Charlie's brows furrow. "The glass is cracked? That's no

good." He scans around the room and spots an open Amazon box near my recycling bin.

"May I?" he asks, gesturing toward the box.

"Sure," I say, wondering what he needs the box for. Some kind of burglary scarecrow?

Charlie scoops up the cardboard, along with the tape and scissors the robber conveniently dumped onto the floor nearby. He heads to the patio door and holds the box up to it, gauging the size he needs.

"You don't have to do that," I say, although I don't really mean it. I am grateful to have someone taking charge while my brain is still so scattered. It hasn't even occurred to me that I'll need to deal with the broken glass.

"Actually, yes, I do," Charlie replies. "Can't have you getting robbed."

I laugh again. "You're right. That would be terrible."

Charlie nods at the mess as he breaks down the box. "I'll prep it now, and then put it up once the police are done. Do you know what got taken?"

"I haven't even looked yet," I say. "I don't know how I'll be able to tell. It's all so mixed up."

"Start with valuables," Charlie suggests.

"That won't take long," I quip. "I haven't got any."

"Excuse me, you have a graph of iced coffee expenditures, and I saw you've got Bruno Mars on vinyl, so you've got a lot worth stealing."

"Don't knock Bruno Mars!" I warn, quickly kicking the Jonas Brothers VIP pass out of view. I sigh. "I guess I'll check the bedroom."

I head off as Charlie breaks the cardboard down to size.

There is a loud pounding on the door.

Charlie calls over to me. "I bet that's the cops. Want me to get it?" he asks.

"Yes, thank you. Actually, wait," I call from the bedroom. "That might be my—"

Charlie opens the door, coming face-to-face with my father just as I come racing out of the bedroom.

They stare at each other, totally frozen for a second. Then Charlie holds out his hand. "Good to see you, sir," he says.

Coach Peter eyes Charlie's hand as though there might be a bomb concealed inside of it. "Haskell?" he asks. "What are you doing in my daughter's house?"

"I was just—she texted and I—because you see—" Charlie fumbles.

"Hi, Dad, you remember Charlie. He's helping me with that kids' charity thing, and we were texting about it when I got home and saw this, so I told him and he was nearby and came over to help," I explain all in one breath. Then I throw myself into my dad's arms before he can question it. "Thank you for coming," I say. I mean it, although Coach Peter and Charlie Haskell are the last two people I want to share a room with under literally any other circumstances.

"Of course, sweetheart," Coach Peter says. He looks around, taking in the sheer chaos. "Well, Annie, I would not say you've been hit by a smooth criminal." Charlie chuckles. I roll my eyes. My dad drops the comedy routine and looks at me with the intensely furrowed brow I usually only see on him in third period. "Have the police come by yet?"

"Yes, we have," says a gruff female voice from the open doorway. We turn to find two uniformed officers: a no-nonsense woman who looks like she's seen it all, and a gangly kid who looks fresh out of the academy. "I'm Officer Cooper. This is Officer Moran. May we come in?"

"Oh, yes, please, thank you," I say, gesturing.

Officer Cooper swaggers in, trailed by the awkward Officer Moran. Officer Cooper looks around wearily. "Yup, it's a break-in."

Officer Moran scribbles that down on a pad. Officer Cooper turns to me. "You're the homeowner? Can you tell me what they took?"

I shrug, helpless. "Honestly, I'm not sure they took anything. I mean, maybe something small, but all my valuables are still here."

Officer Cooper purses her lips. "Hmm. Is there anyone in your life who might wish you any harm? Or might want to get in here for some reason?"

I shake my head, bewildered. "Who would want that?" I blink back tears. The thought that someone would specifically target me is even harder to process than a random break-in. I feel so vulnerable, like the four thick walls around me are nothing but tissue paper.

Officer Cooper looks over at the patio door. "This is how they got in?" she asks as Officer Moran scribbles. "Any of your neighbors have camera doorbells or anything?"

"Maybe? I'm not really sure," I say. I don't have much time to socialize with my neighbors.

"Well," says Officer Cooper, sounding resigned, "we'll take your statement and see if anybody in the complex saw anything. But if they didn't take anything and didn't show up on any cameras, there's really not much we can do."

This time both Charlie and Coach Peter step forward, looking ready to throw down. Officer Cooper does not look intimidated, but she holds up a hand before they can launch into anything.

"I'll have my colleague dust for prints on the door as well. We'll check it against our database. Sound good?" she adds.

Charlie and Coach Peter nod.

"Appreciate you checking on my daughter," Coach Peter says to Charlie begrudgingly, clearly not quite meaning it.

"Any time," says Charlie. "I mean, not *any* time. Only the proper times," he adds quickly. "Anyway, I should probably get going."

"You probably should," says Coach Peter.

Charlie glances toward me, then nods at Coach Peter. "Glad you have everything in hand, sir. Have a great evening," Charlie says. "I mean, not a *great* evening. Just, well, okay, bye."

He flees without saying goodbye to me.

"Your new charity thing, that's with him?" Coach Peter asks me, glaring daggers at the door.

"It happened by accident," I explain. "But he's not a bad guy," I add, hopeful that Charlie made a good impression on my father tonight.

Coach Peter, however, just shakes his head. "I don't

want you getting too close to the Shredders. For all we know, Coach Ryan's using that kid to get dirt on us. I wouldn't put it past him."

For all that I am uncertain about Charlie, the idea that he is leading me on is one thing I do not worry about. The way he looks at me can only be sincere. "I really don't think—"

"I'm serious, Anna Banana, you have to be more careful," my dad says, gesturing to my wreck of an apartment. "Now pack some stuff. I want you staying with me till you get that door fixed." Fatherly declaration over, he moves to the patio door to tape up the cardboard after Officer Moran finishes eagerly dusting the handle.

Grateful as I am to not sleep here tonight, I feel the sting of resentment for his words about Charlie. It isn't a surprise, but I hate that all he sees is a Shredder and a little girl who can't take care of herself. Break-in aside, I can handle myself. Charlie can see that. Why can't my dad?

My phone buzzes, and I set down the plant I picked up from the patio. Officer Cooper looks at me like I am crazy when I explain that the burglar hadn't stolen anything, but instead carefully moved and watered this plant. I could think of no other explanation for how it had levitated off my terrace wall and gotten misted. It never even occurred to me to mist a plant.

What on earth kind of burglar is this? I have no idea who would break into my condo just to water my plants. Notorious Batman villain Poison Ivy? What could it mean?

Did they just really like plants? Were they feeling guilty and did something nice before leaving? But what were they feeling guilty about if they didn't take anything? I did not understand.

I pull out my phone, hoping for a text from Charlie, but this time it is a text from Alison.

Made it back home, I respond, *but my condo got broken into!!*

What?!?! Alison shoots back, with a series of shocked emojis. *What did they take??*

Nothing, that's what's crazy
    They watered my plant tho

WHAT? They watered your PLANT?

Yup

I watch as the three dots appear and then disappear as Alison tries to figure out how to respond.

. . .

Send them to me tomorrow? My plants are a mess

I laugh. I might not feel safe in my apartment, but at least I have good people in my life. And well-watered plants.

~

In the three days since the break-in, my father had my door repaired, and I was finally starting to feel normal again.

Craving my routine, I pick up a large, iced coffee from Stumptown and demand Stinker from an overprotective Alison, promising the dog would stop any burglars in their tracks. Although, I think the worst Stinker would do is drool on their shoes.

It is a gorgeous winter morning. The sky is clear, and the mountain is out, Mt. Ranier's snowy peak on full display. I have my coffee and my borrowed pooch, and as he squats next to a bush with his tongue sticking out in concentration, I feel over the moon. Of course, the real reason isn't Stinker's contribution to the ecosystem.

I have a date tonight.

Ever since the break-in, Charlie has been incredible. He texted me later that night to make doubly sure I was okay, then he followed up the next morning.

I have been holding back with him out of fear of what it will do to my carefully constructed life, but the burglary has made me realize something. Life is unpredictable and uncontrollable. There is nothing I can do about that. So, if

I find someone who makes me happy, why run from it? My single life has been great, but I have been playing it safe. I want to try something new and see how it feels.

So, when Charlie asked if I wanted to meet up, I responded with a resounding yes.

Chapter 22

Seven Minutes in Heaven

CHARLIE

I bounce on the balls of my feet in front of one of my favorite Portland hot spots, Powell's Books. I popped into the city block-sized bookstore when I first moved to Portland. After intending to take a quick peek, I stayed the whole day wandering all four floors of the massive space. When I got a parking ticket for overstaying at my meter, I said I got stuck at Powell's on the written appeal. The appeal was granted.

When Anna agreed to meet up with me, I knew this was perfect. There is no better way to leave your troubles behind than a bookstore, and after the haunted look she had on the night of the break-in, that is all I want for her.

I have been so worried about her that when I finally see her emerge from the crowd—her coat pulled tight, her hair lit like a halo by the streetlights—I half-expect to see evil shadowy figures following her. But Anna looks better than ever. Her eyes are sparkling, and her creamy skin glows. Her beauty mark makes her look just like a Portlandian Marilyn Monroe. My heart pushes its way up into my throat. I know she wants to take things slowly, but I can't help it. The sight of her does something to me.

She stops in front of me and holds up an empty tote bag.

"You came prepared," I say.

"You know it. I'm using the break-in as my excuse to shop."

"You sure you're okay?" I ask, genuinely concerned. "I know it's only been a few days."

Anna nods. "It's a little freaky, but I'm okay. I got a better lock and a security camera. But what I really want is for this date to take my mind off it."

My eyebrows spike and fireworks burst in my insides. "This is a date? Like a date-date?" I ask, barely daring to hope. Could she possibly have changed her mind? My dreams are coming true.

Anna gives me a sultry grin. "Well, it all depends," she whispers, sending shivers down my spine. "Let's see what your taste in books is first."

She turns and sashays into the bookstore. I groan as I follow her swaying hips inside.

Once we cross the threshold into the warehouse-style space, we both pause to inhale deeply. The smell of musty paper wafts through the store, and I close my eyes to savor it. I open my eyes and see Anna watching me, a dreamy look on her face that makes me feel gooey inside.

I clear my throat. "First things first," I say. "What's your color?"

I am referring to Powell's nine color-coded rooms. Anna doesn't even have to think about it.

"Gold," she says.

"Of course the competitive girl would pick the gold room," I tease. "Let me guess, your favorite genre is science fiction? Because that's the only world in which the Freezers win the league."

"Oh, so you chose violence today." Anna laughs. "And no, it's mystery. Because it's a mystery why you think the Shredders have any hope of beating us."

I hold up my hands in surrender. "Is mystery really your favorite? Not sports or photography or something?"

"Non-fiction?" Anna asks. "No, thank you. Why read about things I can see in the real world? Why? What's your color?"

"Me? Gold. Definitely gold." I say, suddenly nervous to tell her.

"Oh, come on. I told you mine. Spill."

"Okay, fine." I sigh. "It's Orange. I like film books."

Anna looks confused. "You like books about film? Can't you just watch the films?"

"The books deepen the viewing experience," I explain. Anna looks skeptical. "Hey, I was a film and video major in college. You're talking to an expert."

"I'm talking to a nerd? Is that what you said?" Anna teases. "Alright, I'll bite." She looks at her phone. "We've each got seven minutes to go find a book for the other person, and we'll see about this film book thing."

I nod. "Prepare to have your horizons widened."

"Is that what they're calling it these days?" Anna asks.

I blush so strongly that I almost match the color of the room we are standing in. I wasn't expecting her to take the lead tonight. Seeing this, Anna dissolves into giggles. "You're bad," I say. "Be careful, or I just might make our next game seven minutes in heaven."

I wink before heading upstairs toward the Orange Room. I quickly lose myself in the glory of the Film and TV section. Only the allure of my stunning date will get me out of here in seven minutes. Otherwise, I'd risk another ticket to stay here all night. Hockey is my life now, but movies are my first love. It might seem silly to read books about them, but there is so much churning beneath the surface that I love to uncover. Isn't *Jaws* an even better movie once you know that the shark barely appears on screen because Bruce, the mechanical version, kept breaking down in the salt water, forcing Spielberg to get creative? It is just like hockey . . . and relationships. Great things happen when you are forced to forget your plans and improvise.

I know exactly the book I want to get for Anna. It is one I have been coveting for a long time but keep talking myself out of buying. My shelves are screaming from the weight of the books I already own, but this is the perfect excuse to pick it up for her.

I am so fixated on making it back to Anna in seven

minutes that I nearly run straight into my teammate Quentin as I descend the second flight of stairs.

"Whoa, Chuck," Quentin says. "This is a bookstore, not a demolition derby."

"Sorry, Quentin, blame the books," I say apologetically. "What brings you to Powell's?"

Quentin holds up a thick cookbook entitled *The Once Peaceful World Cookbook: Over 150 Vegan, Macrobiotic Recipes for Vibrant Health and Happiness.*

I paste on a smile. "Sounds . . . delicious?"

"You know it. I'm heading home to cook page fifty-three from this bad boy right now. You want in?"

Even if I wasn't on a date, I have sampled enough of Quentin's cooking to know the correct answer is no. "Wish I could, but I'm busy tonight."

"Oh, yeah?" Quentin asks. "You here with someone? I thought I saw you with—"

"Nope, nobody, just me," I blurt. With Anna finally coming around to the idea of a relationship, the last thing I want is for our status to be blasted all over the hockey-verse.

Quentin gives me a look. "If you say so, man. Listen, I gotta head out. This tofu lasagna won't cook itself."

I nod, keeping my grin fixed and watching Quentin until he reaches the checkout counter. Then I turn and sprint full bore back to meet Anna.

I rush to catch up and she looks at me curiously. "Are you okay?" she asks.

I wave her off, heart still racing. "I'm great," I promise. "Let me see your book."

"Well, I don't mean to make you feel worse, but my book just so happens to be the greatest mystery ever written," she says.

She holds it up. I whistle. "*Murder on the Orient Express.* I've seen that movie. Johnny Depp gets stabbed."

Anna shakes her head. "That's exactly my point. The book is so much better. Agatha Christie is the absolute master of mystery. She was the first mystery author I read when I was a kid, and I've read every single thing she's ever written. I think my dad actually started to worry I was plotting to kill him."

I take the mystery, feeling the age and weight of it in my hand. I realize Anna isn't just giving me a book, but a meaningful piece of her childhood. That is kind of perfect, given the book I have behind my back.

"Thank you," I say. "I'm excited to read it. But first I'm excited to see your face as I absolutely crush your book with mine."

I hold up my book with both hands like it is Simba from *The Lion King.*

Anna squints at the title, then looks at me blankly. "Okay?" she asks.

I stare at her. "Triple deke? Cake-eater? The Ducks fly together?"

"Are those words supposed to mean anything?"

I lower my book, *Birds of a Feather: The Making of The Mighty Ducks.* "Anna Green, are you telling me you've never seen *The Mighty Ducks*?"

Anna shakes her head. I put my hand to my heart and stagger around the row.

"What?" Anna asks. "It's a kid's movie."

"It's THE kids movie. There is no greater hockey movie in existence."

Anna looks skeptical. "*Miracle*? *Slapshot*?"

"Not even close. I can't believe you call yourself a hockey publicist. Does your dad know about this? And he hasn't disowned you?"

Anna laughs. "It's really that good?"

"It's necessary," I declare. "And it's happening." I take my book and her book and set them down, then grab both of Anna's hands in mine. "For our second date, I hereby cordially invite you to my place of residence for a screening of *The Mighty Ducks*."

Anna giggles, my fingers tingling as her thumbs lightly stroke my hands.

"I accept," she says. "On one condition."

"Anything," I vow, curious. Is she going to go back on this being a date?

"If you're going to make me watch this kid movie, you're going to have to put out," Anna begins. My eyebrows jerk up in shock. "You're in charge of making dinner. I heard a rumor you make a pretty good pizza."

I grin back. She got me. I am surprised and touched that she remembers my offhand comment about making pizza from our encounter at Munch. Oh, I will make her pizza. I will make her the best goddamn pizza of her life. And if she lets me, I'll do much, much more than that. It was amazing I made it this long through our bookstore date without kissing her, but I've been holding back, trying to be a gentleman while she decides what she wants.

"It's a deal," I say.

"It's a date," Anna replies.

Then, before I can step back, she tightens her grip on my hands and yanks me toward a nearby unoccupied row of shelves, pulling me into a shadowy corner. She leans against the shelf, tugging me close and knocking over several books in the process. I stare down at her, a shocked half-grin on my face, our hands still intertwined.

"Anna Green, you are full of surprises."

"Charlie Haskell," she purrs, "you talk too much."

Anna then lifts onto her tiptoes and pulls my lips down to meet hers. This isn't a slow and sensual kiss but an intense burst of heat, both of us craving the touch we have withheld for so long.

A low growl escapes my throat as I press Anna against the bookshelf. I can't believe how amazing she feels or how quickly her body responds. My tongue and hands quest desperately, wanting to memorize the way she feels and tastes.

I want to satisfy the throb between my legs, but a tiny part of my brain is still functioning enough to whisper that we have to stop. If I do all the things I want to do to her right now, we'll get kicked out of Powell's. Possibly arrested.

With all of my willpower, I break the kiss and pull back to look at Anna's flushed face. My arms are still around her, but now there is space between our heaving chests.

I remove her arm from my waist, pulling it up to my lips. I gently turn her hand over and plant a whisper-soft kiss against the delicate skin on the inside of her wrist.

I want badly to leave right now and give Anna what she wants, but she is special. She deserves to be wined, dined, and romanced. I will do this right if it kills me. And given how hard I am right now, it feels like it could kill me. Nevertheless, she is worth it.

Then I lean forward, my lips tickle her ear, my breath hot on her neck, and my voice is hoarse with desire when I say, "I'm very much looking forward to our next date."

Chapter 23

Goal

CHARLIE

We will not have sex tonight for our second date. I want to prove to Anna I am genuine boyfriend material. Despite the very tantalizing enthusiasm she showed at the bookstore, I know this is a big deal for her, and I want to make it perfect.

It is a pretty big deal for me too. I've had my share of hookups, but I haven't been in a serious relationship for over four years, and that one ended in a screaming fight over my crazy hockey schedule. Professional hockey and dating are like oil and water. Nevertheless, I am determined to prove to Anna and to myself that I can handle a real relationship. I don't want to let her go. In fact, if she'll let me, I think I'll hold onto her all the way down the aisle. But that is exactly why we are going to take it slow tonight.

That doesn't mean I haven't scrubbed down every inch of my apartment over the past few hours or sprayed so much air freshener that I've had to open every window to breathe. But I'll be damned if my apartment doesn't smell like Linen & Sky now.

Every pillow on the couch is fluffed. I bought cloth napkins and watched three YouTube videos about how to fold them. Candles wink from the carefully set dining table that I never use. The pizza ingredients are laid out and ready. I thought of everything. But I am still so nervous I feel like the popcorn bag sitting by my microwave. I want this to be perfect.

The doorbell rings, and I jump. It is go-time. I do a last sweep of the place for anything embarrassing I missed, then pull open the door.

My mouth goes dry. Anna is standing there in a burgundy sweater dress that is loose at the top but hugs her hips and stops midway down her thighs, giving me an incredible view of smooth legs that disappear into cute little black boots. It isn't a traditionally sexy outfit, but she looks gorgeous in it, and I nearly throw out my no-sex rule right then and there.

She holds up a bottle of wine in greeting. "Since you're cooking, I figured I'd bring the refreshments."

"This is perfect," I say, taking the bottle and stepping back so she can come in. I catch the scent of her hair as she brushes past. She smells like coffee and orange blossoms. It is intoxicating.

I tear myself away to open the wine while Anna uses the opportunity to take in my apartment.

She inhales deeply.

"Laundry day?" she asks.

"Hmm?" I say from the kitchen, pouring the wine.

"Never mind," Anna says, joining me. "How's the pizza coming?"

"Excellent. I was just waiting for my sous chef," I say, gesturing to a colorful selection of vegetables arrayed in a rainbow around the counter. "Pick your toppings. And before you ask, no, there's no pineapple. Pineapple on pizza is an abomination, and if you disagree, I'm sorry, but you're going to have to leave."

Anna laughs. "Don't worry. I would never commit such pizza blasphemy."

I mime relief, and Anna considers the toppings. "How about . . . green pepper, mushrooms, and pepperoni?"

I make a chef's kiss gesture, grab the mushrooms, and toss her the pepper.

"You chop; I chop."

Anna grabs a nearby knife and sets the pepper on the cutting board awkwardly and proceeds to cut it down the middle, getting the little seeds from the center everywhere. She fumbles with the seed-covered knife, cutting awkward, uneven slices out of one half of the pepper.

"Did that pepper do something to you?" I ask. "Did it insult your family?"

Anna makes a face. "It's a Shredders fan."

I laugh, and then gently pry the knife from Anna, slice out the seedy center of the non-mangled pepper half, and chop it into quick and even strips. Anna whistles.

I grin and slide over the dough, which is already shaped into a perfect pizza circle. "Wanna get saucy?"

I come up and stand behind her, encircling her with my arms and planting a kiss on her orange-blossom-scented hair. Together we spread the sauce on the pizza, then sprinkle cheese and toppings. Every time her arm brushes against mine, I get a little more breathless. My hips bumping into her back pushes it over the top.

Too soon, it is not enough to just feel my arms around her. Anna turns so that she is facing me and pulls me into a kiss. I love the way she tastes and the way her tongue caresses mine. I let go of the cutting board and wrap my hand around her waist, pulling her in. Anna reaches for the top button on my shirt.

I break our kiss and clear my throat, although I do not let go of her.

"I was thinking we should have a talk about baseball," I say hoarsely.

Anna is very confused. "Baseball?"

"Well, specifically, about bases," I say, blushing and fumbling my words now that I have to say them out loud. My body is screaming for me not to say them. I want her more than anything. "I thought we might want to save the home run for another night. Maybe just stay on first for the time being? Take it slow?"

Anna raises her eyebrows. "You're saying . . . you want to stay in the neutral zone?"

"Just for now," I assure her. "I'm serious about you, Anna. I want to show you that tonight's not just tonight. I'm in this for the long haul."

Anna nods.

I put the pizza in the oven and hand her a wineglass. "Shall we adjourn to the table?"

Anna glances at the table with its two very-far-apart chairs, then at the very-inviting couch that will force us to sit right next to each other.

"Why not start the movie?" she asks. "We can eat on the couch."

My eyes light up. "You are going to love it, I promise."

As I hurry to get things set up, Anna examines the movie posters on my wall. *Raiders of the Lost Ark, Stranger Than Paradise, Double Indemnity, Karate Kid.* Below them is a bookshelf stuffed with books on film.

Anna looks around and smiles.

I pat the spot on the couch next to me, and Anna happily obliges. She snuggles up against me, leaning her head on my shoulder. Just because we aren't having sex doesn't mean we can't get close. Right?

"*The Mighty Ducks*," I announce dramatically. "The 1992 sensation that took the world by storm. Ask any Freezer tomorrow, and I guarantee you that this movie is why 90 percent of them got into hockey."

"I can't wait," Anna says dryly.

"You mock," I say, "but this is important viewing for our charity work. This movie's about more than just hockey. It's about bringing out the best in your team and getting kids to believe in themselves. If I can reach even one kid the way Gordon Bombay does with the Ducks, I'll have done something that matters." My voice hitches. I don't realize I feel this way until I say it out loud. Anna has a way of bringing out my inner voice.

Worried about getting too emotional, I press play. The old-school Disney logo pops onto the screen, the dramatic music begins, and the cheesy blue opening credits play. A kid on-screen misses the key penalty shot. This will traumatize him for life and turn him into a smarmy Emilio Estevez.

The oven beeps and I leap up, pausing the movie and returning quickly with a piping hot pizza. The crust is golden brown, the cheese perfectly melted, and I cut slices for both of us.

Anna takes a bite and moans. "This is beyond good," she says, mouth full.

My chest puffs with pride. There is nothing better than watching my girl eat my pizza with my favorite childhood movie playing in the background. Well, that isn't exactly true, but I took the other thing off the table.

Once the movie credits are rolling, I can't wait any longer to find out what she thinks.

"Well?" I ask.

"Very cute," Anna pronounces.

I roll my eyes. "Maybe we should watch it again," I say, reaching for the remote.

"No!" Anna cries and pulls me to her. And then we are kissing again, a tangle of lips and limbs and couch cushions. I keep trying to keep things PG. I have a hand in her hair and a hand on her cheek, and I keep the pace slow and passionate.

She breaks the kiss and pushes me gently back into a sitting position.

"You're right," I gasp, voice thick. "Flag on the play."

"Do you need to go sit in the sin bin?" Anna asks, and I grin. "Can I join you?" she murmurs in a throaty voice.

At that, my jaw goes slack. Anna pushes herself up and throws one leg over to my other side, seating herself firmly in my lap. Her sweater dress rides way up, exposing the white flesh of her thighs.

My gaze heats. My hands dance just millimeters from her thighs. Caressing the air just above the body I long to touch. Could this really be happening? I thought she wanted to move slowly. But now, Anna looks down at me without a trace of hesitation. Her lips are parted. Her breath is fast. Her eyes are heavy-lidded with need. Seeing her like this might just be the most turned-on I have ever been.

"Is this okay?" she asks me. I just nod. I don't trust myself to speak. In fact, I'm not sure I remember what words are anymore. The only thing my brain can process right now is the look in Anna's eyes, the feeling of her thighs on me, and her firm ass pressing into my lap. I stiffen beneath her. Everything I want is right here on top of me.

Anna leans forward and kisses me, and all conscious thought leaves my brain. Our lips melt into each other. My hands grip her thighs for dear life. There is nothing but pure fire in that kiss. I pull her into me, wanting her closer, wanting no space between us, and cursing the clothes that keep me from sliding my hands along her skin.

We surface for air, and Anna moves her mouth down to my jawline, tracing it with tiny kisses. The featherlight brush of her lips drives me crazy. I turn my head, trying to catch her lips with mine, but she moves with me and shoots out her tongue, sliding it across my ear. I shiver. I didn't realize I could get this impossibly hard.

"Charlie," she whispers into my ear.

I can only make a strangled noise in response. Anna pulls back, a mischievous look in her eyes.

"Would you mind if we took the puck out of the neutral zone?" she purrs. She bites her lip and looks at me sweetly, like she has just asked for another slice of pizza. I could come right then and there.

I clear my throat and try to find my voice. "The referee will have to take that under advisement."

She nods enthusiastically, bouncing her body on top of mine and sending a whole new set of sensations rippling through me. If she doesn't want to wait any longer—and she is essentially holding up a neon sign saying that she does not—I am very, very willing to oblige her.

I grab a hold of her thighs and stand abruptly, lifting her up with me. She lets out a squeak and wraps her arms and legs around me.

"I believe the ref has reached a ruling," I tell her, and walk us toward my bedroom.

Anna frees one hand to thread it through my hair, seeking my lips with hers.

She pulls me into another kiss, and I happily yield. We don't quite make it to the bed. I stop inside the doorway, pressing her against the wall so that I can kiss her more thoroughly.

Anna squeezes me tightly with her thighs so that she can free her hands, and fumbles her way down the buttons of my shirt. She tugs at the bottom of it, but it is caught between us. I try to help, and they only get further tangled. She giggles into our kiss, which only makes me laugh.

Afraid I am going to drop her, I sweep her back into my arms and take the last two steps toward my king bed, depositing her onto the soft down comforter.

She props herself up on her elbows and takes a good, long look at me. I stand over her with my chest heaving as I finish tugging off my shirt. Seeing how much she wants me makes me want this even more. I search my mind for any shred of hesitation, but it has vanished. I am ready for this.

I step forward, dragging my fingers up her thighs until they graze the edge of her dress. I hook the soft fabric and continue to run my fingers up her sides, lifting the dress inch by inch and revealing more of her skin until she is in nothing but a lacy bra and black panties.

I look down at her with such intensity to sear this moment into my memory.

"You're so fucking beautiful," I tell her. She opens her mouth to protest, and I shake my head. "Don't you dare deny it."

I get on my knees before her and spread her legs. "Let me just take a closer look."

I kiss my way up her calf, then run my tongue up her

thigh and back down it, teasing her senseless. My nose brushes her panties, and Anna lets out a moan.

"Charlie," she begs.

I don't make her wait any longer. In one swift motion, I hook my fingers on her panties and yank them down, pulling her to the edge of the bed to meet my mouth. Anna nearly screams as my tongue swirls across her slit. I moan in response.

"God, you taste incredible," I tell her, diving back in before she can formulate a response.

I zero in on her clit, teasing it with my tongue. Her breath is getting shorter. Her moans are getting louder. I am relentless. I suck her clit into my mouth at the same time I plunge a finger inside of her and that is all it takes. Anna clamps her thighs around my head and bucks her hips against my face.

"Oh, fuck. I'm coming!" she cries. I grab her legs and hold on, refusing to let up as my fluttering tongue sends her higher and higher. I only stop when she collapses.

I rise back up, a very satisfied grin on my slick face, but Anna is far from done with me. She is determined to make me lose control too. She slides off the bed and down to the floor, bringing herself face to face with my jeans, which somehow remained on throughout this encounter.

Anna takes the zipper down slowly, prong by prong, and I groan. Seeing her below me like this, biting her lip in anticipation, is almost unbearably sexy.

"Let's get that puck into the offensive zone." She winks.

"If that's where you want it," I murmur.

"I want you to shoot it into the net," she says, looking up and locking eyes with me, a slight smile on her lips. "I want you to shoot it hard, and I want you to score. And if that's not clear enough, I want you to fuck me, Charlie Haskell."

I never thought I'd be turned on by hockey sex metaphors, but everything she says sounds sexy, especially that last part. My mind scrambles around for a hockey term to reply with, but it goes blank when Anna finishes with my zipper and yanks down.

My pants drop, taking my boxers with them. The full length of my cock springs free, and Anna's eyes widen. Before I can even blink, she leans forward and takes me partly into her mouth. Her tongue lashes against my sensitive underside, and I gasp. I could come right now, right in her mouth, but I need more of her. Feeling her writhe, hot and wet, against my lips, and knowing I had caused her pleasure was better than most of the sex I'd had in my life. I want to do that to her again. And again.

I pull her to standing, then reach down and scoop her up into my arms. Pausing for a second, I enjoy the simple sensation of carrying this stunning woman like a bride, then laying her gently down on the bed. I turn quickly to excavate a condom from my bedside table.

"Nice buns," she says, and I clench them for her before doing a little booty shake. Anna laughs.

When I turn back around, my gaze shoots straight to her breasts after she reaches behind her back and unhooks her bra. My jaw drops. "Now that's just unfair."

Anna holds out her hand. "Get over here right now," she demands.

I comply, taking my weight in my arms as I settle on top of her. My legs split hers wide, my tip resting gently against her entrance. I stop there to kiss her again, taking a moment to relish her mouth before working my way down her neck to her breasts. I flick her hard nipple with my tongue, and Anna inhales sharply.

"Charlie, I need you inside me. Now."

She does not need to tell me twice. "Yes, ma'am," I say, and press my hips forward. We both gasp as I slide inside. I am careful to move slowly, but Anna is so soaking wet that she takes me easily. It feels better than I even imagined.

Anna glances up, lifts her hips, and wraps her legs around me, taking me all the way in. I let out a groan that might have been her name if I was remotely coherent. I start a slow rhythm and Anna matches it, thrust for thrust. Heat floods through me, building every time our hips meet. We fit together perfectly. Everything feels so right.

She arches up to kiss me and I kiss her back hungrily, craving even more of her touch. I send my tongue into her mouth, and she sucks it between her lips. At that, I lose the semblance of control I've been hanging onto by a thread. My pace quickens, and my thrusts deepen.

"Yes, just like that," she moans, clawing at my back.

Feeling her tighten around me, listening to her moan with abandon, and knowing I am the cause pushes me right to the edge.

"Fuck, what you do to me," I gasp. "I can't last much longer."

"Come for me, baby," Anna tells me. "I want to feel you come."

Hearing her call me baby is just as hot as hearing her tell me to come. But before I do, I am determined to give her one more orgasm.

I reach back and grab her legs, sliding them up and onto my shoulders, savoring the sensation of her calves against my face. I thrust again, the angle allowing me to go even deeper.

Anna arches, and her head rolls back. But I'm not done. Clinging to my senses as the exquisite pleasure builds, I slide my hand down and my questing fingers find her clit. I draw circles around the bud as I plunge forward.

Anna shudders against me, squeezing me even tighter, and I gasp. "Fuck, Anna, I'm—"

That is all I could get out as I come. My eyes shut and my mouth opens in a silent scream, any semblance of control completely gone.

We collapse together, utterly breathless.

All early relationships have their little awkward moments, such as teeth bumping or uncomfortable elbows. But our bodies harmonize in a way I never expected. It is sheer bliss.

I roll onto my back, taking Anna with me and cradling her in my arms so her head can rest against my chest. This quiet moment feels almost as mind-blowing to me as the sex itself. I feel completely whole, perfectly content. I gaze at her with a tenderness that feels a lot like love.

We spend a long time like that, not speaking, just looking at each other. I feel Anna's heart thundering as mine matches it. My mind is a floaty blank, and I am happy just to lie there against her, free from worry about the future. I then notice a slow grin spreading across Anna's face.

I grin back. "What?" I ask.

Anna says simply, "Goal."

Chapter 24

It Was Strictly a Standard Level of Jolly

CHARLIE

I was not prepared for what waited for me in the Tahoe locker room. I spent the past few days dancing on air. The most gorgeous, sexy, surprising, and absolutely dazzling woman has finally let me in. In more ways than one.

It doesn't matter I haven't seen her since that magical night because the Shredders had to rush off for a weeklong away series with the Nevada Dragons. It doesn't matter that this means a ten-hour bus ride, or that the bus bathroom got clogged halfway through, or that I drew the short straw for sleeping next to said bathroom.

Nothing can bring me down after that incredible date. Not when the feel of her thighs wrapped around me and the sound of her breathy moans are still fresh in my mind, tightening my jeans whenever I allow myself to think too much about it. Not when I know there is no better sleep than drifting off with her resting against me, her hair lightly tickling my nose. I can't wait to get back and prove to her she has made the right choice in taking a risk on me. I am determined to prove it to her every single day.

It doesn't matter that we easily won our games against Nevada, although it doesn't hurt. But we could've been crushed by a bunch of geriatric skaters, and I wouldn't have batted an eye. I am that happy.

I stay on the ice late after the last game to chat with a couple of kids lingering by the rink, being ignored by the Dragons players. The boys are thrilled to get the attention of a real live hockey player, and their little sister lights up when I tell her about the Professional Women's Hockey League. I am excited to text Anna about it as I head back to change.

When I get to the locker room, it goes dead silent. I slow, puzzled. Usually after we win a game, the locker room is raucous, and everyone is amped and jumping around. Instead, a big chunk of players huddle in a tight knot in the center of the room. They have been muttering, but they shut up the second I enter. Gilly is off to the side, taping his leg as he shoots me an apologetic look, then goes back to his task.

"Something wrong?" I ask, genuinely concerned. Has someone gotten injured? Has someone's family member died?

"Yeah," says Tony, my least loquacious teammate. "You."

"Me?" I ask. "What'd I do?" I wrack my brain to think if I missed a pass or accidentally knocked someone on the ice. I assisted in most of our goals, though, and even little Alex scored tonight. They couldn't be mad at me for that.

The knot spreads out, revealing Quentin at the center of it. I sensed something was a little off with him, but I've been too distracted by thoughts of Anna to pursue it.

"I told them," Quentin says.

"You told them . . . I'm the one who clogged the bus toilet?" I guess. It actually was Tony. I have absolutely no idea what I have done.

"No. I told them I saw you with that Freezer girl. Anna something."

"The toilet, too," Tony adds.

My insides ice over. I completely forgot about running into Quentin at Powell's Books. What exactly did Quentin see? I could have sworn I watched him leave before the book date turned steamy. Quentin must have just seen us flirting and jumped to conclusions. Granted, he jumped to very correct conclusions.

"How can you be dating a Freezer?" Alex asks, looking like a kicked puppy.

I think fast. I hate to lie outright to my team, but I can't betray Anna's trust. She wants to keep our relationship quiet until we figure ourselves out. Now I am starting to see why.

"I'm not dating a Freezer. Come on," I say. "We got friendly at the Peewee event. I ran into her at Powell's. I'm a very jovial guy." The team is still glaring. "What? I can't be jolly? That's going to be hard for me."

"It looked a lot more than jolly to me," Quentin notes. I wish I could stuff Quentin's mouth with seaweed and trade him to the Dragons. Tahoe is a healthy place; surely, they'd be thrilled to hear him drone on about toxins.

"It wasn't," I swear. "It was strictly a standard level of jolly, I promise. Besides, the Freezers are still human beings, even if they have the stupidest mascot. Anna's a perfectly normal person." It is the understatement of my life, but I sense any actual compliments won't go over well. "I can't be nice to her off the ice?"

It seems a very reasonable argument to me. If I ever want to have a real relationship with the woman I was falling for, I hope they would be persuaded.

But Quentin shakes his head. "We all saw that interview. We've all read Blake's many thoughts about how we suck. If they can't be nice off the ice, we shouldn't be either."

I open my mouth to argue, but Alex chimes in. "He's right. We're a team. All we have is each other. You can't be loyal to us and to another team at the same time. It doesn't work like that. We need you here."

This hits hard. Alex has been my little duckling ever since I gave him that first piece of advice. He's been following me around, peppering me with questions. The team made fun of him, but I love it. To hear that Alex sees this relationship as a betrayal really stings.

I turn, seeking out Gilly. My best friend will come to my defense, but the tall enforcer will not meet my eyes.

"They're right," Gilly says. "The Freezers have been

playing really well this season. We lose focus, we lose. We can't afford to risk it."

I clear my throat, trying to keep my voice light. "Got it," I say. "Next time I see her, I'll be sure to tell her that her mother was a hamster, and her father smelled of elderberries."

"Nah, elderberries are super good for you," Quentin corrects me, not picking up on the *Monty Python* reference. "Tell her Coach Peter smells like ultra-processed deli meat. That stuff'll kill you."

Most of the team groans, and I'm briefly forgotten as they brace for another food lecture from Quentin. I groan along with them, but my heart isn't in it. I am crushed by the thought I am letting my team down. Supporting my teammates is important. It isn't about winning or losing, or some made up rivalry with the Freezers. Then again, I can't give up Anna, not now. Just the thought of having to let her go squeezes my heart like a vise. I feel like I can't breathe.

"Charlie," comes a sharp voice. Coach Ryan beckons from the hallway. "Walk with me."

As if this couldn't get any worse.

I make my way past the lecturing Quentin, unable to look at Gilly, and follow Coach Ryan out of the locker room. I dread whatever scolding I am about to get for whatever barely perceptible error I made during the game. I am not in the mood.

The two of us stroll for a moment in silence. It is a bit unusual for Ryan, but I'm not exactly about to prompt my coach to yell at me. Coach Ryan keeps opening his mouth to say something and then shuts it again.

211

"This girl that you are intimate with . . . Annie," Coach Ryan begins.

"Anna," I correct, instantly kicking myself. "And I'm not intimate with her. Not in any way. Just ran into her at the bookstore." I try very hard not to picture Anna writhing naked beneath me, her legs entwined behind my back, her hips bucking up to meet mine. We have been very, very intimate. Despite everything, I still feel some blood rushing downward.

Fortunately, Coach Ryan is far from a mind reader. "No? That's good. But maybe . . ."

My head jerks up. Was Satan-incarnate Coach Ryan about to be the only one supportive of my relationship with Anna? That is a twist I did not see coming.

"Perhaps if you can get her to the bookstore again, you can ask her some questions."

"Questions?" I ask, not understanding . . . or perhaps not wanting to.

"If you can make her think you are attracted to her," Coach Ryan says, tripping over his words, "she might be inclined to share some information about the Freezers. Their strategies."

I stop in the hallway. "You want me to use Anna to spy on the Freezers?"

"Yes, exactly," Coach Ryan says, relieved that I understood. "Any edge can help us. They're playing too well this season. I don't want any more surprises. After your sloppy board work in tonight's game, you should be worried too."

"Right," I say, too shocked to protest. I could be locked

in a dungeon and tortured for all eternity, and I would never do that to Anna.

Coach Ryan gives me a curt nod. "Get cleaned up, and I'll see you on the bus."

He heads briskly down the hall. I turn back toward the locker room, but my feet won't take me there. The last thing I want right now is to be with my teammates.

Instead, I meander back toward the rink, where a man who isn't Zane is making his slow Zamboni journey across the ice. I watch him absently, my mind racing.

I've been so invested in wooing Anna, so determined to get her to take a chance on me, that I haven't really stopped to consider the reality of her concerns. Sure, I know her dad might hit the roof, but I figured on some easy ribbing from my teammates, and that would be that.

I wouldn't change what happened between me and Anna for the world, but now I can see why she has been so worried. If the league does find out and censure us, it might hurt my team. If I get banned, it could cost us the championship. Everyone's dreams of getting noticed by the NHL would be dashed.

I can't believe that this all stems from wanting to date another consenting adult. Why should the league have any say in who I spend my personal time with? Anna isn't a serial killer or a reality star; she is an incredibly smart, sophisticated sports publicist. If I ever told my parents, they'd literally jump for joy. I am pretty sure my mother has been praying for me to meet a nice girl like Anna since I entered the third grade.

I have always chafed against the rigidity of the pro

hockey world, and this invasion of privacy is a fresh slap in the face. Ever since Anna called me out in our interview for not being serious about hockey, the thought has been slowly growing within me, gaining ground. What if she is right?

What if I'm not serious about hockey? I adore my team, and it is the only world I really know, but being a player is a harsh and draining life. No free time, strict rules, exhausting practices, screaming coaches, and ten-hour bus rides with Tony and his irritable bowels. That is tolerable. But the thought that it might put my relationship with Anna at risk completely changes the equation.

I found the girl of my dreams through hockey. There is no way I'll let hockey take her away from me. I just have to figure out how to keep both.

Chapter 25

Call Me When You Start Acting Like
a Freezer Again

BLAKE

I overslept. Honestly, I don't know how, given that it feels like an entire Mardi Gras parade is marching through my head. Kyle promised me new intel on Anna—not for the first time—so I waited all night at Wayfinder, drinking to pass the time. That bearded bastard never showed. I wonder if this guy isn't quite as genuine as he claims to be.

So I stumbled home, passed out, and may or may not have forgotten to set my alarm. The bacon-wrapped street hot dog I grabbed on my drunken way back decided it did not want to stay in my stomach, and it woke me up so I could heave it into my toilet. That's when I finally saw the time.

We are playing the Salt Lake Cave Bears in a home

game today. We've played them before, and I had wiped the floor with them, so I'm not too worried. I missed the pre-game practice, but I don't really need to practice, so that isn't a big deal. I'll get there in time for the start of the game, maybe a minute or two late since I might have to stop to vomit more hot dog on the way. But that should be fine. They need me.

By the time I get to the Coliseum, suit up, throw up, re-suit up, and skate over to the Freezers bench, I miss the entire first period.

I skate over to Coach Peter. The score is 1:0, in favor of the Cave Bears.

"Hey, Coach, I'm here. Want me to start second period?" I ask.

Coach Peter turns to me with a glare so intense that I take a step back.

"Are you dead?" Coach Peter asks.

"No?" I answer, confused. Wait, am I?

"Are you grievously injured? Are you coming from the hospital?" Coach Peter continues.

"No," I reply, more confident about that answer.

"Glad to hear it," Coach Peter tells me. "You're benched for the rest of the game. Take a seat." The coach turns away.

I stare, my aching brain trying to make sense of what just happened. "You're benching me? But we're losing."

Coach Peter whips back around and marches right up to me. "Yes, we are, Blake. And since you haven't been able to make room in your schedule to join us for practices recently, I think the rest of this game is a great time for you to sit and think about why we're losing."

"That's insane," Blake argues. "No one's ever benched me before. Put me in the game."

Coach Peter folds his arms. "One more word, and it's the whole season."

I open my mouth to protest, but enough of my neurons have come back online that I manage to close it again.

Coach Peter nods, satisfied. "Take the game and think about what it means to be a Freezer, Blake. Because if you don't shape up right now, that will be your seat for the rest of the season."

Henri, the referee, blows his whistle, and the Freezers' second line jumps onto the ice, purposefully bumping me as they do. The only empty spot on the bench is way down to one side, so I am forced to make the walk of shame past the rest of my teammates, none of whom will make eye contact.

Henri skates by and mutters, "*Tête de noeud.*" I'm not sure what it means, but it doesn't sound like a term of endearment.

A few rows up in the stands, I see the two old fogies that come to every game, Eddie and Ramona, tsking at me. They are arguing over whether or not I am this season's Bobby Holík. It isn't a very nice comparison.

I sit, mind reeling. I am both very nauseous and deeply confused. I'm not an overpaid washout, and I know what it means to be a Freezer. After carrying the team on my back the entire season, I am the only reason we've made it this far. What could benching me possibly accomplish? Coach

Peter is generally a good coach, but he completely lost it. The team must be furious.

I settle uncomfortably on the bench and proceed to watch the Freezers lose their first game of the season.

The atmosphere in the locker room after the game isn't just icy, it is downright arctic. Usually after a tough game, the Freezers build themselves back up, trash-talking the other team with wilder and wilder chirps. But not today.

To their credit, the Freezers played decently. Thanks to Leo, who tapped into his childhood ballet training to pull off some very graceful saves, they managed to hold off the Cave Bears from scoring further until a power-play drop pass got past him in the third period. But their offense was all over the place. They played the entire season around me: getting the puck to me, making opportunities for me, and staying out of the way for me. Without me on the ice, they were unfocused, fumbling the puck and letting the Cave Bears get way too many breakouts. It was embarrassing.

I sit by my locker, fuming. Watching my team miss opportunity after opportunity while I could do nothing felt on par with drenching myself in honey and waltzing into a den full of actual cave bears.

I glare at Coach Peter as he confers with Leo. I hope Coach gets the message. Benching me means losing games. End of story.

Coach Peter clears his throat and gestures for everyone's attention. "Listen up, guys. I know it sucks. But if you never lose, you never learn anything." He casts a long look at me. "I hope we learned what we needed to tonight."

"Yeah, we did," I say. "Think twice before benching me again."

The whole team turns to look at me. I realize what it must feel like to be something unpleasant on the bottom of someone's shoe.

"Are you kidding me, man?" Chad asks. "This is your fault."

"Hey, I was ready to play," I argue.

"You missed first period," Vlad tells me.

"And practice," Chad adds.

"And the practice before that," Vlad continues.

"And the practice before that—"

"Whatever," I snap. I didn't realize how many practices I had skipped. The past few months have been more of a haze of booze and breaking and entering than I want to admit. Sure, I've been distracted, but it hadn't shown up on the ice. "I still win games."

"Yes, *you* win games," Leo says.

"What's that supposed to mean? I do. You're welcome." I don't understand how this could possibly be a bad thing. I glance at Coach Peter, who is just letting everyone attack me. Coach Peter stares right back, arms folded.

"You're right. We should grovel in the presence of the All-Mighty Blake Tyler," Chad grumbles. "Heaven forbid we do anything to upset you. We're nothing but your little yellow minions."

Vlad cocks his head. "We're his what now?"

"What?" Chad snaps. "I mix metaphors when I'm angry."

Leo tries to get the conversation back on track. "Blake, we're a team, right?"

"Duh," I say.

"Then you need to act like you care about us. No more showing up late or hungover. No more trash-talking the other teams off the ice. No more making every game about you."

"What? You want me to stop scoring goals?" I stand up, defensive. I don't understand where these attacks are coming from. We've won every game before this. We have our systems in place. Sure, I sensed the team was a little distant, but I figured they were just jealous. How could they blame me for being the reason for their success?

"No," Coach Peter adds, sounding tired, "but they're your teammates, not your stick boys. If you want to stay on this team, you need to be a part of it."

I take a step back, shocked. *If* I wanted to stay on this team? In twenty-four hours, I have gone from star player to a freaking "if"? They've been riding my coattails all season. They are lucky I am even here. They don't get to tell me what to do. If they want me on the team, they need to show they care about me. Not the other way around.

"I don't need this," I retort. "I'm not the problem. You guys were bottom of the barrel last season. You're a beer league without me."

"I think you've got the beer thing covered, Blake," Chad quips.

"Fuck this," I mutter, locking eyes with the Coach. "You

220

don't want me? Keep me on the bench and just see what happens." I push past the team and storm out of the locker room. I am so done with them.

I try to hold on to my righteous anger, but the hornet sting of their insults burrows deep. The thing is, I never felt at home on my last team in the Czech Extraglia. No one there joked around or spoke much more English than was necessary to talk about hockey. I haven't felt at home in most of the places I've been bounced around throughout my life.

Portland isn't exactly my first choice, but I found a routine. After tagging along with the guys, celebrating the team's wins, and defeating everyone in pinball tournaments, I thought they were starting to like me.

Now I realize they are just selfish and ungrateful, same as the rest. If they don't want me here, maybe I should leave. I can come watch every game and relish the looks on their faces as they lose.

Right now, there is only one person I really want to talk to, but she isn't in her office. I storm the halls, looking for Anna.

Before she talks to her father or to the rest of the team, I have to find her. I am already on thin ice with her, and I don't want them spinning the story in a way that makes me look bad. Benching me was undeserved.

I need Anna to know that, and I need her help to tell the reporters who are probably running off right now to write articles about my downfall. I am an amazing hockey player, the best on the team, and I don't understand why that isn't enough. Why everything seems to be spinning way out of my control. More than anything right now, I want to see Anna's face.

Heels clack down the hall, and my heart lifts. She is coming. Everything is going to be okay.

But when I round the corner, it isn't Anna.

It is Mabeline.

Ugh. I might be having a bad day, but I am still not in the mood for this.

"I'm busy, Mabeline," I growl.

"That's fine." She sniffs, barely sparing me a glance. "I was looking for Leo, actually."

I do a double-take. "For Leo?"

She stops and fixes me with a glare that could cut through glass. I nearly take a step back. I'm not used to seeing her eyes do anything other than make cartoon hearts at me.

"Yes, for Leo. Do you have a problem with that?" she asks, barbed wire in her voice.

"Um, no," I snip. Of course I don't have a problem with it. I never asked for her to trail around after me like a lusty lost duckling. Honestly, this is a relief. Good riddance.

"Great," she says coolly. "Then you won't have a problem if I ask him to exchange our date."

"I don't," he replies, although it comes out a lot more wobbly than I mean it to. I completely forgot I owed her a charity date, so it is no problem if she trades it in for one with Leo. Then Leo can put up with her constant, never-ending stream of obsessive adulation and flattery. Not that I think Leo is the right choice for her. He isn't nearly fiery enough for the devilish, one-of-a-kind Mabeline.

Mabeline turns her nose up at me and continues down the hall. I watch her sashay away, her heels clicking and her purple hair tumbling down the back of the black Freezers jersey dress she made. The name was rather crudely cut out of the back of it, leaving a keyhole of smooth skin in its place. I am pretty sure she purposefully tossed her hair just so she could flash her bare shoulder blades at me where my name should be.

It must have been the shock of seeing that, because otherwise I can't explain what I did next. I called after her.

"You're supposed to be *my* fan," I say.

Mabeline did not stop walking. "I'm a Freezers fan," she replies. "Call me when you start acting like a Freezer again."

When she disappears, it feels like she takes my insides with her.

Chapter 26

We Need Our Evil Queen

ANNA

"Let me get this straight," Coach Peter says slowly. "You want to have a *naked* day?"

I nod, cursing my luck for how this meeting is going. After the Freezers' first loss of the season, my dad was angrier than he'd been the day I pulled all the tape out of his vintage hockey VHS to make doll hair. Losing has brought back the memories of how badly last season had gone, and I know he is worried they are heading straight back down that road.

I wanted to postpone this check-in, but he insisted on keeping their talk, claiming that he was completely fine and ready to focus. It is not going well. I half-expect Snow White to pop in at any moment and ask for Grumpy back.

"Hear me out—"

"Nope. Next. Skip to an idea where the fans have clothes. I see enough of Eddie and Ramona as it is."

"The Portland World Naked Bike Ride draws over 10,000 people every year," I continue, steamrolling over his objections. "And that's to bike six miles in weather that's colder than we keep the Coliseum seating. Besides, it would be optional. Nobody would have to be fully naked the whole time. Plus, we could hand out Freezers branded underwear. There's a local company called Thunderpants that I bet would be happy to sponsor it."

"Minor league hockey is a family-friendly sport. We have kids at games," he argues. "Besides, it's probably not even legal."

"Nudity in Portland is protected free speech under the right circumstances," I explain patiently, trying to ride out my dad's tantrum. "And I think the kids can stand to miss one game. We've done a lot of targeting toward families. A naked game would get people through the door who've never even thought about attending hockey before. It's a great way to build out our fanbase."

"You said our ticket sales were okay." Coach counters.

"Yes, but they are just okay. Our winning streak . . ." He winces. "Has brought back a lot of last season's fans. But to become more financially secure in the long term, we need growth. Something like this would help build out our brand. I know you think it sounds crazy, but that's exactly why we'd get a ton of publicity for it."

"That's what I'm afraid of," Coach Peter grumbles. "I'm sorry, Anna. I don't want to be coaching a game and worrying whether everyone's mouse is inside their house or not."

I sigh. I knew this idea was a hard sell, but I've been hoping to catch my dad after a win. I've been talking to Charlie about my outside-the-box philosophy of hockey publicity, and, after ascertaining that the players themselves didn't have to be naked, he absolutely loved it. It is truly something that could only happen in Portland.

Talking to someone receptive to my ideas and getting validation for them has been a huge boost for me. I didn't realize how much I've been holding back around my father until I got involved with Charlie. While it hurts that I can't share that part of me with Coach Peter, Charlie really is making my life better.

I've been determined to try again with some fresh new ideas for the team. It is going over about as well as Chad and Vlad's pitch for a jacuzzi in the locker room.

"We can table the nudity for later," I allow.

"Yes, please. Put it under the table and leave it there," my dad begs.

"But we're still not out of the danger zone with ticket sales. We need to at least try something," I reason.

Coach Peter sighs and pours himself a glass of the Good Scotch and drains it.

"Can I go through a few more ideas?" I ask, sifting through my notes. "Since we've gotten a lot of fans back, we should capitalize on that momentum."

Coach Peter snaps his fingers. "The Shredders."

My head whips up, and my eyes go wide. Full Bambilevel deer-in-the-headlights. It would have looked incredibly suspicious if my dad was paying attention.

"What about the Shredders?" I ask nervously.

"They haven't lost a game since we played them, right?"

"I-I don't think so," I say, pretending to think about it. "Why?"

"Do you remember that interview you did? With that Chuck fellow? The one who was at your house?" my dad asks, fixing me with a look. If I ever thought my dad would be okay with me dating Charlie, that idea vanished after the break-in. He kept bringing him up this way.

"I remember it vaguely," I lie. In fact, the interview is seared into my brain in vivid Technicolor, as is every silly, sweet, and sexy second I spend with Charlie. I am addicted to him, his charm, and his body. And the things he could do with that body. Just the mention of his name sends thoughts I do *not* want to have while talking to my father.

"That interview was perfect," Coach Peter continues, missing the sudden flush on my cheeks. "How you handled it, I mean. Setting up the rivalry between us and the Shredders. We haven't been hitting that hard enough. If you want to capture momentum, we need to capitalize on that."

"Oh, I don't know," I falter. "Are we sure that's the right direction? I'm not sure it will resonate with fans."

But my dad is convinced. "We're the underdogs this season. We're the Cinderella story. We need our evil queen."

"Cinderella didn't have an evil queen," I point out.

"We're Sampson and the Shredders are Goliath. It's the

Red Sox and the Yankees. It's the Lakers and the Celtics. It's perfect. I want you to blast it on social. Get the guys talking about it in the press conferences. See if Tricia will do a piece. The story of the season needs to be the Freezers facing off against the Shredders, preferably in the postseason. From now on, the Shredders are enemy number one."

Coach Peter is really animated now, his grumpiness completely forgotten. My heart sinks. I've seen my dad latch onto an idea like this before, and it is harder to get him to let go than it is to get Stinker to drop street pizza. They both get the exact same shiny-eyed look on their faces.

I hoped we could leave the rivalry on the back burner until it fizzled out. As if my relationship with Charlie isn't tricky enough, it is about to get much more complicated. I wonder why the universe has decided to throw so many things into my path. Have I stepped on one too many bugs? Did I need to cleanse an evil spirit from my house? Why is everything so difficult?

"I'm glad that's settled," my dad says firmly. "Now, there's one more thing I need you to do for me tonight."

Chapter 27

Sink or Swim

BLAKE

I see her in the doorway, and my dimples come out in force. "Anna," I call, "you found me."

Anna sighs. "Hey, Blake," she says. "We need to talk about something."

"We do," I say seriously, my smile fading. "I'm leaving the team. I'm being framed."

Anna sits down a few benches over. "You're not being framed."

"No? What do you call this witch hunt? The whole team says I'm the problem. They're the problem. They're the ones who lost without me. We need to get ahead of this with the press. Tell me exactly what to say, and I'll say it," I offer.

I am so glad Anna is here. I've been looking for her all

night, and now, like she sensed it, she appears before me. My locker room angel.

I've been drawn to her from the start because of her quiet beauty, from the first time I spotted her curvy figure in that silky red blouse and tight jeans. I feel like she understood me in a way none of the puck bunnies ever had. We are both children of hockey. Even though she hurt me by tossing me and my hockey puck aside for some casual fling with Charlie, I am willing to overlook that. This feels like a sign.

"Here's the thing, Blake." Anna sighs. "We're putting you under an embargo. You can't talk to the press."

"What?" I sit straight up. "Why?"

"It's what makes sense at this time," Anna says.

I stare at her, my eyes narrowing. She didn't come here to help me. She is just like the rest of them.

"Is this because of Charlie?" I ask.

Anna's eyes go wide, and her nostrils flare. "What does this have to do with Charlie?"

I hesitate, at a loss for words. I didn't want to admit I had a journalist following her, and my brain is not in good enough shape to form a better excuse. "I know you're doing that charity thing with him," I say, remembering Kyle told me that is her cover story. "But I can tell you, he's using you to get to me. I bet he wants information on Freezer strategy. You're just a pawn in all this."

Anna's lips purse so tight they turn white. I shut up, sensing I crossed a line. She takes a deep breath and looks me dead in the eye.

"Do you want to know why you're not allowed to talk to the press? Because we can't trust you, Blake. You're combative, aggressive, and volatile. You don't think about anybody but yourself. You blame all your mistakes on other people, which means you never learn. You think you're so great? You could be so much better if you worked with the team instead of against them. You could win us the entire championship right now, and you wouldn't earn anybody's respect for it because you've treated your teammates like garbage. They're not here to hold you back, Blake. They're here to keep you afloat, but you won't let them."

She stands and gestures to the nearly empty glass bottle in my hand. "You're just drowning yourself. And I'm done trying to stop you. So, sink or swim, Blake. It's your choice."

She turns and storms out, her footsteps rattling around my brain just like Mabeline's had.

By the time my ridiculously expensive Uber drops me home, my head is pounding like never before. I half-expect it to crack open and spill my scrambled brains onto the carpet. It will serve everyone right for treating me the way they do.

I throw myself onto the couch and take deep breaths of the plant-perfumed air, but it only makes me more nauseated.

Across the room, two blue orbs stare out from my

forest of planters. Iris watches me, her majestic tail flicking back and forth.

"Here, pretty kitty," I coo. I can really use her support. She is the only one in my life who is always there for me.

But not tonight.

Iris pads out from the plants and gives me the long, appraising look that only cats can give. I feel my soul being weighed. Then her pupils narrow into snake-like slits, and she spins, flicking her tail as she trots away, vanishing back into the greenery.

"Iris, come on," I call. "Don't be like that." I force myself to get up and slump toward the kitchen for a can of sardines. But even with the iconic metal click of the tin opening, Iris does not return.

And the smell of the sardines proves to be too much. I barely make it to the sink.

Mouth sour, throat burning, and chest heaving, I lay my head on the cool kitchen counter. My eyes fall on my grandmother's puck, which I had set next to its glass display case the night I brought it back. I intended to set it back up. A thin film of dust has settled atop the wood grooves.

Every time I look at that puck now, I am filled with an acid rush of shame. Breaking into Anna's to get it back seemed like such a good idea at the time. It was mine, after all. But I saw her the next day, sleepless and shaken, telling Zane about the mysterious break-in. It didn't even occur to me what it might look like to her.

I feel terrible and I want to shut out these awful feelings and tell myself that I have done the right thing.

Convince myself that Anna had been brainwashed by Charlie and deserved her comeuppance. I want to tell myself that she is part of the crazy conspiracy that chewed me up and spit me out tonight. Coach Peter turned against me, my team turned against me, the women in my life turned against me, and it isn't my fault. I am the victim in all this. That's what I want to tell myself with my face smushed against the countertop, breathing through one nostril next to my vomit-encrusted sink.

But I can't.

Because I know Anna is right. They all are.

The real question is, is it too late to do something about it?

Chapter 28

Compensating for Something

CHARLIE

The axe goes flying through the air, somersaulting end over end, before landing with a hard thunk directly in the center of the wood. Everybody screams.

"Bullseye!" I cry, and high-five Gilly's sister Hollis. "And Hollis takes the lead!"

Hollis gives a little bow. With her short blonde hair, athletic build, and eyebrow piercing, she looks like a modern-day axe-throwing Viking. Her team is also crushing it in the PWHL this season. The level of sporting ability in the Probert-Patterson family is truly amazing.

"That was really, really great," Alex says a little too enthusiastically, staring at her with moony eyes.

Gilly fake gags and gives Alex a shove. "I'm eating," he complains.

Alex turns bright red, and Hollis makes a face at her brother.

I turn to Tony, eager to distract the group. "What's the scoreboard look like, Tony?" I ask.

Tony sets down his beer and squints at his piece of paper, then points to each of us in turn. "Hollis, Charlie, me, Alex, everyone else here, then Gilly."

They all laugh. Gilly can wipe the rink with us all, but he cannot aim an axe to save his life. I think maybe his stupendous height throws off his center of gravity.

Hollis musses her brother's hair. "Sorry, G. When the apocalypse comes, I'm not letting you into my bunker."

"Your loss." Gilly shrugs. "I can cook, and I can sew. You tell me what's more useful."

"You can cross stitch," Hollis counters. "What are you going to do? Needlepoint someone to death?"

"You can cross stitch?" I ask. "How did I not know this?"

Gilly waggles his eyebrows. "I'm a man of mystery. And Home Economics is a lost art."

I roll my eyes. "Alex, you're up."

Alex takes the axe and marches up to the throwing line. He is good, but he spends so much time trying to see if Hollis is watching him that half of his throws go wide. Including this one.

Tony clucks his tongue and makes a mark on the scoring sheet. I sip my beer, enjoying the scene. I've been making more of an effort since my team confronted me about Anna. I won't stop seeing her, but I realize I had lost touch with them when I was chasing after her. Not to mention, I am lying through my teeth to them daily.

So here I am at the Hopworks Brewery's Celtic Axe Throwing cages for the night, hurling dangerous weapons around with my friends, and texting my secret lover on the side, determined to have my cake and eat it too.

Gilly rises from his chair and selects his axe. It looks small in his hand. Sometimes my friend reminds me of the giant who lived up the beanstalk.

Gilly bows his head over the axe. "Do or do not," he intones. "There is no try."

Then he lets the axe fly and misses the board completely.

"Do not," Tony announces and makes another mark on the score sheet.

My phone buzzes on the table, and I lunge for it. It is Anna, sending me a picture of Stinker wearing sunglasses and looking very unhappy about it. The text says Stinker is helping her try on outfits for our upcoming date. I grin.

"I know that grin," Hollis pipes up. "That's a girl-text grin. Charlie's texting a girl."

Every head swivels in my direction. "No, I'm not," I object, although it doesn't sound true, even to me.

"What girl could you possibly be texting?" Gilly asks. It kills me, but I can't tell my best friend about my blossoming relationship. Not after seeing Gilly's face in the locker room.

"No girl," I insist.

"It's definitely a girl," Hollis says.

Gilly furrows his brow, thinking back. "That puck bunny from the last game? Or that hot chick from the gala I saw you talking to? The one you said was a baker?"

"Alison?" I ask. It is the wrong thing to say. Now they all think I am texting Alison.

"Ooo, Alison," Hollis teases. "And when do we get to meet her?"

I am spared from answering when Tony throws down his phone in annoyance. They all look up. He only needs to say one word. "Freezers."

I wince. Anna warned me, but ever since her conversation with her father, the Freezers' social media accounts have been clapping back at the Shredders hard.

The Shredders don't have a publicist like Anna. Coach Ryan has some suit on retainer who I have never seen do much of anything, but the coach begrudgingly allowed his son Devin to take the reins of their socials on the weekends. The Freezers and the Shredders are in an all-out internet flame war. Even Tricia Cornwallis took notice.

I think it is kind of funny. The rest of the team does not.

We crowd around Tony's phone to see the latest. It is the classic distracted boyfriend meme. This time, the boyfriend is labeled as the PCHL championship and is staring longingly at the nearby girl labeled the Freezers, while his shocked Shredders girlfriend glares at him. Harmless stuff.

Nevertheless, the Shredders take any post about them as an all-out invitation to war.

"Oh, they are asking for it," Gilly declares.

"It's not even clever," Alex adds, puffing up his chest for Hollis.

"It's a little clever," Hollis responds.

"Maybe just a little," Alex amends quickly. "But not a lot."

"You guys better get your twelve-year-old on it," Hollis teases, alluding to Devin.

"Thoughts, Charlie?" Tony asks. All eyes return to me. I know that anything less than a total disavowal of the Freezers will send me straight back to Benedict Arnold status.

"It's tired and unoriginal, just like them," I say, hating myself. "At least our twelve-year-old uses memes that aren't ancient. They need to spend their energy coming up with something new on the ice if they want to even think about beating us. All this Instagramming makes me think they're compensating for something."

Everyone laughs.

They seem satisfied, but I feel sick. I make a mental note to text Anna that her latest chirp hit the bullseye, then pick up my axe.

The throwing instructor returns, leading a new group of rowdy guys—Leo, Chad, and Vlad—back to the cages. They are laughing at something on Leo's phone.

Both groups freeze. The Freezers' eyes go straight to me and the axe in my hand. I make an urgent silent wish to any listening genies or fairies to immediately airlift me anywhere else. It does not work.

The oblivious instructor keeps walking and gestures to the only cage open. The one right next to us.

"Alrighty," she says. "You guys are right over here. We've gone over the rules. Do you want me to walk you through some throwing basics?"

"No thanks," Chad says loudly, his eyes still locked on us. "We're pros."

"Are you?" Gilly asks dryly. "It's nice to hear you're good at something."

"Great!" the instructor says cheerily, refusing to pick up on the vibe. "I'll leave you to it, then."

She vanishes back into the bar. We all continue our glaring contest. The tension is so thick you can cut it with, well, an axe.

Leo, ever the diplomat, finally breaks the silent bro-off. "Gentlemen," he drawls, "shall we all go back to our evenings?"

"We will if you will," Alex replies.

"Sounds good to me!" I exclaim loudly, and step forward, tossing my axe at the target as quickly as I can. The sooner we start ignoring each other, the better.

I'm not as good as Hollis, but even with my nerves, I manage to hit just shy of the bullseye. My friends let loose a cheer so loud I briefly wonder if I somehow won the Stanley Cup and not just scored well at axe-throwing.

"Looking good, Chuck!" Gilly crows.

Not to be outdone, Vlad grabs two axes and marches up to the line. Without hesitation, he whips them at the target. They tumble through the air like sharpened synchronized divers and thud on either side of the bullseye.

Chad whoops, grabs Vlad, and throws him over his shoulder for a mini victory lap.

It does not seem like we are going to ignore each other.

With steam practically coming out of his ears, Gilly rises to go next, but Tony executes a lightning-fast block. "Not you," he says. "Her."

We all turn to Hollis. She picks up an axe, walks up to the line, and turns so that her back is facing it. With a wink, she tosses the axe behind her, and it lands dead center. The Shredders erupt.

Chad goes through some exaggerated stretches as he prepares for whatever elaborate axe throw he is planning. But he doesn't get that far.

"Hey, Freezers," Alex calls, with a quick glance toward Hollis. "Charlie thinks you guys are compensating for something."

The three Freezers turn to look at me. Nothing gets a manly man's attention faster than implying he has a tiny package.

I send another frantic silent wish to any gods or devils listening to strike me with lightning or open a portal down to hell right now. It does not work.

"I didn't quite catch that, Chucky," Chad says, taking a step forward. "Would you care to repeat it to my face?"

I can practically see the rock in front of me and the hard place right behind me. The last thing I want to do is antagonize Anna's team. But if I don't step up right now, not only will I betray my teammates, but I will also betray Anna's and my secret. As much as I want to shout about our relationship from the rooftops, I can't do that to her. Not like this.

So, I do what I have to. "I have no problems with your penis, Chad. I'm sure it's great," I say lightly. "In fact, I bet you handle it much better than you handle your stick on the ice."

Chad's fists clench, and he takes a menacing step forward. The Shedders step up to meet him. It is very lucky no one is currently holding an axe.

Leo puts a hand on Chad's arm. "Forget them," he says. "They're just having one last hurrah before they head off to the retirement home."

"Oh yeah? You really think you can beat us?" Gilly asks.

"Let me see," says Chad. "Oh, that's right. We already have."

"At least we fight our battles in the rink," Alex shoots back, "instead of letting our publicist do it for us."

"Oh really? You don't have a girl fight your battles for you?" Vlad asks, looking directly at Hollis.

Gilly does not take that. He takes another step forward, towering over Vlad.

"What are you trying to say about women in sports?" he thunders. "Because if you want to talk sports legends, let's start with Nneka Ogwumike, Chris Evert, Serena Williams, Mia Hamm, Lindsey Vonn—"

"Jeez, I wasn't impugning women's sports," Vlad snaps, feeling cornered. He casts around for an insult and remembers something Blake had been muttering about. "All I'm saying is our team doesn't send players to sniff around our publicist and to use her for dirt on our systems." He looks straight at me.

I can't help it. I see red. Anna is not someone to be sniffed around and used. I would *never* do that to her.

I lunge for Vlad. Gilly and Tony leap forward to restrain me. Gilly picks me up, my feet dangling.

"Our time's up, guys. Let's leave these jerkoffs to the one thing they're good at," he says, and hauls me toward the exit.

Gilly doesn't let go of me until we are through the exit and out into the frigid Portland air. The air blows through me, calming my thoughts.

"Thanks," I tell Gilly. "Sorry I let it get out of hand."

"Believe me, I would've let you at him," Gilly says. "But it's best if none of us get arrested before the postseason. Not if we want to beat them."

I look at the others. Tony gives me a nod of respect. Alex is staring at me with nothing short of awe. Only Hollis looks thoughtful.

"Can you believe they thought you'd chase after that Freezers chick? And to get their forecheck systems? Like we need to stoop that low?" Gilly laughs. The others join him, forgetting they'd accused me of exactly that. Not to mention, Coach Ryan actually wanted me to do it. But again, I would never.

"So crazy," I say weakly. I started this evening so sure that Anna and I could pull off balancing dating in secret while working for rival teams. It is already proving so much harder than I thought. I escaped by the skin of my teeth tonight.

"Respect, man," Gilly says. "You shredded in there. Oh," he adds, reaching into his pocket. "I grabbed your phone off the table."

He holds it out to me just as the screen lights up with another text from Anna. I rush to grab the phone back, but it is too late.

Gilly glances down, and I can tell by how quickly his smile disappears—he saw Anna's name.

Chapter 29

Not Even Vancouver is Safe

ANNA

I never thought it would come to this. I am in Vancouver. I haven't willingly set foot in the Couve for years. I, like every other Portlandian, insist there is nothing worth going across the river for, especially not during rush hour. Yet here I am, meeting Charlie.

I eye the coffee shop he suggested, RLVNT, with suspicion. Was Vancouver too good for vowels? I have to admit it smells delicious, though. Sending a mental apology to Stumptown for the betrayal, I know I have no choice. Portland never felt so small until I started trying to keep a giant secret.

Everywhere Charlie and I turn, we run into someone from the PCHL. I tried to meet him at Stumptown last week, only to walk right smack into Zamboni Zane.

Running out the door so fast for a fake work emergency, Nayeli chased after me with my coffee. After Zane tried to bribe her into making it a hot coffee, of course.

We attempted Salt & Straw next, only to discover Charlie's crazy fans, Nick and Nate, who have expanded their hockey podcast to include food after the recording at Munch. Their new Dutch friend is a regular guest. I managed to duck out before being spotted, but Charlie got stuck there for a solid hour, assigning ice cream flavors to various NHL Hall of Famers. Wayne Gretzky is Cinnamon Snickerdoodle.

Yesterday, we figured maybe an early morning walk with Stinker would be safer, but Chad and Vlad were training for the marathon. Their route took them past all of Stinker's favorite sniffing spots. Charlie had dived into a bush with as much dignity as he could muster while the guys stopped for a "quick" chat. I suspect they chatted with me for so long because they didn't actually want to run the marathon. By the time I finally got rid of them, Charlie's hair was full of pine needles. In the moment, I thought it was cute, but I know it is not sustainable.

So here we are, meeting in Vancouver, the only place we can guarantee no one from Portland will find us.

Except right there at the counter is Michael, the PCHL official who I coordinated the Charity on Ice events with.

I bend my knees, preparing to dash back out the door, but it is too late. Michael turns around and spots me, giving a tired wave. I plaster a smile on my face and walk over.

"Michael!" I squeak. "I didn't know you were in town."

Michael nods wearily, rubbing the bags under his eyes. "With the playoffs coming up, I just wanted to ensure that the Shredders would be returning the Kerry Cup."

I nod, sympathetic. The PCHL still has not gotten over the Colorado Buzzards claiming they "lost" the cup one year. I hope Coach Ryan is not thinking of following in their footsteps. From what I hear, this has been a tough year for the league officials. They handed out more Category One suspensions so far this season than they have in any previous. A player in the Western Division was arrested for assaulting a ref. Tricia Cornwallis recently wrote a long feature questioning the rise in game penalties. It went viral. No wonder Michael looks so stressed.

Out of the corner of my eye, I spot Charlie heading toward the coffee shop doors. I quickly put a comforting hand on Michael's shoulder, pivoting him so that he can't see the front of the shop.

"It hasn't been an easy season for you, has it?" I ask him, while trying to waggle a finger in Charlie's direction without Michael noticing.

Fortunately, Michael isn't particularly perceptive at the moment. He yawns and nods. "Lord, no. Between you and me, I'm not sure we can handle another scandal."

I nod distractedly, half-watching him and half-watching Charlie, who realizes something is wrong and is backing away. "Absolutely," I say, letting go of Michael's shoulder.

"Luckily, I don't have to worry about any of that from you," he tells me. "It's nice to have some true professionals in the league. And, hey," he adds, "the Freezers are doing great. Maybe I'll be handing the Kerry Cup to you guys this April."

"Here's hoping," I say weakly.

Michael checks his watch. "Well, I'd better run. At least I got a chance to stop in Vancouver. Such a beautiful place, don't you think?"

I nod, refusing to breathe until Michael safely exits the coffee shop without running into Charlie. No more scandals this season indeed.

I text Charlie that the coast is clear, and he hurries inside.

"Who was that?" he asks, pulling me in for a much-needed kiss.

"Just one of the people who has the power to fine you and fire me," I tell him, dying a little inside. It means a lot to me to be seen as a professional in such a male-dominated sport. The fact that I am throwing the rulebook out the window to date a guy is completely contradictory to me. Except that guy is Charlie, and I see a real future with him. If we can ever get that far.

Charlie winces. "Freakin' Couve. I should've known."

I go to order coffees while Charlie stakes out a table. It feels like we are dating forty hockey players, two coaching teams, about 5.4 million fans, and one incredibly bossy Zamboni driver. I would much rather just date Charlie.

I return with two iced coffees. Charlie takes a long sip.

"This isn't bad, I guess," I admit, begrudgingly. "Any luck with Gilly?"

Charlie shakes his head.

"Any luck on your end?" he asks. I have been trying to

convince Coach Peter to tone down the anti-Shredder rhetoric before the two teams draw blood.

"Nope," I tell him. "Now they've got a dart board with your picture on it in the locker room. They're getting pretty good at it."

"Oh, great," he laments. "Ten points for my face?"

"Actually," I say, "they're aiming a bit lower."

Charlie's hand moves automatically to cover the body part in question.

I grin. "Believe me," I say, "I'm protective of that, too."

I smile ruefully at him, wishing I could shove the iced coffees off the table and grab him right then and there. Every time I am near him, my body heats up and my mind slips underneath his clothing, longing for more of him. The problem is being near him for long enough to make that happen.

Charlie clears his throat, and I can tell his mind has trailed down a similar gutter. "Not quite the right time to go public yet, huh?" he asks.

I sigh. I hate the lying and the sneaking, but just the thought of telling my dad makes my stomach flip like it did the first time he talked me into trying the Oaks Park Adrenaline Peak coaster. I lost my lunch, my breakfast, and possibly my previous dinner. I don't want to repeat that.

"Maybe not quite yet?" I say apologetically. I just want some time to figure out who Charlie and I are together. Could this relationship go the distance? I want desperately to keep this handsome lumberjack of a man in my life. With our crazy careers, I need to figure out how to make it work. So far, I don't have any brilliant ideas.

Charlie gives me a supportive smile. "April's not so far away, you know. A few months? Maybe we can go public then."

"Maybe," I say, although I worry that even the season ending won't make our relationship safe because of the way both teams have embraced the Shredders-Freezers rivalry. I wonder how far we can take our secret relationship. Could I keep my dad from noticing if we move in together? Maybe if Charlie keeps his toothbrush in the medicine cabinet and his clothes stuffed in the back of my closet. "You're a guy. You don't have a lot of clothes, right?"

"Uhhh, I have a normal amount, I think?" Charlie says, confused.

"Ignore me," I say. "I'm thinking crazy things."

"Hey, your creative thinking is one of the things I—uh—strongly like about you," he tells me.

The blood drains from my face as I look out the front window. "You've got to be kidding me," I say.

"Oh no, who is it?" Charlie asks.

"Get up right now and go out the back. Don't turn around," I whisper, frantic.

"What if there isn't a back exit?" he asks.

"I don't know. Climb out the window?" I say, dead serious. My eyes widen. "Go, go now. Now, now, now."

Charlie rockets out of his seat and beelines for the back.

No more than a second later, I exclaim, "Dad! Hi!"

After what feels like an eternity, I run around to the back of the building. Charlie is hovering amongst the dumpsters.

"I can't believe I forgot his dentist is in the Couve," I puff, out of breath. "I walked him all the way to his appointment."

"Do you think he saw me?" Charlie asks.

I shake my head firmly. "Your head would no longer be attached to your body. But he does think I secretly like Vancouver now," I say with the same distaste as if I let my dad think I liked eating dryer lint.

Charlie reaches out and pulls me close. I bury my face in his broad chest, drinking in the warm, strong feel of him.

"Can't we have one full date to ourselves?" I lament. "How are we supposed to figure out what this is if we can never have a "this" in the first place?"

Charlie plants kisses in my hair. "We'll figure it out," he promises.

"How?" I ask. "Not even Vancouver is safe."

"Then we'll go farther," he says. He pulls back so he can look me in the eyes, taking my hands in his. "Come on a trip with me."

"A trip?" Anna asks. "Could we? Should we? Our schedules—"

"Surely, there are at least two consecutive days we both have off," he says. "I just want a chance to be with you and only you. I want to give us a real shot."

My body goes tingly, hearing the conviction in his

voice. He cares about this as much as I do. "Where should we go?" I ask.

Charlie grins. "Wherever you want."

"How about the Oregon coast?" I suggest, dreaming of sweeping views, ocean spray, and no Freezers anywhere. "I've always wanted to go to Florence."

"Florence it is!" Charlie declares. He pulls me back into his arms, lifting me up and spinning me around. I laugh and throw my arms around him.

He sets me down and pulls me into a kiss so intense that it curls my toes and leaves me gasping.

"Anna," he murmurs, kissing my neck.

"Hmmm?" I try to respond.

"If we run into any of your family members in Florence, we're fleeing the country."

"That works for me," I say, and pull his lips up to meet mine.

Chapter 30

Another One Bites the Dust

BLAKE

Time always moves more slowly in the last minute of the game. Above me, the last sixty seconds of the Brawlers-Freezers game tick down in huge glowing numbers. Fans leap from their seats, shrieking at the top of their lungs. Sweat pours down my brow in a slick waterfall. My muscles scream for mercy, but there is no going back now.

I have the puck as I race toward the goal. Boise Brawlers seem to multiply with every step I take, surrounding me. I don't have a shot. Cursing, I pivot and wheel around to the back of the net, hoping to confuse the defense and snipe in a shot from the side.

Arcing behind the net feels like soaring through the air. With no defenders in front of me, I fly across the ice in a perfect, weightless moment. The puck sails along in front of me like it is seeking its target. It is the goal we need to clinch the game.

But as I clear the net on the other side, reality—in the form of Brawlers defender Niederman, the massive slab of a player who hates my guts—slams back into me. The man takes up my entire vision and looks ready to give me another black eye. My plan is deteriorating fast.

I can sense which way the Brawlers goalie is going to lunge. If I can time the shot exactly right and slice it through the tangle of tree trunk limbs before me, I can still score. But I'm not sure.

Out of the corner of my eye, I clock Leo bombing down the ice. Coach Peter pulled the goalie up to join the offense, but one of the other Brawlers' defenders swings out to catch him, leaving Chad open.

I don't hesitate. I deke right then swing left, whipping the puck over to Chad. Chad catches it with his stick and snaps it over to the goal. The Brawlers goalie is angled toward me, but he lunges to correct. The buzzer goes off just as the puck goes in.

We win the division playoff. We are going to the conference finals.

The stadium erupts. Freezers fans in every direction, more and more every game, holler their heads off. Freddy the Freezer does a backflip that Olympic figure skating has banned. Players pour onto the ice, cheering. They swarm Chad, but an equal number break off to swarm me.

I get lifted off the ice. I am grinning ear to ear, dimples

on full display. My stats won't show it, since I didn't score, but this just might have been the best game of my life.

It doesn't seem possible, but the party gets even louder in the locker room. The entire twenty-man team belt the lyrics to "Bohemian Rhapsody" at the top of their lungs. We've already been through "Don't Stop Me Now," "Another One Bites the Dust," and "We Are the Champions." "Bohemian Rhapsody" isn't as relevant, but it is my favorite, and when I start it, everyone joins in.

I stand in the center of them all, crooning my heart out into my water bottle microphone. Chad and Vlad jam on their hockey sticks. Mascot Gordie hops around, doing some kind of interpretive dance. Leo has his camera out, recording blackmail for later, but he sings along with the rest of us. I am on top of the world.

Granted, I was on the bottom of the world just a few weeks ago. The look of disappointment Anna had given me in the locker room with my bottle of whiskey still burns in my memory. Usually, I can chalk up pissed-off hockey teammate complaints to inadequacy and jealousy. But I couldn't brush off Anna or the anger in her wide hazel eyes. Hearing how she really saw me cut to my core.

I didn't want her brutal honesty playing on an endless loop in my head. I didn't want to spend another period— let alone another game—glued to that uncomfortable bench. And I didn't want to be the person that no one included in their private jokes or their pinball tournaments. So, after throwing up several more times that night, I decided to do something about it.

When I showed up early to the next practice, Coach Peter just gave me a nod. I also stayed late to work on my passing drills. As good as I am on the ice, passing isn't my strong suit. I came early again to the next practice, and the next. Coach Peter didn't openly acknowledge it, but he didn't stick me back on the bench.

The team seemed skeptical at first, but after a few scrimmages where I didn't hog the puck, they began to change their tune. Chad begrudgingly invited me to come back to Ground Kontrol, although I was pretty sure Leo forced him into it by pinching his arm the entire time. Still, when I asked him to explain the rules of pinball and then actually listened to them, Chad came around. Pretty soon Chad, Vlad, and I were closing down Ground Kontrol, spending hours at the Indiana Jones pinball machine and trying to activate the dancing frog Easter egg. Doing the Michael J. Frog dance became our first inside joke. We soon nicknamed ourselves the Green Line and didn't explain it to anybody.

Now, the entire team stands on the locker room benches, each half-dueting like we are on stage at Live Aid. A stone-faced Coach Peter elbows his way through the high-pitched madness of twenty men trying to sing in falsetto and holds up his hand, expression grim. Everyone falls silent.

He snatches Vlad's hockey stick away from him, takes a breath, and unleashes the most epic air guitar solo we have ever seen.

The whole room cheers and the song resumes in full force, with Coach Peter warbling on enthusiastically with the rest of us.

After the grand finale with many more fake guitar riffs, Coach Peter congratulates the team. Before leaving, he tugs me to the side and claps me on the back.

"Good to see your head back in the game," he shouts over the din. "Keep this up, and I think MVP could be in your future."

"Really, Coach, you think so?" I ask. I didn't want to hope, after everything.

Coach Peter nods. "Just so long as you don't lose your shit again, of course."

Chad and Vlad appear on either side of me, throwing their arms around my shoulders. "Don't you worry, sir," Chad assures Coach Peter. "The Green Line's keeping a firm lid on Blake's shit, sir. It will not get lost again."

I will never admit it, but my heart swells three sizes when I hear that. I vow to keep their promise.

Coach Peter grins and makes an exit. Vlad hums the *Indiana Jones* theme, and Chad turns to me.

"What do you say? Ground Kontrol in thirty? There's an *Attack from Mars* mode that swaps the flying saucers for cows."

I shake my head. "Sorry, fellas, I can't stay out late tonight."

Vlad boos. "Why? You got a hot date tomorrow or something?"

"Actually," I say, "yeah."

A massive "oooo" goes up from around the entire room.

Gordie grabs his water bottle and begins to sing "Somebody to Love." I discover how hard I can blush.

Munch is deep in its lunch rush, but Alison moves like molasses taking my order. I can tell she doesn't like me, although I have no idea as to the *specific* reason why. In all honesty, I guess there are any number of reasons, given my track record this season. I try to smile at her, show her I am a different person now, but she only gives me a side-eye.

"You said *two* steak sandwiches?" she asks.

"That's right," I say, handing over my card. I am weirdly nervous about my date. Honestly, I am surprised she agreed to it. Now that it is here, I feel more pressure than I expected to make a good second impression.

A throat clears behind me. I turn, and there she is.

"I like your hair," I say.

"Thanks," says Mabeline, her hand going to her now jet-black locks. "I was in kind of a dark mood."

"I ordered you the best sandwich," I blurt. I realize maybe I shouldn't have ordered for her. "The steak sandwich. It's really good."

Mabeline regards me standing nervously before her. Then her scarlet lips tilt upward into a brilliant smile. "The steak sandwich is my favorite, too."

"I'll bring them over to your table," Alison chimes in, suddenly acting a lot perkier. She glances back and forth from me to Mabeline. Self-conscious, I steer Mabeline over to a table. I don't know why I have so many butterflies fighting for room in my stomach, but I figure I just feel guilty for how I treated her.

"Thanks for doing this date," I say, voice gruff.

Mabeline shrugs, trying to act aloof. "I did pay for it." She sniffs.

"So . . ." I say, trying to remember all the things Leo told me about Mabeline. "You play roller derby?"

Mabeline nods, her face lighting up. She looks quite pretty when she smiles. Her dark eyes glow, and between those luscious lips are perfect teeth. "I play for the Rose City Rebels," she tells me. "We're undefeated this season."

"Roller derby's like where you skate around and punch people?" I ask.

"Pretty much," Mabeline says seriously. "Just on a track and not on the ice. I'm a jammer, so I'm on offense, but it's defense too. We do a lot of cannonballing, seal clubbing, soul crushing . . . eating the baby. I hip-checked a girl so hard once that she went to the hospital," she says with pride.

"Very cool," I say, genuinely impressed. I don't know what any of it means, but it sounds a lot like hockey. I knew Mabeline was hardcore, but I never realized how similar we were.

"You think so?" Mabeline asks, warming up. "Maybe you can come to a game sometime."

The image of Mabeline racing down the track with her full lips pursed, and her dark eyes narrowed in anger, swarms into my head. I don't know what seal clubbing is, but her raising a massive caveman club with her sculpted, tattooed arms does seem kind of sexy. I might actually enjoy going to one of these Roller Derby things. Mabeline watches me hopefully, pretending and failing to still look mad.

I give her my signature grin. "Maybe I—Kyle?"

Kyle Brodie is standing by the baguettes, staring at me. I blanch.

"Maybe what? Sorry?" Mabeline asks, confused. "Was that a yes? Because I can get you a ticket. Are you free next Saturday? I can call them right now." She reaches for her phone.

"Uh, yeah, maybe, let me, uh, just one second." I stand abruptly before Kyle can come over.

"It doesn't have to be next Saturday," Mabeline offers, her bright smile twisting into an anxious frown. "You can come to any game you want."

"Right. Yes. I just need to, uh, bathroom." I hurry away, making eye contact with Kyle and then jerking my head toward a dark corner of Munch near the bathrooms.

Kyle takes his time skulking back to join me, enjoying making me squirm.

I am positively volcanic when Kyle finally arrives.

"I'm busy," I growl.

"Apparently," Kyle snaps back. "We had an arrangement."

"Maybe I don't need our arrangement anymore." I move to push past Kyle and get back to my table.

"Oh, so you don't want to hear about Anna and Charlie's upcoming getaway?"

I freeze in my tracks.

"Those love birds are taking a trip together. I think it's

getting serious. And after all you've done for her. But if you no longer care ..."

The vein in my temple feels like it is doing the polka. Finally, I grind out, "I care."

Kyle nods. "I thought so. I'll see you at our usual spot before your next game. Enjoy your sandwich."

Kyle vanishes into the shadows as I fume. I made a mistake getting into bed with Kyle. I should be letting both Anna and Kyle go. But I don't quite know how to do either. Even if Anna doesn't want to date me—which I hoped would change when I changed my behavior, but even if it didn't—I still hate the idea of her dating Charlie. But what I hate more is Kyle Brodie and how dirty I feel after talking to him. Even my soul could use a shower after seeing Kyle. Do I need to come clean?

Maybe I should tell Mabeline. She does seem genuinely—if terrifyingly—interested in me, and she clearly knows how to deal with people who get in her way. Maybe I can ask for her help. Maybe she is worth letting in.

But when I get back to our table, Mabeline is gone. Her sandwich is gone too. Mine remains, although it looks like someone tore it into little bits. And then ground mustard into it. And then some sugar packets. And then some grape jelly. Something tells me she figured out that I didn't need to go to the bathroom.

I stare down at the abstract technicolor vomit that used to be my sandwich and realize I made a real mess of things.

Chapter 31

Never Bargain with a Horse

CHARLIE

My trip with Anna has gone incredibly well so far. A three-hour road trip, complete with an Outkast singalong and an intense debate over whether Eminem, Beyoncé, or The White Stripes had sung the best anthem of our millennial childhoods (although Anna made an impassioned plea for P!NK.) I insist we stop in Newport to pay a visit to the intensely colorful Aquarium Village, home of Nessie the Crown Lizard and a particularly bizarre statue of a shark-cow hybrid eating a human leg. Anna takes several pictures of me looking like I am being attacked by various metal sea creatures.

I never had so much fun on a trip before. My family loved taking road trips when I was younger, but those ended with my baby sister having a meltdown after my dad got lost for the fourth time. Anna is a much better trip companion and very good at directions.

We finally check into our cute bed-and-breakfast in Old Town Florence, and Anna's face lights up at the front desk's advertisement for horseback riding on the beach. I can't resist the joy in her eyes and sign the two of us up for a romantic sunset ride. I've never ridden a horse before, but I am a star minor-league hockey player in very good shape, and it will give me a chance to wear my cowboy hat. How hard can it be?

I thought being friends with Gilly got me used to being around people taller than I am—until I meet Popsicle. The mottled gray mare stares down at me with her wide-set chocolate eyes and twitching ears. From a distance, Popsicle looks sweet and harmless. But up close, there is something unsettling about the big horse eye tracking my every move. I feel like she is daring me to pull something I'll regret. I take a step closer, and she takes a step back with her big, heavy hooves. She could stomp me in half.

"Everything okay?" Anna calls down, after easily hopping onto her horse, Lollipop, several minutes ago, with no assistance whatsoever. "Do you need a hand?"

"No, I'm good," I call back, psyching myself up. If Anna can do it, I can do it. We saw a family with two gangly young kids setting off as we got here. Piece of cake.

I take a deep breath, then grab the saddle with one hand and jam my left foot into the stirrup. I heave upward, swinging my right leg over the saddle and reaching for the right stirrup. I don't feel it with my foot, so I keep reaching.

And slide right off the other side.

Thankfully, the sand dunes cushion the blow to my butt, but not to my ego. I hear a strangled cough from Anna and look up. It looks like she swallowed a bug. I am concerned for a second before I realize she is just trying very, very hard not to laugh.

"Are you okay?" she asks, her eyes watering and her voice shaking as she fights to choke down a grin. She barely gets the words out.

I push myself out of the sand. "Absolutely. I meant to do that," I tell her. Popsicle stares at me with a look of disdain. She flicks her tail as if to say, "That's what I thought."

"Sit down in the saddle first, then reach for the other stirrup," Anna suggests.

I nod and heave myself up a second time. This time, I sit firmly in the saddle before finding the stirrup with my right foot. I successfully make it onto my horse. Finally.

"There we go," I say. "Just had to find my centaur legs." Popsicle flicks her tail again, unimpressed.

"Yeah?" Anna asks. "How long has it been since you rode?"

"Hmm, let me think . . ." I say. "That would be about six years and never. I have never ridden a horse before."

"You've never ridden before? Why didn't you tell me?" Anna chides. "We could have gotten an instructor to come with us."

"Well," I don't quite meet her eyes, "I figured it would be easy." I shift in the saddle, trying to get comfortable. I didn't realize quite how big horses are. How does anyone sit like this for very long? I'm not sure my legs have ever been this far apart. Plus, the saddle is rock hard.

"It is easy," Anna tells me. "Once you get the hang of it anyway."

"How exactly did you get the hang of it?" I ask. "I thought you were a hockey kid. Coach Peter doesn't exactly strike me as a horse guy."

Anna laughs. "He definitely isn't. But my grandparents were. They took my mom riding when she was little. It was a nice way for me to feel close to her," Anna says wistfully.

"So, what you're saying," I say. "Is that you've been able to kick my butt at horseback riding since you were like ten?"

"Six, actually," Anna corrects.

"Oh, great. Six is much better."

"You'll be fine, I promise," Anna tells me. "Shall we? We'll take it slow."

She sets off at an easy walking pace, Lollipop moving with her body like they were born together. I admire her petite form on the horse, her hair flowing in the light breeze. I picture the two of us together, galloping along the sands and water splashing in our wake. Maybe this won't be so bad.

As Anna gets farther away from me, I look down at Popsicle and realize I have no idea how to get the horse to move. Is there a start button? Is there a gas pedal?

I give Popsicle a little pat. "Giddyup, Poppy," I say, feeling stupid. Popsicle seems to agree and does not move. "Pretty please? Don't you want to walk with Lollipop?"

Popsicle, it seems, does not.

I hear the squish-crunch of hooves on the sand. Anna and Lollipop circle back around.

"Oh, hey," I say. "We were just taking a quick breather. Popsicle tires easily." Popsicle snorts in disagreement.

"You sure?" Anna asks. "Because I'm happy to help."

"I suppose I could use a tiny bit of help," I admit, "with starting the horse."

Anna swallows another laugh. "You just cluck at her."

I am confused. "Like a chicken?"

"Uh, no, not like a chicken," Anna tells me with as straight a face as she can manage. "Like this," she clicks her tongue gently. "And then bounce your feet lightly on her sides."

Anna starts forward again, demonstrating. I click my tongue experimentally. Popsicle doesn't seem to register. I bounce my feet very gently at her sides. She ignores me. So I bounce harder.

Popsicle jerks her head up and rockets forward at lightning speed. I can swear we are galloping. Anna would later tell me it was a brisk trot. I cling to the saddle for dear life as my butt bounces up and down like I am strapped to the world's most uncomfortable, most repetitive roller coaster. We fly past Anna as my beloved cowboy hat blows off into the dunes.

"Looking good!" Anna calls supportively, nudging Lollipop into gear behind me. "How does it feel?"

"Um, actually," I call back to her, trying to remember if I've made out a will, "I could use part two of our lesson."

"Part two?" Anna asks.

"How do I make it stop?"

I can tell Anna is calling out instructions, but with the wind and the rush of the ocean around us, not to mention the blood pumping in my ears, I cannot hear her. I try the only thing I can think of: bargaining with the horse.

"Popsicle, listen up," I tell her, trying to sound cool and collected instead of terrified. "I promise I will never ever ride you again if you will do me this one tiny favor and please, for the love of god, stop."

As quickly as Popsicle began, she halts. I lurch forward, slamming into the back of her neck, being forced to hug her for dear life or slide right back off.

"Awe," Anna coos, catching up. "Look at the two of you! How sweet! Wait, I want to take a picture."

I swear Popsicle's ears twitch with evil glee. I turn and fake a frail smile in the direction of Anna's phone. "Hey, what do you say we finish the rest of the path on foot?"

Chapter 32

A Voyeuristic Raccoon?

ANNA

Oranges, pinks, and yellows dye the sky in glorious glowing hues above inky black water frothing with waves. It is more beautiful than even the most famous painter's imagination. Charlie and I walk along the damp sand barefoot, holding hands as the waves tickle at our toes.

We return the horses early, then Charlie purloins a bottle of wine, and we continue into the sweeping Oregon dunes on foot. With the sky darkening around us, it feels like we are the only two people on earth. I wouldn't have it any other way.

"So, after this season is over, you're going to retire and become a jockey?" I ask.

"I think I'll try my hand at rodeo, actually," Charlie quips dryly.

"Oh, that's a great idea." I laugh. "You and Popsicle were really vibing."

"That horse is a demon in a horse suit, I'm telling you. Probably sent by the Freezers to sabotage me. Our whole relationship has been an elaborate ruse, leading up to this."

"You're right," I tell him solemnly. "I did all of this, the hockey season, the Peewee game, the gala, the sneaking around, all just to get you to fall off a horse."

Charlie pulls me close, burying his nose in my saltwater-flecked hair and breathing deeply.

I lean against his firm chest, feeling his heartbeat. He is silent for a long time.

"Penny for your thoughts?" I ask him. He seems unsettled, and I hope I haven't triggered regrets about our relationship.

"It's just . . . I thought I'd be better at horseback riding," he says, embarrassed. "I was all ready to show off for you."

I pull back so I can look him in his deep blue eyes. "Let me guess, you don't usually have to try to be good at sports?"

"I guess not. Honestly, never."

"Well, let me ask you this," I say. "Does it bother you that *a girl* can ride circles around you?"

"Actually, it turns me on." Charlie grins. Then his look turns serious. "You're right. I've never really been good at being bad at things. But if I'm going to be bad at something, I'm glad it's with you."

My heart swells to bursting in my chest. Surrounded by high-testosterone hockey players my whole life, I never expected Charlie to get so vulnerable. The fact that he feels safe enough to drop his armor around me makes me feel giddy.

As I bring my face up to meet his, I realize I am falling for Charlie Haskell.

"My precious," Charlie whispers in a cracked, eerie voice. He is hunched over as he reaches toward the squirrel at the base of the ancient tree. It chitters angrily at him and sprints up the trunk, only to turn around and chitter down at him again.

He shakes his fist up at it. "Stupid hobbits."

I watch with a bemused look on my face. After our adventure with the horses yesterday, I agreed to let him pick today's activities. When he saw the Hobbit Trail on our hotel's brochure, he couldn't resist.

Charlie comes toward me, crouched low, and waggles his fingers. "My precious."

I laugh and dart away, giggling as he chases me down. My sneakers thud as I crisscross the mossy trail. The branches curve around the trail like they are protecting it. It really does feel like a magical place.

I reach a small stream and pretend to be trapped. But I surprise him, lunging for a fallen branch and slamming it like a staff on the ground before me.

"You shall not pass," I cry.

Charlie stops dead in his tracks. "Did you just quote *Lord of the Rings* back to me?"

I shrug, grinning. "One does not simply walk into the Hobbit Trail."

Charlie pretends to swoon. "Alright, that does it. Anna Green, you are the perfect girl."

I blush and shake my head. "They're just good movies, that's all." I've never been called the perfect girl before, nor do I believe it is remotely true. Me? Scared to tell the truth about our relationship, addicted to iced coffee and work, and can't get my hair to look nice if I won the lottery? Boring clothes and a ridiculous mole on my face? I feel as far from perfect as I can get.

Charlie lets his jokey smile fall away and looks at me for a long beat.

"They are not good movies," he tells me. "They are perfect movies."

Charlie holds out his hand to me and lets a grin slide back across his face. "Now come on. Time for the special bonus surprise."

I take his hand, and he pulls me back along the trail. "Charlie, you know you can give me the special bonus surprise anytime you want."

Charlie pretends to be scandalized. "Get its mind out of the gutters-es," he says, reverting to his Gollum impression.

I roll my eyes. "If there's some sort of Mordor trail you want to drag us on, I'll meet you back at the hotel."

"Believe it or not," Charlie tells me. "This is even better than Mordor."

"That shouldn't be hard," I grumble, but I let him drag me along. Then I let him blindfold me for a five-minute car ride and guide me with my eyes still closed over a series of rocks that smell like rotting seaweed. I am pretty sure we are actually going to Mordor. But I realize that the more Charlie turns my safe little world upside down, the more I like it. I don't have to be the one responsible for putting out every single fire. Thinking fifteen steps ahead is exhausting. Now I can't even see one step ahead of me. It feels freeing.

He guides me to a stop and angles me. The air around me is musty, damp, and mysterious.

"Are you ready?" he breathes in my ear.

I nod, a thrill running straight through me.

He gently slips off the blindfold, and I open my eyes. At first, I have no idea what I am looking at. We are in some kind of cave, with craggy rock faces that really do remind me of Mordor.

Charlie points, and I gasp. Ahead of us, sprawled out on the rock, are dozens and dozens of snoozing sea lions. One of them stirs, shaking its head and looking right at me with its molten brown eyes.

I clap my hands in sheer glee. I feel so joyful I can burst. "Look at them!" I squeal, getting closer. I turn back to Charlie. "This is amazing."

Charlie clears his throat and nods, blinking rapidly. "I thought you might like it," he says hoarsely.

I tear my eyes away from the sea lions to squint at him. "Are you crying?" I ask, touched that he is tearing up at the sight of sea lions.

271

"No," he swears, blinking faster. "The cave air just irritates my eyes."

As incredible as our day has been, I am pretty sure nothing compares to lying in bed with Charlie's body pressed against mine while watching a movie. I lift my head slightly on his chest, giving him a heavy-lidded smile, as though I could sense his thoughts. I shift my thigh, brushing up against him, and realize the touch has sent a lot of blood downstairs. Despite a very *thorough* shower we have just taken together, just lying together is getting him semi-hard again.

"Enjoying the movie?" I ask.

Charlie grins down at me. "Enjoying the view."

I trail my nails from his shoulder up to the back of his neck, wrapping my fingers in his thick hair and pulling him into me. We melt into each other, legs intertwining, hands exploring, and lips tasting ears, necks, and shoulders. Not rushing, just enjoying the feel of each other.

I feel perfectly safe and warm in Charlie's muscular arms. We've had such an incredible day together, even if his *Lord of the Rings* impression was terrible. I am willing to overlook it to be with this man who listens to my ideas and encourages them and who always finds something to laugh at, even if it is himself. The way he can't stop looking at me, like I am some goddess instead of an ordinary girl. I forget to feel ordinary with him. I never want to leave this trip, this room, this bed.

I let out a low moan as Charlie's lips circle lower, finding my breasts. Heat swirls through my body, the need for him growing. I reach down with my hands, feeling the rock-hard length of his erection. Tracing the tip with my fingers, I spread the drop of pre-cum across the head. He growls low and hungry as he teases my hard nipples with his expert tongue. I want to dive lower, replace my fingers with my mouth, see what kinds of noises I can get him to make, and feel the way he shudders. But just the thought of it is almost too much.

I didn't want to wait. I want him inside me now.

Since I am on the pill and we confirmed we could do away with condoms, I urgently pull Charlie toward me. I wind my fingers back into his hair, tugging him back up to meet my lips, trying to snake my legs around his waist. But Charlie is enjoying the taste of my skin too much. He runs his tongue along my collarbone, my shivers making him even harder. He nibbles at the ticklish spot he discovered at the base of my neck. I squeak and wriggle, my legs untangling from his.

As I twist away from him, Charlie pulls my back to his front, kissing his way along the back of my neck and my shoulders. I moan again as he encircles me with his arms, his firm chest pressing against my back, and the hard length of him twitching against my ass. It is heart-poundingly sexy, and yet caring and gentle at the same time. I never really considered it "making love" until right now.

I part my legs, rubbing my wetness along him, and Charlie presses forward, sliding inside of me. We both moan at the feeling of him entering me, stretching me, filling me. He begins a slow, rocking rhythm as he pulls me tight against him, his arms around me, his hands caressing my breasts, and his lips buried in my neck.

I press back, my body on fire. His stubble scratches against my neck thrill me, and the angle hit spots inside of me that feel like lighting fireworks. I moan again, and Charlie answers me with a deep moan of his own.

"So good, Anna, you feel so good," he groans into my neck. "I don't know how much longer I can go."

I pant. Feeling him pumping into me from behind and hearing how crazy my body drives him sends me spiraling.

"Oh, Charlie, oh god," I cry, grinding my ass into him. My body contracts, and I come, squeezing him for dear life as I ride the white-hot pleasure crashing over me.

Feeling me buck against him sends Charlie right over the edge. He clutches me, pushing deep inside me and coming hard.

Completely spent, we both collapse back into each other. I feel protected in Charlie's embrace. We could have been on a dungeon floor, and nothing would feel cozier. I stretch, wriggling my ass back against him.

Charlie nuzzles into my neck. "Don't start that unless you're ready for round three."

"Is that a challenge?" I ask, giving another little wriggle. I relent, though, content to lie in his arms for the moment.

We lay like that, breathing together, for a long quiet beat.

"How about we don't check out tomorrow? How about

we don't move ever again?" he asks, his lips against my back.

I sigh, and pull away to flip over and face him.

"I don't want to check out either," I tell him. "This has been a perfect weekend. I don't want to go back to sneaking around."

"I hate it too," he tells me. "All I want is to shout from the rooftops that Anna Green is my girlfriend."

I am surprised. "Oh, are we girlfriend/boyfriend? I didn't realize we were exclusive."

Charlie stammers, "Oh, uh, I guess we never talked about it, I mean if you don't—"

"It's just I've been sneaking around with Zamboni Zane too," I tell him, a slow grin slipping through my mock sincere face.

"Oh, have you?" Charlie asks, weak with relief. "Can he do this to you?" He went right back for the sensitive spot on my neck. I squeal and bat at him before he pulls me into a deep kiss.

The conversation is forgotten for several searing minutes before I finally come up for air. "You win," I gasp. "I'll break it off with Zane asap. You can be my boyfriend, Charlie Haskell."

"What do you think would happen . . . if we did tell people?"

I frown, thinking it over. I want to tell people so badly, but it is also terrifying. "Well," I say, "assuming we could keep my dad from killing you—"

"I'll buy a suit of armor," he promises.

"And assuming our two teams would get over it—"

"They'd have to, right?" he asks. "The season's almost over, anyway."

"There's still the league," I finish. "That's the biggest problem."

Charlie pushes himself up on his elbows, thinking. "It's not outright banned, right?" he asks. "What if we told them formally? Filled out some HR paperwork? They couldn't object to that, could they?"

I sit up as well, thinking it over.

"It could work," I say. "It's probably the best shot we have, to approach them directly."

Hope swells in my chest. I want to hold onto Charlie, to hold on to the way he makes me feel alive and ready for anything. I hadn't realized how closed off I'd been before him, so afraid to make waves. Going back to that is unacceptable. But I am still afraid that this relationship will topple everything we've both worked so hard for. I hate the idea of hurting either of our teams, but I also hate hiding this part of myself.

"Why don't we sleep on it?"

I look at him with wide eyes. "Really? Do you mind?"

"Of course not."

"Should we?" he asks, reaching for me. "Sleep on it?"

I am tempted, but the sex and the intense conversation left me wide awake. I've been thinking of him as my boyfriend for a while, but hearing him say the word "girlfriend," and that he wants to go public keeps me buzzing.

Maybe I'm not yet willing to take that risk, but I want to

have one last adventure. An idea flashes through my mind, and I give Charlie a wicked grin.

"We could go to sleep, or . . ."

"Or what?" Charlie asks as I leap up and out of bed to peek through the blinds.

"Or, the hotel pool is empty," I say. "Fancy a little swim?"

"We didn't bring our suits."

My grin turns downright devilish. "Are you going to let that stop you?"

The second Charlie realizes what I am saying, he rockets out of bed.

We giggle like school kids as we slip out of their hotel room in bathrobes and nothing else. My heart pounds at my daring, but we don't see a soul.

The pool glows a gentle turquoise under the moonlit sky, a beckoning oasis shimmering in the darkness. I dip in a tentative toe.

"How is it?" Charlie asks.

"A little cold," I admit. "You'll have to keep me warm."

"Yes, ma'am." Charlie reaches into his robe pocket and extracts a small bottle of minibar champagne.

My jaw drops. "Are you kidding?" I squeak. "Do you know how expensive those are?"

Charlie shrugs. "You're worth it," he says simply.

I blush. "We still could have picked something up at a liquor store," I grumble.

Charlie laughs and pulls me in for a kiss. "I promise next time I'll get you the cheapest champagne I can find. Now get in that pool, or I'm going to drag you back up to the bedroom and have my way with you again."

"I don't think they're mutually exclusive." I wink. Charlie nearly groans. I am amazingly good at getting him hard.

He starts to open the tiny champagne, and I disappear with a splash. The turquoise water ripples and my head pops back up in the center of the water.

"Come on in, the water's fine," I purr, starting to lift my shoulders out of the water.

There is a rustling in the trees, and I freeze, chest still submerged. I look at Charlie with wide eyes. "Is someone there?"

Charlie squints into the dense canopy, but he doesn't see anyone. He throws off his robe and plunges into the chilly water, swimming to me in a few strokes of his muscular arms.

He sweeps me up into his arms as my legs wrap around his middle.

"I don't see anyone," Charlie assures me. "It's probably just a hotel guest or a voyeuristic raccoon."

"A voyeuristic raccoon?" I laugh. "I guess we better give him a show."

I lean forward and our lips meet in a hungry kiss. We enjoy the weightless sensation of bobbing in the swirling water, limbs wrapped around each other. Wet skin on wet skin. It is a moment both of us want to last forever.

After a long and breathless embrace, I finally pull back

to squint into the bushes once more. If there was someone or something, it is completely still now. We are alone in the pool, nothing between us but the luxurious water and the warmth of our bodies.

I give Charlie a sinful smile. "Do something that scares you every day, right?" I ask seductively. Tonight is a swim to remember.

Chapter 33

Why Is Your Dad Sending You Links to Cheese Graters?

ANNA

"I just feel like I'm cheating right now," Alison mutters, glancing around the room and looking supremely guilty.

I roll my eyes. "You are allowed to eat lunch at other places than Munch."

"Don't say it so loud," Alison insists, sinking lower into our little green booth. "Someone will hear you."

Our waiter swings by the table, choosing to ignore Alison's melted posture. He deposits our steaming plate of Mother's Bistro fried ravioli and gracefully vanishes.

"The whole point of meeting here is that no one will hear us," I remind her. "No one comes to this side of the river for lunch."

Alison inhales deeply, eyeing the crimped golden pasta

pillows and their little well of ruby-red sauce with begrudging respect. "I can never get these to come out right, anyway." She spears a forkful, shoves it in her mouth, and moans in ecstasy.

Now it's my turn to look around, but the bustling yellow restaurant hasn't registered her friend's *When Harry Met Sally* moment. I turn back to find my friend has already eaten half the plate. "Hey, save some for me!"

Alison waves me off. "You ordered mac and cheese. You don't need two pasta dishes."

"I absolutely do," I argue, battling with my friend's fork. "Keep hogging the ravioli, and I will take a picture and send it to Sal."

Alison glares at me and reluctantly pushes over the plate. "You're lucky I love you. Now tell me some hot hockey-boyfriend gossip, or I will change my mind."

I glance around the restaurant one more time, reassuring myself no one from our circles were listening in. I told Alison about Charlie the day after our *Mighty Ducks* date, unable to contain my glee. Alison squealed so loudly that I am pretty sure I'll never hear that frequency again. But after subjecting me to a few minutes of a very energetic "I Told You So" dance, Alison calmed down and has been incredibly supportive.

I am very grateful to have this nosy, bossy foodie in my life.

Alison is still staring at me, her fork inching toward the last fried ravioli on the plate. I spear it first. My friend sits back and folds her arms expectantly.

"Boy. Details. Now," Alison demands.

"Okay, okay," I relent. "We had our trip to Florence this weekend."

"And?" Alison asks.

"And . . ." I blush deep crimson.

Alison grins. "That good, huh? Did you leave the room at all?" Alison waggles her eyebrows.

I blush so strongly that I am pretty sure all my blood has just re-routed to my cheeks. "We left the room! Lots of times."

"Name one."

"When we hiked to the lighthouse. And when we went to see the sea lions. Don't tell anyone but I think he teared up when he saw them. How cute is that?"

"Awe, I love him even more," Alison coos. "Only real men cry at sea lions. And the rest of it was spent in bed?"

"Well," I clear my throat, "we did leave our room on Saturday night to go swimming."

Alison frowns. "Swimming? I thought you told me you weren't bringing a suit."

I look at my friend meaningfully.

Alison's jaw drops straight to the table. "Anna Banana, you absolute fiend. I am impressed. I'm pretty sure the last time you did anything this crazy was the day you wore a blue shirt to work instead of a red one."

"That was laundry day," I insist. "I changed at lunch." But I can't keep the smile off my face.

"Thank goodness," Alison deadpans. "But look at you! You're practically glowing. You must really like him."

"Honestly? I really do," I admit. "He's so funny and

sweet, and I actually feel like he gets me. I've had so many new publicity ideas since we started dating, it's crazy."

"Yeah? Is that where Naked Day came from?" Alison asks, laughing as I blush again.

My expression slips as I think about how I still haven't told my dad—or anyone except Alison—about my new relationship.

"It kills me that we have to keep it a secret," I tell Alison. "I worry he thinks I'm ashamed to be dating him."

"I'm sure he doesn't," Alison reassures me. "It's just the stupid league and their stupid rules. And the fact that your dad might still own that old hunting rifle."

Charlie claims to understand why we keep things a secret, but I still worry that he resents it deep down. Every time I think about what will happen when we tell people, my stomach climbs up into my throat.

I look down at my hands, not quite able to meet Alison's eyes. "We did talk about it. Going public."

"Really? Wow, you do really like this guy. What do you think?"

I sigh. "I don't know. Part of me really wants to. But the rest of me . . ."

"Still hasn't found that old hunting rifle?"

I give a small laugh. "Pretty much."

"You really think your dad won't be okay with it?"

I shrug. When my mom died, my dad was there for me 110 percent. He learned how to braid my hair, buy the right tampons, and sing the lyrics to the Maroon 5 songs I loved. He has never excluded me from his hockey world, welcoming me into his office every day after school, letting me blow the whistle for the players during practice drills, or running the game tapes. Even though he carries the pain of my mom's passing with him like a scar that never heals, he made my childhood as happy as he possibly could.

So, I did everything I could to make my dad happy. It was easy to take a job with the Freezers when I loved the team so much. It was also easy to take on more responsibility so my dad could focus on coaching and nothing else. I made the team all I thought about, so I didn't bother branching out on my own. Even when I have dated in the past, I picked safe, low-risk guys who had no chance of upending my routines. Until now. Until Charlie.

"I just don't know that he's ready for me to date someone seriously," I say.

"So? Are dads ever really okay with it? He'll love Charlie when he gets to know him."

"Will he? He loves me, and he loves the Freezers. Charlie interferes with both of those things."

Alison frowns. Fortunately, the waiter reappears with our entrees: southwestern mac and cheese for me and crab cakes for Alison. Alison digs into her crab cakes with glee, but I've lost my appetite.

I keep psyching myself up to tell my dad, then chicken out every time he goes on another tirade against the Shredders, their coach, and their tactics. Maybe after the playoffs. Maybe after the championship. Maybe after I flee to Boston to work for the Bruins, I'll send him a text. Or better yet, a European team. Not that I ever want to leave Portland.

Alison's fork snakes over and digs into my mac and cheese. "I say rip off the Band-Aid. Your dad might surprise you."

I nod, but I'm not so sure. Alison snipes another forkful of mac and cheese.

"Oh!" she exclaims, her eyes filling with glee. "Speaking of hockey player boyfriends, you'll never guess who I saw in Munch the other day."

"Who?" I ask, utterly clueless. I didn't even realize Alison knew any other hockey players.

"Mr. Blake Tyler," Alison tells me, buzzing with gossip. "On a *date*."

"A date? Are you serious?" I search myself to see if I feel any pangs of regret. After all, if Charlie hadn't come along, it's possible I would have fallen for Blake. But I feel nothing but relief that if he'd ever been interested in me, he isn't anymore. Charlie makes me lighter in a way Blake only ever made me feel heavier, stressed over whatever he said or done this time.

"Deadly serious," Alison assures me. "He was on a date alright. A date . . . with Mabeline."

"Get out. With Mabeline?" I have only ever seen Blake run in the opposite direction of his biggest fan. Then again, the more I think about it, the more they seem like they would be a good couple. They are both so intense and single-minded, and they could both probably kill someone without much effort. It might be the perfect match. "How did it go?"

Alison scrunches up her nose. "Not well. I'm pretty sure she left halfway through. And I'm pretty sure she took most of his lunch with her."

I laugh. Maybe I'll see if I can sneak some relationship coaching into our next publicity coaching discussion. I have a feeling I can get Mabeline to give Blake a second chance. Actually, it probably couldn't hurt to give Mabeline some coaching too.

Either way, I am happy there might be another hockey couple to take the attention off me and Charlie. Then my eyes go wide, remembering something.

"Wait," I say slowly. "Weren't *you* supposed to be going on a hockey date?"

Alison's eyes are suddenly glued to her mostly eaten crab cakes. "It's getting late. Should we head out soon?"

"Nice try." I'm not about to let my friend get out of this one. Not after the months of teasing I have endured. "Come on. Have you gone out with Leo yet?"

Alison looks at the ceiling and then at the floor.

"Well?" I press.

"No," Alison mumbles, almost inaudible.

"That's no problem," I say, reaching for my phone. "I'll just text him. Maybe something like how you're dying to go on that date with him, but you're just too shy and sweet to ask and you need a strong, sexy man to get the ball rolling."

Alison lunges for my phone. "Don't you dare. I will ban you from Munch."

I relent, but I fix my friend with a stern look. "Set up the date or I will, and it will sound a lot like that."

"Do I have to?" Alison whines. "It was an accident. I don't want to date a big dumb jock."

I know that Leo has a degree from Harvard in ethno-musicology, but I keep my mouth shut. Maybe I can talk Leo into clueing me in on where their date will be so I can hide somewhere nearby and film my friend realizing all her hockey stereotypes are wrong.

"You have to," I tell her. "Think of it as karma for demanding that I go out with a hockey player so often."

"That is different," Alison grumbles, even though it isn't.

"Oh, really? Come on, what would Eleanor do?" I ask, playing the Roosevelt card.

"Probably date a woman instead?" Alison mumbles.

I fold my arms and stare at my friend. The seconds tick by.

"Fine," Alison mutters, yanking out her phone and dashing out a quick text. "Done. Happy?"

Lightning quick, I dive across the table and grab Alison's phone. Alison's text to Leo reads: *Hey, Anna says we have to go out or the money doesn't go to charity so hit me up, I guess.*

I sigh. Well, it doesn't exactly scream Alison-Leo/Anna-Charlie co-wedding on the beach, but it is a start. I'll have to leave the rest to Leo.

My own phone buzzes, and in retribution, Alison snatches it. "Ooo, please tell me it's a sext from Charlie."

"It definitely isn't!" I cry, although Charlie hadn't *not* sent me the occasional innuendo-filled text. But I don't think I can handle blushing any more today. My cheeks would turn permanent cartoon-figure red. I wonder what Charlie would say. He'd probably like it.

Alison sighs in disappointment and hands the phone back. "Why is your dad sending you links to cheese graters?"

My heart sinks as I take the phone. I thought I got my dad to drop this. "He wants me to get a bunch of branded 'shredders' so our fans can boo and grate cheese at the Shredders. No, it doesn't make sense," I say in response to Alison's confused look. "And I told him it would be a bad idea to hand out sharp objects at a hockey game." I rub my temples. "I'd better go before he places a bulk order on Amazon that I have to figure out how to return."

I am thrilled that the Freezers are so close to the Kerry Cup finals, and so proud of my dad. But a tiny—okay, a large—part of me is dreading the almost inevitable Freezers-Shredders rematch that looms in the very near future. Not only does it mean I'll have to hide my relationship from TV cameras and thousands of fans, but it also means my dad has turned me into his personal anti-Shredders war machine.

The Freezers have momentum, which means this is prime time to recruit new long-term sponsors and cement new fans, but Coach Peter is focused on cheese graters. I mentally add this complaint to the list of things I never dare bring up with my father. I sigh and stand.

"See you tomorrow?" I ask. "I'll come by and grab Stinker, and you can tell me where you and Leo are going on your date. And you can't lie, because I'll ask him too."

Alison wrinkles her nose at me. But I am confident Alison will change her tune once she actually gets up close to the charming and very buff team captain. If only my own love life was going that smoothly. I push the worry out of my mind and go to shut down some cheese graters.

Chapter 34

Why Are You Being So Normal?

CHARLIE

We are going to lose. I feel it in my bones. I watch the Bears' offensive line barrel the puck toward our goal. Above us, the seconds tick down. It is the final period of the final game of the playoffs. Whoever wins this game will go on to the championship.

But time is running out.

The game is tied 2:2, with me scoring both of the Shredders' goals, but the Bears are playing hard. I can feel my bruises more than I can feel my legs. Tomorrow, my whole body will be purple. I am fighting as hard as I can, but with the insane penalties the Bears have been pulling, the game is slipping away. I'm not sure my team has a third goal in them. I should be glad Anna can't show her face at my games to witness this, but not seeing her cheering in the crowd always cuts my heart like a knife.

The Bears' notorious first offensive line earned the nickname the Grizzly Three for their massive frames and brutal play style. I spitefully dub them Yogi Bear, Cindy Bear, and Boo-Boo in my head, but it doesn't make them any less good at hockey.

Yogi Bear snaps the puck toward the net and Tony blocks it. Cindy Bear backhands it on the rebound. Tony lunges into a full split, just barely keeping the biscuit out of the basket. But Boo-Boo goes in for the kill shot.

Quentin sails toward the puck, trying for a last-ditch breakout to get the puck away from the wall of Grizzlies. It is a Hail Mary, but then Alex shoots deep into the defensive zone to join me.

Watching my determined protégé beeline for Boo-Boo, a man twice Alex's size, I force myself to rally. I swing around, making eye contact with Gilly. Despite our disagreements, I know Gilly understands exactly what I am thinking. I kick off after Alex while Gilly falls back. The only way out of this is to work together.

With Alex's help, Quentin gets the puck away from Boo-Boo and whips it toward me. I catch it and immediately send it sailing toward Gilly, then kick off toward the neutral zone. The forecheck works. We are back in play.

We work in perfect sync, passing the puck backward between us, ducking and weaving through the Bears, crossing over the blue line and into the offensive zone. I don't have a spare second to glance up at the clock, but I know we only have one shot at this. Gilly maneuvers into place by the goal.

The massive enforcer comes out of nowhere with murder in his eyes. My half-crazed brain immediately dubs him Winnie-the-Pooh. I act on instinct, swiveling toward the boards, keeping myself between the Pooh and the puck. But I am running out of room. I am about to become a Pooh pancake.

With no other options, I flip my stick, trying for a toe drag to pull the puck back to me. It isn't my strongest maneuver, but thankfully it works, and Winnie slams into the wall where I used to be. No honey for him.

I spin back around, catching a glimpse of the clock as I twist. There are only six seconds left. I am at a terrible angle. I need to get the puck to Gilly or Alex for them to have any shot of scoring, but I can barely see my teammates. Defenders Paddington and Fozzie have them completely covered. It is down to me.

With my muscles screaming, sweat pouring, and blood pounding in my ears, I have room in my mind for one thing: Anna. Time slows as the thought of her cheering face sears through me. With the last of my strength, I do the thing I do best. I shift the right-handed stick into my left hand and chuck.

The puck flies across the ice. The goalie—the Bear in the Big Blue House, obviously—flies forward to meet it. The buzzer goes off.

And the puck sails straight through his legs.

I did it. We won.

I blink away the image of Anna as the stadium roars

around me. The entire crowd is on their feet. Only when I see the hats raining into the rink did I realize I pulled off a hat trick: three goals in one game. Run DMC's "It's Tricky" blasts over the PA system, almost drowned out by the crowd singing. Carla, in her Ted the Shredder costume, executes some jaw-dropping breakdancing moves.

My teammates slam into me, lifting me off the ice. My eyes swing through the crowd, and I catch my family jumping up and down in sheer glee.

It should have been an incredible moment.

But all I can think about is the one person who couldn't be there. I know my teammates think that dating a Freezer would throw off my game. But Anna makes me better. Anna gave me the strength to take that shot.

If only they could see that.

The Shredders' victory lap takes me straight over to my family, and I break off to skate toward the trio. My parents, Sandy and Harold, beam with pride. Even my teenage sister Emmie looks impressed.

"Well, fry me in butter," my dad calls out. "That was a hell of a hat tip."

"Hat trick, honey," Sandy corrects. She leans forward. "I thought you were a goner for sure. What a toe-drag! Your team has the best breakouts in the league. I won't let anybody tell me different."

"Thanks, Mom." I lean forward to hug Emmie, but she wrinkles her nose.

"You stink, Charlie!" she whines. "But you were pretty good," she amends, grinning.

"Oh, pretty good?" I mock, noticing my sister's

"Everyone Watches Women's Sports" hoodie. "Thanks, and nice hoodie, by the way." Emmie rolls her eyes.

"She's joking," Sandy tells me. "She loved you. Honestly, I was a little worried your defense couldn't handle the Cave Bears, but those forechecks in the second period were so clean. Have you been drilling those?"

"Sandy, come on, let's not drag Charlie into a deep dive on forceps," Howard says, slapping me on the shoulder, right on one of my bruises. "He should be celebrating!"

My mom waves her husband off. "He can celebrate after he beats the Freezers in the championship."

My smile suddenly becomes fixed. In all the excitement, I forgot what our win would mean. Going head-to-head with the Freezers for the Kerry Cup. Very possibly my worst nightmare.

Emmie gives me a suspicious side-eyed look. "You're being weird."

"What?" I ask, surprised. "No, I'm not."

"Yes, you are," Emmie persists. "You're usually a lot more obnoxious after you win."

"Emmie—" Sandy scolds.

"What? He is," Emmie insists. "Why are you being so normal?"

I curse my extremely perceptive little sister. She hit the nail on the head. I did not feel like celebrating. But what hurts the most is I can't tell my family why.

I've been longing to spill the beans to them about Anna, but my mom weaseled her way into the social circle and social media of every single Shredder. She also happens to be notoriously bad at keeping secrets. I have to binge-watch every television show I like to avoid her spoilers. I still haven't forgiven her for ruining the Red Wedding. If I tell my family about Anna, Sandy would DM my teammates for their wedding tux sizes the next day.

So, I pull a face at my sister and lie. "Sorry, sis, I'm pretty sure those cuddly little Care Bears broke every bone in my body. I promise I'll be back to embarrassing you as soon as I'm healed."

Emmie narrows her eyes. But she pinches her lips together and is silent instead of pressing. I suppress a sigh of relief.

My mom leans forward, clearly about to launch into a deep-dive, play-by-play of the entire game. I feel my guilt and the many bruises rearing up. I start to skate backward.

"Anyway, I gotta go change. Love you guys. See you at dinner tomorrow?"

My dad tugs my mom back from the edge of the rink. "Sure thing, Chuck. Congrats on getting to the Stanley Cup!"

As my mom and my sister turn to correct my dad, I make my speedy exit.

It isn't until the locker room empties out that I finally deem it safe enough to check my phone.

It feels like my teammates have been celebrating for the past ten hours. They relived every single play, piled every hat they could find on top of my head, and trashed the Freezers in every conceivable way. Quentin even tried a freestyle rap. I never expected to hear the word "Freezer" rhymed with "Kale Caesar," and that was one of Quentin's better ones. My cheeks hurt more from fake smiling than my body hurt from board battles with Fozzie Bear.

Nevertheless, I make it through the team's jubilation and the post-game press conference's invasive questions. Anna did her job well, and everyone is fixated on the Shredders' upcoming match with the Freezers. If one more person asks me how I feel about going up against Blake again, I'll take one of the hats on my head and shove it into their mouth. At least it would quiet them.

But the chaos finally dies down, and I beg off the post-game bar crawl. I sit heavily, trying to find a position that doesn't exacerbate any of my bruises and failing. But the pain fades away when I reach for my phone and see the series of ecstatic texts from Anna. There are so many different hat gifs that it takes me a full minute of scrolling to find her all-caps, exclamation-mark-filled congratulations message. For the first time in hours, a genuinely dopey grin fills my face.

"Good game."

I freeze at the gruff voice from the doorway. I know that baritone like the back of my hand.

"Thanks, Gilly."

I slip the phone into my pocket, feeling guilty. Gilly ducks into the locker room, coming a few steps closer.

"Are you going to be good to go against the Freezers?" Gilly asks.

I clench my jaw. I hate that my best friend doesn't trust me after everything we've been through together.

"Of course," I say lightly. "You heard the reporters. It's the rematch of the century. The Red Sox vs the Yankees. Muhammad Ali vs George Foreman. Rocky vs Communism."

Gilly rolls his eyes. "I hate reporters. The only thing they ever ask me is if I'm really taller than Juraj Slafkovský."

"Are you?" I ask.

Gilly gives me the finger, but he smiles. My friend takes a step closer, still not quite meeting my eyes. "You seem less happy this season." He says quietly.

I bristle. "Not because of her. Because of the rest of it. Believe it or not, Anna's the only thing keeping me sane."

My mind flashes through the past few months. Every good moment has something to do with Anna. Laughing with the sea lions. Kissing at the gala. Making fun of Vancouver together. Coaching those Peewee kids. I never even thought about coaching before she came along. It was her nudge that sent me there. Her early assessment of me pushed me to help out Alex. She actually helped me make the Shredders better. But Gilly is right. Playing for the team doesn't make me happy anymore.

I sigh. "I love you guys, you know that. I'll do anything for the Shredders. But the pressure, the invasive questions, the loyalty tests. Is it worth it anymore?"

"What would you do instead?" Gilly asks.

I shrug, my mind drifting back to Peewee Day. "I don't know. Coach? Is that crazy?"

Gilly makes eye contact for the first time since he

entered the locker room. "It's not crazy. You'd be better than Coach Ryan."

I bark out a short, hard laugh. "That's not hard." I stand, wanting nothing more than to collapse into Anna's bed and her arms. I am willing to add any number of bruises to celebrate with her. She is the only person who accepts me for me right now.

I walk past Gilly, not saying goodbye. I wish my friend would come around, but I refuse to force it. Still, I slow down before I reach the doorway, needing to say one last thing.

"I wanted to tell you about her," I say. "I'm sorry I didn't. But that's the only thing I'm sorry about. Well, that and the fact that you almost got creamed by Fozzie Bear."

I leave before Gilly can respond. Tomorrow, I'll be a Shredder getting ready to take on the Freezers. But tonight, I am just a very bruised boyfriend who wants to see his girlfriend.

Chapter 35

The Cat Who Ate the Canary

BLAKE

Tomorrow, I'll go back to being a Freezer on the brink of pounding the Shredders into the ice, but today, I am just a guy smelling roses.

If anybody finds me at this moment, I will have to admit I finally found one thing I like about Portland. It is Washington Park, and the Portland International Rose Test Garden specifically. I have the morning off, so I bought a massive cinnamon-sugar pretzel from a street vendor and let my feet lead me down the tree-lined path to the garden. At this time in April, the roses haven't reached full bloom, but I love the promise they hold. The sense of anticipation will soon unfurl in bursts of dusky pinks, vivid reds, and charming corals, like little floral fireworks.

Finishing off my pretzel, I stroll along the perfectly

neat rows. I admire their carefully cultivated bushes, resisting the urge to google again how much it would cost to purchase an English manor house and replicate these roses. It isn't something I can afford with the meager PCHL salary cap. Still, I can dream. Maybe the NHL will see me crush the Kerry Cup and swoop me up into the world of big contracts and bigger sponsorships. A few commercials for Home Depot's outdoor department, and I can probably retire as Lord Blake Tyler, king of the roses.

I skim the tiny name signs, hunting for my favorites. I pass by the red and yellow Ketchup & Mustard, the many-petaled Sexy Rexy, and the neon-bright Pink Floyd before stopping at the Dark Night roses with their velvety, nearly black petals that dance around a pale-yellow center. I was initially thinking of Anna as I wandered the rows, but this particular rose reminds me of someone else entirely.

I lean forward to take a deep sniff, but freeze when a throat clears behind me. I know that weaselly throat clear all too well. The smell of the roses falls away, replaced with the haunting taste of stale beer and bitterness.

"I thought we were meeting later," I say, turning around.

Kyle shrugs. "I got impatient."

I don't understand how the beady-eyed reporter always knows exactly where I am, like a smirking, bearded bloodhound.

Kyle eyes the roses disdainfully.

Before Kyle can start, I shake my head and turn back to the black roses I have been inhaling.

"I was gonna text you anyway. I don't want to hear

about Charlie and Anna anymore. I gotta focus on the game."

I like my new, less angry self. Vlad recommended a meditation app I've been using every morning. I finally understand what people are talking about when they use the term "inner peace."

I am still looking forward to wiping the ice with Charlie Haskell's face, but I want to do it for purely professional reasons.

Kyle feigns indifference, swiping open his camera app and navigating to several photos with turquoise backgrounds. He selects one and holds up the screen.

"I get it, man. But I just want you to see what you paid for."

My veins turn to ice at the image of Anna and Charlie, kissing in a dark pool. There is nothing revealing about the photo, but it is an intimate and deeply private moment between the couple, who seem to glow just as much as the water around them.

I search myself for the lightning bolt of rage that usually strikes at the mention of Anna and Charlie, but the nauseating churning in my stomach is something different. Not rage. Not undigested cinnamon-sugar pretzel. It is shame.

"Hotel security guard was doing a sweep, so I had to run before I got the full show," Kyle explains, sounding disappointed. "But I think that paints a pretty good picture."

I take several deep, calming breaths to unclench my

muscles and respond. "Whatever. We already knew she was dating him."

I turn away, back to the roses.

"Sure, we knew that. But nobody else does."

I jerk back toward Kyle. "What do you mean?"

Kyle widens his eyes, all innocence. "The article you're paying me to write, remember? My editor is still not interested. However, I found a few outlets who are very excited to get these photos."

My stomach drops deep into the thorny rose beds. I forgot this was all for an article, one that I realize could completely ruin Anna's career and possibly take down the Freezers with it. I don't usually accept blame for the bad things that go on around me, but I have a sneaking suspicion that this might be all my fault.

"I paid you, right?" I ask, thinking fast. "So those are my photos. And I say you can't publish them."

There. I have saved the day. Only for some reason, Kyle still looks like a cat who ate the canary.

"You paid me to *take* the pictures," Kyle clarifies gleefully. "You want the pictures themselves? That costs extra."

"Okay, fine." I glower, trying to remember how much I have in my bank account. Kyle has done an excellent job of draining it already, but I can swing another payment. Maybe I can sell one of my rare plants. I hate to part with a single one. Still, I got my team into this mess, and it is up to me to get them out of it.

"Great. That'll be $15,000."

"Fifteen *thousand* dollars?" I ask, hoping somehow I heard the reporter wrong. "But, but I don't have that." I'll have to sell all my plants. And the rest of my belongings. And probably a kidney. Maybe two kidneys. I can live without my kidneys, right?

This is bad.

Kyle shrugs, nonchalant. "No? That's a shame. But don't worry, your article's going to do great. After all, that's what you wanted. Isn't it?"

I wasn't ready to give up and let Kyle ooze his way to victory. I shake my head. "You can't publish those photos. They're private."

"Then why'd you tell me to take them?" Kyle asks.

"I made a mistake," I mumble, the unfamiliar words sounding strange on my tongue.

"I get it, man," Kyle tells me. "The photos can be yours. For $15,000. Cash. I take Venmo too. No Zelle though."

My hand shifts to the part of my abdomen where I think maybe my kidneys are. "Just give me some time."

Kyle holds up his hands. "I'd like to, but I can't. I've already got buyers lined up. Sorry, man. No more money? No more photos. It's been great doing business with you, though."

As the shock wears off, my face darkens into something stormy and dangerous. Thunder flashes in my black eyes. I am not a man to be taken advantage of. I point a finger in Kyle's face.

"You're extorting me," I spit.

But Kyle just laughs, the sound as greasy as his beard. "Bruh, did you only just realize that?"

I blink. My finger wavers, reevaluating my entire relationship with the friendly and encouraging journalist who so kindly offered to help me out with my would-be relationship. Has Kyle been this sleazy all along? I wouldn't have missed that, would I? My stomach skyrockets from under the earth to right back up my throat. I really shouldn't have eaten that pretzel.

I force myself to swallow the carb-laced bile. Somehow, I have to fix this. Grabbing Kyle hard by the wrist holding the incriminating phone, I tower over the sniveling journalist.

"You're going to give me those photos," I growl.

Kyle doesn't laugh this time, but he doesn't quake in apologetic fear either. He simply lifts his other hand up to the one I am squeezing like a lemon, taps his phone, and starts swiping.

"Honestly, I'm not sure why you're so worried about those photos when I have these."

Kyle tilts the phone. I look and blanch.

There I am. Grainy Blake scaling Anna's terrace wall. Grainy Blake jerking open Anna's patio door. Grainy Blake emptying Anna's drawers onto the floor. Grainy Blake delicately misting Anna's plants.

Pictures are supposed to mean a thousand words, but these only need one.

Checkmate.

I am utterly fucked. The worst part is that I signed my own death warrant months ago. Kyle didn't force me to break into Anna's apartment. I did this all to myself. Granted, it didn't help that my journalist buddy turned out to be a psychopath. But still.

The muscles in my fingers cease to work, and Kyle peels them off his wrung-out wrist.

Kyle shoves the phone back into his pocket as I stand there, staring at the reporter in abject horror.

"Listen, my man, I'm not a monster," Kyle tells me. "How about this? You've got twenty-four hours to get me my money. After that, Anna's relationship status goes public. No one has to see your little breaking-and-entering adventure. Unless you try to stop me, of course. Sound good?"

I can only stare. A small sound seeps out of my throat, like a mangled frog is lodged there.

Kyle pats me on the shoulder. "Good! Anyway, I've got to run. This place is such a dump."

With one last sneer at the roses, Kyle melts back into the park, as though he was a poltergeist haunting my dreams. But this is no nightmare. This is a real shit creek, and I am heading straight for the waterfall.

I hate myself for getting into this mess. There is no way I can get $15,000 by tomorrow. The only thing I know about selling kidneys on the black market is that I can't figure out how to do it in twenty-four hours. Especially not with the championship game in three days. How can I play while recovering from surgery?

I can only hope that no one will care about Anna and Charlie's relationship. After all, I got over it. Mostly. Surely everyone else could? Maybe the fallout won't be so bad, and they can all laugh about it someday.

But I have a nasty feeling that won't be the case, and

that I have just set something very bad in motion. I try to take a calming breath, but I can't remember how.

My stomach clenches down into a tiny pretzel-filled fist. I lean over and heave my super-sized snack onto a bush of half-bloomed Betty Boop roses. I reach over and wipe stomach acid off the red-tipped petals apologetically. Throwing up doesn't make me any less queasy. Disaster is coming up fast, and, just like my pretzel, I have no idea how to stop it.

Chapter 36

Actually, Where Is Belize?

ANNA

The day started out so well, but by 10 a.m., it tipped right over a cliff. I get up bright and early, with enough time to scoop up Stinker and a large iced coffee before work. The skies dawn crystal clear and Mount Hood is out, its peak winking in the sun. We have forty-eight hours until the Kerry Cup final, and I have engineered a nearly sold-out stadium. I even have several sponsors expressing interest in next year's season. Everything is moving smoothly.

I stroll down the sidewalk with a spring in my step, letting Stinker sniff at every nook and cranny, his tail an exclamation mark of happiness. The end is in sight. I decided that after the game, I will tell Coach Peter about Charlie. If the Freezers win the Cup, I'll tell him immediately. If the Freezers lose, I might give it a few days. But either way, the secrecy has an expiration date.

I will have to deal with telling the PCHL next, but with the season over, what could they do? Relationships are frowned upon but not formally banned. I am more worried about telling my dad, but I have to believe when he sees how happy Charlie makes me, he'll come around. Maybe he'll even be excited. After all, the last person I ever expected to bring home was someone he could talk hockey with.

I hold open the Coliseum doors for Stinker, who trots in like he owns the place. I tip my iced coffee at Zane, who makes a face at me from his Zamboni. Following in Stinker's wake, I head for my office, giving a friendly nod to everyone I pass. Chad and Vlad hold their hands out for high fives. Only Blake won't meet my eyes. I don't think too much of it. Blake surprised everyone with his metamorphosis after the infamous benching, but he still isn't a ray of sunshine. He is probably focused on the upcoming game.

Then I check my email.

Tricia Cornwallis's name sits at the top of my inbox. I thrill at the sight, even though I assume *The Oregonian* journalist just has additional questions about the pre-Kerry Cup press conference. I already received three such emails from her.

That is why, when I open the message, I don't understand what I am seeing at first. Why is Tricia Cornwallis sending me a random photo of two people in a pool? Has she been hacked?

Then I realize. My whole body goes numb. I take an automatic sip of my coffee, but it tastes like cold concrete in my mouth. I can barely breathe.

My phone buzzes. Tricia's name is on the screen.

I dully lift the phone to my ear.

"I wanted you to know that I am encouraging my fellow journalists not to run these photos that Mr. Brodie has been pedaling all over town," comes Tricia's clipped voice. "Am I correct in my assumption you were unaware that they were being taken, Ms. Green?"

"I didn't know," I tell her. My voice comes out faint and far away, exactly how I feel.

"I thought not. Unfortunately, others do not share my scruples. I believe Mr. Brodie has gotten significant interest from the tabloids. *The Globe* and *TMZ* will have it up by tomorrow at the latest." There is a lengthy pause on the line. "I'm sorry I could not do more."

I hang up the phone with clammy hands. I manage to shakily cross the rest of the distance to my office and sink into my chair before my knees give out. Stinker cocks his head up at me, his bushy eyebrows high. He can tell something is wrong.

All of Charlie's and my careful planning. All of the effort we put into not being seen by anyone. We drove three hours outside of Portland just to have a normal date together. All of it flushed straight down the drain with a single photo. How did that smarmy nematode Kyle Brodie catch us in Florence, of all places? I don't know, and I don't have time to figure it out. There are forty-eight hours left before 12,000 fans descend on the building to watch Charlie's and my teams go head-to-head, and Kyle Brodie has just hit my life with a giant wrecking ball.

I force myself to pick the phone back up and make another call. Even the warm sound of Charlie's voice caressing my ear does not make me feel better.

"Hey, babe, what's up?" he asks, completely unaware of the punch coming straight at his face.

"They know," is all I can manage to get out.

"What? Who knows what?" Charlie's tone flips to concern. "Is everything okay?"

"No," I tell him, hitting forward on Tricia's message. "Check your email."

I wait. Then his voice returns, much lower. "Oh."

"Uh-huh," I continue numbly. "Anyway, I was just calling to tell you it's been nice knowing you and I'm moving to Belize."

"Anna—"

"Actually, where is Belize?" I am too hysterical to remember. "Is that in South America? That might not be far enough. Maybe Bali? Bali's pretty far, right?"

"Uh, I think so?"

"Bali, it is. You can come if you want. I know you really like Portland, though."

"Anna," Charlie interrupts firmly. "I am so sorry."

I shrug, helpless. "You didn't take those photos."

"No one should have taken those photos," he tells me gruffly. "That was a private encounter between two consenting adults. It's nobody's business but ours."

I blink back tears. I feel violated. One of the highlights of my year is about to be permanently inked onto the internet for all to see, just because Kyle Brodie wants to make a few bucks. Anybody who looks me up until the end of time will see this. It is hard enough to be a woman in the world of sports already.

"The league won't see it that way," I say, fear spiking through me in icy shards. This is the polar opposite of the HR-friendly way I was planning on telling the PCHL about our relationship.

"Anna, listen to me." Charlie's voice is a soft blanket around me. "Have you been conspiring to rig the Kerry Cup?"

"No." I sniff.

"Great, neither have I. Problem solved, case closed. They can yell and wave their arms, but we've done nothing wrong. That reporter, on the other hand, is going to get shoved down my garbage disposal." His anger rumbles over the line.

A shaky smile spreads across my face. Charlie can always make me feel better, no matter what. "Let's wait till after the Cup. I don't think the league will love it if we become convicted murderers on top of everything."

"Fine, I can wait," he grumbles. His voice turns serious again. "Anna, are you going to be okay? Do you want me to come over there?"

Stinker perks up beside me, thumping his tail. I glance toward my doorway. My body goes numb again.

"Gotta go, Alison. I'll call you later," I tell Charlie, hanging up over his confused protests.

I turn to face the door. "Hi, Dad."

Coach Peter hovers in the doorway, studying his shoes.

There is a line between his eyes that only ever appears when the Freezers are down in the third period. I feel my insides crumple.

"Is it true?" he asks.

I can only nod, hating that this is the way my dad finds out about the best relationship of my life. I stare at the ugly carpeting, wishing it would swallow me whole. No such luck.

Coach Peter strides over to Stinker, looking anywhere but at me. The dog thwacks his tail furiously and drools on the coach's shoes, happily oblivious.

I sigh. "I was going to tell—"

"I just got off a call with the PCHL. They got a very unusual email forward this morning."

I wince. Everything is going wrong. "They're upset?"

"Upset? They're livid. They threatened to suspend both teams. Forgo the finals and just give the cup to the third best team by default."

"What?" my jaw drops to the floor. This is so much worse than what I expected, even in my nightmares where the PCHL chases me around with knives. "That's crazy. They can't do that. That's an insane overreaction. I'll call Michael, let me talk to him—"

"I took care of it."

"You did?" I sag in relief. My dad has been my protector all my life. I should have known he'd step up in my time of need.

"Of course. I told them it would be crazy to cancel the final when we're so close, that you'd made a horrible mistake, and that whatever relationship you had with that

Shredder was over. They've paused the suspension for now, but I think they'll feel better if you issue a public apology."

I stare at my father like I've never seen him before, my heart closing up in my chest. "You want me to issue an apology?" I ask, incredulous.

"I think it would help. They need to see that you feel bad for what you did."

"What I *did*?" I am seething. Whatever guilt or fear I thought I'd feel if the PCHL found out about my relationship is nothing compared to how I feel about my father branding me as some kind of hockey jezebel. Like I should be wearing a scarlet jersey for daring to go on a date.

Coach Peter finally notices that I don't look particularly apologetic. "Anna, we're two days away from the Kerry Cup, for crying out loud. This is our chance to finally show people what this team is made of."

"I know that," I snap. "But I don't see what that has to do with a private relationship that has nothing to do with my job. Do you really think the old men of the Pacific Coast Hockey League should get to dictate what I do with my personal life? I mean, come on, Dad." I look at him pleading.

"I do when it jeopardizes our team's future."

I can't believe it. "You think I don't care about this team?"

Coach Peter squares his shoulders, finally looking me in the eye. "You've got a funny way of showing it if you've been running around with that Shredder menace."

I swallow hard, betrayal scraping my insides. I always

knew Charlie would be a tough sell, but because I am Coach Peter's little girl. Not because of this.

I take a step toward him. "I have done everything for this team. I've worked early mornings. I've worked late nights. I've poured myself into boosting ticket sales even when you've ignored all of my ideas. I've spent hours coaching your star player to take his foot out of his mouth. My life is the Freezers."

"I know that," my father argues, "so I don't understand why you had to risk all that by lollygagging around with the enemy."

I am so upset I don't even stop to mock my dad for using the word "lollygagging."

"Because it has nothing to do with him being the enemy. Charlie Haskell is a good man. He supports me, he believes in me, and he never questioned my loyalty to the Freezers."

"I'm not questioning your loyalty. I just think you made a mistake—"

"It's not a mistake! I'm in love with him!" My declaration shocks both of us into silence. I didn't expect to say it. I haven't even admitted to myself that I feel it. But once the words are out there, I know it is true. I am in love with Charlie.

Despite all my fears and anxieties, Charlie stands by me, never wavering once. He brings out the best in me. My dad may have known me for my whole life, but he doesn't see me the way Charlie does. He sees only what he wants to see, and maybe that is my fault for hiding so much from him. But I refuse to hide anymore.

"I'm sorry I didn't tell you. I really am. But the thing I'm the most sorry for is that after everything we've been through, my dad didn't stand up for me when he should have." I sit back down heavily in my chair and point to the door. "Now, if you'll excuse me, I have a lot of work to do to get my team ready for the Kerry Cup."

Chapter 37

I'm Afraid That's All We Have Time For

ANNA

"So they're not backing down?" Charlie asks.

"No," I fume, glaring at the computer like it has personally insulted me.

"Shit," Charlie agrees.

The Kerry Cup final is tomorrow night, and both of us should be focused on the game. Instead, ever since those pool photos splashed across the front page of every tabloid Kyle could sell them to, I have been fighting tooth and nail to keep the PCHL from canceling the Cup altogether.

The League is stubbornly sticking to their demand that our relationship end—or else they will suspend the final and award the cup to the team with the third-best record: the Tallahassee Eclipse.

I point out again and again that there is no actual rule

against player-manager relationships, and that Charlie and I have done nothing wrong. But Coach Peter remains unsupportive, and the press battered the league all season thanks to the players' bad behavior that led to the penalty and assault scandals. The League decided to choose our relationship as the battle they could not lose.

I retrieve my computer and hold it up for Charlie to read the email I just received. Michael has quickly become Charlie's least favorite league official and second least favorite person on the planet, after demon-incarnate Kyle Brodie. He skims the novel-length missive, and his eyebrows nearly shoot off his forehead.

"Are they serious? They're citing page 273 of the league handbook? I didn't even know the handbook went to page 273."

I roll my eyes. "Since there's no actual rule against player-manager relationships, they've decided to make something up. They found a random line that implies our inter-team relationship is a 'failure to preserve the integrity of the matches' and allows them to suspend the final. I'm pretty sure that page in the book is about stadium maintenance." I shove the computer away again and bury my face in my hands. "I don't know what to do. The game is tomorrow. I really think they might do it."

"I'll quit," he declares. "Fuck them. This isn't Colonial New England, and they don't get to tell us what to do with our lives. I'll quit in protest." He looks up to see what I think of his valiant and noble sacrifice, but I shake my head.

"You're the Shredders' best player. They need you."

"You sure?" he jokes bitterly. "If I let the Freezers win, your dad will probably start to like me. We'll kill two birds with one puck. I'm getting sick of it all anyway. Being a pro isn't worth it if it means I can't be with you."

I give him a sad smile. "Neither of us is quitting. Too many people rely on us. The whole point is that our relationship hasn't hurt anybody. I refuse to prove them right and do anything to hurt either team's future."

"What do we do, then?" he asks me.

"I don't know," I whisper, eyes watery.

"We can ignore them and hope they just drop it," he suggests without much optimism. "It really would be crazy for them to cancel the final over this. They'll change their minds."

"But what if they don't?" I ask.

"I guess, maybe we . . ."

He trails off, working up the nerve to say it. I look up at him.

"Maybe we what?" I ask.

"Maybe we break up." He forces the words out, each one falling between us like a stone.

"Oh," I say, sitting back. It is as if the light winks out in my eyes.

"After the season is over, we can talk again. Decide what we want to do going forward." The words come out in a rush, but they sound hollow.

"Sure." I give a small nod, my voice sounding just as hollow. I pull my hands back from Charlie's.

I stand, wanting to be anywhere but in the apartment of the man I can't have. I know Charlie is right to break up with me. Of course, he is right. There is no other solution that doesn't end in one or both of our teams getting flushed right down the toilet. All my dad's hard work doesn't deserve to be flushed down to the sewer rats.

I know it is the right thing. But then why does it hurt so much? Part of me wants him to rail and scream and fight for me, no matter how futile. He fought for me through our whole relationship, overcoming every obstacle in our path. Until now.

I hear the finality in his words. We won't be able to just get back together after the final. Not if we cave like this. We will have to deal with the same problems all over again come next season. This is the end.

And I haven't even told him that I love him.

I grab my laptop and beeline for the exit. Charlie stands but doesn't try to stop me. I reach the door and pause for one last look back.

Charlie looks at me like a lost puppy. I feel the need to say something, but I have no idea what I can even say.

"I'll email the league," I offer lamely, "but we'll probably have to address this at the pre-game press conference tomorrow." Charlie nods, his face turning serious. I hate not seeing any laughter in his eyes.

"I'll take care of it," he tells me.

And that is it. I force myself to tear my eyes away, turn the knob, and step into the chill of the hallway. One step, and we are done.

I stand at the end of the hallway for a moment, watching Charlie's door. Just in case he changes his mind and comes after me. But the door doesn't open. Finally, I turn away.

I stand off to the side as the press buzzes around me like a swarm of obnoxious hornets. I didn't sleep a single second last night. There isn't enough foundation in the world to make me look less like warmed-over death.

I sigh, waiting for the press to finally stop jabbering at each other and take their seats. After emailing Michael and the PCHL to inform them of Charlie's and my decision, I delegated as much of the remaining press conference duties as I could. If I have to be out there glad-handing reporters as they ask me about Charlie and whether or not I have a bikini body, I will draw blood. Plus, I have barely spoken to my dad since our argument, which only makes me feel worse. At least this way, I can suffer silently on the sidelines.

Finally, Tricia Cornwallis sweeps into her customary front-row seat, and the rest of the press follow suit. I turn back and nod. My dad and the Freezers file past me, most unable to look me in the eye. Only Leo gives me a quick sympathetic nod. Blake practically sprints past. I have to use all my publicist tricks—including picturing the men doing Olympic figure skating—just to keep my face neutral.

I slip for just a second when I glance over to see the Shredders taking their seats. My eyes snap straight to

Charlie's blue-eyed gaze like they are magnetized. I force myself to look away, and I swear he winces as I do.

The room bursts into its usual frenzied cacophony of chaos. A number of reporters mutter over their phones as they read some new update, probably more of Kyle's photos of me and Charlie. There is that look in their hyena eyes, the one they get right before they go in for the kill. Charlie points to Tricia, but before she can give voice to her question, he holds up his hand. My heart clenches.

"Hi, everyone," he begins, voice ragged, "I figured I might spare you the trouble of asking some of your questions by just giving you the answer." He clears his throat and looks down at the small, worn notecard in his hands. "I can confirm that Anna Green and I were in a relationship, and that our relationship has . . . ended. Anna is an incredible woman and an incredible publicist and at no point did our relationship compromise the integrity of her work or mine. Nevertheless, we apologize for the pain that our secrecy has caused. We want nothing more than a good final, and we hope everyone can keep their attention on the game where it belongs. Thank you."

His voice cracks, and he clears his throat again. Refusing to acknowledge the teary sheen in his eyes, he turns back to Tricia. "Did I about cover it?"

"Actually," she begins, "my question is for Mr. Tyler. Mr. Tyler, do you care to comment on the pictures that were just released that appear to show you breaking and entering, and quite frankly obliterating, Ms. Anna Green's apartment?"

Every single head swivels toward Blake, who sits with his mouth agape, looking like a computer program that has just crashed. There is half a second of utter silence, then the room explodes in another deluge of noise. Every single reporter stands, shouting at the top of their lungs. More than one of them asking, "And why did you water her plants?"

My mouth goes dry, and I dive for my phone. Sure enough, Kyle has just done another photo dump, but this one isn't me and Charlie. This is "Blake Tyler Behaving Badly." I reel. After everything that has happened in the last forty-eight hours, I barely even remember the condo break-in, let alone comprehend that Blake was behind it. Blake, of all people? Why?

I shove my swirling emotions aside. I only have room to do one thing right now, and that is my job.

"Thank you, everybody. I'm afraid that's all we have time for," I say, diving into the fray and using my loudest camp counselor voice. "We've got a big game to prepare for, so we need you all to get going." They stare at me. I stare back, folding my arms. "Now."

Thunderous chair scraping and complaining fill the room, and I turn away, refusing to look at Charlie or Blake. I am determined to make it through this damned Kerry Cup before more shit hits the fan.

Chapter 38

I Am Not a Duck

BLAKE

It was supposed to be the biggest game of my life, and I turned it into a complete and utter disaster.

Honestly, I am surprised I even make it to the ice. Anna turned into some kind of Publicity Hulk after the press conference, forcing the reporters to retreat while somehow simultaneously sweet-talking the very thin-lipped PCHL officials into allowing the game to move forward as scheduled.

I try to talk to her, although I have no idea what I am going to say. But Coach Peter grabs me, shoves me in the locker room, then straight onto the bench with barely a word.

Having the break-in come out like this feels like a physical punch to the stomach. I am dazed and winded, but my biggest feeling is relief. The break-in has been eating away at me like a worm in my soul ever since I did it. It got so awful that I ended up shoving my grandmother's puck into my own side table drawer to not have to think about it. Knowing I will get rightfully punished feels less painful than continuing to punish myself in secret. All I want to do now is make up for my epic mistakes.

But instead, I am watching this game unfold without me.

Second period ticks away as the Freezers' second-line offense loses control of the puck *again*. The Shredders lead the game by one point, but if the Freezers keep bumbling like this, every single Shredders player will get the chance to score a hat trick. Blindfolded.

Coach Peter's jaw tightens even further. The worry line between his eyes has lodged itself on his forehead with the first Shredders' goal and never left. Despite telling me he would "deal with me later", he hasn't let me out on the ice.

As the Shredders whip past us with the puck, I throw myself at Coach Peter, practically begging. "Come on, Coach, please put me in. For the team." The Coach doesn't make eye contact, but he does finally shout out for a line change, waving me, Chad, and Vlad onto the ice. Finally. I shoot off the bench like it is a circus cannon, and within a minute the puck is back with the Freezers where it belongs.

I execute a quick pass to Chad and race up the ice, readying to catch the puck again. But Chad passes to Vlad. Lightning quick, I readjust my position, dodging the Shredders' defense.

Vlad scans the ice, his eyes skimming right over me as he slaps the puck back to Chad. I swear into my helmet. Chad tries for a quick shot, weaving around the defense, but the angle is all wrong and Tony bats it aside like a pesky fruit fly.

The buzzer sounds. I scream.

One more period to go and we are still losing by two points.

Not to mention that my team decided I am invisible.

Oh, and there is the small fact that everybody now knows I have committed a felony.

Utter disaster.

The mood in the Freezers locker room, with only twenty minutes left in the game and the Shredders ahead, is downright dire. On any other day, for any other game, it would be the perfect time for a rallying motivational speech straight out of the movies. Coach Peter would set a fire in our hearts, and then we would leap to our feet—cheering and united as one—ready to take on the world.

But this isn't that movie, and that's not what the exhausted, sweat-drenched Freezers are getting. Instead, they get me.

"What the hell, guys?" I storm into the locker room, oozing fury. "We suck this game. In case you didn't notice, we're losing the Kerry Cup. To the freaking Shredders."

I glare at the nineteen other players I've finally begun to call my friends. Not one of them acknowledges me.

Chad turns to Vlad. "Hey, Vlad," he asks loudly. "Did you hear something?"

"Yes—I mean—no," Vlad says. "I mean, I just heard you asking me if I heard something. But I didn't hear anything else."

Chad rolls his eyes. "You got there in the end, buddy. I didn't hear anything either. Anybody else hear anything?"

There is a chorus of nos around the room. Leo doesn't say no, but he doesn't stop them either. Chad stands up, deliberately bumping into me as he makes his way over to grab his water bottle.

He picks it up and puts it to his lips, only to have me punch it out of his hand. Water sprays down Chad's chin.

"Fuck, Blake," Chad sputters.

"Oh yeah? You can hear me now?" I ask.

Chad grits his teeth and lunges for me. Leo leaps to his feet and grabs the furious winger, holding him back.

"Let me go, bro," Chad hollers.

"Why aren't you passing to me?" I challenge, getting in Chad's face.

Chad squirms, but Leo's grip is iron. The rest of the team is on their feet, surrounding us.

"Why aren't you passing to me?" I ask again. "We're gonna lose."

"Oh, I don't know," Chad finally spits. "Maybe because you broke into Anna's house? Because you're a psycho who only thinks about himself and that's never going to change?"

I step back, almost as stunned as if Chad head-butted me. I know what I did to Anna was bad. But I always thought it was just between us. Well, Anna and me and Kyle, the putrid cockroach who blackmailed me into silence, then released the photos anyway. I didn't give the team a second thought when I did all of that, which seems to be exactly what Chad is mad about.

Leo loosens his grip on Chad, who shoves Leo off and pushes his way through the crowd.

"You should be suspended, man," Chad mutters, slumping down on a bench and glaring at the wall. Vlad retrieves Chad's water bottle and joins him.

"You guys think I'm a psycho?" I ask meekly.

Leo sighs, returning to his seat. "You *are* a psycho. For a minute, we thought maybe you were our psycho. But teammates don't do shit like that to each other. And Anna's our teammate, too."

I scuff at the floor, feeling two inches tall. Kyle isn't the putrid cockroach. I am the putrid cockroach. Or we both are, which is almost worse. I decided to change, but I haven't made amends for who I was before. I didn't appreciate how much my actions impacted everybody around me.

I have been playing hockey for over a decade, but this is the first time I know how it feels to be a part of a team.

"You're right," I mutter. "I'm sorry." I glance up and do a double-take. Instead of ignoring me, all nineteen pairs of eyes stare at me with identical expressions of surprise.

"Can you say that again?" Chad asks. "Much, much louder?"

I take one of my deep, calming breaths. "I'm sorry. You guys are right. It was selfish and stupid and maybe a little psycho. I did that a long time ago, when I was trying to be somebody else. But I don't want that anymore. I want to be a Freezer. Can you forgive me?"

The Freezers look at each other, uncertain.

"That depends. Are you going to apologize to Anna?" Leo asks.

"Yes, absolutely," I promise. "As soon as the game is over."

All eyes in the room turn to Chad, who is staring intensely at his water bottle.

"Chad and Vlad," I ask, "can I still be on the Green Line?"

They look at each other, communicating in their telepathic bro-twin way. Standing simultaneously, they turn to face Blake.

"We only have one thing to say to you," Chad says somberly. He walks forward until he is toe to toe—kiss or kill distance—from my face.

"If we're gonna be the kings this season, we need to see your inner Queen." He hands me his water bottle.

By the time Coach Peter and Assistant Coach Sylvia walks into the locker room, the entire team is up on the benches singing Queen's "Don't Stop Me Now" at the top of our lungs. Me, Chad, and Vlad are in the center, doing our frog dance and belting into our fake mics.

Coach Peter takes in the scene, amused, while we finish the song. The line between his eyes relaxes slightly.

"Well," he says, when we finally finish, "I was working on something awesome and inspiring to get you out of that slump, but honestly, I don't think you need me to. So, let's get back out there and kick some ass."

The team cheers.

"Welcome back to the Kerry Cup with your host, Ike the Mic. I'm telling ya, folks, the Shredders might be up by two points coming into third period, but if you think you know where this game is going, get back in that buffet line because it's time to think again."

The Freezers burn through third period. The whole team is on fire. Me, Chad, and Vlad own the ice, moving in sync like telepathic bro triplets, getting the puck away from the Shredders on a breakout, and scoring almost immediately. We need just two more goals to win. The game is on.

The Green Line cycles the puck along the boards, whipping the puck backward to each other in passes so fast we nearly break the sound barrier.

"Well, butter my bagel and call me Betty. Look at how fast that puck is going, folks. I can't even keep track of it. Do not try this at home," Ike booms.

Chad races the puck over the blue line and shoots it back to me to take it to the net. Defender Quentin forces me to pivot over to the boards, but I'm not going to give up that easily. I fly along the wall, making Quentin chase me. Chad and Vlad hollers at me to "wheel," and I sail around the back of the net.

I clear the net and take my shot. Tony zooms forward

but isn't fast enough. The puck whips past him and into the net.

"It's in! That's a goal, folks! With minutes to go, the Freezers have tied the game! Holy guacamole, I did not see that coming."

The fans roar in the stands. Queen pours from the speakers. The Freezers cheer. I scan the crowd for any flashes of Mabeline.

That is the only reason I spot the angry blur skating toward me. There is one other person who would have taken Anna's break-in to heart. Someone I was protected from while stuck on the bench, but not anymore.

Charlie barrels into me at full speed, slamming me into the boards and knocking the breath right out of my body.

"You asshole!" he roars, pummeling me with glove-blunted fists. "You broke into her apartment. What's wrong with you? Why did you do that?"

The question is valid, but my newfound sense of Zen does not extend to letting my nemesis pound me into the ice. I bend low and ram into Charlie, sending the two of us skidding. I pummel Charlie right back, spitting out words between gloved punches.

"None." *Punch.* "Of." *Punch.* "Your." *Punch.* "Business."

We sail across the ice in what looks like a hug. Henri the referee trails us across the rink, shouting in annoyed French.

Charlie shoves me off of him, and we glare, circling each other. I vaguely register the crowd chanting. They do love a fight. I regret that my date with Mabeline ended before she could teach me what seal clubbing entails.

Charlie lunges, and I swing away. "None of my business?" Charlie growls. "Of course it's my business, you leaky refrigerator."

"Oh, yeah?" I try and fail to think of a shredding-related insult. "No, it's not, because you're not even dating anymore."

Charlie flings himself toward me again, tipping my balance and sending the two of us crashing onto the ice. We roll across the rink and right into Henri.

Time seems to slow as Charlie and I watch Henri teeter, arms flapping before falling backward.

I close my eyes, waiting to die, but Henri never hits the ice. Instead, he gently thunks into an incredibly tall Shredder, who carefully sets him back upright.

Henri gives the player a stiff nod, then turns back to Charlie and me, sitting on the ice staring up at him like terrified toddlers.

"Are you done, you enfants? Zeese is a major pénalité," Henri declares in a thick accent. "Five meen-oots in the box. Both of you. Zut alors! Imbéciles!"

"Five minutes?" Charlie cries. "That's the rest of the game."

"Yeah, and both of us?" I groan, hauling myself to my feet. "He's the one who started it. Just send him."

Henri gets up in my face so fast I don't even register he has moved until he is spitting on my nose.

The referee unleashes a stream of such rapid French that I can only blink back. I catch words like "merde," "dégage," and "connard," which I think means duck, but based on the context, most definitely does not.

"I'm not a duck," I argue lamely.

Henri points toward the penalty box. "Both of you. Vite."

We turn and trudge toward the penalty box. I feel Charlie's glare burning into my back. I can't believe I am about to spend the last five minutes of the Kerry Cup final stuck in a plastic box next to my mortal enemy. My only shot at playing again is if we go into overtime, unless Charlie kills me first.

A lot could happen in five minutes.

Chapter 39

Get Over Here and Let Me Punch You

CHARLIE

A banged-up piece of plexiglass is the only thing sparing Blake Tyler's life right now. I glare into the Freezers penalty box, willing the plexiglass to melt.

How dare Blake hurt Anna like that, then have the gall to say I am the problem. He deserves to be marched onto a pirate ship and made to walk the plank. He deserves to be shot into space without a suit. He deserves to be fed to a pack of angry squirrels.

The last one makes me smile.

Blake gives me a funny look. "Why are you smiling? Are you happy we're missing the rest of the game?"

"I'm smiling because I'm picturing your elaborate death," I shoot back. "And my team's doing just fine."

I glance at the ice. To be honest, play has been sluggish since we were banished to the sin bin. With the minutes ticking down to the end of the championship game, neither team has managed to regroup and break the tie. I can only hope that the Shredders will push the game into overtime so I can get back onto the ice. I like the idea of a sudden-death game against Blake.

Henri swings by every minute to mutter more rapid French in our direction. Superfans, Nick and Nate's seats are way too close for comfort. I am pretty sure they were livestreaming the entire penalty, hurling insults that I couldn't hear.

This isn't the end of the Kerry Cup that I pictured. My fantasies involved more winning, grabbing Anna, and dipping her into a passionate kiss as I received MVP.

I look toward her spot in the stands, but I feel a pang as I remember that even if we do win—and by some miracle I still get MVP after this debacle—there will be no dipping and no kissing. Me and Anna have broken up, just like Blake said. I made that sacrifice to protect her, not wanting to force her to choose between me and the job she loves so much. But that doesn't make it any easier. It is honestly a miracle I managed to play this well.

I feel held together by duct tape and a determination not to let my team down any more than I already have. Given my current position, even that isn't going so well.

But when I saw Blake score and flash that stupid dimply grin, I completely lost it.

Honestly, I'd like to lose it again, if it wasn't for that piece of plexiglass.

Blake shifts on the bench. The surly man seems uncomfortable with my glare.

"Sorry," I spit. "Am I bothering you?"

"You are," Blake growls.

"Good," I snap. "Then it's working." Blake turns back to face the game, but I can't let it go. "I can't believe you broke into her condo. What kind of a person does that?"

Blake studies his knees. "She had something of mine."

"Oh sure. That's a great excuse for a felony."

"Why do you care?" Blake complains. "You broke up with her."

"We broke up so that the league didn't suspend the final over those photos. You should actually be thanking me that we're even here at all."

Blake grimaces. "I tried to get him not to publish those. That's why he sold the ones of me, too."

"Wait, what? What did you have to do with it?" I ask, confused.

Blake's gaze drops from his knees to the floor.

My eyes go wide as it all comes together. "You? You got him to take those pictures?" Before the thought has fully registered, I am on my feet, slamming my fists into the divider. Plexiglass be damned, I will pulverize Blake into hamburger meat and grill him. The man is about to become a smashburger.

Ike's voice booms, "Look at that, folks, the fight seems to be continuing in the penalty box. Good golly, Miss Molly, I haven't seen that in a Portland minute. Reminds me of the time that . . ."

"Get over here and let me punch you!" I scream. "What

the fuck is wrong with you? You completely violated both of our privacies. You had no right to take those pictures."

"I'm sorry, okay?" Blake screams back, cowering despite the unbendable plastic between us. "I guess I was maybe a little bit jealous."

"Oh, a little bit jealous? That's your excuse? Write a nasty comment online next time, asshole."

My pounding on the plexiglass slows. Watching Blake snivel without being able to unleash any actual punches or squirrels on him loses its appeal. I give the plastic one last half-hearted kick, then sink back onto the bench, defeated.

"You cost me my relationship with the love of my life," I tell Blake. Saying it brings back all the pain of the last twenty-four hours. The cuts on my heart reopen and bleed.

Blake glances at me. "Look, I've done a lot of growing and meditating since all of that," he starts. I snort. "I'm sorry, but I did not cost you your relationship." He finishes firmly.

"Are you seriously saying that to me right now?" I ask, incredulous. "If you hadn't gotten that reporter to take those pictures, we'd still be together."

"Maybe, but you chose to break up. The pictures didn't break you up," Blake reasons.

"They nearly cost us our jobs. They nearly cost us this game."

Blake shrugs. "Yeah, but wouldn't that have happened anyway as soon as somebody found out? It just happened to be me. You're the one who broke up with her." He turns back to the game, and I just barely hear him mutter, "I wouldn't have."

"That's not—you're completely—how dare you—" I sputter. But I have a sinking feeling in my stomach so awful it makes me nauseous. Is the obnoxious idiot Blake actually right?

"I did it for her," I say, but it sounds weak. She didn't ask to break up. I felt so guilty for the pain I was causing, and so scared she would suggest breaking up, that I said it first.

I chose a sport I'm not even sure I want to play anymore over the girl who lights up my life like the diamond I dream of buying her. Anna was right from the very beginning. I take the easy path. I hate myself.

"What do I do?" I say to myself, reeling.

Blake eyes me. "You love her?"

"I wasn't talking to you, stick head," I snap. "But yes."

"Then prove it," he says, ignoring the insult. "Prove it and get her back."

Although every fiber of my being resists admitting it, Blake knows what he is talking about. I am in the penalty box for two infractions today. One against Blake, which is still totally worth it, and one against Anna. That one just might be the biggest mistake of my life. The second the game ends, I need to figure out how to win her back.

The buzzer sounds, signaling the end of the third period. The score remains three to three. Me and Blake will have another chance to face off in sudden death overtime.

I glare through the scratchy plexiglass. "We're still going to beat you," I say.

Blake shrugs, meeting my eyes. "Not if we beat you first."

We regard each other with begrudging respect.

Henri skates back over, looking wary. "Are you going to fight again as soon as I let you out?" he asks.

"No," We dutifully chorus.

"Then go. Get out of my sight." He opens the boxes and mutters, "Crétins."

We clamber back onto the ice. We stare at each other for a tense moment. Then I nod and turn to skate back to my team. Blake does the same. Henri sags in relief.

I reach my bench to find my team already huddled. "Listen, guys, I'm sorry," I say. "I don't know where my head's been at. I've been letting you down. But it stops now, I swear."

Coach Ryan steps forward, eyes blazing. "You're goddamn right it stops now—"

Gilly's giant hand on his shoulder cuts him off. "No," Gilly says. "We're the ones who are sorry. We made you hide a piece of yourself from us. That's not what real team-mates do."

Quentin nods, joining Gilly. "That sucks they made you break up just to play. Not cool."

Alex steps forward, too. "We've got you. Whatever you need."

I can only manage a nod, my throat clenched and tears in my eyes. This right here is what I love about hockey. Bringing people together. Suddenly, I know exactly what to do after the game is over. But first things first.

"So, boss," Gilly says, "what now?"

I grin. "Try to win this thing?"

The Shredders cheer.

Chapter 40

Are You . . . Paying Attention to the Game?

ANNA

"Anna, sweetie, you are going to break my hand," Alison says through gritted teeth.

"Sorry, sorry!" I force myself to let go. I've never been so nervous watching a game. Ever since the press conference, I've been in a daze. The breakup aches like someone amputated a limb, my body mourning a piece of itself. Then on top of that, to learn that Blake, of all people, trashed my apartment. Why? Did I do something? Is he crazy? I can barely process it all.

I wasn't sure I could watch the championship final, but Alison nobly volunteered to watch it with me. My friend even manages to keep her eye rolls and bored sighing to a minimum.

I try to stay focused, watching the game mostly through my camera. I snap photos of Mabeline, down in front sporting ombre red and blue hair now and a very low-cut DIY Freezers jersey jumpsuit. I even catch a few of Nick and Nate, leaping up and down in the stands, pounding their orange and teal painted chests, and waving their equipment.

Eddie and Ramona sit below us in matching Freezer red and navy pom-pom hats that Ramona knitted, turning around every so often to offer comforting statistics.

"The Los Angeles Kings were eighth seed when they won the Stanley Cup in 2012," Eddie tells me as they settle in at the start of the game. I try to smile.

Then when the second period ends with the Shredders up by two, he says, "You know the Toronto Maple Leafs came back from 3-0 to win the Cup in 1942."

Ramona smacks him. "That was back in '42! Is that supposed to make her feel better?"

"And that Kings' player Jarret Stoll married a sports reporter. He won the Cup."

Ramona smacks Eddie again. Eddie holds up his hands in defense. "What? I'm just saying."

"Thanks, Eddie," I say, although Ramona is right. None of this is making me feel better. Every time the Freezers stumble, and the Shredders get ahead, my heart lurches with worry. But every time Charlie loses the puck or misses a shot, my heart lurches all over again. My heart has no idea how to react to Blake, who is the Freezers' best chance for victory and also the man who broke my patio door, so it gives me what feels like a prolonged heart attack all game.

Until Charlie charges Blake toward the end of third period, and my heart nearly stops altogether.

"What a game, folks! This is turning out to be a real bloodbath," Ike calls out.

That is when I start squeezing Alison's hand, and I haven't let up for the entire penalty.

My mind races as the five-minute overtime period begins. I don't know what to feel about Charlie attacking Blake. I know he did it for me, but we agreed to break up. It was Charlie's idea. Taking it out on Blake, even if he did something bad, doesn't change anything. I wish we found a way to fight the PCHL, but we didn't.

I need to let it go, and so does Charlie. Except that my eyes keep seeking him out on the ice, tracing his broad muscles as he races down the rink. I watch his blue eyes flash as he lines up a shot and chucks it.

Leo dives for the puck, and Alison tenses beside me. The goalie gets there just in time and blocks the shot. Alison relaxes.

I stare at my friend. "Are you . . . paying attention to the game?" I ask.

"What?" Alison jerks back, trying not to look guilty. "No. Of course not. Hockey's still stupid."

I study Alison, noticing she is wearing red. Alison never wears red. "Oh my god," I realize. "You went on your date with Leo."

"No, I didn't."

"Yes, you did. You did, and now you love hockey."

"No, I don't!" Alison denies, but her face turns as red as her outfit.

I pull my friend into a side hug. "This is so great," I squeal. "You're going to come with me to every game next season."

Eddie leans back over. "Justin Braun from the Canucks married that woman from *MasterChef*. She almost won."

"What have I done?" Alison groans.

I squeeze my friend even harder. At least love conquers all sometimes, even if it doesn't work out for me. I try not to think of all the double dates me and Alison could have gone on with Leo and Charlie.

If nothing else, dating Charlie taught me the importance of stepping outside of my comfort zone. I promise myself I'll keep doing it, whether that means a new hobby or a new boyfriend. Maybe I'll try rock climbing.

The buzzer sounds again. My attention snaps back to the game. Both teams pour their hearts into the overtime period, playing harder than they have through the whole game. But the underdog Freezers and the powerhouse Shredders are too evenly matched. The game still sits at a tie.

I gulp. That means only one thing.

"There you have it, ladies and gents. This game's going to end in a shootout. Leaping lizards! I can't remember the last time that happened. What a night," Ike booms.

The energy in the stadium crackles with electricity. Twelve-thousand fans lean in as one. Silent and staring.

Below on the ice, the three shooters for each side assemble, faces as solemn as though they are about to duel. Charlie, Alex, and Gilly for the Shredders. Blake, Chad, and Vlad for the Freezers. Leo and Tony take their places in their goals.

I think I might pass out. I glance over and notice Alison looks the exact same way. I offer my hand, and Alison squeezes it gratefully.

Chapter 41

Give It Your Best Shot, Stick Head

CHARLIE

Alex is up first. He grips his stick so tightly his knuckles turn white, and it vibrates from his shaking. Gilly subtly steps behind him.

I swing around to the front, giving Alex no choice but to look me in the eyes. "Hey," I say. "You've got this. Don't even think about it. Just try to miss Leo."

Alex nods robotically. "Just try to miss Leo," he mumbles. "Just try to miss Leo."

I slap him on the back and send a small prayer to any gods who are listening.

Alex steps forward, and the stadium goes deadly quiet. All eyes on him. He really does look like he might pass out.

Then he bends low and whips toward the goal like he's been doing this all his life. I cheer. Leo moves with him, anticipating the shot, and I squeeze my stick for dear life. But at the last second, Alex pivots, dragging the puck back with his stick, and skates around a shocked Leo to score. A perfect fake out.

The stadium roars.

Little Alex Gonzalez zooms back toward his team, looking like he could fly. We pile on him in a big bear hug.

But the game isn't over.

Chad steps up to the puck next, looking like this is just another practice and not the biggest game of the season. He casually skates toward the goal, picking up speed as he goes, snaking from left to right and back. Tony stays on him the whole time, watching like a hawk. I wonder if Chad plans to deke at the last second and fake Tony out, but no. We both realize what he is doing too late. He goes straight for Tony and slides the puck straight between his legs. A five hole.

The crowd goes mad.

But after that, things take a turn. The goalies aren't about to get bested twice in a row. Gilly tries to distract Leo with his stickhandling and deke him out, but Leo isn't fooled. No score.

The nail-biter continues. Vlad goes in for a tricky shot and misses, and the shootout score remains 1:1.

It is down to me and Blake.

I stare down the ice at Leo, knowing an ordinary chuck won't cut it here. I think fast. Leo will expect me to mix it up and be ready for that too. An idea forms. My eyes flash toward Anna, the woman who inspires me to take such giant leaps of faith.

I can just make her out in her usual spot, looking stunning in her signature Freezer red. Her chestnut hair glows, catching the light as she leans forward, glued to the rink. She probably isn't rooting for me, but it doesn't matter. Seeing her is all I need.

I bend low and skate forward with the puck, exactly as I always do when lining up my signature move. Leo watches me, but I can see he isn't buying it. As I get closer to the goal, I give Leo exactly what he expects. I flip to a forehand shot. Leo looks victorious for catching my deke and angles toward the shot, low and ready. But at the last second, I deke again, switching from forehand to backhand and snapping the puck off my stick so fast Leo doesn't even have time to realize he is wrong.

The puck sails past Leo, but I miscalculated. The puck hits the side of the goal and bounces out.

My heart drops. I missed. Just like little Gordon Bombay at the beginning of *The Mighty Ducks*. I am a failure.

But funnily enough, I don't feel like a failure. Because I know when this is over, win or lose, I am going to get the girl.

I catch Blake's eyes across the ice. "Give it your best shot, stick head."

My mortal enemy gives me a nod, then turns toward the goal.

Blake doesn't even give Tony time to think. He blazes up the ice faster than I've ever seen him skate before. It looks like Blake is going for a classic slapshot. In a shootout, that is insane. Does he want to force another round of shots?

Tony seems to be thinking the exact same thing. There is no way anyone would be crazy enough to do a slapshot in a shootout. He is so sure that Blake is deking that he drops into a split to catch the trick shot, and the puck soars past him.

Blake scores. The Freezers win the Kerry Cup.

The entire stadium leaps up onto their feet, cheering. Red and navy confetti rain down. The Freezers swarm Blake, lifting him up off the ice. Coach Peter is dancing and hollering his guts out, looking like his dreams finally came true.

We watch the joy all around us with stoic faces. Gilly claps me on the back. "They played a good game. We'll get 'em next year."

Alex joins in. "You bet we will. Hey, Gilly, is your sister here? Do you think she saw me score?"

I grin as Gilly groans. We turn to scan the crowd for Hollis, but I know who I am really looking for. I can't wait another second.

I turn and skate toward the exit, eager to change and win back my girl. That's when I notice the police officers. Two of them. The same ones that were at Anna's house the night of the break-in.

I freeze, wondering if the PCHL called the police on me for wanting to defy them. But they aren't there for me.

Officer Cooper has her eyes on the Freezers' raucous bench. "Blake Tyler," she calls, her clipped voice cutting through the celebration. "You're under arrest."

Chapter 42

Can We Do This in the Back?

ANNA

The last thing I expect to be doing right after my team wins the Kerry Cup for the first time, is begging a police officer to arrest our star player more discreetly.

"Please," I whisper. "There are so many reporters here, and about 12,000 smartphones pointed right at us. Can we do this in the back?"

The young Officer Moran straightens and puffs out his chest toward the crowd. Thankfully, at this exact moment, I am pretty sure most of their phones are pointed at Chad and Vlad drenching my dad in ice water.

Officer Cooper gives me a weary look, like she arrests celebrity hockey players every day of the week.

"We did let him play the entire game. You know we're

arresting him for breaking into your condo, Ms. Green?" she asks. "I assume you saw the same pictures we received several hours ago?"

"Yes, I do know that," I reply, although the reality of the whole situation still hovers somewhere in the ether, waiting to hit me. I never knew being in shock would feel so surreal. "Which is why I'm hoping you'll do this for me."

Officer Cooper sighs the deepest sigh I ever heard. "Fine. We'll be in the hallway. If he's not there in five minutes, I'm pulling out the cuffs and coming back. And you better be right behind him. We need you to come down to the station to make another statement."

"Absolutely. I can't wait," I promise. Officer Cooper grits her teeth and signals Officer Moran to head for the hallway.

Sagging in relief, I turn to deal with my next problem —getting Blake to willingly be arrested. I step inside the Freezers bench area and my feet leave the floor as someone picks me up and spins me around in a dizzying circle.

I have a heady moment of thinking it is Charlie before remembering with an icy splash of disappointment that he is the last person it would be. Instead, I am in the very sweaty, very wet arms of Chad.

"We won!" he hollers in my ear.

"I know!" I holler back. "Can you put me down?"

"Anything for you, my queen," he shouts, setting me down. I turn to look for Blake and immediately feel myself lift back up.

"We won!" an incredibly damp Vlad hollers in my ear.

"Down, Vlad!" I shout, and he obeys.

Back on solid ground, I regain my footing as I scan the sea of players for Blake. His sharp features usually stand out from the rest, but not tonight. I elbow my way through a forest of shoulder pads, trying to find him.

I feel a hand on my shoulder. "Don't pick me up!" I shout preemptively, tugging away.

Leo regards me with raised eyebrows that suggest he doesn't understand why I needed to say that. "Wouldn't dream of it."

"Good." I straighten again. "Have you seen Blake?"

"He's not here."

"Just great," I grumble. "I need him for . . . something."

"Might be hard to get him," Leo deadpans. "I think he just went to get arrested."

My eyebrows skyrocket. "Leo, did you just tell me that Blake Tyler voluntarily left the Kerry Cup to go get arrested quietly?"

Leo shrugs. "That about sums it up. He's not a bad guy, you know. I mean, he's a psycho, and I used to hate him, but I think he's getting better."

I nod, not entirely sure what to say to that. I didn't think this night could get any stranger.

Leo suddenly becomes very interested in studying his feet, unable to look me in the eye as he asks, "Did, um, did your friend from Munch come to the game?" He tries to sound casual and fails completely.

I beam. "I think she likes you, Leo. Don't screw it up."

Leo grins. "I'll do my best."

"Now if you'll excuse me," I say, "I'm late for the police station."

Leo gives me an apologetic smile and rejoins the conga line of Freezers heading for the locker room for what promises to be a very long and very loud night.

I give them one last look and hurry away.

Officer Cooper slides the paperwork over to me and waits. I stare down at the pages, my brain sliding right over the words. I should feel better knowing that Blake is the one who broke into my condo and will now pay the price. But something doesn't sit quite right. As freaked out as the robbery made me, I still can't explain why he would break into my home, toss all my stuff around, and then leave without stealing anything. Or no, not leave, but water my plants first, and then leave. I realize with a pang that I probably haven't watered them since.

The station door bursts open, and Coach Peter hurries inside, still soaked through from his victory drench. "Is it over? Did I miss it?" he asks, breathless. "You all left so fast, and I was so . . . soggy."

"Mr. Tyler and your daughter have both been willing to cooperate with our investigation," Officer Cooper informs Coach Peter. "I would suggest you do not get in the way of this arrest."

"Sorry, Coach. I know it's bad for the team," I say. The publicist in me knows it is very, very bad news for a player to get arrested, even discreetly. Another way I am letting down my dad.

"Are you kidding?" Coach Peter asks. "He broke into my baby's house. Give me the handcuffs. I want that SOB drawn and quartered."

I am so shocked that I can only stare.

My dad comes over to me and grabs my hands. "I'm so sorry for not being there for you, Anna Banana. I got those photos of you and the Shredder, and I just saw red. But I never should've doubted you. I was so set on winning I lost sight of the fact that I'm your father first, and that's the best coaching gig there is. You've come so far, and I couldn't be prouder."

Tears well in my eyes. "Thank you, Dad." I throw my arms around him. I haven't realized how much I've been hurting from our fight, but hearing him say he is proud of me refills my soul.

Officer Cooper clears her throat. "This is very touching, but frankly irrelevant. Ms. Green, can you please just sign the statement? My shift's almost over. And it's a Saturday."

"Got a hot date?" Coach Peter jokes.

Officer Cooper does not respond, but Officer Moran nods emphatically. Anna looks back at Officer Cooper, who simply taps the paperwork.

Coach Peter gives me an encouraging smile, but I hesitate over the signature line. Even with my father's support, something doesn't feel quite right.

"Could I talk to Blake before I sign?" I ask. "Just for a minute."

"You're not his lawyer or his phone call." Officer

Cooper sighs another one of her heavy sighs. "But I'll give you five minutes. My shift ends in ten."

I nod. "Five is all I need."

I expect to be shown into an interrogation room, like *Law & Order*, but Officer Cooper simply ushers me and Blake into a cramped office. Honestly, it is only slightly bigger than a closet and just as full.

Coach Peter offered to talk to Blake on my behalf, but I had a feeling that would end badly. I sent him off to rejoin the celebrations with promises of immediate text updates. This is something I need to do for myself.

I sit on a squeaky chair and study Blake. For someone who just won the game of his life, he looks utterly miserable.

I try to figure out how to start the conversation, but Blake gets there first.

"I'm going to confess, I promise. I'll plead guilty."

"You are?" I ask, surprised.

"I'm sorry," he replies. "I shouldn't have done it. It was stupid. Really, really stupid."

I don't contradict him, but it isn't the full story. "Blake, why did you do it? Why did you break into my home and tear it apart? It really scared me, you know. I didn't feel safe there for a while after that. Knowing that someone had come there and destroyed all my things for no reason. I mean, you didn't even take anything."

Blake looks at me woefully. "The puck."

I stare at him, not understanding. "The what?"

"The puck I gave you. That's what I took."

"The puck you gave me," I repeat, trying to remember.

"It's just . . . my grandmother gave it to me when I was in high school. It was my good luck charm. She found it at an antique shop." He smiles fondly. "My grandmother meant a lot to me."

I realize with a rush of guilt that Blake is talking about the weird square of wood he gifted me all those months ago. I shoved it in my drawer and completely forgot about it.

"I wanted you to have it. I did," Blake continues. "Actually, I wanted a lot of things from you."

"Oh," I say, my cheeks warming. "Blake, listen—"

"I know," he tells me. "It wouldn't have worked out anyway. You have bad taste in guys." My lips quirk, but my smile fades as Blake continues. "I was mad about it at first. Mad enough to ask that reporter for help."

My eyes widen. "You mean Kyle? You're why he took those pictures?"

"I didn't know he'd do all that. I tried to get him to stop once I realized," Blake tells me quickly. "I just wanted him to find out if you and Charlie were really dating. And make sure he wasn't using you to steal team secrets or whatever."

My head spins. I don't know what to think.

"I'm so sorry, Anna," Blake tells me. He really seems like he means it.

"Look, I am really sorry I didn't realize how much the puck meant to you," I tell him. "But it doesn't excuse you from breaking into my apartment or invading my privacy like that. You could have asked for the puck back. You could have just talked to me."

"I know," Blake says miserably. "But I guess that would have meant admitting I made a mistake."

I study the man in front of me, both so tough and so vulnerable. At the beginning of the season, he wasn't willing to be anything but tough. As upset as I am with him, Leo is right. He is trying to change.

Still, I have one question.

"Blake, why did you water my plants?"

Blake looks shocked I would even ask. "They needed water," he says, like it was the most obvious thing in the world. "How are they now? They must be doing better since it's spring again."

"Oh yes, much better," I lie. I resolve to water them the second I get home, and I hope they have some cactus DNA in them. I stand. "Thanks for being honest, Blake."

"Whatever you need. Tell them I'll sign a confession as soon as they're ready."

"I'll let them know," I say, wheels turning as I walk to the door.

"Oh, and Anna?"

"Yes?" I ask, turning back toward him.

"What are you going to do about Charlie?" Blake asks.

The question stops me in my tracks. "What do you mean?" I ask carefully. "We broke up. You know that."

Blake shrugs. "I know. But I think you're kind of like his puck. I don't think he's going to give you up that easily."

My heart flutters, and I shove it down. "I've gotta go," I

tell Blake, and flee before anything else surprising happens.

The second that I reappear, Officer Cooper impatiently slides the paperwork over again, pointedly eyeing her watch.

I hesitate. "Actually," I say, "I think I'm good."

Officer Cooper stares. "Come again?" she asks.

"I don't want to press charges."

Officer Cooper pinches the bridge of her nose. "You know that's up to the state, right? A crime was committed."

"Maybe, but I talked to Blake, and he didn't take anything of mine. And I think maybe I left the patio door open."

"The patio door with the broken lock?" Officer Cooper asks, voice dripping with skepticism.

"Yep, that's the one." I stand firm.

Officer Moran looks back and forth between his boss and me, eyes wide.

I glance down at Officer Cooper's watch. "I believe your shift's just ending, Officer?" I ask.

Officer Cooper sighs again and smooths her hair. "If I release him, he's your responsibility. I'm not driving him home."

"Don't worry," I reassure her. "I'll get him a ride. And before you go, there is one more thing I'd like to talk to you about."

"Hey, Blake." I stand on the police station steps, waiting.

"Anna, listen, I vow—"

I hold up my hand. "Save it. You are going to make this up to me with a significant number of community service projects I have planned that you will do without complaint." Blake nods emphatically. "But for tonight, I found you a ride."

I move aside, and a vision in navy and red steps into the light. Mabeline. Blake's breath hitches, taking her in.

"Hi," he says. "You look nice."

"Thanks," she replies, clearly wary. "You need a ride? Back to Anna's house to break in again?"

Blake winces. "Actually, I was thinking we never really got our auction date. Maybe I can make it up to you? After your next roller derby game?"

A slow smile spreads across Mabeline's deep-red lips. "Maybe you can."

Blake grins back. "Good."

Mabeline holds out her hand, back to her usual insanely giddy self. "Now come on, let's go. I finally figured out where you live. Um, I mean . . ."

I watch them head off into the darkness. They really are a perfect match. Between Blake and Mabeline, and Leo and Alison, a lot of love happened tonight. I take a shaky breath, feeling the dull ache in my chest that will take a long time to heal. I think about what Blake said about Charlie. Will he change his mind and fight for me?

I try to put him out of my head. Happy endings only happen on the hockey rink.

Chapter 43

I'd Rather Talk About Hockey

ANNA

J ust one more press conference, I tell myself, and then it will all be over. It is two days since the Freezers won the cup, and this is the last official event of the post-season. I will have to face Kyle, that greasy parasite, but I am prepared for that. Charlie will be there too, and I am much less prepared for that. But still, in one hour, this bittersweet chapter of my life will close.

I stand in my same spot in the stained multipurpose room, with its unflattering lighting and unbalanced folding chairs. But I feel entirely different from the person who stood here only six months ago. I have more confidence in myself and my ideas now. I even reached out to Tricia Cornwallis about collaborating on a series of lunches and lectures for women in sports media. Tricia has proven surprisingly supportive and even has an encyclopedic knowledge of all the good ramen places in Portland. We have the first event planned for next month, and there is already a waiting list of attendees.

I wish things worked out differently between me and Charlie, but so long as he is a Shredder and I am a Freezer, I know he made the right decision. Even if it makes my heart clench.

The reporters begin to file in. Tricia takes her usual seat, giving me a nod that manages to be both professional and encouraging in the same motion. Both of our expressions turn cold as Kyle strolls in and slouches nearby, stroking his beard like a skeezy, self-satisfied Santa Claus. How he can cause so much hurt and look so serene is a depressing mystery, but I plan on dealing with him later.

I glance back toward the hall, checking the time. I left the Freezers in their locker room singing Lady Gaga. They ran out of Queen songs, so Chad and Vlad jumped to their other favorite queen of pop. By the time I left, they were rocking out to "Bad Romance," which is not something I expected to see in my lifetime. Even my dad joined in.

I didn't check on the Shredders, putting that in the hands of Assistant Coach Sylvia. Just one last hour of staring into the face of the man I can't have. Then it will all be done.

At least it will be a good press conference. The Freezers pulled off quite the Cinderella story this season, winning the cup in one of the biggest comebacks the league has ever seen. Voodoo Donuts even made a Voodoo Doll donut frosted in red and blue in our honor. I can't prove it, but I have a sneaking suspicion Coach Peter bought every single one of them.

That isn't the only thing the teams are celebrating. My mind slips straight to Charlie with another flutter of nerves. Despite the Skateful Shredders' loss, Charlie was voted MVP, news that Blake accepted with surprising grace. Blake even muttered something about Charlie being a "not terrible player after all."

Despite everything, I can't help feeling proud of Charlie. He truly deserves it. Coach Ryan's constant screaming wasn't the thing that propelled that team to the finals. Charlie was. It is nice to see him get some recognition.

I bite my lower lip, trying not to miss him. Just one hour. It should be a simple, easy press conference. Surely, there couldn't be any more surprises left.

Just as I pull out my phone to check the time again, I hear the thunderous stampede of hockey players behind me. The Freezers have their championship shirts on, and they look like the happiest kids in the candy store.

"Anna," Vlad says very seriously. "We need to have a Gaga day next season."

"I'll make a note, Vlad," I tell him. I glance toward the other side of the room. Sylvia has the Shredders lined up and ready. I fix my eyes on Sylvia, determined not to look for Charlie, and nod. I turn back toward the Freezers and signal them. Coach Peter gives my shoulder a comforting squeeze as he moves past me.

The men file onto the rickety stage, and my eyes go straight to Charlie. The sight of his broad, open face with his thick brown hair and lumberjack jawline sends shivers straight down my spine. He looks eager and confident. I try not to be resentful that he doesn't look as tired and distressed as I feel.

Charlie's gaze slips toward me for a second as he walks, and the shock of his blue eyes sears straight through me. My mouth goes dry. Just get through the press conference, I tell myself for the thousandth time. One more hour before he is out of my life, and I can figure out how to move on. By the time the Freezers take on the Shredders again next season, I am determined to be over him. Somehow.

Everyone takes their seats, but Charlie remains standing. He holds up his hand, holding off the usual cacophony. "Before we get started, I have a quick announcement I'd like to make," he declares, his voice a little hoarse. Charlie looks down at a small stack of dog-eared notecards and takes a breath.

I can tell he is clearly not as confident as he looks, matching the nerves simmering through my body. What on earth is he going to say?

"I'd like to thank everyone here for naming me MVP. It's an incredible honor at the end of an incredible season . . . for the Freezers." Everyone laughs. Charlie grins and continues. "But seriously, I could not be prouder to be a member of the Skateful Shredders and to have made it all the way to the finals with this amazing group of people. As a professional hockey player, I could not ask for more." Charlie takes another deep breath. "Which is why, now that the season has ended, I am officially announcing my retirement."

Shocked gasps explode from every corner of the room. I feel like I turn to stone, rooted to my spot on the stained carpet with my entire being concentrating on what Charlie has to say next.

"I have loved being a hockey player," I continue over the noise, "but what I have loved most has been the people I've had the privilege to get to know. My teammates who inspire me, my competitors who challenge me, and others I've met along the way," his gaze slips to me again, "who have helped me realize what I want in life. So long as I have those people, I don't need to chuck any more pucks, even though I am really good at it." More laughs. "So, I'm hanging up my skates and looking forward to trying something new. The next time you see me, I'll be starting a new career as a coach in Portland's junior league." It sounds like the entire room is murmuring.

He clears his throat and sets down his cards. "Now, if you'll let me take up just a little bit more of your time, I have one more thing to say."

He steps off the platform and walks straight to me.

As several dozen reporters' heads turn to follow, I feel myself leave my body. I can't move from this spot—or from Charlie's blue-eyed gaze—if I try.

"Anna Green," Charlie declares, taking my clammy hands in his warm ones, "please forgive me for being a complete and total idiot. Letting you go was the biggest mistake I've ever made. I don't expect you to take me back right away, or at all, but if you're willing, I would love to buy you an iced coffee sometime."

He stares into my shocked hazel eyes with his open, honest, sky-blue ones, running his thumbs back and forth across my knuckles and making them tingle.

My throat goes dry. My mouth is a desert. Breaking up with Charlie has been devastating. As incredible as our time together has been, our lives are incompatible. And when he just gave up, it hurt. Five minutes ago, I was determined to put it in the past and move on.

Now here he is, declaring himself in front of all these people. Fighting for me. It is everything I want if I am willing to trust it. Could I?

Charlie leans forward, closing the distance between them until his lips rest by my cheek. My breath hitches.

He whispers into my hair, "I hope you say yes, because I'm in love with you."

Hearing that, my whole body comes alive. Charlie pulls back to see my reaction. My face lights up like the sun. My eyes sparkle. I grin from ear to ear.

From the stage comes a very loud throat clear. We look up, startled. It is Gilly.

"Well?" he asks. "Are you guys gonna kiss? Because if you're not, then I'd rather talk about hockey."

"Gilly," Charlie complains loudly, "you are rushing my big romantic gesture."

"No, he's right," I say. "We do need to talk about hockey."

For a second, Charlie's expression wavers as worry

replaces hope. Then I give him a wicked little grin. "So, we better hurry up and kiss."

I pull his lips down to meet mine, and the room erupts in cheers. Charlie lifts me into his arms and swings me around as the hockey players hoot and holler. Even Coach Peter applauds, although he keeps a sharp eye on Charlie. I can't help but laugh into the kiss.

Charlie finally sets me down, although he does not let me out of his arms.

I grin at him. "We probably should actually start the press conference."

I feel a tap on my shoulder and turn. Officers Cooper and Moran snuck into the room while everyone was distracted by the kiss. Officer Cooper looks annoyed, but Officer Moran looks almost teary-eyed.

Seeing them, Blake turns white.

"Oh, sorry everyone," I say, regretfully pulling away from Charlie. "But we do actually have one more bit of business to take care of before we can get to questions."

I step aside, and Officer Cooper swaggers up to Kyle.

"Kyle Brodie, you are under arrest for trespassing and extortion," she announces.

"And for generally being a conniving weasel," Tricia Cornwallis adds.

This time, the applause is deafening.

Charlie and I haven't let go of each other since the press

conference earlier that week. Which made it very hard to plan this surprise for him.

"Come on," I demand, dragging him toward Ground Kontrol.

He makes a face. "A whole night at a Freezers party when I could just spend a whole night in bed with you? Are you sure you don't want to just turn around?" he asks, pulling me into him and nuzzling my neck.

"I am sure," I tell him firmly, although I can't resist him kissing my neck for a second. Then I push open the door.

"Good riddance!" everyone inside cries.

In front of us aren't just the Freezers, but the Shredders as well, for a post-season party for both teams and a send-off for Charlie. Even his family is here.

I whip out my phone to capture Charlie's shocked face. I know I'll be framing that one.

Tony steps forward and pulls him into a bear hug.

"Oh, please," Charlie says. "You can't wait to get rid of me."

"Yup," Tony confirms, but he sounds very emotional.

Gilly, Hollis, and Alex hurry over to join them.

"Can I be team captain now that you're quitting?" Alex asks, one eye on Hollis, hoping she notices he is rocking an "Everyone Watches Women's Sports" T-shirt.

Charlie laughs. "You have my vote, kid," he tells him. "If the NHL scouts don't get you first."

"Really?" Alex asks, glowing.

Gilly rolls his eyes. "Don't give him ideas, Charlie. I'm the one who's going to have to deflate his head to get it to fit in his helmet."

"Don't worry, I'll help," Hollis volunteers. Alex's eyes widen in fear.

Charlie laughs and grabs my hand, pulling me toward his giddy parents, who are sporting sweatshirts with Charlie's face screen-printed on them.

"Come on, I want you to meet my parents," Charlie tells me, unaware that I've become fast friends with Sandy and Harold in the past twenty-four hours of planning this party.

The Freezers' side of the party quickly devolves into their favorite Ground Kontrol activity. Drinking and defeating each other at pinball.

Chad holds up a quarter and declares, "Whoever wins this gets to drink their beer out of the Kerry Cup!"

Vlad looks up from where he is already doing that. "Oops," he says.

Chad sighs. "I try so hard."

"I've got something," says Blake in the corner. He digs into his pocket and holds out a worn wooden square. The team crowds around to look at it.

"It's a vintage hockey puck from the 1800s. My grandmother got me one when I was a kid. I, uh, lost it for a bit, so I went on eBay and found another one. I thought maybe it could make up for some of the shitty stuff I did this season. Although," he adds, "it was weirdly cheap."

Vlad picks it up, wide-eyed. "This," he declares, "is awesome."

"We play for the puck!" Chad announces at full volume.

Blake looks up to find Leo appraising him thoughtfully.

"You're not so bad, Blake," he tells him. "I'm glad you joined the Freezers. Just don't commit any more crimes, and I think we'll have a good season next year."

Blake nods.

"Hurry up," Chad groans. "I'm late to beating you."

"Oh, yeah?" Leo claps back. "You don't even stand a chance."

"Neither of you do, actually," says a female voice.

The men turn. There stands Alison, leaning on the pinball machine, looking stunning in flowing pants and a tailored vest. Leo clears his throat.

"What are we playing for?" she asks. "Because none of you can beat a high school state pinball champion."

She smiles flirtatiously in Leo's direction, although her smile drops when she sees the square puck.

"Actually," she backtracks, "maybe I'll just watch."

"Oh no, you don't." Leo takes her hand and gently places a quarter in it. "We're taking this all the way." He gazes into her eyes until Alison clears her throat too.

Chad leans forward and snatches the quarter. "Thanks, guys. I'll take it from here."

Ignoring the groans, he slots the quarter into the machine and pulls the lever. Gilly wanders over, digging out a quarter of his own.

"I'm next," Gilly declares. "We're not letting you take the cup and pinball." He leans over and hollers, "Hey, Charlie, come play!"

Charlie looks up from where he is grabbing drinks at the bar and shakes his head. "I'm busy being in love," he shouts back. But he grins since the Freezers-Shredders rivalry seems to have defrosted.

Gilly rolls his eyes and goes back to watching Chad. Charlie winds his way over to me with our two beers.

"Your adult bev-er-age," he says goofily, then leans close. "So, you wanna get out of here?" he asks, waggling his eyebrows.

I blush. "Actually, there are a few people who'd like to say hi first."

I step back, revealing Coach Peter and Coach Ryan.

Coach Ryan steps forward and stiffly holds out his hand. "Congratulations, Charlie, you had a good career," he says, stilted. "Could have been better if you'd stayed, but it's your choice."

"Thanks, Coach," Charlie says, taking his hand and willing the interaction to be over. Of course, when Coach Ryan wanders away, it means Charlie has to talk to my father.

"Good to see you again, sir," Charlie says, slightly terrified.

Coach Peter looks at the two of us, then down at his shoes. "I actually wanted to apologize. To both of you. Anna Banana, you're my little girl, but you're so much more than that."

I pull my dad in for a hug. "Thank you, Coach," I whisper. We have been back on good terms ever since the police station, but it still means the world to hear him say it.

Coach Peter turns to Charlie, holding out his hand much warmer than Coach Ryan had. "Charlie, you're a hell of a player. And from what I've seen, you're gonna make one hell of a coach."

"Thank you, sir," Charlie says sincerely, grabbing Coach Peter's hand.

"Hurt her," Coach Peter tells him as he firms his grip, "and I will come for you."

"Dad!" I exclaim.

Coach Peter relaxes his hand. "Just kidding," he says, although he clearly isn't. He nods to the two of us. "I'll leave you two kids alone. Oh, and, Anna, I'll call you tomorrow about that Naked Day you keep going on about. Make it Naked Third Period, and you've got a deal. I can stomach twenty minutes of naked fans. Especially if we can do it against one of the New England teams. They're such prudes."

I beam as Coach Peter melts back into the crowd of partiers.

Charlie pulls me close, pressing his forehead to mine. "So Naked Day is on?" he asks. "Where do I sign up?"

"Don't worry," I reply, "you can be my test subject."

I turn to survey the party, which has already devolved into a giant pinball competition. Even Charlie's mom is playing.

I laugh. "You know, I never thought I'd see the day when a Freezer and a Shredder would find love. But I'm very, very glad I did."

"You mean Gilly and Chad?" Charlie asks. He pulls me

back to him, brushing the hair out of my eyes. "You forget, I'm not a Shredder anymore. I'm just yours."

I grin as I reach for his lips with mine. "You're right. We're a team."

It is the scariest team I've ever been on and already the greatest. I can't wait to see where the next season will take us.

Six Months Later

ANNA

Pizza for breakfast has never been so romantic. I awake slowly, the smell of baking bread filling my nostrils and working its way up to my sleepy brain. I smile and stretch out in my empty bed, luxuriating in the feel of my skin on the soft sheets.

Pots clang in the other room as I force myself to sit up and shake the sleep out of my head. My eyes focus on the photographs I took that Charlie convinced me to frame and hang up opposite the bed. I even got up the courage to enter a few competitions. I don't know yet if I've won any, but it feels nice to take real pride in my work instead of dismissing it as a hobby. He helped me see that.

A meek October sun peeks through my window, as though ready to flee at the first sign of rain. Most people I know get depressed as the weather worsens and the nights creep up earlier. But to me, it means only one thing.

Hockey season is coming.

And this one is going to be good.

The door bursts open as Charlie kicks his way inside, his arms laden with a silver tray of breakfast pizza. I was very skeptical the first time he made one, but I quickly discovered that flatbread makes a mouthwatering vehicle for sunny-side-up eggs, roasted garlic, and sizzling bacon. I dragged Alison over for a demo, and now there is a kimchi breakfast pizza permanently on Munch's morning menu.

"Breakfast is served, my love," he chimes, setting down the tray on the bed with a grand sweeping gesture and bowing. "I made it to celebrate your big day. Five hundred boyfriend points for me, please."

I roll my eyes and mock applaud. "Nice try, but you made this because you're nervous about *your* big day, and you needed a distraction. That's only one hundred boyfriend points, and you know it."

Charlie puts his hand on his heart. "You see right through me." He sighs and flops down on the bed, grabbing the slice with the most bacon on it.

"You have no reason to be nervous," I tell him. "The Green Juices are going to do great."

Charlie's youth charity idea has turned into a full-blown intramural league across the Portland public school system. There is plenty of interest, and more than a few local hockey players willing to lend a hand.

Charlie, of course, dubbed his team the Green Juices, and

his first draft pick was Devin Roberts. Out from under his dad's thumb, Devin proved a first-class player and an even savvier recruiter with the occasional tip from me. The kid has a bright future. Not to mention that Coach Ryan gave Charlie a photo of him and Devin wearing matching Green Juices jerseys. It is Charlie's favorite photo, aside from the photos I take. The one I snapped of Charlie at his sendoff party was indeed framed proudly and rests on my office desk.

"I know. Really, I just want the kids to have fun," he agrees. "But I wouldn't mind if they also won every single game."

"Sorry," I say. "That's a Freezers' thing."

Charlie playfully withholds the pizza. "The Shredders are coming for you, Green."

I shrug, grabbing for my breakfast. "Maybe. Depends on how good their coach is."

Charlie narrows his eyes. "What do you mean?"

I widen my eyes in response. "A little birdie told me that Coach Ryan got an offer from an AHL team and might take it."

Charlie points an accusing finger. "You've been texting with Gilly? But he's *my* friend."

"Not anymore," I say cheerfully. "Besides, players shouldn't get too friendly with their coaches. Then again, maybe that will change if their coach isn't a meanie who yells all the time."

"Oh, I yell. The Green Juices are deeply traumatized," Charlie says solemnly.

"Just think about it," I say. "Maybe you can do both.

The intramural league is practically running itself already."

Charlie shakes his head. "I'm not ready for that."

I push myself up and take his hands in mine. "Charlie Haskell, you're the one who taught me not to run away when things get interesting. The man I fell in love with can do anything he puts his mind to."

It is cheesy, but true. I have no doubt whatsoever that whenever Charlie wants to step up to coaching the pros, he'll be sensational. He'd give my dad a run for his money, and I have no problem with that. Coach Peter could use a run after all those donuts.

Charlie sets the pizza aside and pulls me close to him, threading his hands through my hair and nuzzling his favorite beauty mark with his nose.

"You get one million girlfriend points for being so amazing," he murmurs, kissing along my earlobe.

I laugh. "That's too many! I'm pretty sure I already have about three billion."

"Not enough," Charlie replies, shifting until he is on top of me, holding his weight on his elbows. He leans in to kiss me senseless.

I wrap my legs around him and flip the two of us over, so I am on top, pinning his arms with mine. I grin seductively down at him, my hair dancing along his cheeks. Charlie growls in response, trying to press himself up to kiss me.

"Stop stalling," I chide. "We are both going to be late."

"How dare you, I would never," Charlie claims, but he relents, and I slide off. I wiggle my butt at him as I go to find clothes. My hand hovers over my usual red blouse, but I reach instead for a yellow sweater dress.

I finally allowed Alison to take me shopping recently. I'm still not sure about the more adventurous additions to my wardrobe, but Charlie's dazed expression every time I wear one has convinced me that Alison was right. Like always.

"Actually, I do have a real present for you," Charlie tells me. "Not just the pizza and the points."

"Oh, really?" I ask. My heart flips when I turn around to find him standing behind me, his hands hidden behind his back. It is way too early for a ring, but I can't help wondering as he stands earnestly before me, his blue eyes looking straight into my soul.

He takes a breath and reveals what he is hiding.

I laugh at the 64oz navy-blue insulated tumbler with a custom Freezers logo on the front. He offers it to me reverently. "For your iced coffee. You're going to need it."

I take it and pull him into a hug, delighting in his strong arms wrapped around me.

This season, my dad gave me free rein to make his hockey champs as Portland Weird as I want. It still makes him nervous, but he is determined to trust me, and I am determined not to let him down.

So, I took the brief and ran with it. I use Tricia's and my women in sports media lunches to strategize ways to bring in more women to hockey, and over 50 percent of our new season ticket holders this year are women. The upcoming Naked Day has proven so popular that seats for that game sold out almost as soon as we opened ticket sales. But most of all, I can't wait for what I am unveiling to the press today. My greatest achievement yet.

The official sponsor of the Freezers and brand-new owner of the Memorial Coliseum's snack bar: Stumptown Coffee.

I approached dozens of iconic Portland businesses, including Voodoo Donuts, but Stumptown has always been my top choice. To be able to combine my two loves— hockey and iced coffee—is a dream come true. The fact that I can now buy my favorite drink two feet away from my office is the absolute cherry on top. I'll have to be careful to do it when Zamboni Zane isn't around, or he'll try to change my order to hot coffee, but that is a risk I am willing to take.

The Freezers are about to become very caffeinated. With the new season around the corner and the Shredders itching to take back their throne, we will need it.

Charlie grins, watching me pull my yellow dress on and puzzle over how to fit the massive tumbler into my bag.

I head for the door, but he grabs my hand one last time, pulling me close.

"I'm really going to be late now," I chide. "And so will you."

"So, we'll be a little late. I promise, this is important."

"What is it?" I ask, resigned.

Charlie lifts me up and spins me around, his lips on mine, kissing me senseless. When he finally lets go, I offer him a dazzling smile.

"You're right. I guess we can be a little late." I lean in for one more kiss.

Ten minutes later, we finally get out the door. I wave goodbye as I hurry toward Alison's to nab Stinker for the big Stumptown reveal.

I slide into my seat, relishing the feeling of the first game of the season. I love sitting on the edge of the hard plastic chairs, feeling the chill of the ice, and the thrill of excitement from the crowd. Below us, Zamboni Zane makes his slow, stately way across the ice as the players get ready for combat. The air buzzes with anticipation.

I lean forward and tap Eddie Mullins on the shoulder.

"What do you say, Eddie? Do we have a shot this year?"

Eddie frowns, surveying the ice and thinking the question through. He shrugs. "Lotta newbies on the team this year. Fresh legs can go either way. I'd say maybe fifty-fifty."

Ramona shakes her head and whacks her husband. "Fifty-fifty? With a coach like that?" She swivels around to shake her head at me. "Don't listen to him. He was wrong last season. He'll be wrong again this season."

"I guess we'll just have to see," I tell her.

Zamboni Zane finishes his run, and Henri skates to the center of the ice, looking even more aggrieved than he usually does. He signals, and the two teams pour onto the ice.

I pick up my SLR camera, zooming in. Usually, I like to

shoot in black and white, but this game is special. I want to capture the players in all their bright-green glory.

As the twelve-year-olds shoot onto the ice with their exaggerated game faces on, I flip my camera lens over to the coach. There is Charlie, singing the Green Juice theme song at the top of his lungs, cheering encouragement, and looking so incredibly alive.

I grin and snap a picture. Henri shouts to get ready for the puck drop. I briefly debate about upholding my tradition of closing my eyes to drag out that one last perfect moment before the season begins.

But this isn't an ordinary season, and I'm not the girl I used to be. I keep my eyes open, lifting my camera back up.

I don't want to miss a thing.

Also by Lolu Sinclair

A Sanctuary for Fire & Fate

Naked in Naknek

Lost Love on 6th Street